Eagle & Crane

By Suzanne Rindell

Three-Martini Lunch
Eagle & Crane

Eagle & Crane

SUZANNE RINDELL

Allison & Busby Limited
12 Fitzroy Mews
London W1T 6DW
allisonandbusby.com

This edition first published in Great Britain by Allison & Busby in 2018.

Published by arrangement with G. P. Putnam's Sons, an imprint of Penguin Publishing, a division of Penguin Random House LLC.

Copyright © 2018 by Suzanne Rindell

The moral right of the author is hereby asserted in accordance with the Copyright, Designs and Patents Act 1988.

A CIP catalogue record for this book is available from the British Library.

First Edition

HB ISBN 978-0-7490-2322-5
TPB ISBN 978-0-7490-2327-0

Typeset in 11/16 pt Adobe Garamond Pro by
Allison & Busby Ltd.

The paper used for this Allison & Busby publication has been produced from trees that have been legally sourced from well-managed and credibly certified forests.

Printed and bound by
CPI Group (UK) Ltd, Croydon, CR0 4YY

In memory of my grandfather, Norbert

1

NEWCASTLE, CALIFORNIA
SEPTEMBER 16, 1943

They bump along the country road, rolling through golden hills that are punctuated with granite boulders and dotted with clusters of oak trees that appear blackish green from afar. Every so often the road dips through a marshy patch here, a thicket of wild blackberry bushes there. Broken branches and nibbled leaves; the signs of beaver and deer. Verdant meadows and white flashes of cabbageworm moths. As they near the orchard, clouds of sparrows and finches make nervous, disorganized dives at the soft yellow weeds around the plum trees, little groups of them assembling like constellations and abruptly breaking up again, each and every tiny nervous body keeping one eye turned to the sky for the shadowy shape of a hawk soaring high above.

When they reach the break in the low split-rail fence, the sheriff steers the car onto the property and along the dirt drive, through the many rows of trees, and toward the leaning peak of the largest foothill. The morning air is laced with the sharp, peppery scent of dry grass burning.

'Awful smoky out,' Agent Bonner remarks, once the automobile comes to a stop.

'Rice fields,' the deputy says as the three men step out of the sheriff's old Model A. 'Somewhere down in the valley. It's after harvest, see. This is when they burn 'em. Smoke gets trapped up here, against the foothills. Kind of sets around a spell.'

The sky is indeed filled with a thick haze, turning it the color of dull gunmetal; the sun is a flat white disc, small as a dime and lost in a sea of gray.

'It's routine farming business. The rice fields aren't Jap-owned,' Deputy Henderson continues. 'Or if they were, they aren't anymore.'

He is young, the right age for a soldier, but there is an air of being excluded about him, and of lingering teenage angst. Probably flat-footed. Or poor eyesight, Bonner thinks. Those are the most common 4-Fs, when you can't tell by simply looking at a man. Henderson's hair is the color of tarnished brass; his face and neck are very pink, the flesh cratered, ropey and swollen with acne. Just to look at him, a man could feel the sting of what it must feel like to shave.

'Let's get this over with,' Sheriff Whitcomb says. At least it is obvious why *he* isn't marching around in a uniform on the front: too old. He is thin, with haunted blue eyes. A pair of jowls and one tuft of white hair sprouting from an otherwise shiny dome. Bonner spied the tuft back at the station, before the sheriff reached for his hat and offered to drive the group out to the ranch. Every town seems to have a pair like this, Bonner thinks. Henderson and Whitcomb. One will eventually replace the other, and the cycle will begin again.

'You said Louis Thorn is living in the old farmhouse now?' the sheriff calls over his shoulder, speaking to Henderson. He is polite enough to Agent Bonner, but it is clear he prefers to pretend the agent is invisible.

'Yes.' Deputy Henderson answers the sheriff in a quick, eager voice. 'Old Man Yamada signed it over to him, before they lost legal rights. So Louis owns it fair and square.'

'That's mighty interesting,' Agent Bonner remarks. Bonner's certainly heard of cases where Japanese families had signed over their property to their white neighbors before being evacuated to the camps. In every single case, the Japanese were hoping to eventually have their land, homes, and cars returned to them, which implied a kind of special trust in one's neighbors.

'It ain't how you think. The whole town was mighty shocked the Yamadas did that,' Henderson says. 'The Thorns and the Yamadas had a long-standing dispute over this land.'

'Why'd he sign it over to the Thorn family, then, if there was bad blood?' Bonner asks. He looks to Whitcomb, but Whitcomb shrugs and looks away, his gaze dilating with disinterest. Bonner can tell the sheriff finds explaining town gossip to an outsider tedious.

'Louis Thorn and Harry Yamada was friends – sort of,' Whitcomb says, dispassionately. 'Maybe Old Man Yamada put some stock in that. The old man didn't have any friends who weren't Japanese, himself. Maybe he figured it was worth a shot.'

'Took a fat chance on that,' Deputy Henderson grunts, reaching one hand up to rub at his pimply face. 'I say Louis ain't givin' this land back. His father and grandfather always told him this land was Thorn property in the first place. They'd likely roll over in their graves if he was to think about giving it back.'

'All right,' Whitcomb says, pulling out his revolver, spinning the cylinder to ensure all six rounds are there, and putting it back in his holster. 'Let's just see if he knows anything. Keep it civilized. Should be pretty straightforward. We're talking about a law-abiding citizen here; I don't have any reason to believe Louis Thorn'd lie to us.'

They begin walking up the incline of the foothill toward the tidy white clapboard house nestled into the hillside just below the top. Louis Thorn might be living in it now, but Old Man Yamada had originally built it half a century ago – back when the latter was still a baby-faced young man, an early settler to the area. The house sits into the hill in a slightly cantilevered fashion, with a small wraparound porch from which a person can look out over the orchards below; neat rows of plum trees extend below one side of the house, a grove of satsumas in the middle, and almond trees on the other. The property consists of some fifty-odd acres, and as the three men climb the foothill now, they can see that the trees eventually peter out to reveal a wide, flat pasture some distance away. As they pause to look, three sets of eyes fall upon the far-off shape of a small, impromptu hangar down below, looking as though it had been thrown together hastily from available materials.

It is the place where the Yamadas kept their biplane, and where Louis Thorn purportedly still keeps it now. Or so Agent Bonner has been informed. The FBI took special note of the biplane after the two remaining members of the Yamada clan – Kenichi and Haruto 'Harry' Yamada – broke out of the Tule Lake Relocation Center, where they were being detained. The plane made the FBI more nervous than usual, but either way the Yamadas were to be tracked down and returned to the segregation center, and as soon as possible.

The three men arrive in front of the house and climb up the twenty or so stairs that lead up to the porch. No need to knock; their boots make a good deal of noise on the wooden planks. The screen door swings open on creaking hinges before the third man reaches the top stair.

'May I help you fellas?'

The door claps shut. Louis Thorn, dressed in a long-sleeved undershirt and trousers, his suspenders hanging beside his hips, looks at the men standing on his porch, glancing searchingly from one to the next. One half of his face is dewy, clean-shaven. The other half is covered in lather. He is still clutching the straight razor in his left hand.

At the sight of the razor, Whitcomb lightly touches a hand to the butt of the gun on his own hip. 'Mornin', Louis. The way I hear it, you got the run of things here these days,' the sheriff says, taking the lead.

'That's right,' Louis responds. There is a note of caution in his voice. He looks over the sheriff's shoulder, taking in the unfamiliar sight of Agent Bonner. For a brief instant Louis appears startled to see the FBI agent, but quickly recovers himself.

'Looks like you settled into the place pretty good,' the sheriff presses on.

Louis returns his gaze to the sheriff but doesn't reply.

'I take it you heard about them Yamada boys already.'

'I heard,' Louis says. His voice is low, steady.

'Then you know we're here to ask you if you seen 'em.'

Louis blinks. 'Harry and Mr Yamada?'

'Yes.'

'I reckon this is the last place they'd come.'

'So you're telling me you ain't seen them?' the sheriff prods.

'No.'

'And you wouldn't be inclined to help those Yamada boys if they came knocking?'

'I told you, I haven't seen them since.'

'All right, all right,' the sheriff relents. 'You understand, we gotta ask, Louis. Agent Bonner here can't go about his business till them boys have been found.'

'Mr Thorn.' Agent Bonner introduces himself, clearing his throat and extending his hand. Louis hesitates, then passes the straight razor to his other hand. The handshake is curt.

'Look here, Louis,' the sheriff continues, 'I don't know what you got goin' on in that head of yours. Maybe you got it in your head to protect these fellers, even if they're Japs. Or maybe,' he says, lowering his voice, 'you've gotten accustomed to being a property owner. Ain't no crime in that. Maybe if they came back here they wouldn't exactly be welcome. Like I said . . . I don't know what you got goin' on in that head of yours. But, to tell you the truth, I'm an old man, and I could give two shits.'

Whitcomb pauses, certain that he has everyone's attention now.

'What I *do* know,' the sheriff adds, 'is that it would make all of our lives a hell of a lot easier if you let us take a look around the property and see if we can't prove you're telling us the truth.'

Louis is silent a moment. 'All right,' he finally answers.

The sheriff nods. Louis moves as if to go back inside the house to finish his shave.

'The biplane,' Agent Bonner says, reminding everyone.

'Oh,' the sheriff says, turning back to Louis. 'The agent here has to ask you some questions about that airplane being kept on the property . . .'

'Yes?'

'How'd that plane come into your possession?' Bonner begins.

Louis hesitates. 'Bank auction,' he says.

Bonner has read the file: he knows that Louis is skipping details, leaving out the part where *Kenichi Yamada* – not Louis – bought the plane at a bank auction, and only later signed it over to Louis.

'We used it for our flying circus act, but I don't do that stuff anymore. I work for the US Army Air Corps as an instructor up at the Lincoln airfield. I train flyboys headed to the Pacific, mostly.'

Bonner already knows this, too, but does not interrupt. It was always better to let people do their own telling.

'Do both Yamada men know how to fly the plane?' Bonner asks.

Louis shakes his head. 'Only Harry.' He pauses, then repeats Harry's full name as though to clarify. 'Haruto Yamada.'

'And before your instructor days, you and Haruto Yamada' – Agent Bonner flips open a notebook – 'you charged spectators to watch you perform stunts in this plane? That's how the two of you became friendly?'

Louis shrugs. 'Originally, we both worked for Earl Shaw and put on a barnstorming act for his flying circus. Later we had our own act . . . it was called Eagle & Crane.'

'Eagle & Crane?'

'Uh-huh.'

'Sounds mighty . . .' Agent Bonner pauses, looking into the air for the proper word. 'Showy.' Louis narrows his eyes just slightly at Bonner, but Bonner presses on. 'What sort of tricks did you perform?'

'Oh, wing walking and barrel rolls and such,' Louis replies. 'With Earl's show, sometimes we flew two planes in formation, did loop-the-loops. Later it was more choreographed stunts. Parachute jumps, that type of thing.'

Bonner nods. He scribbles a note.

'Say . . .' Louis asks, his eyes narrowing again. 'Why so many questions about our business with the plane?'

'Well,' Bonner says, clearing his throat, 'it goes without saying that the Bureau feels an escaped evacuee who knows how to fly an airplane might be a liability.'

Louis doesn't comment. Bonner knows he's obligated to ask the questions the FBI expects him to ask, so he presses on.

'Do you have any reason to believe Mr Yamada might attempt to gain access to your biplane?'

Louis pauses, considering. He shakes his head.

'If Haruto Yamada *was* able to gain access to the biplane, do you have any reason to believe he might use his flying skills to commit an act of war?'

'*An act of war?*' Louis repeats. 'You mean hurt folks with the plane somehow?'

'Yeah,' Deputy Henderson suddenly chimes in. 'I'll be damned if Pearl

Harbor ain't taught us all about how vicious those Japs can be – can't put anything past a-one of 'em!'

Louis's head snaps irritably in Deputy Henderson's direction. His hand holding the straight razor twitches.

'No,' Louis answers, returning his attention to Agent Bonner. 'I don't think Harry would do anything along those lines. It's not . . . it's not Harry.'

'You sound defensive on Harry's behalf,' Bonner remarks.

'I'm not defensive.' Louis stiffens. 'I'm just not going to say something is one way when I know it's another. Harry ain't about to steal the Stearman and crash it.'

As if by the most absurd cue, their ears suddenly prick to the sound of an airplane engine droning in the distance. Louis knows from the sound of it that the plane is flying at an unusually high altitude, the steady whine of the engine humming like a dying mosquito.

All four men – Louis included – hurry to the railing at the edge of the porch and look up. Sure enough, there in the sky is the familiar silhouette of the Stearman. The group stares at the plane, powerless and immobile as they watch it inch across the sky, all of them mute as they listen to it drone along.

But then they hear an even more alarming noise. The engine sputters and coughs, and for one long, horrendous second shudders loudly, until finally it goes silent. It is a sequence of sounds Louis has never heard the airplane make before, a noise ever so slightly different from the stalling noise it makes if you pull up too hard . . . and yet, the second he hears it, Louis recognizes the sound with a sick feeling in his gut: it is the engine running out of gas.

What happens next is baffling. The biplane falls from the sky, a flying thing no longer, like Icarus and his melted wings. No one pulls up on the nose or raises the wing flaps. Instead it drops like a stone, or – even swifter – like a bird diving on purpose. But a bird can recover from such a dive. A small biplane cannot – that is, not without an expert pilot intent on maneuvering the contraption for all it was worth.

The men standing on the porch hold their breath as the biplane plummets. Then all four of them reactively wince, steeling themselves as it makes impact, nose-first, directly into the makeshift hangar. A small fireball leaps into the air, then transforms into a sea of black smoke.

The smoke adds to the thick haze in the air, completely blotting out the September sun.

'Well . . . *shoot*,' Whitcomb mutters. He spits onto the porch and turns now to Louis Thorn. 'You care to revise your statement, son?'

2

The crash site belches black, oily smoke while the local fire engine nearly pumps the well on the Yamada ranch dry. When the color of the thick smoke finally changes from black to white, the firemen begin to breathe more easily behind their homemade masks of wetted cloth, knowing they have turned the tide on the fire. Now it is only a matter of time until the entirety of the charred mass quiets down to a steamy hiss. The air for miles around smells strange, laced with ash, the sickly scent of burning rubber, and the queer metallic odor that usually precedes a large thunderstorm.

Of the two bodies found in the wreckage, one is clearly that of the elderly Jap, Kenichi Yamada. The other is presumed to be the body of his son, Haruto Yamada. The body itself is badly charred, but a singed, tattered version of the US Army uniform that had been issued to Haruto Yamada shortly before he went AWOL still clings to the remains as they pull the body from the burning mess.

Despite the chaos at the crash site, Bonner takes care never to lose track of Louis Thorn. In particular, he studies Louis's expression carefully when the two bodies are covered with sheets and lifted away on stretchers. *Maybe you've gotten accustomed to being a property owner . . .* Sheriff Whitcomb had said to Louis earlier on the porch. *Maybe if the Yamadas came back here they wouldn't exactly be welcome.* Bonner had wondered if Louis was helping to hide the escaped evacuees. Now Bonner must consider the possibility that Louis is, in fact, involved in a much darker crime.

When the commotion begins to die down, Bonner sidles up to Louis.

'I think we ought to continue our conversation, Mr Thorn,' Bonner suggests in a firm but gentle voice.

Louis turns to stare at Bonner with a dazed expression. He is still half-dressed and half-shaven. Smudges of black grease and specks of tar from the crash complement the few smears of shaving lather still clinging to his cheek.

'How about we go back up to the house and sit down?' Bonner presses.

Louis's dazed expression melts, then sharpens, as though coming back into focus. He looks down at the ground. His brow furrows.

'All right,' he agrees.

Several minutes later, the two men sit down to talk in the front parlor of the old Yamada house. They are perched across from each other on a pair of matching pink silk settees. In fact, the entire room is a study in symmetry. Two silk settees. Two small square glass coffee tables between them. Two bookshelves made of bamboo. Four beautiful silk scrolls hanging on the walls, all of them displaying inky watercolors of cranes and fish and far-off mountains. It is a curious blend of East and West: a series of treasured heirlooms presumably brought over from Japan, intermingled with the bulky pink settees and Western-style coffee tables.

With the other half of his shave yet to be completed, Louis managed to splash some water on his face once they got up to the house, wiping away the crust of dried lather and smudges of black grease. Despite the fact that half his face is still covered in thin, fair stubble, he'd put on fresh clothes and quickly wetted and combed his hair, too, and now, sitting across from Bonner, Louis seems cleaner, more collected. Bonner takes a closer look at Louis, assessing the details.

Louis is twenty-three, but looking at him now, Bonner notices he is distinctly boyish. With his dark blond hair, freckled nose, and blue eyes, Louis embodies the popular image of an all-American boy. Now Bonner wonders if that wholesome impression is part of a façade.

Louis can't know it, but he is the reason Bonner requested the Yamada case. In recent months, Bonner had developed an aversion to fieldwork and specifically requested desk duty. His fellow agents said he was nuts to volunteer for such drudgery, but Bonner was relieved to work in an office, away from the Japanese segregation centers, away from the manhunts for Japanese Americans considered uncooperative with the order to evacuate. Bonner didn't care that his peers predicted he would get bored. Boredom was a better feeling than some of the other feelings he'd had since his job began to revolve around the enforcement of Executive Order 9066.

However, when reports of two escaped evacuees from Tule Lake meant the FBI was going to send an agent to Newcastle, California, and interview the young man living on the Yamadas' old property – a fellow by the last name of Thorn – Bonner asked to be put on the case, back in the field, because the name and location held a special significance for him.

I figured you'd come to your senses sooner or later, his boss, Reed, said in an approving tone, oblivious to Bonner's ulterior motive. Reed approved his request and assigned Bonner to the case, which was how Bonner now found himself sitting across from Louis Thorn.

Louis is visibly nervous; it would be natural for the crash to set him on edge, but perhaps it is something more than that, Bonner thinks. Perhaps he senses Bonner's special interest in him. Or perhaps Louis had something to do with the crash and has something to hide. Louis turns his head as though he hears a sound outside, and the unshaved stubble on one half of his face catches in the light from the window, the hair gleaming with slight traces of red and gold. It is Louis's complexion that draws the agent's attention now, and not because of Louis's comical shave. Bonner is surprised he didn't notice before: bruises bloom over both cheekbones, and Louis sports a fresh cut under one eye.

'Looks like somebody roughed you up pretty good,' Bonner comments.

Louis touches a self-conscious hand to one cheek – the more naked, clean-shaven one.

'I went to get a drink at the saloon in town the other night,' Louis says. 'Got into a little scuffle.'

'How many nights ago?'

'Three.'

The bruises and the cut look more recent than that, but Bonner nods with brisk affability.

'I hope you don't mind if I verify that.'

'Sure,' Louis replies. 'I'll give you the name of the bartender down that way – will that help?'

Bonner thinks to himself, *Louis Thorn is either telling the truth, or else is a clever, cool customer. He has an earnest air, but something doesn't sit right.* Aloud, Bonner says, 'I'd be much obliged.'

Sensing Louis's distracted mind-set, Bonner clears his throat. A broadcast squawks loudly from a Zenith radio perched on the mantel – one of the few objects in the room without a symmetrical twin. War updates, turned up to top volume.

'That yours?' Bonner asks idly.

'Course,' Louis replies. 'The Yamadas turned theirs in.'

Louis means the Yamadas obeyed the order to turn the radio they owned over to the US authorities as an item of contraband that those of Japanese ancestry were not allowed to retain after Pearl Harbor.

'They complied and never did anything fishy,' Louis adds. He pauses. 'Till now, I suppose.' He shifts on the settee and changes tack. 'Anyway, some weeks back I bought a new radio so I could follow—' His voice breaks off. 'Well, so I could follow all the news about the war, I guess,' he finally finishes.

The kid must've been listening to it while he was shaving – maybe for the company, Bonner thinks. Bonner does that himself from time to time; it is a lonely thing to live alone, probably even more so in a strange house. But now it feels as though the radio is a disturbance, a small but terrible shrieking emanating from the corner of the room, intruding upon any real shot at conversation. Bonner rises from the settee and points.

'May I?'

Louis nods, and Bonner switches off the radio. A dense quiet floods the room in a cool, relieving wave. Bonner lets the silence settle a little before breaking it again. He clears his throat once more.

'Earlier you insisted the Yamadas weren't likely to try to commandeer the biplane,' Bonner says.

Louis raises a wary eyebrow at the agent but says nothing.

'Doesn't look like that turned out to be the case.'

Louis remains silent.

'What do you think caused the crash? Do you believe it was an accident? Or do you think there was a target that the two Yamada men had in mind?'

'I don't know,' Louis repeats. 'I think I made it pretty clear I don't think they had the inclination to hurt anyone.'

Agent Bonner pauses. The railroad lines that came up from Sacramento through the big station in Roseville were regularly used by the military to transport ammunitions manufactured in the Bay Area. Such a target would be ideal for a Japanese spy. And yet, that was not where the biplane had ultimately crashed. If they were trying to hurt someone other than themselves, they had failed spectacularly.

'Seems lucky for us that it crashed directly down on the empty hangar,' Bonner says now.

Louis grunts. 'Easy for you to say. Weren't *your* hangar.' He pauses and grunts again. 'Or your biplane.'

'You said Harry was the one who knew how to fly the biplane?' Bonner continues.

'Yes.'

'And his father did not?'

'No.'

Agent Bonner must admit: the crash hadn't hurt anyone except the two men in the plane. This means all possibilities must be explored and ruled out in his report. He clears his throat. 'Do you have any idea whether Harry or his father may have been . . . well . . . despondent? Ready to give up on the world?'

Louis looks at Bonner for a moment before answering. 'You mean ready to die by his own hand? That don't sound like Harry to me.' He pauses, then continues: 'But I don't imagine he or Mr Yamada were too cheerful about the camp they were in.'

'So you *do* or you *don't* think someone crashed that biplane on purpose?'

Louis shakes his head, reticent. 'I don't think anything. All I know is what I saw today, same as you.'

Bonner leans back and sighs. 'Well, that's just it,' he says. 'I don't know much about planes, but I've always been under the impression that they don't just drop like that from the sky – that even if the engine dies, there's some sort of maneuvering a pilot will try to do.'

Louis appears to relent. 'That's generally true, I suppose,' he says.

'And as far as I could tell, Harry didn't attempt any of that,' Bonner says. 'He didn't try to perform any emergency maneuvers.'

'No. It didn't look like it.'

'Why wouldn't he?'

'I can't answer that,' Louis says.

Suddenly, the men are interrupted. A back door slams, footsteps move swiftly through the house, and a young woman rushes into the front parlor.

'Oh!' she utters, stopping short when she catches sight of Agent Bonner perched on the settee opposite Louis. The young woman freezes, a deer caught in headlights. Something about her suggests a sense of urgency abruptly put on hold. It is as if she has blown in on a gust of wind; a fresh hint of the day outside – the Indian summer, the crisp leaves, the terrible burning scent of the airplane crash – swirls in the rush of air that arrives with her.

'I didn't know you had a guest,' she says to Louis.

Bonner takes a closer look at the young woman. She is pretty, but in a spritely, tomboyish manner. Her red hair is smartly bobbed, its coppery color as bright as a flame. She is skinny as a whip, and attired in a crisp white shirt and a pair of men's riding trousers.

'Did you see the crash?' Louis asks, a note of wary caution in his voice.

'Yes,' the young woman answers. 'Isn't it awful?'

'Harry and Mr Yamada . . .' Louis says.

'Yes,' the woman replies in a somber tone. 'I know.'

The young woman lowers her eyes to stare down at the rug beneath her feet, and after a second or two Louis follows suit, leaving Agent Bonner to glance back and forth between the two of them as though trying to make up his mind about something. He stands.

'I'm Agent Bonner,' he introduces himself to the young woman, holding out his hand. 'The Federal Bureau of Investigation sent me here to make some inquiries about the Yamadas.'

'Oh!' the young woman exclaims, accepting Bonner's hand and shaking it firmly. 'Of course. I'm so sorry. My name is Ava Brooks.'

Bonner racks his brain, trying to guess at the relation between Ava Brooks and Louis Thorn. *Sweethearts? Neighbors?* She certainly entered the room as though she were familiar with the place.

'Ava has been helping to run the orchards while the Yamadas ain't here,' Louis offers, as though reading Bonner's mind.

'Oh.' Bonner nods and sits back down. 'I see. And you . . . live on the property?' While he has no reason to doubt them, Ava doesn't exactly look like a typical foreman. Bonner wonders if there still isn't something more between them.

'I live nearby,' Ava replies. Her tone has shifted and is slightly stiff, brusque. Bonner considers perhaps she was offended by what his question implied. 'It's a lot of work, keeping the orchards running without the Yamadas,' she adds defensively.

'"Without the Yamadas"? It sounds as if you knew them.'

'Of course I knew them.'

This catches Bonner's attention. He retrieves his notebook and pencil again from his inside jacket pocket. 'If you're aware of the crash, then I assume you're also aware of the fact that the two Yamada men left the camp at Tule Lake without permission. I'm investigating their case.' He pauses. 'Would you mind telling me how you knew them? Have you always helped out in the orchards?'

Ava bites her lip. 'No. I suppose I first met Harry Yamada when he joined my stepfather's barnstorming troupe.' She glances at Louis. 'Louis and Harry joined at the same time.'

Bonner takes this in, slightly caught off guard. 'I see. You were all members of this . . .' He struggles to recall the details Louis gave him earlier, in order to describe it properly. '. . . flying circus act?'

'Yes,' says Ava. 'More or less. That's how we met.'

'Interesting,' Bonner remarks. 'Did you also perform daredevil stunts?'

Women didn't ordinarily fly planes – much less dance on the wings – but from the looks of Ava, Bonner wouldn't put it past her.

Louis cuts in. 'No – Ava doesn't fly. She's afraid of heights. Never been up in the air, as a matter of fact.'

Agent Bonner frowns and raises an eyebrow. 'You were employed by a flying circus troupe, but you're afraid of heights and won't go up in an airplane?'

'I sold tickets for airplane rides,' Ava answers. 'And to use the word "employed", Agent Bonner, is to imply that I was paid for my work. It was my stepfather's nutty idea to start a barnstorming act. Back when Earl first started the show I was still a kid, and my mother and I were just along to sell tickets and lemonade.'

'Traveling with a flying circus . . . Sounds like a rather remarkable childhood,' Bonner says.

Ava shrugs. 'It beat standing on the breadline,' she replies.

She has a point: the Depression was unbearable for most families. If there is one thing good about this war, Bonner thinks, it's the effect on the nation's economy. Not exactly a fair trade-off, but still.

'Your stepfather – *Earl*, was it?'

'Earl Shaw,' Ava says. She nods, but something in her face hardens at the same time.

'Yes.' Bonner flips a page in his notebook. 'Louis mentioned him earlier. He was the founder of the flying circus and originally the owner of the biplane that crashed today?'

'I reckon that's the way of it, yes,' Ava replies.

'Can you arrange for me to speak to him?' Bonner asks.

'Why?'

Bonner blinks. 'Well, two Japanese detainees broke out of the Tule Lake Relocation Center, stole a biplane, and crashed it. And that biplane just so happens to have belonged to your stepfather at one point – not to mention the fact you just told me Haruto Yamada once worked for your stepfather. That seems as good a reason as any to want to talk to him, doesn't it?'

Ava frowns. 'All right, sure,' she says. 'But the problem is, I haven't the faintest idea where to find Earl, so I'm not certain I can help you.'

'No one's seen Earl in over three years,' Louis supplies.

Agent Bonner is silent, thinking. During this brief pause, something shifts in Ava's demeanor. She suddenly becomes bolder. She straightens her spine and takes a breath, all business.

'I don't mean to be rude, Mr Bonner,' she says, 'but if you're nearly finished with your business here . . . ?'

Again Bonner blinks at her, surprised. He realizes he is being thrown out.

'I'd like to talk to Louis,' Ava continues, 'and there are things that need doing around the orchard . . .'

Bonner shakes himself, hiding his irritation. 'Of course,' he replies. He stands and straightens his suit. A tall man, Bonner dwarfs the room. 'But I'd like to talk to you more at a later date,' he says to Louis. He turns to Ava. 'I'd like to talk to both of you more.'

'Well, you've proven you clearly know where to find us,' Ava says, a hard note in her singsong voice. The rote words are supplemented with a plastic smile. After ten minutes with the young lady, Bonner already knows: she is not the type to hide her disdain.

Louis stands, looking embarrassed by Ava's behavior. 'I'll see you out,' he says.

Ava retreats to the kitchen. At the front door, the two men shake hands.

'I'll be in touch,' Agent Bonner promises.

'All right,' Louis says.

'Oh,' Bonner says, pausing and turning back. He fishes out his notepad and pencil one last time. 'What was the name of the man you said tends bar in town?'

Louis blinks.

'You said you could give me the name of the bartender who was there the night you got into that scuffle we discussed,' Bonner prompts in a helpful tone.

There is a pause as Louis stiffens.

'Joe,' he says finally. 'Joe Abbott is his name.'

'Very good,' Bonner says, scribbling the name into his notebook.

'And the name of the bar?'

'Murphy's Saloon.'

Bonner nods and scribbles that down as well.

'All right, then. You take care, now,' he says to Louis.

'You, too.'

Bonner steps out onto the porch where, hours ago, he first met Louis Thorn, and hears the porch door slap shut behind him.

And with that, Agent Bonner finds himself alone again. Looking around and seeing no car, he remembers that the sheriff drove him over to the former Yamada property and that Bonner left his Bureau car parked in front of the sheriff's office. He shades his eyes and glances up at the late-afternoon sun beating down with surprising heat despite the thick smoke now in the air.

'Well, I'll be damned,' Bonner mutters, putting his fedora on. He sighs and takes his jacket off, folding it over his arm and beginning the long, dusty walk back into town.

3

Louis and Ava peep through the curtains, watching the shape of the FBI agent moving down the drive. Bonner is ambling slowly – probably on account of the heat, Louis thinks.

'I reckon I ought to have offered to drive him into town,' Louis comments.

'No. I think you ought to stay away from him,' Ava says. 'As much as possible.' She drops the corner of curtain and steps away from the window, lowering her voice. 'He'll be back for certain. He may have located the Yamadas, but he believes you had something to do with the crash.'

Louis looks at her. She waits for him to say, *I didn't*, but he says nothing. The air between them is awkward. First there is the oppressive weight of the crash, the deaths . . . not to mention, the last time Louis saw her, Ava was in a bed, naked. That was only twenty-four hours ago. But neither of them will talk about that now. Not directly. It feels like a lifetime has passed since then.

'That agent,' Ava says now. 'He looks an awful lot like—'

'I know,' Louis snaps in a low voice.

Feeling sympathetic, Ava reaches out to touch his shoulder, but the second she makes contact, Louis flinches as though she has stung him.

Fine, Ava thinks. She walks to the kitchen and frowns at the pile of dirty dishes in the sink. Louis has kept the rest of the place pristine but, like a typical man, has turned a blind eye to the kitchen. *The bachelor life*, Ava thinks. She sighs and rolls up her sleeves, then fits the shallow metal washtub into one half of the sink, filling it up with hot water.

'You don't have to wash those,' Louis says, following her into the kitchen and eyeing what she is up to.

'Somebody has to,' Ava says. 'Besides, Mrs Yamada would not approve of her kitchen being treated like this.'

'It's not all my mess,' Louis reminds Ava, speaking to her turned back. 'I wasn't here by myself.'

She freezes where she stands at the sink, looks down at the filling water, and sighs. She turns the spigot off. 'I know,' she says. She plunges her hands into the water and sets about washing a plate. *Plates and cups first*, her mother always said, *and pots and pans last*. Ava is hardly the domestic type, but after years of traveling up and down California and making camp with a group of barnstormers, cleaning up after men has become ingrained in her, like it or not.

'Honestly,' Louis says, 'you don't have to do that.'

'Go and shave the other half of your face,' Ava replies. She turns to look at him and manages a weak smile, an imitation of her normally jaunty self. 'You look ridiculous. Even more ridiculous than usual.'

Louis knows this isn't an accurate slight against his looks. This is simply how Ava used to joke – with both of them: Louis and Harry. She is trying to put him at ease, attempting to force a small flicker of normal life in the midst of gruesome disaster.

Louis walks away without saying anything further, and Ava is left alone to ruminate over the rapidly graying dishwater.

Over the kitchen sink is a large window. It faces west, lining up almost exactly in the direction of the airplane hangar, the latter still sending a dirty column of leftover smoke into the sky. Ava finds it impossible not to stare out the window at the hazy plume as she washes, rinses, and sets each dish absentmindedly on the drain board.

Since the moment she rushed into the parlor and found him sitting with the FBI agent, Ava hasn't been able to read Louis. *Is he even sad?* She knows this is Louis's way: when emotions run high, he retreats into a stoic shell of himself. But she also knows Louis was angry with Harry . . . so very angry. And he had his reasons to be angry. She tried to decipher his expression when he'd said, *Did you see the crash? Harry and Mr Yamada* . . . She'd held Louis's gaze for only a moment or two, but then something she glimpsed in his eyes made her look away, acutely uncomfortable. She can tell the FBI agent suspects Louis had something to do with the crash, and Ava understands that the agent has a reason to wonder.

Ava rinses the final frying pan and dries her hands on a dish towel as she continues to stare out the window. The firemen were able to extinguish the blaze; she knows there are no more flames, but the crash site is still so hot, smoke continues to rise, the dirty haze like a permanent smudge marking the sky. Looking at it, Ava feels utterly hollow. Not only is it terribly grim to think of the two dead bodies the firemen pulled from the wreckage down there, but Ava is also aware she is watching a part of her past turn to ash.

The fact of the crash means that the last of the two biplanes, *Castor* and *Pollux*, are gone: two twins, forever separated. The first biplane vanished into the black pit of Earl's debt, and the second is now a strangled heap of engine parts and smoldering metal. It is strange to comprehend: so many of Ava's formative years revolved around those two airplanes.

Sounds like a rather remarkable childhood, Agent Bonner had said. Perhaps it was. Ava can hardly remember a time when she didn't hear the thrumming whine of airplane engines or wake up to two planes sputtering through the air as a pair of pilots practiced trick after trick: loop-the-loops, barrel rolls, falling leaves, harrowingly close fly-bys that, during shows, made the spectators down below gasp. All of these aeronautical feats were commonplace in the realm of Ava's life – as was the constant camping, traveling from farm town to farm town. They would start at one end of California's Central Valley and travel down to the opposite end, then start back north again. They took only the stormiest months of the winter off, and only then because Earl had yet to figure out a way to draw a crowd when it was pissing down rain.

It had been a simple outfit, at first: Earl hired Buzz and Hutch, a pair of pilots who were hard up for work, and the idea was mainly to sell airplane rides to curious farmers (and their wives and children), to fly into town with the festive air of a carnival, and then disappear before the authorities came sniffing around. Mostly, the main thing Ava recalled from her 'rather remarkable childhood' was a sense of loneliness.

27

But everything changed when Louis Thorn and Harry Yamada joined their barnstorming act.

'Eagle' and 'Crane' – those were the names that the other two pilots eventually bestowed upon Louis and Harry. Buzz and Hutch had insisted every pilot worth his salt needed a 'call sign.' They nicknamed Louis for his blond, freckled, all-American looks, and Harry . . . well, they named Harry after a bird, too, to match Louis. But being about as sensitive and diplomatic as a pair of sledgehammers, Buzz and Hutch declared it ought to be a 'Jap' bird – hence Crane.

With Louis and Harry on board, the show escalated, eventually growing into something bigger and more extraordinary than anything Earl had ever imagined. Ava, too. Her life had been unexpectedly changed by Eagle & Crane; she had, in her own way, fallen in love with them both.

Eagle & Crane. Louis and Harry. Ava continues to peer out the window, full of the awareness that her love for the two young men – and one in particular – is the cause of the smoke she is watching now, steadily rising into the air.

4

LOS ANGELES, CALIFORNIA
1924–1934

There had, of course, existed a time before Ava and her mother joined the traveling barnstorming spectacle. When she thought even further back, Ava could remember a time before they lived like vagabonds out of a caravan, a time before the view out her window changed weekly, a time before the sound of biplanes constantly droned overhead.

When she closed her eyes and concentrated, Ava could remember all the way back to a little Spanish-style bungalow in Los Angeles. She remembered the bright green of the small, sloped lawn, how the afternoon light burnished the house in gold and how bougainvillea crept along the champagne-colored stucco, enveloping the arched doorway in fuchsia flames. She remembered how ripe oranges materialized in winter: giant, heavy globes, they bent the limbs of a tree in the backyard, bobbing on the branches like Christmas ornaments. A suit of armor stood at attention in one of the hallways inside the house – a prop auctioned off by a movie studio and the sort of faux-medieval décor preferred in those days by plenty of respectable Angelenos, who seemed bent on creating their own mythologies and coats of arms.

For the first five or six years of Ava's childhood in that house, the atmosphere was routine, cheerful. Her mother left the radio switched on all day while she puttered about doing chores; Helen Kane chastised folks to 'button up your overcoat' and Cole Porter insisted, 'Let's misbehave!!!' as her mother hummed along and pinned laundry to a line outside. It was difficult to remember rain ever falling during her childhood – in that backyard, or upon that roof, or even in Los Angeles more generally; it seemed the sun shone every day, except in June, when a dull fog rolled in off the Pacific and hung persistently in the air, thick and shapeless, gray as a dull nickel.

Ava remembered her father – red-haired, like Ava herself – as he sat bent over a desk, doing calculations while wearing a green banker's visor. Ava was still quite young, but she possessed a dim understanding that the visor fit in with her father's profession somehow. His job had something to do with the banks; it seemed he was always on the telephone to New York. He worked in an office downtown, a tall-ceilinged, mahogany-paneled space that was perpetually hazy with cigarette smoke, the blinds partially drawn against the brash glare of the blinding Los Angeles sunshine outside. Ava's mother took Ava to visit him there a handful of times, and her father had always looked busy, distracted. He kept very early hours, often rising before the sun to work, but he also finished early. *Bankers' hours*, he called them. In the evenings he sometimes took Ava and her mother to a baseball game, or else a picture show. If they were bound for the movie house, her mother liked to dress up, to set her dark hair in pin waves. More often than not, she even reached for the garden scissors and clipped a pair of camellias from one of the shrubs that grew on their front lawn, insisting they each tuck one over an ear.

Ava's father, usually a fairly serious man, would laugh, and grin, and wolf-whistle at the two of them, and say things like *What a pair of movie stars! How'd a fella like me ever get so lucky to be surrounded by two such gorgeous dolls?*

Perhaps all little girls believe their mothers are glamorous, but Ava suspected hers was more glamorous than most. Ava's mother's name, Cleo, was short for Cleopatra. Her mother looked the part: a full red mouth, regal cheekbones, and thick, black, silky hair – the opposite of Ava, whose pale pink lips made a small, demure bow, and whose red hair sprouted from her head like a flame. Cleo also possessed the kind of hourglass figure that was difficult to hide, no matter what she wore. It was difficult not to notice the way people reacted to her mother. Even when she was only running simple errands, men and women alike constantly threw looks at her mother.

Unfortunately, Ava's mother was fickle when it came to the kind of attention she received: sometimes she liked it, but more often than not it proved too much for her to bear. The contradiction puzzled Ava. Her mother had a fanciful nature and loved to dress up, yet she could be painfully withdrawn. Finally, one day, it dawned on Ava: her mother wasn't dressing to attract notice; she was 'playing dress-up.' Too much attention gave Cleo clammy hands and a tight feeling behind her eyes. When life made demands on her, Cleo got terrible headaches. During such times, she retreated to her bed and drew the curtains, transforming day into night.

Let's allow your mother to rest, Ava's father would say if he was home when Cleo got one of her headaches. He would take Ava for a walk or buy her an ice cream, and by the time they returned, her mother would be back on her feet, humming a quiet tune and cooking some supper.

The Great Crash of '29 happened on a Tuesday, around the time of Halloween. Ava remembered the three pumpkins they had carved and set out on the terra-cotta steps that led up to their little Spanish bungalow. Ava had arranged the pumpkins in descending size to resemble her family: a daddy, a mommy, and a baby.

That afternoon, Ava's mother walked to the kindergarten schoolyard to fetch Ava once school was out, and on the walk home they stopped at the corner store to buy a few groceries. When they approached their house, Ava noticed her father's Ford coupe parked at the curb, indicating he'd finished the workday and come home. This wasn't terribly unusual: Ava figured he was keeping 'bankers' hours,' just as he said. Recently he'd explained to Ava, too, that clocks kept different time in New York, so that while it was one time here, it was a different time there.

She skipped happily enough up the steps, but as she passed the three pumpkins, Ava felt a curious chill.

Inside, all was quiet. Ava went to her room to play. She assumed her mother would pop her head into her father's office to chirp out a quick greeting, then stow the market items in the kitchen icebox. Only a minute or so had passed when Ava heard the bloodcurdling scream. She dropped the hard plastic horse figurine she was holding and ran toward her mother's cries.

A half dozen eggs were splattered on the hallway floor just outside her

31

father's office, yolks oozing from their broken shells. Her mother had fled to the front parlor and sat sniveling on the settee, shuddering as though the bullet had ripped through her, too. Black mascara was already beginning to run down her face. No one stopped Ava from looking into the office, and so she did, just to check. Her father's forehead was slumped over his desk, lifeless. His hand still clutched the revolver. Ava was five at the time – much too young to understand what she was seeing. And yet, somehow, she did.

Seeing her father, his head tipped upon the desk, his skull looking as fragile as one of the eggshells lying in a shattered heap on the floor, Ava only understood one thing: something had broken her father, and as a consequence he had gone someplace she and her mother could not follow. He was no longer in the room, and he was not coming back anytime soon.

They remained in the little Spanish bungalow for a time. Policemen came and went and her father's body was taken away, but there was little way for life to resume as it had been before. When Ava's mother learned that her husband had died with not a penny to his name and owing debts, she contracted one of her terrible headaches and retreated to her bedroom. When Ava checked on her, Cleo was curled up in bed like a child. Ava remembered peeking through a crack in the door and staring at the curve of her mother's back, her mother's birdlike bones showing through her satin nightgown, the ridges of her spine like a sagging string of pearls.

Ava turned six. Unable to rouse her mother from bed in the mornings, Ava found the jar where her mother kept grocery money, purchased milk and white bread from the corner store, and walked herself to and from school. But she sensed even this arrangement – reduced as it was – could not hold up for very long. Unopened mail was piling up at their house. Notices appeared, tacked up to their front door. Collectors began knocking, while Ava's mother only burrowed deeper under the bedsheets, hiding like a frightened animal, until finally one day the collectors returned with the police.

The officers put them out on the street with only what they could carry. Ava felt a pang to realize yet another of her mother's mistakes: perhaps they might've sold their possessions. Fake Hollywood prop or not, she wondered what the suit of armor might've fetched in price.

All they had left now was the cash Ava's mother had long ago squirreled away in an old hatbox. They found an apartment for rent by the week, but by the second week it was already too expensive, so they moved to a seedier apartment, in a seedier neighborhood, and then still a third apartment, in an even worse part of town. It became obvious to them both that Cleo would have to look for a job, some way to make an income. Ava knew her mother was terrified; she had never worked a day in her life, and felt qualified for nothing.

Fortunately, there was one industry that continued to boom in Los Angeles in spite of the Depression, and that was the movie industry. Cleo was able to get work on one of the studio lots as an extra, and she became a pretty face floating in the background of Sherwood Forest, scurrying along the bustling streets of New York, even – ironically – posed amid Queen Cleopatra's court. Once or twice, she even got to speak a line. At one point, a studio executive caught a glimpse of her legs and thought she might make a good chorus girl, but Cleo's stint there was short-lived. It turned out her legs were nice to look at but not very coordinated, and her singing voice was a weak, nervous whisper. Back to the pool of stock extras she went.

None of it paid very much, and they were still painfully poor. Ava turned seven, then eight. They managed to squeak by – but sometimes with a little help from a new habit Ava had begun to cultivate. She began to go on short outings alone, returning to whatever dingy apartment they were living in with a couple of apples or a can of soup.

'However did you afford these?' her mother would ask, biting into a Red Delicious.

'I found some loose change in the lining of the hatbox,' Ava lied. She reused that lie several times, and her mother never questioned it. Never mind that the hatbox would have had to have some distant relation to the fairy-tale goose that laid the golden egg for it to be true.

Ava had learned: there were certain advantages to being a scrawny, invisible eight-year-old girl. She knew she ought to be ashamed of herself. She also knew she was hardly the only hungry waif in those days to develop a case of sticky fingers. Times were tough.

As she grew, Ava found other ways to help them squeak by, coming up with small tasks she could do. By the time she was nine years old, she had begun taking in other people's ironing for a few extra nickels here and there. When her tenth birthday approached, her mother began to worry that Ava was growing up without a proper childhood. It made her sad to see her daughter concentrating so hard on other people's laundry when she should be outside, playing with other children.

And so, one day, when Ava's mother overheard a gaggle of girls talking on the studio lot about a carnival that had popped up on the beach near the Santa Monica Pier, her ears perked up. Perhaps a visit to a carnival would lighten her daughter's heavy mind. Children liked carnivals, didn't they?

'I spent less than I would have at the actual pier, and I had twice as much fun,' one of the girls said.

'Well, that math sounds good to me,' a second girl agreed, snickering.

'And you know what else? They sold the most marvelous bags of caramel corn for only a penny,' the first girl said.

Cleo, a woman who had always possessed a highly suggestible sweet tooth, felt her mouth water. She made up her mind. A visit to a carnival! Ava would be thrilled, she thought.

When she came home that evening and announced to her daughter that they would take the Red Car over to Santa Monica and see the carnival on Sunday, Ava was not particularly tickled. But Ava saw the expression on her mother's pretty, hopeful face and bit her tongue. Perhaps a carnival would ease her mother's worries and lift her spirits. Cleo had recently begun to revert to the habits she'd adopted just after the death of Ava's father: sleeping in quite late, avoiding the pile of bills that were accumulating in a corner of their shabby one-room apartment.

'All right, we'll go,' Ava agreed to her mother's invitation, sounding like an adult succumbing to the will of a child.

Ava resumed her ironing. Neither of them gave a thought to how a single visit to a makeshift carnival might in fact change their lives.

5

SANTA MONICA, CALIFORNIA
JUNE 3, 1934

The carnival consisted of a ragtag group of performers that had found a measure of success by setting up shop in the echoing shadow of the Santa Monica Pier. They were a true vestige of the Depression, a company of players starved for a hearty meal and a good night's sleep; their desperation to survive manifested itself in the way they dazzled their audiences with a riotous, nearly unhinged hilarity. During the afternoons, the sun beat down brightly, and a wet, briny breeze blew in over the festivities.

There were several jugglers, a fire-eater, and a sword-swallower. A strongman lifted various weighty objects and pumped a woman over his head like a barbell. A crone dressed as a Gypsy read fortunes. Another woman danced on stilts, swathed in a diaphanous costume that fluttered in the Pacific breeze like a moth's wings. In the evenings, they performed by torchlight, everything around them glowing with new magic. Every so often the Santa Monica police would come around, insisting that the carnival perform its entertainments elsewhere, but the carnival had proven itself resilient, taking down their tents sewn from bedsheets and disbanding, only to reassemble not more than an hour later in the same place. They made their money by performing for nickels and dimes, but also through confidence games: there is nothing a man will spend more on than the chance to bet on his own good fortune – especially when he is down and out.

It was in this carnival that Earl Shaw came to eke out a living. He did not perform anything so obvious as card tricks or the old shell game wherein cups swirl on the table in mad figure eights and winning is an utter impossibility. In fact, Earl Shaw did not appear to 'perform' anything at all. He went in for a more elegant approach and gave the people what they really wanted: a chance to buy a miracle in a bottle.

There was a special zeal for health products in California. Perhaps it was something in the air, something in the sunshine and water. In earlier years, people had come to Los Angeles looking to reap the health benefits, hoping to cure tuberculosis or stave off rheumatism and asthma, and something of the old desires and beliefs persisted, even as the city built itself up and forsook the soil and orange groves for asphalt and palms. Even as the Depression took hold of the nation – or perhaps *especially* when the Depression gripped the nation – the people of Los Angeles stubbornly dreamed of becoming better, healthier, more fabulous versions of themselves. Earl Shaw was intimately acquainted with the California philosophy of health: he understood all too well the impulse to be rejuvenated, reborn, and remade entirely – shedding an old, dumpy, failed self in order to shine again as the phoenix rises from the ashes. And, having a keen grasp of this brute desire that stirred in the people who populated that particular state, Earl Shaw endeavored to make his living by capitalizing on it.

Ava and her mother made it to the carnival later than they'd expected; Cleo had slept in that morning and lazed about during the early afternoon. Now late afternoon slipped quickly into dusk. The sky had been slightly hazy all day long, making for a brilliant and bloody sunset over the Pacific. They spent the first hour gaping at the dancer on stilts, the jugglers, the fire-eater whose flames began to glow electric as the sun slipped into the sea. Eventually, they heard a man hollering suavely from a caravan with the voice of a true salesman. They drifted in his direction, boats called to the shore.

'Witness the true miracle of Pandora's Wonder Tonic!' he cried. 'Health, beauty, and happiness will all be yours after a week of taking Pandora's Wonder Tonic! Just a spoonful twice daily, and in seven weeks you will see incredible results! Cataracts? *Cured!* Gout? *Gone!* Blemishes? *Banished!* Makes your nose slimmer and your eyes brighter! Turns back the clock ten to twenty years!'

36

He paused and held up two photographs. 'A skeptic at heart? Just lay your eyes on the evidence of the effects of the true miracle that is Pandora's Wonder Tonic!'

Ava inched closer, curious, and squinted at the two yellowing photographs. One was of a grimacing old lady with frowsy hair, lesions on her face, and pustules on her lips. The other was of a young girl, fresh-faced and smiling.

'That's meant to be the same woman in both photographs?' Ava asked, raising an eyebrow.

'Of course!' The man swiveled his head and took in the precocious ten-year-old girl with a quick head-to-toe gaze. After a fleeting pause, his shiny pink lips broke out in a knowing smile. His white teeth flashed and he reached a hand up to twist the ends of his black moustache.

He turned to look at Ava's mother, and his eyes lit up as he took in her dark, silky pin curls and shapely red mouth. 'I see you're raising quite the young critic, *madame*,' he commented. He took off his hat – a somewhat ridiculous old-fashioned top hat with a silk band – and gave a dapper bow. 'Unless you are, of course, her older sister . . . a fact which, now that I look at you, I can see is quite possible. Please, *mademoiselle*, pardon the mistake!'

Ava's mother laughed and gave a warm smile.

'No need,' she said. 'You got us right the first time. This is my daughter, Ava. And my name is Cleopatra.'

Ava frowned. Her mother only introduced herself with her full name when she wanted to impress someone; why she wanted to impress *this* loud huckster of a man was beyond Ava's comprehension. When he heard the fanciful name, his eyes widened in appreciation.

'What a fitting name for such an imperial beauty,' he said.

Ava watched with irritation as her mother's cheeks flushed.

'I humbly submit to you my own name. I am Earl Shaw.'

He bowed to each of them in turn, a pair of smaller, more cursory bows, like punctuation in a sentence.

'I don't believe they're of the same woman,' Ava interrupted the introduction, having resumed squinting at the two photographs.

'Ah, yes – I'd forgotten! Our young inspector!'

He leaned over and put his hands on his knees to address Ava directly. This irritated her even more. She was not the sort of child who took comfort in condescension.

'That's the power of the tonic, girl! Pandora's Wonder Tonic! I tell you: it works such amazing miracles, people can hardly believe what they're seeing! It's quite understandable you have doubts. Why, none of us ever knows what to make of a true and utter miracle, do we? Defies the imagination!'

'Well, that's for certain,' Ava snorted, still glaring hard at the photographs, almost as though one of the two ladies had come to life and whispered something offensive to her.

'Ava!' her mother snapped. 'Don't be rude to the kind gentleman!'

Earl waved this off.

'Nonsense,' he said. 'I have dealt with cynics set in their stubborn, dismissive ways before; by now I do believe I have developed something of an immunity.'

He hesitated and looked Ava's mother over once more.

'But perhaps your miniature critic would be more reasonable on a full stomach. Might I ply the two of you with dinner?'

He licked his lips. Ava wasn't sure if this was because he was contemplating dining or was thinking of her mother.

'Dinner?' Ava's mother blinked.

Was this tonic salesman asking to take her mother on a date? Ava had watched her mother turn down impossibly handsome actors and powerful producers; she was secure in the knowledge that rejection was coming.

'Yes, dinner!' Earl persisted. 'Unless, my dear Lady Cleopatra, there is . . . *ahem*, a Mr Julius Caesar or a Mr Mark Antony in the picture who might take my invitation as an affront?' Earl said, probing.

'No,' Ava's mother said, blushing again. 'There isn't.'

'Then it's settled. I'll shut the shop right now. I'm taking you both to the Brown Derby!' Earl added, seeing he would need to up the ante. 'My treat.'

Ava looked between the two of them, stunned. The Brown Derby was a famous restaurant in Hollywood. Ava knew her mother had always wanted to go, having read in the newspapers that Clark Gable was a regular. Somehow

Earl Shaw had found his way straight to her mother's Achilles' heel.

'Oh, I don't know,' her mother said now, softly, shaking her head. 'We only just met you. We couldn't let you take us out or pay for our meals.'

There now – *that* variety of response was more familiar. Ava sighed an inward breath of relief. But then she watched as Cleo bit her lip, then understood that her mother was in fact tempted by his invitation and already reconsidering.

'Nonsense!' Earl exclaimed, brushing off Cleo's refusal in one deft, sure move. 'You can and you will! Fret not, for you are in good hands: I happen to be a most honorable and upstanding host. Why, my dears, have you ever seen a more honest face than this?' He pointed to his visage and grinned, his white teeth flashing from under his dark moustache.

Ava thought she absolutely *had* seen a more honest face, but held her tongue.

That was the first – but certainly not the last – they saw of Earl Shaw. He took Ava and her mother out for more meals at more restaurants, until one day Earl took her mother out for dinner alone. The two of them returned with a bag of leftovers for Ava and a slightly scuffed gold ring on Cleo's finger.

'Earl and I are going to be married!' Ava's mother announced proudly. She gathered Ava into her arms and squeezed her daughter tightly. 'Isn't that wonderful news?'

A protest bubbled up in Ava's throat but stopped at her lips when she saw her mother's radiant face.

A week or so later, the three of them went to city hall. Once the ceremony was complete, Earl gave Ava a pocketful of rice and instructions to throw it at him and Cleo as the two newlyweds stood grinning together on the city hall steps. Her mother wore a simple white cotton dress and laughed a lot, while Earl's hair gleamed with even more pomade than usual. Ava threw the rice with an unsure, halting hand.

'You have a stepfather!' Cleo said, squeezing her daughter close as the three of them had their photograph taken. 'Aren't you glad?'

Glad wasn't exactly the word for how Ava felt. *Cautious* might've been a better word, but Ava reminded herself: things hadn't been so swell before

Earl came along. For now, at least, her mother was laughing.

The first change came when Earl insisted they all live together in his caravan – which, as he pointed out, offered 'rent-free' accommodation. Earl was correct about the lack of rent, but the caravan was hardly fit for a family. An old, rickety wooden contraption, the wagon dated back to the Civil War and consisted of one long, rectangular room, divided lengthwise by a curtain. Two very narrow beds that folded down on lengthwise planks hung from the side of either wall. The straw mattresses were ancient, and over time had turned damp and hard. If Earl and her mother wanted privacy, they drew the curtain, but as this was a poor partition, Ava found herself taking long, rambling walks in the evenings, or hauling a bedroll outside to sleep on the beach under the stars.

Exactly five days after they moved in with Earl, he turned to Cleo, claiming to have had a sudden epiphany: an attractive woman and her comely daughter would likely sell Pandora's Wonder Tonic better than he could alone! Soon enough, Ava and her mother found themselves spending most of their time working the tonic stand on the beach by the pier. Ava kicked herself for not guessing that this was Earl's plan all along. All told, though, Ava felt it wasn't so terrible. She'd always been an industrious child. And besides, they were in the middle of the dog days of summer: the beach wasn't such an awful place to be.

But Ava hadn't given much thought to what would happen when the carnival pushed on. As fall approached, she learned Earl intended to travel with it, and expected her and her mother to follow along as well, living out of the caravan. The final pretense of Ava's old life – a public school education – was dropped altogether. She'd always done well in school; she was angry, but was quickly reminded she had no say. Earl insisted her gain was far greater than her loss.

'What does she need school for, anyhow?' he roared in a loud voice to Ava's mother one evening, as if Ava weren't on the other side of the thin fabric partition and plainly able to hear every word. 'Why, the world is her oyster now – she's got the best school of all: the School of Life! She'll travel to places she's never been! No education better than that, I guarantee . . .'

They traveled with the carnival from Los Angeles to San Diego, then over to Phoenix and Tucson and Albuquerque. Ava watched her skin turn unusually tan and freckled under the strong desert sun. Living in the caravan essentially meant a life of camping, of not knowing when your next bath might come; it felt like her skin was constantly coated in a layer of dirty, sandy residue.

In Santa Fe, their circumstances changed a second time when Earl came home late one night after winning a very lucky hand of poker. Drunk and merry, his heavy footsteps rocked the caravan as he climbed inside.

He roared to Ava's mother, 'You won't believe it, my dear! I really hit it big this time!'

Ava's mother smiled, happy to see him happy. 'How much did you win?' she asked in a cheerful voice.

'Not *how much* but what!' Earl replied. 'Come with me!' he said. He grabbed Cleo's hand and led her through the little fairgrounds where the carnival had set up shop, to a dusty desert field. '*There!*' He pointed.

Ava, who had followed along as Earl excitedly dragged her mother to the empty field, blinked in the direction of Earl's pointing finger. It was night out, but a bright, flat moon hung in the sky. As Ava looked, she thought she saw the shapes of two biplanes.

'Airplanes?' Cleo asked, bewildered.

'No more of that Pandora's Wonder Tonic business for us!' he exclaimed with the sudden force of a man who'd just made up his mind in that very moment. 'Why, we'll break off on our own! Travel as we please, selling airplane rides to old Farmer John and the little missus. There's money in these airplanes, I tell you!'

'I don't understand,' Ava's mother replied, laughing nervously and shaking her head.

'A flying circus!' Earl said. 'I'm talking about a flying circus!'

'But . . . do you know how to fly?'

Earl waved a dismissive hand. 'We'll find a couple of pilots, pay them a cut of the profits,' he said, then added as though thinking aloud, 'A *small* cut, that is . . .' He walked over to the airplanes and began to circle them, rubbing his chin and thinking of the best way to plumb every penny he could from

41

the two mechanical wonders. Together they were, without a doubt, the largest windfall Earl had ever chanced upon.

Ava and her mother drew closer, both of them trying to get a better look at the biplanes. In the moonlight, she could see one was red and the other was blue. *CASTOR* and *POLLUX*, their names glittered in gold lettering. They seemed so still and heavy; Ava stared at them, slightly awed to picture them flying high in the sky.

6

EARL SHAW'S FLYING CIRCUS
CALIFORNIA'S CENTRAL VALLEY, 1935–1939

As it turned out, Earl was blinded by optimism when he declared, 'There's money in airplanes.' The second he laid eyes on the biplanes he'd won, his mind carried him back to his younger years and the first time he'd seen a flying circus. People had crowded around, waving dollar bills at the pilots, begging for airplane rides.

'Where was this?' Ava asked. She was curious about Earl's past. It seemed he had traveled all over the country.

'Hush now, child! I'm in the middle of a story,' Earl replied, and launched again into a detailed account of the enormous riches he was sure the flying circus had made that day.

'*Barnstorming*,' he said, shaking his head in admiration of the memory. 'Going from town to town, flying stunts and offering airplane rides. They call that barnstorming, and the folks who do it are called barnstormers.'

Earl couldn't know how dated his memory was and how much barnstorming had changed over the years. The novelty of airplanes had worn off for some folks, and new federal regulations had put the kind of informal flying circuses Earl was remembering out of business. Moreover, Earl hadn't considered how the Depression had taken its toll on the barnstorming business, too. He was only thinking back to that day he'd seen a pair of pilots mobbed by admirers clamoring for rides, the flying circus looking like it was making money hand over fist. If he had known better, maybe he would've sold the pair of Stearman Model 75 biplanes straightaway. Earl had always maintained a fondness for quick cash.

Since he didn't know better, his heart was fixed on the idea of running his very own flying circus and raking in all the profits that came with it.

The first people to hint that Earl's notions weren't entirely accurate were the pilots Earl hired. They were a couple of characters – two fellows who went by the names 'Hutch' and 'Buzz'.

'I dunno how much money you're countin' on us makin' . . . I kin fly the stunts you're describin' and take folks up for rides, but it's gonna be up to you if we get a fine,' Hutch said when Earl approached him.

'Fine? Why would we be fined?'

Hutch explained. Earl listened and looked slightly cowed, but quickly hid it once Hutch was done talking.

'Of course,' Earl said, as though nothing Hutch had said came as a surprise. 'You worry about the flying. I'll worry about the rest.'

He hired the two pilots and the group began to travel together, with Earl determined to make a go of it.

'Those are awfully funny names,' Ava remarked when Hutch and Buzz first introduced themselves. Those were their *call signs*, they explained to Ava. They laughed and told her: pilots typically went by nicknames. Hutch's was simply short for his full last name, Hutchinson, while Buzz had earned his name due to the fact that he'd developed a reputation for buzzing the flight tower wherever he went.

Hutch was the older of the two pilots and had flown for the Army. He was middle-aged, with touches of gray at his temples. He was more rugged than handsome, and ambled like a cowboy. Kind but stern, Hutch didn't smile too often, but when he did, crinkles appeared at the corners of his eyes and lent him an oddly charismatic, Santa Claus air.

Buzz was in his mid-twenties, with dark blond hair he meticulously combed into a slick side sweep. He'd worked here and there as an instructor, but, according to him, wanderlust and 'skirt chasing' had kept him from holding down a solid regular job. It was easy to see Buzz was a ladies' man: his head nearly swiveled off his neck whenever a pretty girl walked by. There was a little swagger to his every movement; it was visible even in how an airplane moved while under his control.

Hutch and Buzz already knew how to fly a decent repertoire of aerial stunts: barrel rolls and loop-the-loops, spiral dives and harrowingly tight fly-bys. Once they showed him what they could do, Earl insisted the flying circus hit the road without further delay, still full of the idea that barnstorming would make him rich. So the group set out, heading west back to California. They traveled from town to town, attracting whatever impromptu audience they could by flying stunts, with Earl trying to convince as many members of the crowd as he could to purchase a scenic ride in the clouds.

Earl was almost immediately disappointed by the size of his profits. By the third town, he had to face the reality that his expectations had been overblown. He grew irritable and began to snap at Ava's mother in particular.

'We're making more than we were with Pandora's Wonder Tonic,' Cleo ventured one evening, trying to cheer up her husband.

'*Barely*,' Earl sneered. His head jerked in her direction and his eyes narrowed. 'And what do you know about it, anyway? Keep your nose out of our business matters. You know nothing about it.'

Those first few weeks, Earl talked regularly about quitting and selling the biplanes which he had decided he should've done in the first place. But then, around the time they passed through Sacramento, something changed and he seemed to settle down. Ava guessed that he had come around to seeing her mother's point: that they *were* making slightly more than they had with the Wonder Tonic and a steady income was nothing to scoff at, given how the rest of the nation was doing.

Soon they fell into a routine as they moved from town to town. Hutch and Buzz scouted the next location from above, circling back and signaling to Earl as he towed the caravan with an old Model A down below. When they found an empty field that fit the bill, they landed the two biplanes. Eventually, Earl, Cleo, and Ava caught up, motoring along in the Model A.

If the field belonged to a local farmer, Earl typically worked out a deal to pay the farmer a little money to use it – an expense he almost always grumbled about later, despite the fact that it was unavoidable. By trial and error, he learned to vary the price of the rides they offered; a handful of customers at a cut rate was better than no customers at all. To no one's surprise, Earl was very good at sizing people up and guessing what each town could afford to pay.

During those early days, both Hutch and Buzz urged Ava to come up for a scenic ride. She was vaguely panicked by the thought of soaring into the sky in one of the two heavy metal contraptions that seemed more likely to be earthbound. But she was also tempted. She felt something within her issuing a morbid but exciting dare.

'Bah!' Earl said, if he was within earshot when Hutch and Buzz began to rhapsodize about the pleasures of flying. 'The girl isn't a paying customer,' he pointed out. 'She doesn't need adventure; no reason to frighten the child! Unless . . . of course . . . *you'd* like to pay for the wasted fuel yourselves?'

Ava did not push for an airplane ride; she was both fascinated and terrified of the idea anyway, a true mix of emotions. After a while, Hutch and Buzz stopped inviting her to go up for a quick flight. The days and weeks and eventually months went by. She had a good head for numbers, and Earl put her in charge of the cashbox. Day in and day out, she sold scenic airplane rides . . . without ever having taken one herself.

They passed their first summer season of barnstorming without incident. But Earl's frustration returned as fall gave way to winter. Cold, rainy weather left them without any business, sometimes weeks at a time. They traveled south again, seeking the sun. By early spring, Earl was desperate to see his bottom line tick upward again. Up to that point, the flying circus had taken care to stick to smaller farming towns.

'You're gonna wanna stay at least a few miles away from anyplace that has an airport or airbase,' Hutch had advised, early on. 'It ain't worth attracting the attention.'

Earl had heeded this advice, but now he was itching to push his luck. From his time selling Pandora's Wonder Tonic he knew that the population of Los Angeles had exploded over the past three decades; Earl couldn't help but be tempted by all those potential passengers willing to pay a buck to say they'd gone up in an airplane. They began to circle in closer and closer to the city.

Just as Earl had hoped, sales indeed increased, until something happened. They were in El Monte, a little town on the outskirts of Los Angeles. Hutch and Buzz had flown a few stunts, and once a small crowd had gathered, they set about taking passengers up for scenic rides. Everything went smoothly and they were almost in the clear – they had already taken the last paying tourist up, the crowd had dispersed, and they were preparing to make camp for the evening – when a sheriff's car came rolling onto the empty field Earl had paid a local farmer to borrow.

The gentleman who stepped out of the car was well over six feet. He adjusted his hat against the midday glare and strode toward them with purpose. He introduced himself. It just so happened that he, Sheriff Thompson, had been a former Army pilot himself. He also happened to know about a little something called the Air Commerce Act.

'I been hearing in town that you folks put on an air show here today,' he said.

'Air show?' Earl roared, as though surprised.

'I hope you know,' the sheriff warned, 'putting on an unlicensed air show would be *illegal* in these here parts . . . I'd be obligated to report ya.'

'Oh, no,' Earl said, shaking his head and waving his hands gracefully. 'No, no – you have it all wrong, I assure you . . .'

The sheriff raised an eyebrow.

'We're just crop dusters!' Earl said with sudden, joyful vehemence. It was the cover story Buzz and Hutch had suggested he use should this very situation arise. His eyes slid involuntarily to his two pilots now, and each gave a tiny nod as if to affirm his tactic. 'Lots of orange groves around here,' Earl continued. 'We thought to avail ourselves to the local farmers . . .'

'Crop dusters, huh?' The sheriff aimed a skeptical look at the two colorfully painted biplanes over Earl's shoulder and shook his head. 'Sorry, but I gotta advise you to push on through these parts,' he said with an air of finality.

'But—' Earl began to protest, but the sheriff raised a hand to silence him.

'Look, let me put this in plain English for you: I'm giving you a chance to clear out of here without any further hassle. I'd take that deal if I were you, you understand?'

Earl backed down. He nodded. 'Well, sir!' he replied. 'We're only trying to make an honest living in the midst of these hard times; any man can understand *that*, these days! But if we're not wanted, then we'll go . . .'

'Good,' the sheriff replied, satisfied. 'Then you'll be moving on . . . I'll be back around on patrol later this evening and I won't expect to see you here. Good afternoon.' He touched the brim of his hat and strode back to his car. As he walked, he called over his shoulder, 'For the record, fellas, crop dusters don't tend to fly circles over the only *fallow* field for five miles in every direction!'

With that, the sheriff pulled the door to his Ford shut and started the engine again.

They had all witnessed the exchange: Ava, Cleo, Hutch, and Buzz. No one said anything. Ava looked at Earl; he looked deflated, but also angry enough that she half expected clouds of steam to shoot from his ears.

'Well?' Earl demanded, glaring at the group as the sheriff's car kicked up a cloud of hazy dust in its trail as it pulled away. 'Useless pack of beggars! Don't just stand there twiddling your thumbs! Pack everything back up!'

They did as they were told.

Later that night, once they had made camp in the San Gabriel Mountains, Earl was still angry. It was a setback. Ava knew it would be at least another day or two before they felt safe enough to try a new town, fly stunts, and sell rides. Earl couldn't stand to lose the money.

That evening, after the group had eaten supper, Ava's mother and Earl retired to the caravan, while Ava remained by the fire with Hutch and Buzz. Earl had been so agitated by the sheriff's earlier eviction he had barely eaten – a bad sign, Ava knew. She was dreading joining them in the caravan, for she suspected Earl was bent on picking a fight. *Picking a fight* was an inaccurate way to phrase it, because Cleo never argued back, really. Sometimes she never even spoke. Earl was capable of working himself into a lather all by himself.

Sure enough, as Ava sat around the fire with Hutch and Buzz, the sounds of Earl's angry voice began to boom from within the caravan. It got louder and louder, drifting toward them through the balmy night air.

Buzz's head jerked in the direction of the caravan, as though contemplating an interruption. Hutch shook his head at him, signaling to Buzz to stay right where he sat.

'I'd keep out of it,' Hutch said. 'It sounds like he's just blowin' off some steam.'

'What if he keeps at it or gets worse?'

'Then I'll step in and have a word with him. But you just stay where you are, Romeo.' He paused and waited for Buzz to contradict him, but Buzz didn't. 'Don't think Earl hasn't noticed the way you been lookin' at his wife.'

'Aw, shoot . . . I look at all women that way.'

'Maybe so, but he ain't gonna thank you for getting in his business now, tryin' to play the hero.' Hutch poked the fire with a stick. He glanced at Ava with gentle, apologetic eyes. 'That business is only between a man and his wife. Let's just let him yell hisself out for now. It'll pass.'

The dying flames danced back to life and the fire threw off a steady wave of cheek-warming heat. Eventually, Hutch was proven right: Earl yelled himself out and the caravan returned to a quiet, still state. Once everything had been silent for a half hour or so, Ava got up, brushed herself off, and went to bed, stepping lightly, careful not to wake her mother or – worse – Earl.

The next morning they traveled north, away from the city of Los Angeles. Having learned their lesson, they restricted their travels to the smaller, more rural towns.

'Like I say: make enough noise to scare up some business, but not enough to scare us up a hefty fine,' Hutch repeated.

Earl was frustrated but seemed resigned to the truth in Hutch's assessment. He was more mindful about keeping a quiet profile and kept them moving quickly from town to town, never lingering to bask in the attention they drew. The barnstormers carried on, carefully making a humble living. The days turned into months and eventually years, and Ava grew up as she always had, ever since the day her father died: with a jarring tempo, in starts and fits, like an airplane engine sputtering to life.

7

NEWCASTLE, CALIFORNIA
SEPTEMBER 16, 1943

The walk back into town is long and sweaty. By the time Agent Bonner makes it back to the sheriff's office, his shirt bears two large rings beneath his armpits. He passes by his Bureau car, still parked where he last left it, directly out front. He pushes his way through the front door of the office and steps inside.

It is ever so slightly cooler inside the building. The walls are painted hospital green, and the blinds are drawn against the September glare, while an oscillating fan lazily churns the air, the rhythmic whooshes of air making a sound like waves lapping a beach.

'There you are,' Deputy Henderson calls from across the room, rising from his desk. The sheriff's office is mostly one simple room, and there are three desks: a large one for the sheriff, a smaller one for the deputy, and an even smaller, unoccupied one for the woman who works as a part-time secretary. *Life in a one-horse town*, Bonner had uncharitably thought during his first encounter earlier that morning.

'We lost track of you at the crash site,' Henderson says. 'Wondered where you'd got off to.'

'I accompanied Louis Thorn back to the old Yamada house,' Bonner replies, shooting a look across the room, to where Sheriff Whitcomb sits hunched over a stack of paperwork on his large desk. Whitcomb doesn't look up. Neither Whitcomb nor Henderson apologizes for not making a better effort to locate Bonner and offer him a ride back into town. Not that Bonner wants to pick a bone with either of them.

'It seemed like a good idea to go ahead and pursue an interview with Thorn,' Bonner continues, allowing this indifference to roll off his back. 'You know . . . get his impressions of the crash while they're fresh.'

'Sure, that makes sense.' Henderson nods.

Bonner hears the sheriff grunt from across the room.

'What was that, Sheriff?' Bonner calls to Whitcomb.

'Learn anything useful?' Whitcomb replies without looking up from his desk.

'Maybe,' Bonner replies.

When the sheriff grunts again, Bonner ignores him. 'May I use your telephone to make some calls? Bureau business, of course.'

Henderson points Bonner in the direction of the unoccupied secretary's desk.

'Just so long as the FBI don't mind payin' for the charges,' Whitcomb reminds them in a loud voice, before Bonner even gets settled in and lifts the receiver.

The first order of business is to make sure the bodies are being taken to Sacramento as instructed – and now Bonner has a few additional demands. Louis Thorn confirmed that Harry hadn't performed any emergency maneuvers. It occurs to Bonner that, instead of being suicidal, perhaps Harry was intoxicated or incapacitated in some way. He wants to have the Yamadas' blood tested if possible. Bonner can feel Henderson and Whitcomb listening in as he gives the coroner instructions to send some samples down to the FBI's laboratory in Los Angeles.

'I'll be staying in town for a few days,' Bonner says, once he has hung up the phone.

'I woulda thought now that you know exactly where your runaway Japs are, you'd be on your way,' Whitcomb says.

'It's not that simple, I'm afraid,' Bonner says. 'Given the crash.'

'I heard you ordering those tests. Can't imagine what kinds of nonsense you're imagining went on, but you ain't planning on harassing any of my citizens here, are you? You know as well as I do, the two Japs in that plane was the ones who crashed it, open and shut. We should all just be thankful no one got hurt.'

No one got hurt. Bonner doesn't point out that two people, in fact, died. He knows it's the wrong point to make, the wrong deaths to count. 'I just need to round up sufficient information for my report,' Bonner says instead. 'It's routine.'

Whitcomb doesn't reply. Bonner is intrigued by the fact that Whitcomb seems to want to protect Thorn from scrutiny.

'Know of any hotels?' Bonner asks, directing his attention to Henderson.

'Sacramento's got plenty,' the sheriff says, pretending to be absorbed again in the paperwork on his desk. Bonner knows Sacramento is a good hour away.

'I'd like to keep closer to the evidence,' Bonner replies. He tamps down his annoyance with Whitcomb and directs his question to Henderson instead. 'Know anybody renting out a room?'

'I heard Lindy MacFarlane is looking to take on boarders,' Henderson offers in a cheerful, eager voice, oblivious to the sheriff's prohibitive evil eye. 'If you like, I'll draw you a map to her place and telephone ahead to let 'er know you're coming.'

'Much obliged,' Bonner replies, earnestly grateful. A fresh thought occurs to him. 'Tell you what, Henderson,' he continues, 'maybe tomorrow evening, after I get settled in, I can buy you a beer to repay you for your kindness.'

Deputy Henderson's face lights up. 'That'd be mighty generous of you,' he says. It is plain he is thrilled at the prospect of being seen out drinking a beer with an agent from the Federal Bureau.

'I believe I heard something about a place here in town . . . Murphy's Saloon, was it? That the place where Joe Abbott tends bar?'

'How'd you know that?'

'Just something Louis Thorn mentioned,' Bonner replies with a nonchalant shrug.

'Funny thing to come up.'

'Indeed,' Bonner agrees.

He sighs, takes the hand-drawn map and the address Henderson has scribbled down, and prepares to leave. Across the room, Sheriff Whitcomb finally looks up from his desk, and Bonner can feel the sheriff's hot glare. Why won't the sheriff help him, anyway? That's another question gnawing at Bonner. For now, he's merely content to track down a place to get a meal, a shower, and a shave.

'Say, is Murphy's Saloon pretty easy to find?' Bonner asks.

'Easy enough.' Henderson nods. 'It's on the main drag here in town.'

'All right. See you there tomorrow around six o'clock,' Bonner says, and, tipping his somewhat damp fedora back on his head, leaves.

8

The MacFarlane house is a small, vertical Victorian cottage located on the outskirts of town, near the railroad tracks. The first thing Agent Bonner notices when he climbs out of the Bureau car is that the house is in a state of disrepair. The most noticeable defect is that the house leans; it is as though a clapboard-sided creature has heaved a great sigh and forgotten to straighten up its shoulders again. It also appears as though the house was once painted white by some unseen optimistic hand, but for want of more whitewash over the years it has now been left to lapse into a weather-beaten gray. Yet, despite the house's obvious lack of regular maintenance, it bears a welcoming air – even if it is a lonesome, almost wistful welcome at that.

When Bonner climbs the rickety porch stairs and raps on the door, he is surprised by the sight of the woman who opens it. He expected an elderly widow but is greeted instead by a young woman close to his own age, with chocolaty-brown curls, a fetching mouth, and large, brooding eyes. There is a flicker of something in them that reflects the house's appearance – something curiously lonely yet welcoming.

As she peers out from behind the screen door, she visibly flinches to see Agent Bonner standing on her porch. Her smile vanishes and the expression that replaces it remains frozen upon her face.

'Good afternoon, ma'am. My name is William Bonner,' he explains awkwardly. 'I'm in town on some business for the Federal Bureau of Investigation, and I've come to see about renting a room . . .'

His introduction peters out as he waits for some response from her. Instead, she stands there, staring, looking him over from head to foot, openly evaluating each detail in turn.

'Yes, I know,' she says finally. 'Dwight Henderson telephoned from the sheriff's office.'

'Then I've come to the right place,' he replies, wondering – if she had indeed expected him – what accounted for her startled expression. He glances at the slip of paper where Deputy Henderson scribbled down her full name next to her address and some bare-bones driving directions. 'You must be Rosalind MacFarlane.'

'I am. Come in.'

She turns and disappears into the darkness within, and after a brief second of hesitation Bonner follows. Inside, the house is as ramshackle as it is outside, but with a wealth of furniture and potted ferns. The stained-glass window over the front door, as dirty as it is, lets in light in a murky kaleidoscope of colors and patterns.

'Would you like some iced tea?' Rosalind asks over her shoulder as she paces through the house.

'All right,' Bonner agrees. He glances around, looking for signs of other boarders. 'Forgive me, but is it just you here?'

'My grandmother passed on not long ago and left this house to me. I had intended to sell it . . .' she says, and pauses. 'But things changed, and I decided it would be wiser to take in boarders instead.'

Her explanation doesn't directly address his question, but Bonner takes it to mean there are no other guests at present.

She shows him to the sitting room and proceeds to rattle about in the kitchen for five minutes or so, then returns with a tray laden with two glasses and a small pitcher of iced tea. They sit sipping for several minutes. It occurs to Bonner that he ought to raise the question of his accommodations and the price. But as his eyes adjust to the dark of the house's interior, he begins to make out his hostess's face more clearly, and something stops him short.

'Have you been crying, ma'am?' he blurts out before he can stop himself.

She looks at him but does not answer.

'I beg your pardon,' Bonner rushes to add, ashamed. 'It's none of my business.'

'You can have the spare room upstairs,' Rosalind answers, as though deaf to both his question and his apology. 'I charge two dollars a night. Three if you want two square meals included. There's only one lavatory in the house, so that we'll have to share. How long do you intend to stay?'

He can't help but feel she has a peculiar way about her. While it is natural to cast the occasional glance at a person's face while engaged in conversation, it seems to Bonner that she is staring at him, and staring quite intently at that. Uncomfortable, he shifts in the worn velvet armchair and clears his throat.

'Well, now, I suppose that depends . . .' Bonner begins to reply.

'On?'

'On how long this investigation takes.'

No flicker of expression passes over Rosalind's face as she continues to hold Agent Bonner in her stare. When she speaks, she says in a matter-of-fact voice: 'And that will depend on how long it takes for you to explain how those two escaped Japs turned up dead in that airplane crash today.'

It is a statement, not a question. Agent Bonner's eyes widen; he is surprised she should know so much and speak with so much authority. He frowns, slightly alarmed. Rosalind waves a hand to put him at ease.

'Dwight likes to gossip,' she explains.

'Dwight?' he repeats. 'Oh – yes . . . Deputy Henderson . . .'

'As I mentioned, he telephoned to let me know you were coming.'

'Sure.'

Bonner considers this. Ordinarily, he doesn't like to discuss the details of an open case. But it occurs to him that just as Deputy Henderson has leaked the day's gossip to Rosalind MacFarlane, she might be the recipient of other town gossip as well. Bonner thinks back to the bruises on Louis Thorn's face. Thorn's flimsy lie struck him as an obvious cover-up.

'The deputy and the sheriff,' Bonner says, 'they mentioned something about the Thorn family having some kind of bad blood with their Japanese neighbors. They said it was more or less common knowledge among folks around here.'

'Yes,' Rosalind answers. She does not elaborate, and the air in the room thickens with the ticking of the mantel clock.

'Well, what I don't understand so much is how those two boys – Louis Thorn and Harry Yamada – got to be friends if there were hostilities between their families.'

Rosalind's gaze is vacant. She shrugs.

'I suppose it was the airplanes that brought them together,' she says.

'How did that come about?'

'Well, first, that flying circus came to town. That was likely the beginning of it,' Rosalind replies.

'That would be Earl Shaw's Flying Circus?' Agent Bonner asks, pulling out his notebook and glancing at his scribbles from earlier.

'I suppose so. Didn't go myself. That barnstorming act came to town and kicked up a ruckus. And rumor had it them two boys got it in their heads to run away with the circus, so to speak.'

'And that's when they became friends?'

Rosalind shrugs again. She sniffs as though irritated. 'That's when they had something in common, I suppose.' She aims a somewhat bitter look at Bonner. 'I can't tell you *why* they became friendly. I don't know that anybody in this town can tell you that. But loving those airplanes gave them a reason to cross paths.'

'May I ask, Miss MacFarlane . . .' Agent Bonner begins. Her words have given him permission to ask what he really wants to ask. 'Do you have any reason to believe Louis Thorn would hurt Kenichi or Haruto Yamada?'

She looks at Bonner, saying nothing. For the space of a minute, she gazes at him in silence.

'No,' she finally replies. She presses her lips together in an expression that Bonner can't quite make out.

Bonner has the distinct impression she is lying.

Hours later, after dusk has come and gone, after the earth has cooled and the air has turned fresh and crisp again and filled with the music of crickets, Agent Bonner prepares to turn in for the night. It is plain that indoor plumbing was an afterthought to the house's architect: the sole lavatory Rosalind mentioned earlier is little more than a small structure accessed by going through the kitchen. In the bathroom, Bonner finds a bar of hand soap and uses it to scrub away the soot still on his skin from the crash site, then splashes some water on his skin and decides to tidy up the remainder of his person first thing tomorrow morning. He pulls the brass chain to switch off the electric bulb overhead and makes his way back up the creaking stairs to his bedroom. Rosalind showed him the room two hours earlier, after the dinner she'd cooked for him as part of his room and board.

She lingered in the room after that initial showing, pointing out the room's various quirks: the nightstand drawer with a broken handle, the best way to open the window for a night breeze. When she ran out of details that might warrant explaining, she simply stood in the middle of the room, waiting, between Bonner and the rickety queen-size bed she had only minutes ago apologized for as she pointed out a couple of lumpy springs.

Bonner had the sensation that she wanted something . . . that she either wanted to tell him something or she wanted something *from* him. He had an urge to reach one hand up and touch her shoulder – lightly, just to reassure her somehow. But before he could do anything, she abruptly turned and, without so much as another word, left the room.

A strange hostess, indeed. She retreated to her own room, and he had not seen hide nor hair of her for the past two hours.

Now, as he slips out of his suspenders, unbuttons his collared shirt, strips the latter off, and pulls his undershirt over his head, he thinks he hears the faint metallic groaning of unoiled hinges. His back is to the door, and when he looks behind him, he notices that it now hangs open a crack. He's nearly certain he pulled it shut after he made his way upstairs from the bathroom.

The dark splinter of doorway stares back at him.

'Hello?' he speaks into the quiet of the room.

No one answers from the hallway. Agent Bonner waits a full minute, listening, but there is nothing. It is an old house; the door doesn't quite fit in the doorjamb anyway, being slightly too small on one side. It has likely cracked open out of regular habit. He pulls the quilts back and slips into bed. The sheets are pleasant against his skin – clean and cool.

He lies there, thinking about the Yamadas, about the spectacular airplane crash he witnessed earlier that morning and about Louis Thorn's cagey behavior both before and after the fact. He thinks about the 'flying circus' that, according to Rosalind MacFarlane, brought the two young men together in an unlikely friendship – or, at the very least, some sort of alliance. He thinks, too, about his new landlady and the strange intensity of her stare.

William Bonner's eyes are closed and he has almost drifted entirely off to sleep when he hears the floorboards creaking just outside his door and the soft footfall of someone hurrying away down the hallway.

9

EARL SHAW'S FLYING CIRCUS
NEWCASTLE, CALIFORNIA, MAY 4, 1940

Two biplanes approached each other from opposite sides of the horizon. They moved in steady progression, both of them exactly the same height above the ground, piloted toward each other over what seemed like an impossibly smooth, invisible road. If they continued on their course, they would meet in the middle of the open field, somewhere just over Louis Thorn's head. As they approached, the whining drone of their engines filled the air as though the sound were liquid and the curved dome of the sky were an empty drinking glass. Each time Louis thought the whine of the engines couldn't get louder, it got louder still. And it wasn't just that the engine noise increased; its reverberation intensified, too, until eventually it felt like a hive of bees thrumming within Louis's own chest. His heart pumped faster.

Louis had first heard the unfamiliar sound – fainter, farther off in the distance – while milking the cows during the early hours of dawn, and wondered what it could be. A few hours later, while on an errand for his mother, he rode the old mare into town and on his way back took a shortcut through Irving Sumpter's fallow field. The two biplanes completely surprised him – not to mention his horse – seeming to abruptly materialize in the sky. Once he'd recovered from his shock, Louis recognized the sound as a louder version of what he'd heard earlier that morning, and realized it must have been these two airplanes arriving in the area.

He climbed down from his horse to watch. Now the two biplanes were almost overhead. It was funny: from a distance it looked like they weren't going that fast – no faster than an automobile, anyway. But as they drew nearer, their true racing speed was revealed. Now they were very close to each other; Louis no longer had to turn his head from side to side to alternately check on one, then the other. Both fit together in a single glimpse of cloudless sky. One biplane was red with white stripes painted on the tail, the other royal blue with a sprinkling of white stars on the tail. The two of them made a deconstructed American flag reassembling itself.

It looked as though they were bound to collide. Louis understood this was purely for show, but he found himself holding his breath anyway. At the very last second, the two planes tipped their wings sideways in a very narrow pass, turning so they flew head to head as they moved past each other, the topsides of their wings appearing to nearly touch. They leveled out again. Then both arced upward, the whining pitch of their two engines changing as it became clear they were intent on executing a pair of loop-the-loops in opposite directions.

Louis watched in amazement, squinting into the cockpits at the pilots, trying to imagine seeing what they were seeing. His stomach lurched a little just trying to picture it: the earth surging away, disappearing, rising overhead like a moon, and eventually rushing toward you again. What only a bird might see. Downright unnatural for a human. Having completed their tandem loop-the-loops, the two biplanes flew on, going in opposite directions yet again. Two circles of white vapor trailed behind in the air where the planes had completed their perfectly symmetrical maneuvers, a pair of wedding rings floating down from the heavens.

'They're just doing all that to draw a crowd,' a voice said from somewhere down in the tall grass near where he stood. 'I hope they haven't alarmed you.'

Louis jumped. He hadn't realized he wasn't alone. His horse whinnied. He stroked the mare's muzzle to calm her again and cast a hurried glance around, blindly looking for the source of the voice and eventually spotting a figure lying flat on its back. The shape appeared to be lounging, cradling its head in its hands and staring up at the sky overhead. A flash of red hair, a pair of men's trousers . . . Louis squinted more closely and realized he was looking at a girl.

She sat up, chewing a tall weed that protruded unapologetically from one side of her mouth.

'They make a big fuss on purpose, flying all the tricks they can think of, see,' the girl continued, her teeth still gnashing away at the weed. 'That way they get people's attention, get their curiosity piqued.'

She crawled to her feet, stood up, spat out the weed, and brushed herself off, finishing the performance by giving a lazy, halfhearted yawn and arch of her back. Louis remained silent, a little dumbstruck.

'I guess it's kind of like their calling card,' the girl added now, since Louis had yet to reply. 'A way to drum up business. They'll fly a few tricks every half hour for an hour or two – see? Hopefully people will get curious enough to come out to have a closer look, until there's enough people to start offering rides. It's how a barnstorming act works.'

Louis cocked his head at the girl. 'How do you know that?' he asked, finally breaking his mute state.

'Oh,' the girl said. 'I thought you'd guessed as much . . . I'm with the barnstorming act.'

He felt like a fool. Of course she was with the barnstorming act. He'd never seen her before, and the towns around those parts were small; new faces were rare. He looked more closely. She was probably only a year or two younger than himself, skinny and on the tomboyish side. She possessed a magnificent bob of red hair that was paired with bright, catlike pale green eyes and rather browned, freckled skin. Louis felt an unexpected sensation of heat rising to his face.

It appeared she was studying him in return. Her small pink bow of a mouth broke into an amused smirk, and she looked Louis over from head to toe as if trying to decide how much of a rube he was.

'My name is Ava,' she said, holding out her hand. 'Ava Brooks. The planes are my stepfather's. I travel around with this act.' She pointed to the sky. 'My stepfather announces the show, my mother sells her homemade lemonade, and our two pilots, Buzz and Hutch, do all the flying. I collect money for the airplane rides.'

'Nice . . . to meet you,' Louis stammered, taking her hand. 'Louis Thorn.'

They shook, and Ava noted the firm grip of his handshake. He was handsome, too, in a clean-cut, all-American sort of way. There was an easy, friendly air about him.

'Listen, if you're interested in going up for an airplane ride, they'll probably start taking folks up in about an hour or so,' Ava said.

'Really?' His face lit up.

'Of course.'

But then a new thought occurred to Louis, casting a small shadow over Ava's suggestion.

'How much is it for a ride?' he asked.

Ava smiled gleefully, and shrugged. 'Well . . . some flying circuses charge their passengers as much as ten or fifteen dollars,' she replied.

'Fifteen dollars?' Louis repeated, incredulous. He coughed and tried to hide his disappointment; he didn't want the fact of his poverty to be obvious.

'But,' Ava continued, 'this one is a little down on its luck. Only, don't tell my stepfather I said that.'

She chuckled but also glanced over her shoulder, as though the stepfather she had mentioned might suddenly materialize. She turned back and smiled again, but this time there was a vaguely awkward, embarrassed element to her expression.

'My guess is, we'll probably be asking folks for a fiver,' she concluded.

'Five dollars?'

'Yep. You think you'll go up for a ride?'

Louis felt his pulse quicken and his palms grow sweaty. Five dollars was a fortune in the Thorn household. He looked up again at the two biplanes as they zoomed overhead in the blue sky.

'I'll have to go home to fetch the money . . . and put the horse back in the pasture, I guess . . .'

Ava shrugged and smiled again.

'There ought to be time enough for all that,' she said. 'Earl likes to make sure we've drawn a decent crowd first before we start to sell individual rides. If you do want to go up, I'll be taking money right over there.'

She pointed in the direction of where a wooden caravan that was hitched to an old Model A was parked some distance away in the field. Someone had set a rickety old wooden table and chair out in the open air. Tied to the table with rope was a handmade sign that read SCENIC AIRPLANE RIDES SOLD HERE!

'Will I see you there?' she asked.

Louis turned back to Ava. Her eyes flashed like a dare. There was nothing to do but grin and nod like a fool.

10

After about an hour's worth of flying stunts, Buzz and Hutch had managed to attract a small crowd. They performed trick after trick, until finally enough people had gathered so that an audible 'Oooh!' and 'Ahhh!' could be periodically heard at the completion of each feat.

Earl stepped up onto a crate and shouted into a megaphone.

'*Let's give 'em a hand, folks!*'

Sensing that enough of a crowd had gathered to merit his presence, he had emerged from the caravan to play host and do the announcing. From where she was sitting, Ava could see that, as usual, Earl was dressed to the nines in a loud red jacket and stood very erect, his shoulders thrust back and his dark hair heavily oiled.

'*Can't say you see something like that every day, now, can ya?*' he bellowed.

The sixty or so people who had congregated in Irving Sumpter's field obediently applauded, despite the fact that it was clear the performers, high up in their biplanes, could not hear their appreciation. Sumpter himself stood nearby, arms folded, taking stock of the goings-on. When the planes had touched down in his field earlier that morning, Sumpter saddled his horse and went out to investigate. By the time he reached the planes, a puttering truck hauling a caravan had come bumping along over the rutted land. Earl hopped out and offered Sumpter a ten-dollar bill to 'borrow' the field for the day.

'*Alllll-righty, folks!*' Earl shouted now. '*Who wants to go up for a ride? Step right up and form a line! Don't push: I promise you, everybody gets a turn! Best scenic tour you'll ever take!'*

'How much?' someone hollered.

'*Why, the ride is free!*' Earl called back in reply.

There was an astonished gasp.

'*But the* landing *will cost you five dollars!*' Earl concluded.

A ripple of good-humored chuckles sounded from the onlookers. It was a common joke among barnstormers; the crowd couldn't know how the tired punch line had been pilfered from a flying circus back east, which in turn had stolen it from yet another circus down south.

'*Step lively, now!*' Earl continued, but sales were temporarily interrupted when the two biplanes came in for a landing. All heads turned and watched as first one and then the other flew lower and lower and eventually touched down upon the yellowing crabgrass of the fallow field. The first plane bounced along, taxied, turned, and rolled to a stop. Minutes later, the second rolled in next to it. Shouts and cheers floated into the air as the two pilots laughed and hollered back and forth to each other.

'*Meet our aeronautical masters of the sky, folks!*' Earl called out, waving an arm toward the two pilots as they approached.

'*Mr Ray "Hutch" Hutchinson!*'

Hutch climbed down from *Castor*, the red plane, and raised a hand in a kindly wave.

'*And his esteemed colleague, Mr Charlie "Buzz" Lambert!*' Earl shouted, gesturing to the second pilot.

Buzz descended from *Pollux*, the blue plane, gave a cocky grin, waved – and quickly added a wink when his gaze fell upon a young lady in the crowd.

'*Now, my friends . . . as I was saying, five dollars is a mere pittance in exchange for the adventure of a lifetime! You won't regret it! Yes, indeedy, folks! Right this way!*' Earl continued in his signature showy tone, '*Step right up and purchase your ride – ahem, I mean to say,* landing, *of course! – from the lovely lofty Ava here!*' He paused ever so briefly to make a sweeping gesture in the direction of where Ava sat presiding over a cigar box of cash, collecting bills and coins. '*That's right, folks! That lil' lady will help you to purchase what is guaranteed to be the most memorable experience of your lives! Around here we call her Lovely Lofty Ava, First Lady of "Avi"-ation, hah!'*

Ava resisted the urge to roll her eyes. She hated when Earl trotted out all that 'First Lady of "Avi"-ation' garbage. Part of the reason she hated it was because it struck her as misleading; after all, Ava had *still* never been up in an airplane – not once.

There was a second reason, too. Earl had only started using lines like that in reference to Ava in recent years. Ava was dimly aware that she was no longer a child; she had grown into a young woman, and she felt the new weight of male eyes on her. She hadn't quite made peace yet with her new role. She had watched Earl use her mother's beauty to charm customers – even back in the old Pandora's Wonder Tonic days – and Ava was queasy at the idea of Earl using her own femininity to perfect his hustle.

By that point, people were beginning to approach her where she sat at the little rickety wooden table. The first stragglers were shy, but soon a lively group began to crowd around, and eventually the aspiring airplane passengers formed a small line. Ava took money, made change, and kept track of whose turn it was to climb into one of the two biplanes.

After helping the first five or so customers, she looked up briefly from the cigar box and felt her eyes scanning the horizon around the field, searching for the young man she'd encountered earlier. Would he come back? If he did, was it because she'd smiled and teased him a little and given him little opportunity to decline? Was she no better than Earl? No, she told herself. Her friendliness was sincere in a way Earl's wasn't. And there had been something about the young man; she'd taken an instant liking to him.

She glanced around the field again, and – as if on cue – her eyes hit upon the figure she sought. There he was: the young man who'd introduced himself as Louis Thorn. Ava watched as Louis picked his way across the field, shading his eyes and watching as *Castor* and *Pollux* took off with fresh passengers in tow.

As he turned back, his eyes caught Ava's and he gave a tiny, subtle wave. She smiled in return. She continued to watch Louis out of the corner of her eye as he stepped into the line that had formed in front of her table. Ava went on selling rides and taking money, keeping note of Louis's position in line. A few more people stepped into the line behind him. Eventually, it was his turn to pay his money and buy an airplane ride.

'Why, hullo again,' Ava chirped, genuinely happy to see him.

'Hi,' Louis replied, sheepish. She noticed that he'd changed his clothes; he was now attired in a nice white cotton shirt and brown slacks. She watched as he felt for his shirt pocket and produced five one-dollar bills.

'Five dollars,' Louis said, as though to verify the number of bills he'd just dropped on the table.

She couldn't help but notice the tremor in his hand. Ava took his money and folded it around the growing wad of bills lumped within the cigar box. She glanced up at Louis and smiled in a manner that she hoped reassured him.

'It's very safe, you know – traveling by airplane,' she said. 'Why, they say it's even safer than traveling by automobile, as a matter of fact.'

'I'm not scared,' Louis said, but he'd rushed to say it and said it a little *too* quickly. Ava looked at him, and in that second the two exchanged a look of knowing.

The moment was interrupted by the sound of an amused grunt – covered by a quick cough – emanating from somewhere over Louis's shoulder. Ava wouldn't have paid it much mind, except for that fact that when Louis turned around to address the person, she noticed Louis's whole body palpably stiffen. She peered over his shoulder and noticed a second young man around the same age as Louis. Ava took a closer look and noticed the other young man was Oriental.

Slowly, Louis turned around.

'Got something to say?' he asked the young man standing behind him.

Ava was surprised by the aggression in Louis's voice: when she'd encountered him alone in the field earlier, Louis had struck her as having an easy, open disposition. She wondered what it was about the second young man that rubbed Louis the wrong way.

Feeling the weight of her gaze, the young man glanced at Ava. As they locked eyes, a small chill ran over her skin and up the back of her neck to the base of her skull, a ripple of . . . *something*. Ava was hard-pressed to identify her reaction. She studied his features as if some answer were to be found there. The young man's dark hair was surprisingly thick and ever so slightly wavy, combed back from his forehead and face to reveal a pair of high, haughty cheekbones. His nose was rather long but flat and narrow, his mouth and chin finely carved, set in a stern manner. But it was the expression inscribed upon his brow that caught Ava's attention the most. His eyebrows were downright cocky and amused. His face struck an interesting contradiction between stern and jovial.

By now Ava had asked the young man for his five dollars, and he had paid it. He was handsome, Ava realized, a beat too late, and she found herself blushing with this obvious albeit belated discovery. Ava forced herself to stare down at the cashbox sitting in front of her with sudden concentration.

'Harry Yamada,' the young man said, extending a forthright hand.

Ava looked at the hand but did not reach to shake it. Out the corner of her eye, she noticed a smug twist of Louis's lips as he observed her snub.

'If you'll both just stand over there while you wait your turn,' she said to Louis and the second young man. She pointed at the accumulating group of future passengers, all of them waiting to go up, and the two young men joined the shuffling group.

Louis nodded and moved in the direction she indicated. The other young man – Harry, as he'd introduced himself – followed. The air of animosity between the two boys did not dissipate, but, for the slenderest of seconds, Ava thought she saw Harry turn back and wink at her – a flirtatious, mocking wink, as though he'd known her blush was for him. She gasped at his audacity, but in the next second he was facing away again, a placid, businesslike expression on his face. It had happened so fast, Ava wasn't entirely certain it had happened at all.

11

How had he not noticed Harry Yamada standing behind him? They'd exchanged less than a handful of words over the last seven years. Both were acutely aware of the feud that existed between their families, and the two took great care to avoid each other.

Now Louis narrowed his eyes at Harry.

The grunt could have meant anything, but Louis took it precisely in only one manner. The resentment ran deep, and it didn't help that Louis had been obliged to quit school a year and a half earlier to help out on his family's ranch full-time, a humiliation Harry Yamada did not have to endure, as his family had a significantly better parcel of land. The Yamadas were well-to-do; Harry and his sister, Mae, always had good clothes and new schoolbooks. By contrast, Louis was one of twelve children born to Edith Thorn, who, ever since Louis's father passed away some eight years earlier, had been left to rely upon her children to run the family ranch.

It didn't help, either, that all the Thorn children had been taught that the Yamadas' superior acreage originally belonged to their grandfather, Ennis Thorn, and that Ennis had been tricked out of the land in an act of grave injustice. The story had been handed down – first from Ennis to his son John, and then from John to Louis and his many brothers and sisters. With their father dead, Louis's eldest brother, Guy, was chiefly responsible for keeping the story alive. Louis looked up to Guy, who worked harder than anyone Louis had ever known. So when Guy warned Louis to 'keep away from the thieving Japs who stole our land,' Louis did his best to oblige. But Louis, being Louis, found that hostility did not come naturally to him.

'Got something to say?' Louis repeated now.

Harry shrugged and shook his head. He raised his hands in a show of innocent ignorance. This much seemed aimed at placating Louis. But there was a hint of some additional gesture – not quite a grin, but almost. It struck Louis as superior. He grew more irritated than ever.

Louis returned his attention to the two biplanes. They went up and down, up and down, flying off into the distance and disappearing for about ten minutes or so at a time. With every landing, they unloaded a fresh, giddy passenger flushed with excitement and loaded up a wide-eyed, uninitiated pale passenger in exchange.

The better part of a half hour elapsed, and finally it was Louis's turn to go up. Both biplanes landed within a minute of each other; each unloaded a passenger. This meant Louis and the person after him – in this case, Harry – would be going up at the same time, each with a different pilot. Louis would rather not go up at the same time as Harry Yamada, but he couldn't think of a way to raise an objection that wouldn't sound childish. So Louis simply eyed the two pilots, who stood up in their cockpits and began to climb down. They approached the waiting crowd and waved Louis and Harry over.

'C'mon, boys!' the older pilot hollered. 'We don't have all day!'

Louis found himself rooted where he stood. Then his feet came unstuck and his legs operated on instinct. He could hear footfalls behind him. Louis gritted his teeth and picked up the pace.

They drew nearer to the planes. On the red plane, Louis saw gold lettering that read *CASTOR*, and the same gold lettering with the word *POLLUX* on the blue plane. Louis wondered which biplane – and, by extension, which pilot – to choose. His heart quickened and his eyes darted back and forth. He thought he felt Harry fall back a bit. A gesture of politeness? Or was Harry just as intimidated?

'Well, hurry up and hop in, kid!' the younger, blond pilot called, staring directly at Louis, solving Louis's dilemma. Louis walked toward the blue biplane, turned his head, and glimpsed Harry walking toward the red.

'The pilot doesn't ride in the front?' Louis overheard Harry ask in a puzzled voice. Louis rolled his eyes. The way it worked, the pilot sat in the second cockpit, in the back, with the passenger up front; Louis knew that much from books and newsreels, and from building models.

The blond pilot clambered up into the cockpit and handed down a cap and goggles to Louis. They were damp with the perspiration of previous passengers and smelled a little like mildew, but Louis didn't care; he received them with a sense of awe. Carefully he fit them over his head, doing up the strap under his chin with hands that were still trembling. The pilot directed Louis to climb into the cockpit and buckle up for safety.

'Okeydokey, kid, you all strapped in nice 'n' tight?' the blond pilot asked.

'Yes, sir.'

'No need for formalities, kid. This ain't the military or nothin'. Say, why don'tcha call me Buzz?'

'Yes, sir – Buzz, sir,' Louis accidentally bleated out. He twisted in his seat just in time to catch Buzz's amused, exasperated expression.

'Well, hell . . . sometimes you can't teach a new dog new tricks, neither. All right. If you're all set, let's get this thing on up in the air!'

Louis forced a stiff nod.

'Contact!' Buzz shouted, and pushed the electric starter.

The engine let out a mighty cough and suddenly the front propeller at the nose of the biplane sprang to life. It gave a puttering whir that was at first quite satisfying, then grew slightly terrifying as the blades began to beat the air in earnest. Buzz dropped a hand lever down and the plane began to roll along the empty expanse of Irving Sumpter's fallow field.

A short distance away, the other pilot, Hutch, yelled out, 'Contact!' and Louis heard the second biplane's engine cough and sputter. He looked over and saw Harry staring straight at him, looking as calm as anything under his own set of cap and goggles. There was no trace of worry etched upon his face, a confident excitement the only legible emotion.

Louis found himself envious of Harry's lack of fear, and his mind reactively flicked back to something his father used to say over and over again: *Damn idiot foreigners.* Now Louis's brother Guy repeated these words, adding, *Those Japs cheated your grandfather out of his land, despite the fact these damn idiot foreigners hardly even know how to run a ranch.* The last part was open to debate. While Kenichi Yamada had planted several varieties of things in his orchards that neither Ennis nor Louis's father, John Thorn, would have ever considered – plums, almonds, satsuma oranges – the Yamada family turned a nice profit. Their orchards meant they always had plenty to sell at the fruit-packing sheds dotted along the train tracks in town, and their cattle grazed, fat and happy, on the remainder of the land that, to his dying day, Ennis Thorn insisted they'd swindled from him.

Louis's attention was brought back to the present as the biplane began to pick up a little speed. After a moment, the second biplane began to drift toward the runway, too. Harry's confident smile disappeared from sight as Hutch steered his biplane behind the first and pumped the brake. Louis understood they were going to follow each other, one plane trailing the other on takeoff.

'All righty, kid. We'll get some speed up and be in the air in no time!' Buzz hollered over the propeller and engine. 'Ready?'

Louis stared stiffly ahead; he couldn't see Buzz behind him, but he nodded.

'And . . . up we go!' Buzz announced.

Bumpity-bumpity-bumpity-bump-bump-bump. Crabgrass and gopher holes. Sumpter's field was hardly a smooth surface, but even so, Louis had not expected the takeoff to be so bumpy or the biplane to bounce so much. He regretted eating breakfast. (His mother, Edith, had served up eggs and ham, along with a no-nonsense expression.) It was rough going for a minute or so, and then . . . all of a sudden . . . the jarring motion petered out and was replaced by a vacuum of friction, a smooth weightless feeling as the biplane lifted off the ground.

Louis felt a sense of exhilaration and euphoria come over him. But it was short-lived. Buzz pulled back on the stick and Louis's stomach felt as though it had detached from his body. His innards seemed to drop away from him as the biplane began to climb higher and higher. His body pressed down in the seat as they continued to rise. Then Buzz descended a bit, and Louis suddenly felt light as a feather. As they leveled off, Louis felt a little more normal and Buzz began to make a scenic tour of the area. The snowcapped Sierra Nevadas hovered in the distance on one side of the plane, the flat, fertile Sacramento Valley on the other. Louis peered over the edge of the cockpit and recognized the American River, and from that was able to deduce the names of the mining towns, one after the other, mostly dots along the water.

After a while, Louis relaxed. To his surprise, he was thoroughly enjoying the tour. But as he stared down at the rolling land below with a dazed expression, his ears pricked to the sound of the second biplane. He twisted in his seat and saw that Harry and the other pilot, Hutch, were floating into formation with Louis and Buzz. Harry appeared exhilarated, like he was having the time of his life. He grinned and waved, but Louis only clenched his jaw. The two biplanes flew along like this for a time; Louis found himself slightly distracted and a little less engaged with the scenic tour he'd paid five precious dollars to enjoy.

'Okay, kid! Time to head back now,' Buzz hollered over the noise of the wind and the plane's engine. Louis turned his head and nodded solemnly, trying to resist the urge to protest. It all felt much too quick; he had just gotten comfortable with the unfamiliar sensations of flying. It couldn't be over already.

Buzz tilted the wings so they did a slow circle, and the mountains that had been on the left side of the plane slowly swiveled so that now they were on the right. But shortly after they'd turned 180 degrees, something happened that caught Louis completely off-guard. Hutch, the pilot of the other biplane, began making hand signals to Louis's pilot, Buzz. The young blond pilot nodded in approval and gave a thumbs-up. Louis heard Buzz chuckling.

'Well, I'll be damned,' Buzz said to himself. 'Got yourself a goddamned daredevil passenger there, eh, Hutch?' Buzz proceeded to pedal the rudders to catch some drag, slowing down and falling behind Hutch's plane as though to give it more space.

'What's wrong with Harry and that other pilot? What're they gonna do?' Louis shouted back to Buzz. But Buzz didn't answer; he only grinned and pointed ahead. Louis turned back to face forward just in time to see Hutch (and Harry) corkscrew through the air in a barrel roll. Louis was shocked, speechless. It didn't matter: Hutch and Harry weren't done. Once they pulled out of the barrel roll, the biplane leveled off, then – to Louis's further astonishment – rocketed up vertically into the sky. Up and up the other plane went, until Louis understood on instinct: they were going to complete a loop-the-loop. And, sure enough, they did. They began in front of Louis and Buzz, arced overhead, and turned up behind the blue plane.

Once the red biplane had made its full loop, it leveled out and pulled back into formation behind Louis and Buzz. Louis could hear Harry hooting and hollering from the front cockpit, euphoric from having turned upside down in the air and lived to tell the tale.

Hutch shouted something to Buzz that Louis couldn't hear, and Buzz shouted something back. When shouting became too difficult, the two of them reverted to their complicated hand gesturing. Louis had a feeling he knew what was coming when Buzz returned his attentions to the passenger in front of him.

'What do ya say, kid?' Buzz hollered. 'Whaddaya say we give 'em a run for their money?'

Louis froze, unable to speak.

'How 'bout it?' Buzz prodded.

'Yeah. All right,' Louis finally said, shaking himself.

'What was that?'

Louis swallowed and clinched his jaw to stave off his nerves. 'I SAID, ALL RIGHT,' he bellowed, trying to brace himself.

'*Woo-hoo!* Attaboy! Man after my own heart. Okay, kid. Let's show them how it's done,' Buzz said, and Louis immediately regretted his decision as Buzz began maneuvering the plane into position.

As Buzz had before, this time Hutch fell back and let Buzz have the sky.

'First things first!' Buzz shouted, and all of a sudden the biplane spiraled into a series of three barrel rolls in succession. Hutch had only done one, Louis dimly recalled, trying to keep his breakfast down for the second time that afternoon. Buzz piloted them through three – a kind of one-upmanship. It wasn't *so* terrible, the barrel rolls. It felt a little like being the meat on a spit, but they were over almost before they began.

Buzz leveled off. Louis realized what was inevitably coming next. As they flew on, Buzz pulled the stick back. They began to climb straight up, as though going up a wall. Louis patted the belts that held him in the cockpit. Suddenly the belts felt very thin; Louis felt strangely naked. But before he could dwell on this feeling, the biplane had pitched so that now the top of his head was pointing directly down at the ground.

This was more of a ride than Louis had been expecting. Only a little while earlier, he had been standing on the ground, trying to envision what the pilots were seeing and feeling as they completed their loop-the-loops. Now Louis was flying one right along with Buzz. It seemed to last forever, and then, at the same time, it was over almost immediately.

Finally they leveled back out, and Buzz piloted the biplane back over to rejoin the red biplane carrying Hutch and Harry. Now it was Louis's turn to hoot and holler at the top of his lungs; he couldn't stop. Harry waved, and in his giddy, elated state, Louis momentarily forgot how much he hated him, and waved back.

12

Once back on the ground, Louis's legs quivered as he tumbled down from the cockpit. The ground beneath his feet didn't seem stationary anymore, as if all along the dirt were really an unsteady sea and Louis had just never known it.

'Ya all right there, kid?' Buzz asked, retrieving the cap and goggles he'd given Louis.

'Sailor's legs,' Hutch commented, ambling over from where he'd landed the other biplane, wearing a friendly smile. 'Except we ain't hardly sailors. But after bein' up in the air, every other element – earth, water, what have you . . . just seems heavy and inelegant. It'll pass. Just give it a minute.'

Harry followed close on Hutch's heels, still grinning. Louis smiled back for the second time that day, but then, thinking of his brother, thinking of his family, forced the smile again from his face.

From across the field, Ava watched the group approach, intrigued by the intense air of excitement that hummed in the air around them. She noticed Buzz and Hutch were more animated and amused than usual; usually they got bored taking passengers up for tourist rides. They were laughing and clapping the two young men on the back, she noticed. She shot Louis a slightly bewildered smile.

'So . . . how was it? Terribly frightening?'

Her question was directed to Louis, but before he could answer, Harry piped up.

'Piece of cake,' he said, grinning.

Ava turned around to take in the sight of Harry Yamada afresh. He was so confident, so cocky. She arched a skeptical eyebrow.

'Piece of cake?' she questioned.

'Sure.'

Ava rolled her eyes.

'Your pilots – Hutch and Buzz, here – even flew some stunts with us,' Harry added for good measure.

This was news to Ava; Hutch and Buzz had performed the stunts out of sight from Sumpter's field. *That* certainly wasn't part of the tourist ride. Surprised and troubled, she looked to the pilots for confirmation.

'Stunts? Which stunts?'

'Just a few barrel rolls and a loop-the-loop,' Hutch answered.

'And . . . that . . . didn't intimidate you at all?' she asked. Her eyes flicked involuntarily to Louis's own; after all, Ava thought earlier she'd detected the sensible sentiment of caution in him.

Louis looked to Ava and then to Harry and back again.

'Nah,' he lied, shaking his head.

'As a matter of fact,' Harry said in a sure voice, 'I'd have liked to do more.'

'Like what?' Ava snorted, annoyed by his overconfidence.

'I don't know.' Harry shrugged. 'Maybe go out for a walk on the wings.'

'Now, don't talk nonsense, boy,' Buzz interrupted with a dismissive tsk. 'That wing-walking business is only for madmen. Even Hutch and I ain't crazy enough to leave the cockpit.'

'Not voluntarily!' Hutch said. 'I done a parachute jump once or twice, sure – but that was the Army's idea, never mine.' He chuckled at his own joke.

'I'd do it,' Harry said. 'If someone'd let me go for a walk on the wings, I'd go up in a heartbeat.'

'You'd honestly wing walk, son?' Hutch asked, shaking his head.

'I would.'

'Hey, Hutch,' Buzz chimed in, 'I think we got these kids too excited – all the blood's rushed to their heads from that loop-the-loop.'

'What's this I hear?'

Ava recognized her stepfather's voice and turned to see Earl. Here he came, his silky jacket completely out of place in the farmer's field, flashing bright red under the afternoon sun. Ava knew he would have something to say about Buzz and Hutch flying a few barnstorming tricks with passengers in tow – but *what* Earl's take on this situation would be, she couldn't guess.

'What's this?' he repeated. 'Am I to understand you performed some stunts with these passengers in your planes?' A stern expression on his face, Earl gave his pilots a questioning stare.

'It wasn't their idea; we asked 'em to,' Harry intervened, not wanting to get the pilots into hot water. 'And it was all very safe.'

'*Safe?*' Earl roared, still using his highly dramatic, carefully articulated announcer's voice. 'Why, of course it was safe! Above all else, my pilots are the *safest* in the state – nay, the nation! My flying circus has been in business for years and is top-notch, I assure you!'

Ava listened with skepticism, aware of the fact that the circus was neither licensed nor legal. Earl paused and gave Harry and Louis a quick once-over.

'Allow me to introduce myself: Mr Earl Shaw, founder and owner of this spectacular barnstorming show.'

Ava watched as her stepfather gave his signature bow. She had witnessed this bow many times throughout her time with Earl. He generally performed it when he was cornering an unwitting 'customer.' Ava knew it was not a bow of subservience; it was Earl's way of asserting himself, of cornering his prey.

'No, no, dear boy, I wasn't at *all* concerned for your safety. As I say, I only employ the safest pilots in the world!' he continued.

He smoothed his dapper black moustache and squinted his eyes, and Ava felt even more certain Earl was silently hatching some sort of plan. She looked at the two young men, wondering if they were savvy enough to catch on.

'It's only a matter of our fee for such embellishments!' Earl said finally.

'Your fee?' Harry blinked.

'Absolutely, my boy! Why, it seems to me, if the ride we furnish for you involves additional entertainments, we're obliged to charge you extra. Otherwise, it would hardly be fair to the other passengers!'

Aha, Ava thought. So that was it. She had to hand it to Earl: he always managed to come up with an angle.

Buzz made an effort to steer the conversation away from money. 'Well,' he said, 'if you can believe it, now these fellas want to go wing walking.' He thumbed toward Louis and Harry with a friendly chuckle. Buzz had miscalculated, however, because Ava saw Earl pause. Then his face lit up even brighter.

'Is this true? Are you boys in earnest?' Earl asked.

'Absolutely,' Harry answered for them both. Ava's eyes flicked again to Louis's face as she wondered if he felt the same.

'Hmm,' Earl mused. 'We would have to charge even more for that,' he said. 'Seeing as how it would be a once-in-a-lifetime experience – wouldn't you agree?' He eyed Harry up and down, making a quick calculation of the maximum the boy might be able to afford. Ava could already guess what Earl saw and what he was thinking: the boy was an Oriental of some kind, but he spoke excellent English, looked very kempt. America was a country of immigrants after all, and there was no telling nowadays who had coin to spare.

'Well, if you have your hearts set on wing walking, we *might* be able to accommodate you boys if you return again tomorrow – for an *additional fee*, of course . . .' Earl glanced in the direction of where Irving Sumpter stood, and Ava guessed that he was calculating how much the old man would demand in order to use the field a second day. Sumpter looked like he'd be glad for the extra spare change, anyhow. Earl returned his attention to Harry. 'So . . . shall we expect you tomorrow?'

'How much?' Harry asked, cutting to the chase. 'How much to go up again and take a walk on the wings?'

'Ten dollars,' Earl Shaw proclaimed.

'Twice the price?' Harry asked.

'Why, yes – and at that amount, it's a steal!' Earl replied, once again twirling his moustache between his thumb and forefinger.

'Just so I'm clear: if I turn up tomorrow with ten dollars,' Harry recited carefully, 'you'll let me go up in your plane with one of your pilots and wing walk?'

'I will! I will indeed,' Earl replied. 'Do we have a deal?'

Harry's eyes twinkled with determination. 'All right, then. I'll be here tomorrow. With ten dollars.'

'Excellent.' Earl smiled, and gave a second showy bow. 'I look forward to your return, and we shall be happy to accommodate you.'

'All right,' Harry said. He began to walk away. Then, as though an afterthought occurred to him, he hesitated, and turned back to Louis.

'Say, what about you?' Harry asked. 'You gonna wing walk, too, Thorn?'

Louis shuffled his feet. His eyes flicked nervously from Harry to Earl Shaw, then to the pilots, and finally to Ava.

'I would,' Louis answered, 'but that's simply too rich for my blood.' Ava suspected this was the truth, and that he'd had a hard time digging up the five dollars he'd already paid for the ride he'd just taken.

Harry thought about this for a moment and scratched his head. He shrugged.

'Well, I'll pay for you to go up,' he said finally. 'Hell, to be honest, I'd appreciate the company up there.'

'I don't need your money,' Louis said, his spine suddenly stiffening.

'Sounds to me like you do,' Harry said.

'I ain't gonna try to talk sense into the likes of you,' Louis said. 'I can't afford to go wing walking and that's the truth of it.'

'That's the truth of it,' Harry repeated, 'unless the truth is that really you're scared.'

'I ain't scared.'

'Well, I don't mind supplying the money if you don't mind proving that you ain't scared.'

'*Fine*,' Louis said. He spoke the word through gritted teeth, but there was a quaver in his voice, and Ava heard it. She glanced between the two boys. There was more between them than a simple dare about an airplane stunt.

'Well!' Harry exhaled. 'I'll see you here tomorrow?'

Louis swallowed. 'Well . . . all right, then.'

Louis and Harry squared off, nodding stiffly to each other.

Earl was plainly pleased. Buzz and Hutch exchanged a look, each raising an eyebrow. As Louis and Harry began to walk away, Ava jumped up from her post at the table and ran after the two of them.

'I assume you're both all full of talk,' Ava called after them. 'And now you've gone and got it out of your system.'

They stopped. Harry trailed a short distance behind Louis. He turned around first and looked Ava over.

'What do you mean?'

'I mean, you're not really that stupid, are you? You don't think you're to go up with Buzz and Hutch, and simply wing walk with zero experience. Do you?'

'Sure,' Harry said. 'Why not?'

Ava snorted. She'd been to countless small towns. Young people developed strange ideas when there was so little to do and no city nearby. There was no way to tell whether these farm boys were crazy or stupid – or both.

'C'mon,' she said, 'you both had your fun. Now it's time to behave sensibly. You'll get yourselves killed trying to wing walk.'

'What's it to you?' Harry asked. He looked at her with an amused smile that somehow made Ava feel stung. 'You care about what happens to us?'

'Hah, hardly!' She was about to launch into a lengthier retort, then paused, realizing her tactic was all wrong. She glanced over a shoulder to make sure Earl wasn't in earshot, took a step closer, and dropped her voice. 'It's just so sad . . . you don't even know you're being taken for fools . . .'

'How so?'

'I know plenty about how Earl thinks. He'll use your dare to see if he can't draw an even bigger crowd tomorrow. And if either of you breaks your necks trying this fool stunt, well, Earl doesn't care! Just so long as he's drawn a big crowd and sold plenty of folks rides before the two of you go up.'

Harry nodded. To Ava's surprise, it appeared he'd already considered this.

'Fair enough. Earl seems like a' – Harry fished for a word – 'a true *businessman*. But don't worry about us. We'll be fine.'

'Oh? And exactly how many times have you gone up in an airplane?'

'Well, now, today would be my first time,' Harry admitted, undaunted. 'How many times *you* been up?'

Ava froze, and her cheeks turned bright red.

'Wait a minute,' Harry said, laughing, incredulous. He searched her face and verified the truth. 'Do you mean to say you travel around with a flying circus and you ain't *never* been up in an airplane?'

Her cheeks still burning, Ava stared down at the ground, humiliated and angry.

'Truly?' Harry exclaimed, continuing to laugh. '"Lovely Lofty Ava, First Lady of 'Avi'-ation" has never been up in an airplane? Not once? Not for a single ride?'

Ava's eyes flashed in Harry's direction, catlike and angry. All the while Ava and Harry had argued back and forth, Louis had listened and watched, remaining silent.

'Aw, lay off her already,' Louis said, coming to her defense. But Ava didn't want his sympathy.

'Know what? You can go hang yourselves – both of you,' Ava said. 'And I suspect you *will* hang yourselves,' she called over her shoulder as she stormed off. 'Tomorrow!'

13

NEWCASTLE, CALIFORNIA
SEPTEMBER 17, 1943

Bonner wakes up and gets dressed, full of one dreaded certainty: he can't put it off any longer. He needs to check in with the office in San Francisco. Bonner knows he's likely to get chewed out by his boss. The thought of Sheriff Whitcomb listening as Reed hollers at him makes Bonner cringe.

Just as he is about to head over to the sheriff's office, Bonner asks Miss MacFarlane if she has a telephone line, almost as an afterthought. She surprises him by showing him to a tidy little closet next to the front door.

'I'll have the operator reverse the charges,' he promises, though she doesn't ask. Rosalind nods and bustles off, but he thinks he can still hear her, hovering out of sight but nearby. She is a peculiar young woman. Bonner had felt her staring at him again over breakfast.

A few minutes later, Bonner has been connected and Reed gets on the line.

'*What are you still doing there?*' Reed's ordinarily commanding voice is thin and tinny over the telephone wire. Cal Reed is a terse, square-jawed man with very little sense of humor – exactly what people thought of when they pictured a Bureau man. '*The local sheriff wired me that they're mailing us copies of the death certificates,*' Reed adds.

Bonner is surprised, in part because he didn't know Sheriff Whitcomb had done any such thing. But of course he did. Whitcomb has made it clear he wants Bonner out of his town, the sooner the better.

'*Called me up, too,*' Reed continues. '*Gave me an earful about how he didn't appreciate you sending the bodies all the way to the coroner in Sacramento.*'

'The man here didn't seem qualified—' Bonner begins, but Reed cuts him off.

'*I'm sure at the very least he can distinguish between alive and dead. At this point, those certificates are really all that's needed to close this case, Bonner,*' Reed reminds him. '*So I don't care much where they come from, so long as they're in the file when you turn in your report.*'

'Well, the truth is, sir, I'm still looking into the nature of the crash,' Bonner says now. 'For my report.'

There is a pause on the other end of the line.

'*I see,*' Reed says finally. '*Is there a lot more to it? I know the older one – Kenichi Yamada – was classified 4-C.*'

4-C. '4-C' is the code for 'enemy alien'.

'Yes, I know,' Bonner replies. 'I saw his Application for Leave Clearance in his file, and the answers he gave to the questionnaire.'

'*Are you saying you've found evidence the Yamada men were involved in treasonous activities after all?*'

Bonner pauses.

'It's not that so much as . . . well . . . the crash itself . . .'

Bonner shifts uncomfortably in the small telephone alcove. He hears floorboards creaking and cranes his neck out the closet door to see if Miss MacFarlane has returned. He doesn't see her, but he also doesn't feel alone anymore. Is she eavesdropping on him?

'The crash itself merits further investigation,' he tries to explain to Reed.

'*Oh? What makes you say that?*'

'There's something not right about it,' Bonner says. He feels the weakness of his argument; Reed isn't the sort of man given to operating on a hunch. Bonner presses on in a hurry, hoping that what he lacks in cold, hard logic he can make up for with enthusiasm. 'If you don't mind, sir, I'd like to talk to a few more of the locals, get an airplane mechanic to come out and look at some of the wreckage.'

'*Let me get this straight: you're thinking sabotage?*'

'Perhaps.'

The line is silent for a moment. Bonner knows Reed is mulling over the situation. They both know the Department of Commerce would not take too kindly to anyone – white or Japanese – causing planes to fall out of the sky.

'*Hmm,*' Reed mutters. '*All right. I want you back here, but I suppose we can spare you for now. See what you can turn up. Put it all in your report.*'

'Of course,' Bonner agrees.

'*Oh, and Bonner . . .*'

'Yes, sir?'

'*I don't need to remind you about the Bureau's budget . . . I don't know what you plan to pay that mechanic, but I'd keep the overhead low. If this turns out to be a simple murder case of a couple of Japs and nothing more . . . political, say . . . then that's a local matter; I'm not sure that's within our purview.*'

'I understand, sir.'

'*I know why you've been hiding behind your desk the past few months, Bonner. You aren't fooling anybody.*'

'Sir?'

'*Look, I can't understand why you feel guilty. Spending time around those camps can't be good for anybody. But you can't go developing Jap sympathies. We don't have that luxury right now. Spying and Japanese nationals are a very real security concern and it's our job to take that concern seriously.*'

'I know that, sir.'

'*All I'm saying is, don't turn this case into something it's not because you think somehow you need to redeem yourself.*'

'I'm not,' Bonner says, and as the words come out of his mouth, he realizes they are partly true. The case had become about something more than simple redemption for him; it's also about Louis Thorn. For reasons he can't explain to Reed, Bonner needs to know who Louis Thorn is, and whether or not Thorn is capable of murder.

'*Fine,*' Reed says, easing off. '*I've said my piece. Now get what you need to wrap up the case and get back here.*'

'I will,' Bonner replies.

He hangs up the receiver and sighs. He knows one thing for certain: Reed is going to be steamed when he sees that Bonner ordered lab tests on the Yamadas' blood. But Bonner will deal with that later, when he has to. He stands and straightens his suit. As he steps out of the telephone closet, he sees the briefest flash of Rosalind MacFarlane's skirt as she hurries back into the kitchen.

14

EARL SHAW'S FLYING CIRCUS
NEWCASTLE, CALIFORNIA, MAY 5, 1940

Word traveled surprisingly fast – catching on faster than one of the terrible grass fires that periodically plagued that part of the California foothills – that Harry Yamada and Louis Thorn had dared each other to walk on the wings of a biplane. The sun came up that morning bright and blaring, the herald of a warm, dry day under a cloudless sky. By noon, well over a thousand people had gathered in Irving Sumpter's field, and the air vibrated with the steady buzz of people speaking in excited, jittery tones.

Ava watched as Earl greeted people with plenty of dapper fanfare, urging folks to buy a scenic ride and herding them into line. His scheme was working; by noon, Ava had sold more scenic airplane rides in one hour than she had during the entire previous month – she had to put sales on hold briefly when Earl sent her back into town to fetch more gasoline, as no one had anticipated the planes would need so much. Buzz and Hutch had their work cut out for them, chauffeuring what seemed like an endless stream of passengers up into the clouds and back down onto solid ground. Making and selling lemonade, Ava's mother could barely keep up with demand. Twice she was forced to send a boy for a fresh block of ice from the icehouse and more lemons.

It was plain to Ava that Earl was delighted with the bargain he'd struck. She found herself surprised that it had not occurred to him before: that he could simply invite a pair of crazy farm boys to wing walk (or attempt to, anyway) and instantly draw larger crowds than he'd ever managed to draw before. He'd always wanted to hire stuntmen, but this proved too difficult. All of the quality men who regularly did wing walking only wanted to work for Hollywood, which not only paid more handsomely than your average flying circus but also immortalized the stuntmen's daredevil tricks on the silver screen. Earl's shoddy flying circus held no appeal, and was illegal, besides.

But now, as Ava watched her stepfather flit around the field, a greedy smile curling his pink lips under his moustache, she knew Earl had had an epiphany and that he was thinking these two crazy farm boys might as well be dipped in the legendary gold that had been mined from the Sierra Nevada foothills all around them. And yet, for all the free publicity they'd accidentally drummed up, when Harry Yamada arrived on the field that day with the sum Earl Shaw had previously named clutched in his hand, Earl did not hesitate to take that, too. He was, above all else, a businessman.

'Very good, my son!' he exclaimed, coming over to clap Harry on the back and supervise as Ava accepted the money. Earl's eyes were glassy with excitement as Harry handed over a twenty-dollar bill. 'That'll fetch you one extra-special premium flight! Indeed, it will!'

'You mean *two*,' Harry reminded Earl. 'Ten each, and that's twenty. Twenty dollars was the price you named for *both* of us to walk on the wings.'

'Of course, of course, you're quite right,' Earl hastily added. He smiled, his white teeth flashing under his groomed moustache. 'Where is your friend?' Earl asked, glancing around with an air of innocent inquiry.

'Louis?' Harry repeated.

Harry stiffened as he pronounced Louis's name, yet cast a glance around as though anxious for him to arrive. The mixed reaction puzzled Ava.

'I expect he'll turn up . . .'

'Wonderful!' Earl replied in a distracted manner. 'Now, why don't you take a walk around, have a lemonade—' A sudden atypically generous impulse gripped him. 'On the house! Everyone will be wanting to shake your hand! Your friend hasn't arrived yet, and I assume you'll want to go up together . . .'

At this, Harry gave a small nod. Again there was that air of ambivalence. Ava wondered again about the ties between the two young men. The mystery intrigued her.

'We'll have you boys go up for your rides once all the other customers have had their turns,' Earl continued. 'Seeing as how your rides are' – Earl searched for a way to phrase it – 'more *deluxe.*'

Ava shot Harry a look, wishing he'd heeded her warning. She knew Earl wanted Louis and Harry to go up last for a reason: if they fell to their deaths – and it was clear that Earl believed this was a possibility – it would be the end of Earl's sales for the day, and those who had paid for a scenic ride but hadn't gone up yet might even demand their money back.

Harry, however, appeared to understand Earl's master plan and the motivations behind it. *Earl seems like a true businessman*, Harry had remarked the day before. He might very well be crazy, Ava thought, but at least it seemed like Harry Yamada was not a dupe.

About an hour or so later, around one o'clock, Ava spotted the familiar shape of Louis Thorn making his way across the field. While Harry had approached with a confident swagger, Louis looked slightly miserable and terribly pale. Ava felt more nervous for him, just seeing the state he was in. Nerves could get a fella killed, she thought.

'You know,' she said as Louis approached her table, 'common sense is an admirable and brave quality, too. You *don't* have to do this.'

'I . . .' Louis hesitated, looking into Ava's eyes. 'I want to.'

'You sure?'

He laughed. 'Not entirely. But, hell . . . I reckon I won't get this chance again. And if Harry Yamada can do it, well—'

'*There* you are, my boy!' Earl interrupted, hurrying over to Louis's side, just as he had done earlier with Harry. When he clapped Louis on the back, Louis flinched.

'Your friend, Harry – he's already paid,' Ava piped up, before Earl could mislead Louis.

'He's not my friend,' Louis said, as though murmuring a memorized line.

Noting his vehemence, Ava cocked her head. 'Well, you're about to risk your lives together,' she said, 'so what would you call him?'

Louis didn't answer.

'What are you two on about?' Earl asked, clearly disinterested in the reply.

His head swiveled as he scanned the field, pleased by the number of spectators. 'Your friend, the young Chinaman, is somewhere yonder.' He pointed.

'Harry's not Chinese,' Louis stated. 'He's Japanese.'

'How fascinating!' Earl replied, though it was plain he was not fascinated in the slightest. 'If you'd like to join him, that would be splendid . . . Everyone here is keen to get a look at you both.' Earl patted Louis on the shoulder, simultaneously nudging him in the direction of the table where Harry stood and Cleo sold lemonade. 'I'll fetch you both when it's time for you to go up!'

Louis nodded and obeyed, walking to where Earl had pointed as though in a trance. He'd woken up in a cold sweat that morning, remembering his foolish pledge from the day before to walk on the wings of an airplane. The sharp edges of terror had worn off, but now he was a bit numb and dazed. Harry spotted him approaching and smiled.

'Ready to make history?'

Harry's tone was amicable, and Louis recognized an old vestige of the short-lived friendship the two boys had once shared – a happy alliance between two neighboring kids many years ago when they were boys. Louis felt the forgotten glimmer of something familiar but pushed it away.

'We're hardly making history,' he replied. 'Plenty of people have gone wing walking before.' Louis had collected several newspaper and magazine clippings over the years. He'd been fascinated with airplanes, with barnstormers and stuntmen – fascinated, that is, from a comfortable armchair distance. But just because he'd read about it didn't mean he was eager to do it himself. Why had he agreed to this insanity? He'd been baited.

'Must mean it's perfectly safe!' Harry replied with a smile.

Louis glared at him.

'I take it you're nervous.' Harry smiled. 'Me, too.'

But Harry did not look nervous. Harry never looked nervous. Louis knew all too well: if Harry had nerves, they were made of iron. Louis felt all the more rankled. As they continued to wait, Louis made an effort to avoid further interaction with Harry. It wasn't difficult. Earl Shaw had been right: people all wanted to get a look at the two boys, shake their hands, wish them luck.

* * *

Over an hour and a half elapsed as Earl made certain to beat the bushes for every paying customer he could. Buzz and Hutch loaded up each passenger in turn. Finally, there were no more people standing in the line waiting to go up for a scenic flight.

But the crowd had not dissipated – if anything, it had steadily grown. Everyone was waiting to see what would become of Louis Thorn and Harry Yamada. The air was filled with electric anticipation tinged with a hint of morbidity.

Louis listened as Earl began to address the crowd.

'And now, ladies and gentlemen, the moment you've all been waiting for . . . two of your very own local boys will take to the skies in an attempt to perform a harrowing, hair-raising act of bravery! Will they or won't they – that's the big question, folks! Will they find the courage to walk in the footsteps of barnstormers and daredevils everywhere, and step out onto the wings as they fly high, high, high above the earth . . .'

Louis couldn't hear the rest; the whoosh of blood in his ears had drowned everything else out. Earl's voice droned on. Spectators whispered excitedly to one another. Louis stared straight ahead, seeing nothing and comprehending nothing as the minutes ticked by. The next thing Louis became aware of was Harry's elbow gently prodding him in the ribs. Louis intuited the elbow's message: *showtime*.

'Lads!' Earl Shaw swooped over to them both. 'Are you quite ready? Your grand adventure awaits!'

Louis took a breath. He and Harry exchanged a look and nodded nearly in unison. Earl shepherded them off in the direction of the two biplanes.

'Good luck!' someone from the crowd shouted.

'Don't break yer necks!'

Louis walked toward the blue plane, where Buzz was waiting. Harry walked toward the red plane and Hutch.

'So here's what you want to do, kid,' Hutch was saying to Harry. He pointed to the wings of the biplane. 'Walk out on the lower wing here; that way, if you need to, you can steady yourself with the struts or the cable wires that run between the two wings. Try not to be too rough if you can help it.'

'Hear that?' Buzz said to Louis. 'Listen to what Hutch is telling him.' Louis nodded.

'And walk slowly,' Hutch continued, 'so I can feel 'er as she goes and correct for your weight. That way I can keep 'er level. Don't just shoot out to the tip of the wing; you'll make my job difficult. Understand?'

'Yes, sir,' Harry replied.

'We'll put both planes on a nice, steady course, directly over the field. You can start your walking a little before we get near the crowd. We'll tell ya when.'

Hutch climbed up into the cockpit of the red plane, and Harry followed suit. Buzz and Louis did the same.

'Get all that?' Buzz asked Louis.

Louis nodded, though he couldn't feel his neck. The cold, numbing sensation was spreading. 'Anything else we oughta know?' he asked.

Buzz thought about this for a second and shrugged. 'You know how to walk?'

'Yes.'

'Well, I imagine that's the long and short of it. Only you'd better lean just slightly into the wind. Don't want to get blown off the wing.'

'You ever wing walked before?'

'Hell, no,' Buzz said, pulling on his cap and goggles. 'I ain't an idiot.' Before Louis had a chance to respond, Buzz yelled out, 'CONTACT!' and pressed the electric starter. Louis felt his stomach turn over, churning in sync with the propeller. He cast an anxious glance at the red plane, where Harry sat in the cockpit in front of Hutch. Harry's stoic face was unreadable. His eyes behind the goggles seemed unseeing.

In no time flat, they were in the air. Buzz's takeoff was smooth and steady. Louis was too nervous to appreciate it, fixated as he was on the task before him. Suddenly the cockpit seemed impossibly steep and snug. How was he supposed to climb out and crawl onto the wing? he wondered. He was aware, too, of the wind whipping over his face: had it been that forceful during yesterday's flight? Louis felt himself starting to sweat under his clothes. His forehead and cheeks, too, were sweating, but the wind dried them instantly, chilling him in spite of the warm spring sun overhead. He twisted around again to get a look at Harry. The red plane floated just behind them. Harry looked like a statue, his expression focused but serene.

Buzz and Hutch flew a distance away from Sumpter's field and then circled around. They fell into formation side by side and dropped a bit lower to the ground, then leveled out, both of them flying a steady course, just as Hutch had promised. When they were still some distance away from the field, Buzz and Hutch signaled to each other and traded a thumbs-up.

'Okay, kid!' Buzz shouted to Louis. 'Time to climb out onto the wing.'

Louis nodded and clenched his jaw but didn't move. He glanced over at the red biplane. Presumably, Hutch was hollering the same instructions to Harry. As Louis looked on, Harry carefully kneeled on the seat, then stood, leaning forward at the waist and clutching the rim of the cockpit. He swung first one leg over to the wing, then the other.

'Hey, kid!' Buzz shouted. 'Did you hear me? Time to climb out on the wing.' He followed Louis's gaze and spotted Harry. 'See! Like your friend there is doing.'

Louis didn't move. Frozen, he watched as Harry gripped the strut – the bar running between the cockpit and the upper wing – and slowly straightened up, testing his footing on the wing. After a few seconds, Harry removed one hand from the strut, then the other. He staggered just slightly, got his bearings, and tilted forward into the wind.

'Say, kid,' Buzz hollered. 'It's now or never!'

Louis willed himself to move, but nothing happened. Meanwhile, Harry began to inch his way farther out on the wing, sliding his feet over the metal surface rather than lifting them. They were drawing near to Sumpter's field now. Louis could make out the crowd of onlookers far off in the distance.

'I don't blame you, kid, but I gotta warn you: this is your last chance,' Buzz called. 'Do you want to leave all the wing walking to your friend?'

Oh, hell, Louis thought. He finally willed himself to move. First he did as Harry had done, climbing so as to stand on his seat and gripping the rim of the cockpit. His legs felt absurdly weak and rubbery. Doubled over like that, he placed one tentative foot on the wing, then the other, his knuckles white where he gripped the strut overhead. He caught a glimpse of the ground below – it was only when you looked directly down that you could tell how fast the plane was traveling – and his mind silently and involuntarily strung together a sequence of more expletives than Louis had ever realized he knew.

He stood there for several seconds, gripping the strut where it made a diagonal slash above his head. They were now nearly over Sumpter's field. What looked like a blur of colorful dots turned into people, and Louis could see a sea of upraised arms, all of them pointing and waving with excitement. He looked over and saw that Harry had made diligent progress, moving all the way to the tip of the wing and on the verge of initiating his return voyage. Something surged in Louis.

All at once, he released his grip on the bar and made a speedy beeline all the way to the tip of the wing as fast as he could.

He had forgotten the warning he'd overheard Hutch give Harry: not to dash out to the tip of the wing too suddenly. The biplane tipped with the abrupt weight redistribution, and for a brief, terrifying second Louis lost his balance. He pitched forward on his toes and his arms wheeled in the air. Down below, spectators screamed and various mothers clapped quick hands over their children's eyes.

But Buzz quickly righted the plane while at the same time one of Louis's wheeling arms caught hold of the vertical struts that braced the far end of the biplane's two sets of wings.

'Ho-leee shit, kid!' Buzz shouted. 'You gotta take it more slowly out there! Or, at the very least, give a fella some warning!'

Louis nodded. His heart was in his mouth by that point. A few more seconds went by as he continued to grip the bar at the far end of the biplane's wing.

'Now inch your way back to the cockpit,' Buzz hollered. 'SLOWLY. If you need to, use those guide wires there to steady you.'

In all the commotion, Louis had lost track of the other biplane. He looked for it now and saw that Harry was already crawling back into the cockpit. Once safely within, Harry raised a hand and waved. Was he taunting Louis or encouraging him?

Either way, a flicker of something Louis believed he glimpsed in Harry's wave triggered him, and he found himself letting go of the outer strut and shuffling inch by inch back toward his own cockpit. His knees still quivered but he made sure progress. As Buzz had instructed, he steadied himself with the wires. After a minute or so, he reached his destination, grabbed on to the rim of the cockpit, and felt a flood of relief wash over him. Resisting the urge to scramble, he climbed back in deliberately and carefully.

'Wooo-hooo, kid!' Buzz shouted. 'Attaboy! You did it! I almost thought we were going to have to clean you up off of that farm field down there. I'm overjoyed we ain't gotta!'

Louis did not reply. They flew on for another minute or so.

'Well, kid? Cat got your tongue? How do you feel?'

Louis turned around to face Buzz. He was still wordless. But the giant grin on his face did all the talking for him.

15

Earl was clearly surprised that Louis and Harry had not fallen to their deaths. Nonetheless, Ava was a little horrified to observe *how* surprised.

Once *Castor* and *Pollux* touched down, an enormous roar of applause spontaneously erupted from the crowd. All four of them – Buzz, Hutch, Louis, and Harry – were instant celebrities, but Louis and Harry especially. Ava noticed that Earl kept close tabs on the two young men as folks all around clapped them on their backs, shook their hands, and even hoisted them into the air and once or twice upon people's shoulders.

'Well done, fellas!' Earl said, steering Louis and Harry away from the adoring crowd. 'Well done! Say . . . are you boys free this evening? Your rare feat calls for a celebration – booze and food on me! Whaddaya say?'

Ava watched Louis's and Harry's faces as they exchanged a look. Their icy stand-off seemed to melt, if only slightly.

'I'll convince my pilots to come along, too,' Earl pressed. 'Hutch? Buzz?' he called. They nodded.

'Well,' Louis said, shrugging. 'All right. I suppose dinner'd be all right.'

After a brief pause Harry nodded his agreement, too. Ava wondered what Earl was up to now.

Earl insisted they all clean themselves up and reconvene. Two hours later, when they returned at the appointed time, he instructed Buzz to help him unhitch the Model A from the caravan. He offered the front seat of the truck to Louis and Harry, but both boys firmly declined.

'The women should ride up there,' Louis insisted awkwardly. 'Especially seeing as how they got those nice clothes on.'

As he mentioned Ava and her mother, Louis's eyes flicked reflexively in Ava's direction, his cheeks flushed red, and he immediately dropped his eyes to the ground.

Doll yourselves up, Earl had ordered earlier. Cleo was wearing a silk dress and fresh red lipstick. Ava had changed out of her men's trousers and was uncharacteristically attired in a navy velvet dress with an elegant, low-cut bib of lace that fluttered around her neck and shoulders. Her mother had brushed Ava's short bob for her and pinned it neatly into pretty waves. Ava suspected it was a cheap tactic and that Earl hoped to intimidate the boys. In Louis's case, at least, Earl's plan appeared to be working.

'You two are our guests of honor,' he said now, gesturing to the front seat.

But Harry shook his head as well. 'Wouldn't be right.'

Ava watched as Earl's gaze slid over Harry's face. She could see him pause as he took in the specific shape of Harry's eyes, remembering the racial difference between Harry and the rest of the group.

'Hmm,' he said. 'Maybe you've got a point.'

So Ava and her mother climbed into the front seat, and the truck bounced heartily as the four remaining men piled into the back. Earl put the Model A in gear and picked his way to the roads that led to Auburn, the town that contained the restaurant the locals had recommended. The old truck coughed and sputtered its way up the steep incline of the increasingly large foothills. They must have made a funny picture: everyone all dressed up, piled together in the jalopy.

Auburn revealed itself to be an old mining town with a rather grand courthouse and a row of cozy brick buildings that served as a downtown. It was a charming, dusty village still haunted by the ghosts of the forty-niners who'd settled it, but compared to Newcastle it was practically metropolitan. They found their way past the round-domed courthouse and a half mile down a sloping road that led to the Freeman Hotel, which contained the only 'fancy' restaurant around; the hotel, with its tennis courts, was the closest thing to a country club in the area. As they pulled up, Ava took a good look at the building. It was a large, white two-story structure, a railed balcony wrapping around the entire sprawl. Earl found a place to park the Model A, and the group poured out.

Inside the hotel was a bar, a dining room, and a small dance floor. While it was all nice enough, the hotel bore an air of wistful decay. One could detect the money that had once poured into the hotel during its more prosperous days and how the upkeep had subsequently taken a hit during the Depression along with the rest of the nation. Now the facility was mainly keeping up the pretenses of its golden era.

Unfortunately for Louis and Harry, one of those pretenses turned out to be the requirement that male diners wear dinner jackets. Earl was wearing a splendid jacket, and even Buzz and Hutch were wearing jackets – or, at least, slightly threadbare garments that passed for jackets. Louis and Harry had spruced themselves up, certainly; Ava thought they looked nice in their crisp clean shirts, snappy suspenders, and carefully combed hair. But within minutes of the group's arrival, a maître d' scurried over and made it clear that their lack of dinner jackets was not to be overlooked. They were hurried off to a coatroom while the rest of the party was shown to a table.

'You could've told them, Earl,' Ava said as they slid into a large round booth with silver-grommeted red leather seats.

'Those fellas could've borrowed something at the very least,' Cleo chided softly.

'How was I to know?' Earl protested. But the wide grin on his face betrayed him. By now Ava had caught on: Earl wished to strike some sort of deal with the two boys. At the moment, he was out to impress Louis and Harry, and one way to do that was to remind them that without Earl to shape their respective futures, they were just a pair of unsophisticated farm boys.

A few minutes later, Ava watched as Louis and Harry emerged from the coatroom and walked self-consciously across the dining room. Something had shifted ever so slightly in the rapport between the two of them; a truce had been called, if not quite an alliance. Ava saw Harry lock eyes with Louis, and the two smirked as though stifling a couple of snickers. The jackets were both several sizes too large for the boys, lending them a clownish air. As they drew nearer, Ava overheard the tail end of a muttered exchange.

'I don't see how this is any better than what we've already got on.'

'You look like an elephant lost in its own skin,' Harry remarked, raising an eyebrow at the pathetic gray jacket hanging on Louis's shoulders.

'You ain't one to talk,' Louis replied.

As they neared the table, a different maître d' – one who appeared more senior, presumably the hotel manager – hurried over to intercept Louis and Harry as they prepared to sit down.

'May I help you?' he inquired in an unfriendly tone. His gaze was fixed on Harry's face in particular.

'Kind sir, the Chinaman and his friend are with me!' Earl intervened from where he sat in the booth. 'They are my guests tonight.'

After a second's pause, the maître d' bowed. 'I see. My apologies.'

Still not entirely convinced, he turned back to Louis and Harry with a cold, unwelcoming expression and walked stiffly away. Ava frowned. She looked at Harry, but his eyes were cast downward. She wondered if these occurrences happened regularly. She wondered if he was embarrassed, or angry, or perhaps . . . both? He gave no sign.

'Sit down, sit down!' Earl roared, ready to play host.

He smoothed over the awkwardness of the situation by waving down the nearest waiter and ordering two bottles of champagne, which promised a pleasant amnesia for all. Crystal coupes were immediately brought out, a couple of pops were heard, and, soon enough, sudsy golden liquid filled each glass.

'I propose a toast,' Earl bellowed, raising his glass in the air.

Everyone obediently followed suit and raised their own glasses high in the air, the light from the chandeliers glinting down through the champagne coupes like half a dozen or so golden eyes.

'Here's to two of the craziest farm-boy tourists this barnstorming spectacle has ever hosted!'

'To Louis and Harry,' Ava added.

'To Louis and Harry!' everyone repeated.

A chorus of clinking glasses followed but was interrupted when a sudden sputtering came from Louis. He had never sipped champagne before and had not anticipated it would be so bubbly. Harry clapped him on the back as though to aid him, and for a second it was as if the two young men were friends. There it was again: that hint that the frosty hostility she'd initially noticed between the two boys was melting.

As Ava mused on this, she sipped her own champagne timidly, cautiously peering around the dining room to see whether anyone noticed or cared. By the letter of the law, she, Louis, and Harry were not quite of legal age. But in her travels, Ava had noticed that folks in smaller farming towns cared significantly less about enforcing this rule than people in big cities did. Small-town folks figured if somebody was old enough to bale hay or break a horse, he was old enough to have a drink at the end of a hard day's work. Now, even if the maître d' were to return and give them further trouble, Ava suspected Earl would slip the gentleman some money to make the problem go away. The bribe would cost Earl – as had the champagne itself, and the evening out on the town in general – but after six years of living in a cramped caravan, Ava knew Earl and knew exactly what he was about. Ava had spent the entire day stuffing cash into a cigar box. She was perfectly aware that there had been a steep uptick in sales today, and Earl, for all his flaws, was a clever man. That was how the champagne would prove useful: a pair of farm boys tipsy on champagne and bowled over by the fancy setting were likely to agree to just about anything.

Earl reached for the bottle where it sat in a bucket full of melting ice and hastily refilled Louis's and Harry's glasses as though to confirm Ava's suspicion. The actual subject, however, did not come up until midway through the meal, after a small orchestra had assembled and begun to play. Every so often a well-dressed couple rose from their respective tables and floated around the polished wooden floor. The atmosphere was still elegant, but now it had turned from somber to gay.

Buzz observed the couples dancing for a few moments, then turned to Ava's mother. He grinned. Ava knew perfectly well: men loved to flirt with her mother, and Buzz was an incurable ladies' man who flirted for the sheer sport of it sometimes.

'May I steal a dance?' Buzz said to Cleo.

Cleo blushed and looked to Earl. He waved a magnanimous hand.

'Oh, go on – enjoy!'

Buzz and Cleo rose and joined the other dancers.

'Well, if you all would excuse me,' Hutch said, producing a cigar from his inside jacket pocket. 'I reckon it's awful nice out, now that it's cooled down some. I'd like to go smoke this outside and stare up at those stars a spell.'

Earl nodded and away Hutch went, ambling in that bowlegged cowboy way he had. Just as it was plain that Buzz was a ladies' man, it was also clear that Hutch was a man who enjoyed solitude. Before the flying circus he'd been an Army pilot, and before that he'd driven cattle for a living. He spoke fondly of those days – long days, without another human in sight for weeks on end. Ava suspected Hutch had reached his limit on small talk an hour or so earlier.

The table suddenly seemed more intimate. Now they were four: Earl and the two farm boys, with Ava looking on. Earl quickly stretched his wrists and cracked his knuckles, preparing to spring into action. He took out his pocket square and refolded it with meticulous precision. He ran the flat of his palm over his carefully combed and oiled hair. Finally, he leaned in over the table toward the two young men with a confidential air.

'You boys had *some* kind of fun today,' he commented in a casual voice. 'It got me to thinking perhaps we might come to some sort of arrangement together.'

Harry's lips twisted in amusement while staring at Earl with skepticism. 'Arrangement?' he asked, raising an eyebrow.

'Yes, I was thinking of perhaps extending our stay for a second weekend of performances and rides and letting you fellows try wing walking a few more times . . . I believe Sumpter would be amenable to the idea, and we could even try some fields farther away, in neighboring towns.' He paused, wearing the innocent expression of a man who has just hit upon an idea. 'Why, I'd even be willing to consider giving you both a hefty discount on the established price.'

Louis didn't say anything, but Harry began laughing – a deep rumble that began somewhere low in his diaphragm and bubbled up along his throat.

'*Discount*, eh?'

'Of course! I don't see what is so amusing about my generous offer of a discount.' Earl looked irritated. He reached a hand to his moustache and twirled the ends.

'You'll have to pardon me,' Harry said, 'but it sounds an awful lot like you're looking to hire yourself two stuntmen, only instead of paying them you expect *them* to pay *you*.'

Ava looked at Harry and suppressed a laugh of her own. She was impressed. Not only was Harry's assessment razor-sharp and wholly accurate, but few people confronted Earl Shaw so directly.

'Surely you're not suggesting I hand out money in exchange for the privilege of an airplane ride? Dear fellow, I'm afraid I must inform you: that is *not* how a barnstorming spectacle works. Not at all.'

'Well, now, seems to me we'd be entering into the 'spectacle' part of that equation,' Harry replied.

Earl did not respond. Throughout this exchange Louis remained silent, watching and listening, too stunned to speak.

'Look here,' Harry continued. 'We're no fools. We know what's in it for you; we saw how much money you made today.'

'Indeed,' Earl replied. 'And what do you propose?'

'I propose that if you're going to ask a couple of fellas to come and work for you, you make them a proper offer.'

Earl leaned back in his chair and squinted his eyes, measuring up his opponent. He let out an aggravated sigh. A minute or two passed in silence.

'All right,' he said finally, in a dry, businesslike voice. 'Five percent of ticket sales each.'

'What do Buzz and Hutch get paid?'

'Ten.'

'Then we want the same.'

'Nonsense! Buzz and Hutch are pilots! That's *skilled* labor.'

'We've skills of a particular variety, too.'

Earl snorted.

'We'd be risking our lives on a regular basis,' Harry argued. 'That's gotta count for something.'

'Fine. Seven and a half each,' Earl countered. 'And not a penny more.'

Earl tossed his napkin on the table and let out a tsk, making a supercilious face as though he were put out, but in truth he had to work a little at feigning his petulance. His share had just gone down from eighty percent to sixty-five . . . and yet, sixty-five percent of four times the regular proceeds nonetheless amounted to a significant increase.

'We'll try out this arrangement this weekend and see if it comes to anything,' Earl said. 'Who's to say, after all, whether the attendance today wasn't a simple fluke?' By then the dishes had been cleared and he summoned the waiter to bring a cordial, along with some coffee to sober up for the drive home.

'Oughtn't you fellas shake on it, to make it official?' Ava piped up to ask. She had been silent throughout Earl's entire exchange with the boys, and he gave a slight jump as though he'd forgotten she was sitting at the table with them. He realized, with a small inkling of irritation, that this also meant there was a witness who could hold him to his offer of seven and a half percent each.

'Yes,' Earl replied. 'Let us shake on it, boys.'

He extended a hand to Harry, who took it and gave it a curt but firm shake, a calm smile on his face. Then Earl turned to Louis. Louis hesitated for the briefest of seconds.

'I don't know . . .' Louis said. 'I got . . . responsibilities. To my family's ranch.' Again he averted his eyes, as though embarrassed. 'It's why I had to quit school in the first place.'

'Tell me, boy,' Earl said, sensing a bit of extra urging might be necessary. 'How much you gonna make this weekend on that farm of yours?'

Louis cast his eyes down at the polished wooden floor and shrugged.

'You will make far more money with our outfit, and you can send it home to your dear old Ma and Pa, if you insist.'

'Well, that's a good point, I suppose . . .'

Everyone could see the imaginary wheels turning in Louis's head as he debated first one side of the argument, then the other. After a few moments he looked up at Earl, then Harry, and finally Ava. His brother Guy would blow up when he found out what Louis was up to. But maybe Guy would let it go, if only Louis could send some real money home. The orchestra stopped. Louis clenched his jaw and shook.

'You sign some new talent, Earl?' came Buzz's voice as he returned from the dance floor with Cleo.

'That I did.'

'Well, this oughta add some extra color to our outfit.'

Buzz grinned and nodded at Louis and Harry. He liked to make money, too. Hutch came back in from his solitary smoke break outside, and a final toast was proposed with the dregs of the champagne, barely a swallow in each glass. Noisy, irregular clinks sounded all around.

The rest of the evening wound down with all the energy of a contented celebration. There was only one sour note. After Buzz and Cleo returned from the dance floor, they slipped back into the booth together, rejoining the group. Buzz was feeling relaxed and had laid his arm to rest around Cleo's slender shoulders. Earl, far gone by then on the combination of champagne and cordial, was in the middle of a cackling laugh over something Buzz had said when his eyes fastened on Buzz's arm around his wife. His mouth snapped shut in mid-cackle and a dark shadow immediately descended over his face, turning his expression from merry to enraged with remarkable speed.

'For heaven's sake, woman! Haven't you any sense of propriety?' he snapped at Cleo.

Cleo froze, then averted her eyes, her whole body wilting miserably like a leaf of lettuce suddenly thrust into a hot oven. Ava cringed to see her mother looking so embarrassed and apologetic. Meanwhile, Buzz took the hint and retracted his arm.

'I didn't mean anything by it, Boss,' Buzz said. 'I was only stretching out for comfort. This booth is a little cramped after sitting in a cockpit all day.'

'Not to worry,' Earl said. '*You* aren't the one to blame.' He smiled around the table, but only at the men. 'It's *her* I've got a bone to pick with. She always has to act the belle of the ball everywhere we go. I can't take her anywhere.'

The smile faded as he turned to stare at Ava's mother. Cleo's eyes remained downcast, as though she were making a careful study of a small brown ring stain that had been left behind by a gravy boat a busboy had cleared earlier that evening.

'She forgets that she was living in squalor when I found her, and that if she prefers, she can always go back to nothing again.'

A beat passed as no one at the table dared to speak.

But then Hutch chivalrously cleared his throat and changed the topic. The group of them resumed their earlier, more lighthearted, celebratory mode. If she had been stung, Cleo let it go, shyly but steadily brightening as soon as a smile returned to Earl's face.

Ava, however, was not so quick to forget. Earl didn't notice her smoldering like a hot coal where she sat quietly in the booth. He downed the last of his cordial, slapped the table with an air of finality, and stood up to go – impervious to the growing hatred in his stepdaughter's eyes.

16

Louis Thorn and Harry Yamada had officially joined Earl Shaw's Flying Circus. At first, Earl pretended the boys were hired only on a trial basis. This was all for show, to keep them on their toes. But after a couple of successful performances, he quickly forgot all about his posturing and began to treat Louis and Harry as permanent members of the barnstorming act, as if they had always been his stuntmen.

Ava was secretly glad to have Louis and Harry aboard – 'secretly' only because Ava didn't want to give them the satisfaction. Especially not Harry. She hadn't forgotten about the day they'd all met – the day she'd warned them about Earl's mercenary interest in their proposed attempt to wing walk; instead of thanking her, Harry had only teased her and scoffed at her. Ava wasn't one to stand for being mocked.

During the day, Louis and Harry spent most of their time in the air with Buzz and Hutch – performing or traveling to the next destination – while Earl, Cleo, and Ava puttered along down below in the Model A, towing the caravan behind them. The shows began to follow a routine. Now that Earl was no longer convinced Louis and Harry were destined to die in spectacularly grotesque fashion, he often arranged for them to perform earlier in the day, rather than as a finale. Earl had discovered that the sight of Louis and Harry walking safely on the wings of *Castor* and *Pollux* emboldened spectators, particularly young men. And in his tremendous announcer's voice, Earl had no trouble spelling it out for those who were slow to draw their own conclusions: if the flying circus's two stuntmen were brave enough to take a walk on the wings, only a coward would decline a scenic tourist flight! At the conclusion of Louis and Harry's stunt, a fresh wave of business came pouring in as young men bought rides, hoping to impress their sweethearts.

At first, there was very little opportunity for Ava to engage Louis or Harry in conversation directly. At night, Ava typically slept in the caravan along with Earl and her mother, while Louis and Harry made camp outside with Buzz and Hutch. Still, there were times in the evenings when everybody sat around together as Cleo cooked supper over the campfire, Hutch got out his harmonica, Buzz sang along and chewed tobacco (sometimes while sneaking a peek at a girlie magazine), and Ava read a book (her favorite pastime) that it would abruptly dawn on Ava: the two newcomers were now present during these evenings as well. There was an additional hum of new energy. This hum was felt more than heard; after all, when they weren't shouting insults and challenges to each other from a pair of biplanes, the two boys rarely exchanged words. Ava noticed they maintained a standoffish air while at the same time making camp side by side, right along with Buzz and Hutch.

Ava also began to note their interests and habits. Louis regularly had his nose in a comic book – often one of the same five comic books he owned. And Harry . . . well, Harry also read, or else spent his time whittling away at something. Occasionally Ava attempted small gestures of friendly curiosity, but only with Louis. She wandered over to their side of the campfire and sat down. Louis was easy enough to talk to; he would blush but also try to hold up his end of the conversation, bringing up topics he thought might interest her. Harry never chimed in, but she could feel him listening. Ava stole furtive glances at the things he read or the items he whittled. She was able to deduce that he liked to read magazine stories about magicians and that he carved unusual wooden box contraptions that operated like puzzles. Like the wooden boxes he carved, Ava considered him something of a mystery.

From the very beginning of the barnstorming act, the money that the flying circus earned had always been handled in the same manner: Ava collected the customers' payments, stuffed the money into the cigar box, and, at the end of the day, handed the box over to Earl. For his part, Earl immediately counted the contents, measuring the money against the number of rides Buzz and Hutch had given that day. He kept careful count; his greedy eyes missed nothing. After he'd counted the contents of the cigar box twice, Earl parceled out the two shares owed to Buzz and Hutch – and, later, two more for Louis and Harry – and pocketed the rest. There were no shares apportioned to Ava or her mother. The reason for this was simple, Earl argued: Cleo and Ava were his wife and stepdaughter – an extension of Earl, really – and he was the head of the household, naturally enough.

The result of all this meant Ava and her mother almost never had any cash. Ava was less than pleased with this arrangement. Complaining to Earl got her nowhere. He either charmed his way out of the conversation or else grew irritable and short-tempered.

Over time, she began to remedy the problem herself, reverting to an 'old habit' she'd picked up during those years she and her mother were on their own.

With two new stuntmen in tow, the flying circus left Newcastle and began to ramble through all the neighboring towns. At first they remained in the Sierra Nevada foothills, working their way south, crossing from Placer County to El Dorado, hopping between the small gold-mining towns dotted about along the tributaries of the American River. The terrain was hilly, but parts of it were still wide and flat enough to land a pair of biplanes; the farmers were happy to accept a little cash for the use of their fields, the locals were bored and starved for entertainment. The barnstorming act was prospering, and with it the members were lining their pockets with more coin than ever – all except Ava and her mother.

Under these circumstances, Ava's 'old habit' grew steadily more regular.

In the town of Folsom, with its compact main street perched on a little hill not far from the river itself, Ava decided to 'liberate' a few penny candies. In the town of Gold Hill, Ava slipped a little wooden pencil up her sleeve. In the town of Coloma, Ava spotted a few mother-of-pearl buttons that would serve nicely to mend her favorite blouse.

But it was in the quaint town of Placerville that Ava found herself in a dry goods store eyeing her most ambitious prize of all: a beautiful leather-bound edition of *The Comedy of Errors* with a pretty gilded finish on the edges of the pages. The store mainly sold sacks of flour, hardware, and textiles, and offered only a handful of books; most were tucked neatly on a shelf. This proud volume had been turned face-out. It was clearly part of a set but had somehow lost its mates over time. Ava involuntarily bit her lip when she saw it. She loved Shakespeare, and this was a play she had yet to read. The title sounded fun, perhaps more lighthearted than the Shakespeare plays she was already familiar with, which were mostly heart-wrenching tragedies. The longer she contemplated the beautiful edition, the more she wanted it.

Instinctively, Ava darted a glance around the store. She hadn't ever dared to steal anything this great in value. It had been easier when she was just a child, a skinny slip of a girl who was invisible to most folks. Maturity had betrayed her; despite her insistence on bobbed hair and men's trousers, Ava knew that in the world's eyes she had grown into a pretty young woman. And pretty young women did not go unobserved. Men and women greeted her and frowned if she did not respond with a gracious air and pleasant smile. Men, of course, demonstrated a spectrum of behavior, from blushing to the tipping of a hat brim to slurred greetings that were downright lewd. Customers and shopkeepers eyed her, curious about the nature of her purchases.

That was what the shopkeeper was doing at the present moment: eyeing Ava where she stood. If she was going to liberate the book, she was going to have to be very careful. It was June, and she wasn't wearing heavy winter clothes that might help her hide the book. Creativity would be key. Ava looked around and spotted an older woman inspecting the store's selection of white and floral-print calico. She wandered over to the woman, leisurely inspecting goods as she went.

'Oh!' Ava exclaimed, once she was beside the woman. 'Are you sewing a dress by chance?'

'I am,' the woman replied, smiling and puffing up with pride to be acknowledged. 'I was hoping to sew something my granddaughter might wear to the church picnic. My daughter seems to think calico is quite old-fashioned, but I haven't made up my mind; I still like it . . .'

'It's a practical fabric,' Ava offered. 'And, for a picnic, nothing's better than white muslin for the heat!'

The two of them continued on in this manner, Ava complimenting the woman's taste, and the old woman pretending not to raise an eyebrow at Ava's trousers. The shopkeeper grew bored and began to wave to other townspeople passing by his shop window. Ava knew what she needed most was a distraction. Her eyes hit upon several bolts of fabric stacked one on top of the other, low down, just behind the front counter.

'Oh! What about those? Have you looked at those already?' she asked the old woman. The woman turned, blinked, and squinted.

'No. I haven't seen those . . .' she mused.

'Is that a sweet little rosebud print on that one? How charming that would be for a young girl!'

Soon enough, the old woman had demanded that the shopkeeper haul up each bolt of fabric and lug it onto the cutting table for inspection. The shopkeeper labored to deliver up the items one by one. As the old woman and the shopkeeper inspected each bolt of fabric in turn, Ava took her cue and quietly drifted away from this new transaction.

Within seconds, she had slipped the book under her blouse and down the back of her trousers. A small tremor passed through her to know she was doing something that wasn't quite right. She wavered for the briefest of seconds. *Needs must*, she told herself. Earl had ensured that Ava and her mother were dependent upon him while at the same time acting stingier than Ebenezer Scrooge. If she wanted anything for herself, she would have to take it, however she could. With this thought in her mind, she recovered her resolve.

But the second she turned around, Ava understood instantly that she had made a fatal mistake. The shopkeeper was looking square at her, glaring, his features quickly filling with outrage. Her blood ran cold with dread.

'I *saw* you, missy!' he said, hissing in a low voice.

'Beg pardon? Saw me?' Ava replied, blinking innocently. 'Saw me what?'

Now the old woman stopped to look and was frowning with concern. Ava felt her heart sink. She felt terrible to let the old lady down; how scandalized the woman would be to know she'd helped a thief!

'You know perfectly well *what I saw*,' the shopkeeper said. His teeth were brown – stained from chewing tobacco, she guessed. He leaned over the counter and leered, his wiry body tense, perching his elbows on the glass display counter as though to ring her up for some invisible purchase.

'I hope you don't think you're leaving my shop without payin' for that book there,' he said. He paused and spit into a brass spittoon in the corner.

Ava felt a thickness in her throat as she swallowed. She couldn't believe this was happening. Not to her – it couldn't.

'See *here*,' she began, her voice betraying a high-pitched warble. 'I don't know what you mean with all this—'

'Oh, I think you know perfectly well what I mean, missy,' the shopkeeper hissed. 'You stole that leather-bound volume I put up for sale over yonder! And if you want to press the matter, I ain't too shy to call in the sheriff.'

'I . . . I . . .' Ava wavered. The words 'Please don't' were on the tip of her tongue, when she suddenly heard a new, familiar voice interrupt.

'You mean this volume, here, sir?'

Ava spun around and found herself facing Harry Yamada. At some point in the past ten minutes or so, Harry had slipped into the shop unseen. Now he stood across the room, holding up the very book the shopkeeper had just accused Ava of stealing. Ava was so shocked by this turn of events, she had to stop herself from patting her waist and backside, where she had put the book.

'I don't mean to intrude,' Harry continued, 'but might this be the book you mean? I'm terribly sorry – I picked it up from its place in your lovely display. I only wanted to get a better look at it.'

The shopkeeper stood up, his spine stiffening, his frown deepening. He squinted at the cover of the book. He looked from Harry to Ava and back again.

'Well . . .' he grumbled, clearly baffled, 'I suppose that's the volume I mean.'

Ava was astonished. However did Harry filch the book off her without her feeling it? Ava wasn't sure how to feel about the idea that Harry might be a better pickpocket than she was. And now there he stood, holding the book up near his shoulder, standing in the back of the shop, near its original place in the display, amused and clearly pleased with himself.

'Look here, young fellow,' the shopkeeper continued. Now he'd had a moment to take in the sight of the book and, more importantly, Harry. He was relieved to see his merchandise had not disappeared, and yet uncomfortable to see it clutched in the hands of a young Oriental man.

'Look here . . . that book is for paying customers in'erested in buyin'!'

'I was contemplating the purchase,' Harry said. Ava looked again at him, and this time it was her turn to raise an eyebrow. 'But I may have to think on it for a while,' he concluded.

'Well, *while you do that*, you can just leave that book right where you found it,' the shopkeeper replied.

'Oh,' Harry said, smiling. He restored the book to its place in the shelf's display. 'Why, of course.'

Ava's cheeks burned to realize: that was *not* where Harry had found it.

Little was said after that. Harry made a few friendly remarks, the old woman carried on with her quest to find the perfect cotton fabric to please both daughter and granddaughter, and Ava hurried out of the shop before anyone could say anything more to her.

She had made it about a block down the street when she heard Harry call her name. She turned around to see him grinning at her.

'Nice work, Robin Hood,' he said. 'But I think you might be a little out of practice.'

'Oh?' Ava replied. 'What would you know about it?'

Harry looked at her, smiling. 'Anyone ever tell you stealing ain't right?'

'Easy for you to say. Louis says your people are rich.'

Harry looked surprised, then regained himself. 'My folks do all right,' he said. 'What of it?'

'Well, you've probably never had to steal just to eat.'

Harry thought about this for a minute. 'No,' he said. 'You're right. I haven't.'

Having won her point, Ava wasn't sure what to do or say next. She felt her cheeks beginning to color.

'But if I may give one piece of advice,' Harry said now.

'Oh, yeah?' she replied. 'I'm not sure I could stop you.'

'If you intend to make a regular habit of this, you need to get better at your sleight of hand.'

Ava was stung. 'That's the first time I've ever been caught!' she said hotly.

Harry smiled, and shrugged. 'At least I was here to make it reappear,' he said, obviously quite pleased with himself. 'That's my specialty.'

'Your *specialty*?' What was he implying – that she should *thank* him? 'Oh, yeah?' she said, irritated. 'Your specialty is that you make things reappear?'

Harry nodded. 'It is,' he said. 'The best magicians not only make things disappear, but they make things reappear – and always know when the time is just right.'

Ava had a flash of the magicians' magazines she'd glimpsed Harry reading and wondered if he wasn't quoting directly from one of the issues.

'Huh,' she grunted, looking him up and down one last time. 'Good to know I've given you ample practice for your skills.'

'Not at all,' Harry said, still smiling his generous smile.

Annoyed, Ava turned to go. Then she paused and spun back around.

'Just for the record,' Ava said, 'you caught me on an off day. When it comes to making things disappear, my sleight of hand is just fine.'

Now it was Harry's turn to raise a cynical eyebrow. 'Is it?'

'You bet.'

And with that, she produced Harry's silver lighter from one of her trouser pockets. His eyes roved her body, looking for answers, confused – not quite comprehending at first – but as soon as they landed on her hand it was clear that he understood. His own hand moved automatically to pat his pocket, but of course his pocket was empty.

Ava laughed.

She pitched the lighter into the air and, on reflex, Harry caught it.

'See you around,' Ava said, and walked away.

Later that evening, the barnstorming troupe gathered around the campfire. For supper, Ava's mother made a pot of stew and put some coffee on. After the last of the stew had been sopped up with a final crust of bread, the group sat around entertaining themselves, as had become their habit.

The warm day had taken on a chilly edge after the sun went down, and Ava went inside the caravan to retrieve both a book and a blanket. She had long since run out of new material to read, and settled on rereading a book she had already read a handful of times – in this case, *The Red Pony* by John Steinbeck. Books were her treasures; she paused as she looked over the stash she'd accumulated, feeling their spines with an idle finger. *Around the World in Eighty Days. Romeo and Juliet. Adventures of Huckleberry Finn. Moby-Dick. David Copperfield. The Count of Monte Cristo.* She tried not to think about how nice it would be to add another volume to her library. Ava knew she should simply be glad the situation did not end worse: she understood exactly how close she'd come to being caught, how narrow her escape had been.

At first, when Ava reemerged from the caravan, everyone was still more or less arranged around the campfire just as she had left them. But when she returned to the spot where she had been previously sitting, she saw something nestled in the tall grass. She reached for it and her eyes lit upon the rectangular, leather-bound shape and glimpsed the familiar gold lettering, *The Comedy of Errors.*

Ava was so shocked, she dropped the book like a hot potato. Her first instinct was to hide the book in the blanket – as though worried that perhaps she *had* stolen the book after all. She threw a wild glance around to determine whether anybody had seen her reaction. Her mother was oblivious, busy doing the washing up. Earl was deep into a glass of whiskey and occupied by polishing his favorite gold pocket watch. Hutch was gazing at the stars as he played his harmonica, Buzz was yodeling along with his eyes closed, and Louis was entranced by a comic book with a brightly colored cover. Only Harry was watching Ava.

She frowned and lifted the blanket up a few inches. There it was: the book she hadn't managed to steal some hours earlier. Curiously angry to see it, Ava stood up and stormed off, intent on taking a walk through the dark field.

Only a few minutes into her walk, she heard footsteps rustling the tall grass behind her.

'Hey!' Harry called to her. She paused, allowing him to catch up. 'Aren't you gonna say thank you?'

'Hah. Hardly! That shopkeeper's suspicions will go straight back to me now, won't they? So, yes – thanks *ever so much*. I expect you couldn't resist proving your point about sleight of hand, eh?'

Harry didn't answer. She pressed on, enraged.

'I'll have you know, I used to steal to *eat*, and only because there was no other way to put food on the table! But it's only a game to you, isn't it? A silly little magic show! And exactly which 'magic trick' did you use this time?' she mocked.

She couldn't make out his face in the dark, but she saw Harry's shoulders move as he shrugged.

'Hmm. Well, I suppose you'd have to call it . . . *Presto Dinero*,' Harry replied.

'Wait a minute . . . you . . .' Ava stammered, recognizing the Spanish word. 'You bought it?'

'It seemed like you wanted it pretty bad.'

Stunned, Ava didn't say anything.

'Well, anyway . . . it's yours, free and clear. No sheriff hot on your trail.'

Ava was still speechless.

'You're welcome,' Harry said finally. She saw his silhouette nod, then he turned and strode back in the direction of the flickering yellow and orange glow of the campfire.

17

The month of May evaporated like morning dew, giving way to the shimmering heat of June. Sunrises were filled with the low cries of mourning doves, the chatter of finches and sparrows. Noon brought near silence, and later, the afternoons thickened with the buzzing drone of insects. The days were growing indisputably hot and dry; nonetheless, the sales of airplane rides rose right along with the temperature.

The flying circus was slowly making its way along the foothills, and they had stopped in Fiddletown, a place that looked to Ava like the set of a Hollywood Western. During their first day there, by late morning, most of the members of the barnstorming troupe had gone into town. Ava's mother reported that they were running low on provisions, and Buzz and Hutch accompanied her in order to help carry her purchases, which were likely to include a sack of flour, a heavy tin of lard, and, of course, always, always, more gasoline. Earl went into town as well, on the pretext of visiting the barber for a shave and a trim. Ava knew that, before suppertime, he would very likely find his way into a mah-jongg game or a hand of poker.

'Where's Harry?' Ava asked Louis, noticing that the two of them had been left alone at the campsite.

Louis shrugged as though he could not be bothered to concern himself with Harry's whereabouts, but then, after a brief moment, relented.

'Well, I overheard him say somethin' about wanting a bath,' he replied.

Ava nodded, comprehending. Bathing was tricky on the road if a person had any modesty at all, and even when the local town boasted a bathhouse, a Japanese man likely wasn't welcome. Over the years, Ava herself had often sought out a secluded stretch of river or hidden lake cove. She sighed and glanced around the campsite.

'Looks like it's you and me and a whole lot of chores, then,' she said to Louis. 'Lend me a hand?'

His face lit up with a friendly smile. 'Sure thing,' he said.

Ava put him to work gathering fresh kindling while she did the washing up. After that, she fetched a wooden tray of tools from inside the caravan and threw an oily rag at Louis's chest.

'What's this?' Louis asked, catching the filthy rag, confused.

Minutes later, the two of them stood peering into the metal innards that allowed *Pollux* to stay up in the air as Ava's hands rubbed various coils and pipes clean with mineral spirits, squirting still other parts with oil from an oilcan.

'Don't you ever think it's all a little unnatural?'

'What's unnatural?' Louis asked, looking confused by the question. Ava, who had long ago learned how to clean and perform routine maintenance on an airplane engine, was now busy showing him how. It dawned on him that this was the irregularity Ava meant. 'Unnatural that you know how to work on the engine of a biplane but won't fly in one?' he asked.

Ava rolled her eyes. 'No. I mean men, airplanes – the whole idea of it.'

'Are you asking me was mankind meant to fly?'

Ava shrugged, a little embarrassed. 'I suppose,' she said. She took a step back from *Pollux* and gestured at the biplane, her hands still holding the oilcan and the oily rag. 'I mean, just think – how does this heavy chunk of metal carry you up into the sky, much less keep you up there?'

'That's easy,' Louis replied. 'It's physics.' He began to explain the laws of aerodynamics in all seriousness, but Ava only laughed.

'Why, thank you, Professor,' she replied, teasing him. 'I happen to know all that.' It was true . . . or mostly true. Ava had read up on the laws of physics as they concerned airplanes – although Louis seemed far more interested and enraptured with the nitty-gritty of the science than she was.

They had been on the road all together for a few weeks now, and over the course of that time Ava had gotten to know a bit more about what made Louis Thorn tick. He was a funny conundrum of opposing qualities. First, there were the physical quirks. Louis was tall and well built, but not necessarily athletic. He was good-looking and clean-cut – folks often used the words 'all-American' to describe him – and Ava got the impression that girls liked him. But she also got the impression that he was the less-confident sibling to an extremely self-assured older brother. There was a careful deliberation about the way he moved that translated into an awkward tempo of hesitation. She'd especially noticed it on the day of Louis's and Harry's first wing-walking attempts: Louis was the one you *expected* to be the better wing-walker, and yet . . . even from far away, you could plainly observe the way his brain second-guessed his every move.

Then there were Louis's hobbies and interests. His tone and expression turned very serious when he talked about science, about physics and mechanics – or, alternately, whenever he talked about his other true love: comic books and their characters, particularly a new character people were supposedly crazy about, called Superman. While these two passions – science and comics – went together perfectly in Louis's mind, Ava was quick to point out how one debunked the other. She had never seen Louis more frustrated than when she insisted that the very premise of Superman – the world's strongest man, who flies around in a cape without the help of an airplane – was hardly a scientifically sound conceit. Ava teased him but stopped short when she saw a vein in his temple throbbing, and realized he might blow a gasket in all earnestness. It was rather endearing, actually.

But when he wasn't explaining aerodynamics or talking comic books, Louis was quite different: rather relaxed and open. He had a friendly way with people and found it difficult to get cross with folks or carry a grudge – which was why, perhaps, it struck Ava as strange that Louis acted so funny around Harry, and vice versa. It almost seemed like Louis had to concentrate all his energies on hating Harry, or else he'd forget to do it.

'Speaking of unnatural,' Ava said now, changing the subject slightly, 'I don't think there's anything more unnatural than how you act around Harry.'

She left the remark dangling, to let Louis absorb it and perhaps return some sentiment of his own accord. But Louis was merely silent.

'It seems as though maybe you actually like him,' Ava observed, trying to nudge Louis along. 'Or, at least, like you don't hate him as much as you let on.'

Louis shrugged. 'It's not . . . There's . . .' He hesitated, as though searching for the right words. 'It's just that there's a lot of history between our families.'

Ava had been trying to tease out this story bit by bit. She tried to get more of it now.

'You said it was about land.'

Louis nodded.

'My father always told us the same story about the Yamadas, over and over . . . He said my grandfather was tricked out of his land.'

'And so that's what you believe – that Harry's family stole your family's land?'

Louis shrugged.

'Sure. They're my kin. Wouldn't you believe them?'

Ava thought about this. 'I don't know,' she said, pondering aloud now. 'It's still just . . . one side of the story . . . and it's not like you or Harry were even alive to witness what really happened.'

'Are you calling my father a liar?'

Ava knew Louis's father was dead. Her instincts told her to tread lightly.

'I guess I was just saying . . . maybe Harry's been told a story, too, and it's a different story . . .'

Louis didn't answer, and Ava fell into an apologetic silence. She went on cleaning the biplane's engine. She could sense Louis beside her but lost in thought, his eyes absently watching her hands.

'We used to be friends, you know,' Louis said finally. His voice was a flat murmur, as though he were only remembering this fact himself.

She'd suspected something like this was possible. Nonetheless, she looked at Louis with genuine surprise.

'Back when we were kids,' Louis explained. 'Since our families' acreage put us right next to each other, we played together out in the little grove of trees at the property line.'

Ava smiled, interested. She wanted to picture it. 'What would you two get up to?'

Louis looked off into the distance and gave a cross between a grunt and a chuckle. 'I remember I'd show him all my comic books; we'd read and I'd explain about *The Shadow*, and he'd show me all his magic tricks . . . He was nuts about Blackstone and the Great Lafayette, and his favorite, Harry Houdini. Taught me a couple of card tricks once, and a bit with a coin . . .' Louis hesitated, lost in memory. 'I always thought it was funny that so many magicians are named Harry, and that was Harry's name, too.' He paused again. 'Of course, that's not Harry's *real* name. He's got a Jap name, too. Haruto, I think.'

Haruto Yamada, Ava repeated in her head. Another interesting fact she hadn't known. She recalled Harry's gift – that pretty gilded volume of Shakespeare, *The Comedy of Errors* – and blushed. She poked her head in closer to the plane's engine so Louis wouldn't see.

'Sounds like the two of you got along pretty well once,' she said, trying to keep the conversation about Louis and Harry.

'I guess we didn't know any better.' He paused. 'Or maybe I did. My brother Guy saw that Harry and I were playing together, and he used to warn me all the time that it wasn't right – that if I kept on, I'd likely catch a hiding from our father.'

'And did you?'

'Catch a hiding?' Louis shook his head. 'No. My father never caught on that I was spending time with our Jap neighbors.'

'Then . . . what changed?'

'What do you mean?'

'Well, when I first met you both, it didn't seem like you and Harry were exactly chummy. So what happened?'

'Oh.' Louis nodded. 'Yeah. We *were* friends – sort of – but then, I suppose, one day I stopped speaking to him.'

'But why?'

Louis looked at the ground. 'It was around the time my father died.' He shook his head, uncomfortable. 'Seemed disrespectful . . . if I were to keep on talking to any of the Yamadas – at least, that's what my brother Guy was awful keen on pointing out. After our father died, he promised he'd give me that hiding himself if I kept on bein' social with Harry.'

'So after your brother said that, you just stopped talking to Harry?'

Louis nodded.

'Did Harry ever complain or ask you why?' Ava ventured.

Louis shrugged. 'School was the only time we saw each other after that. He tried to talk to me a couple of times in the schoolyard, but I avoided him. And then, once we was in high school . . . well, it didn't matter much. I was bound to drop out anyway.' Louis lowered his eyes as though ashamed. 'I was needed on the ranch.'

Ava was sympathetic. She'd had to leave school, too, and wanted to tell him she understood. But before she could find the right words, Louis was looking at her with a funny expression on his face.

'Boy,' he said, 'you sure do ask an awful lot of questions about Harry all the time!'

Ava startled.

'Do I?' she asked.

Louis shrugged and laughed.

'It sure seems like it to me.'

Ava waved a hand. 'I'm sure it's just a coincidence. You and Harry are the most excitement this outfit has seen in years. Only natural to be curious about the two of you – both of you.'

Louis smiled and nodded, and Ava continued to point out various engine parts, giving their names and showing Louis those spots where grime was especially likely to build up. Louis had no reason to doubt any of it. He watched Ava as she talked, noticing how green her eyes looked when they caught the amber glare of the late-afternoon sun.

18

NEWCASTLE, CALIFORNIA
SEPTEMBER 17, 1943

'I reckon I'm under obligation to keep you informed,' Sheriff Whitcomb says, by way of greeting. He gives a disdainful grunt for good measure.

Agent Bonner comes in from the bright sunshine and pulls the door shut behind him. The same hospital-green walls greet him. The fan whirs with an exhausted, overworked air, as though aggrieved by the dent it is unable to make in the oppressive heat.

'Keep me informed of what?' Bonner asks.

'Plenty of that biplane's parts burned up in the crash, but the local firemen collected all the ones that didn't. The fire chief telephoned this morning. He's no expert, but there's a part he thinks is likely the fuel line, and it looks to him like someone cut it.'

Bonner freezes, his brow furrowed.

'Well, I suppose "punctured" is how the fire chief put it,' the sheriff adds. 'It looked to be cut, but not through and through. Just a small vertical slice. Looked to be man-made.'

'Meaning . . . someone tampered with it on purpose?'

The sheriff holds up a hand and shakes his head.

'I figure that's up to you to see about. But I'll caution you . . . I wouldn't go jumping to any conclusions,' Whitcomb says. He pauses and fixes Bonner with a meaningful stare. 'And I certainly wouldn't go pointing any fingers – not just yet.'

It is clear they are both talking about Louis Thorn without either of them needing to mention his name.

'Of course,' Bonner replies. 'I only intend to follow procedure. I'd like to make some calls, see if I can find an airplane mechanic to come up here and verify what the fire chief is looking at.'

Sheriff Whitcomb grunts.

'I assume the FBI will be footin' the bill for that?'

Bonner's jaw clenches, remembering Reed's admonishments about the Bureau's budget. He coughs and nods.

'Spoke with my boss about it this morning, as a matter of fact,' Bonner says.

Whitcomb grunts again. 'Needless to say, until we all decide different, this information is just between us fellas,' he says, casting a meaningful look at Deputy Henderson.

'Of course,' Bonner repeats.

Henderson doesn't speak. His eyes move between the two of them with a sheepish, vaguely guilty air.

Hat still in hand, Bonner glances around the room. 'May I?' he asks, pointing to the receptionist's desk, where he sat the day before to use the telephone.

Whitcomb frowns, but tips his head in a brief nod, giving permission.

'Irene gets into work 'round three,' he warns.

'Appreciate it,' Bonner says, and slides into the desk chair, preoccupied with the sheriff's news about the fuel line. He's already itching to talk to Louis Thorn about that. But Bonner knows he has to be patient, have an expert verify the sabotage, make sure no piece of the case has been overlooked, however small. He reaches into his attaché case, extracting a file folder. In it is every bit of information the FBI possesses about the Yamada family.

Bonner flips open the manila folder and extracts the contents. He clears the desktop before him and begins to lay out each paper and photograph in a deliberate, meditative manner, like a mosaic artist laying tiles. He switches on a desk lamp and peers more closely into the constellation of documents as though he were trying to read tea leaves.

Bonner knows he must eliminate the Yamadas as suspects, even if the notion strikes him now as increasingly unlikely. If Harry Yamada and his father had a death wish, it was simple enough to crash an airplane without having to tamper with the fuel line. Why would they take such a useless additional step? Suicide is a question of will. Sabotage is the sort of action taken by someone with something to gain from hurting others.

Bonner's mind circles back around to Louis Thorn, the man living in the Yamadas' former home, the official owner of the former Yamada property. Bonner hadn't expected any of this when he requested the case. He simply recognized the Thorn name and found himself curious. His curiosity was an idle sort, perhaps a touch narcissistic, but benign overall. It wasn't until Deputy Henderson began telling him about the land dispute between the Thorns and the Yamadas that Bonner got the inkling that his grandmother really hadn't ever told him very much, and that the situation was far more complicated than he had anticipated. He thought he'd get a passing look at Louis Thorn – at most, he might discover Thorn was hiding two escaped evacuees and turn a blind eye.

He never expected to meet Louis Thorn and suspect the young man of murder not more than ten minutes after shaking his hand.

Now Bonner doesn't know what to think. In the wake of the crash, Louis didn't appear shocked or saddened, so much as . . . *distracted*. The cut fuel line did not bode well, either. As far as Bonner can tell, the Thorns were poor and begrudged their neighbors' prized piece of land – land they believed had once belonged to their own family long ago. So many questions swirled around the case, but most of them kept orbiting back to one big question in particular: did Louis Thorn ever intend to give the Yamadas back their land? The Yamadas trusted him with it, but should they have?

Bonner knows the case is becoming an obsession; he can feel the fishhook sliding deeper and deeper under his skin. He knows, too, there comes a point in every obsession where a person stops caring that he's obsessed, a point where a person wants the answers so badly, he doesn't stop to contemplate whether or not he should be asking the questions. Plenty of people – Whitcomb not least of all – would rather Bonner leave well enough alone.

But Bonner has his heart set on digging up more information. He thinks again of those mysterious cuts and bruises on Louis Thorn's face, and looks across the room to where Deputy Henderson is bent over his own desk. Perhaps, Bonner decides, it's time to have Henderson show him the way to Murphy's Saloon and get that beer they discussed.

19

THE THORNS
1869–1930

It was Louis's grandfather, Ennis Thorn, who originally came over from Ireland in 1869 and traversed the vast distance from one American coast to the other. Ennis was thirty-four at the time, and lines had already begun to etch themselves upon his face, especially around his gray, sun-strained eyes, which instantly sprouted two small fans of lines whenever he smiled or looked into the sun. The lines deepened with the years until they ran all the way down the sides of his cheeks, all the way to his hairline. By the time he made it west, the lines had begun to settle in for good, no matter what expression he wore.

Back in Dublin, Ennis left behind a wife, three children, and a sizable group of angry debtors. He loved his wife and, not having told her of his plans to leave for America, nearly changed his mind over breakfast that morning. It pained him to go but, once across the Atlantic, he never looked back. After disembarking in New York, Ennis made his way steadily west over the years, picking up work in the form of manual labor. In Ireland, the Thorn family trade had been blacksmithing, and Ennis had retained enough of the old skills to hire himself out. He smithed for passing wagon trains whenever he could, and when he couldn't, he hired himself out in other ways, moving from town to town, raising barns and baling hay, until he ran clean out of towns and went to work dynamiting tunnels and hauling rocks for the transcontinental railroad that was slowly inching its way across the nation. He drank and gambled at every opportunity without fail, and got himself run out of several Nevada mining camps for his trouble.

By the time Ennis reached California, he was feeling his age and then some. He had developed the perpetually sour stomach of an alcoholic bachelor and was finally ready to seek out the relief of a regular home. When he set eyes on the rolling foothills that lay at the bottom of the tall Sierra Nevada mountain range, he came to the conclusion that he might like to graze some cattle, perhaps have an apple orchard.

It was an opportune time for Ennis to make such a decision, as he happened to be flush with cash, having just won a very lucky hand of poker and taken a small fortune from a fellow Irishman who owned a silver mine in Virginia City, Nevada. The game had lasted late into the night and Ennis had gotten his compatriot good and drunk before relieving him of a large chunk of the man's wealth.

Ennis then pushed onward to California, marveling at the manner in which the dry brown landscape of Nevada suddenly turned green only a few miles over the border. It wasn't as green as Ireland, but it may as well have been; Ennis had been traveling through prairies and deserts and tall brown mountains so long, seeing any bit of green felt like drinking water. He was *home*, he decided. Having just turned forty – and not a tender forty but rather a salty, weather-beaten forty at that – he found himself weary of travel, ready to stay put for a time. He also subscribed to that particular dream countless newly rich men often have in common: that along with his wealth he had been transformed overnight into the variety of important man meant to leave behind a legacy. To this end, he purchased one hundred and fifty acres in the Sierra Nevada foothills and promptly sent word to the Irish communities back East that he was in need of a wife.

To his astonishment, a little mouse of a woman named Nessie Barrett was dispatched from Boston on the very next train. Like Ennis, she was also pale and freckled, with gray eyes and hair pale as straw. Later, all who met them remarked that Ennis and Nessie could easily be taken for kin: besides the years that separated them, the main difference was in their expressions and temperaments; his was bold, hers was timid. She was a funny thing, that Nessie: petite and not quite beautiful, but attractive and feminine in her own way. Her pale hair struck a sharp contrast to her eyebrows, which grew thick and dark, making her tiny upturned nose and little mouth look even smaller than they were. But despite her fragile-looking exterior, she endured the trip west and arrived only slightly the worse for wear, and two short days after she stepped down from the third-class passenger car, Nessie Barrett became Nessie Thorn. This turn of events surprised everyone, most of all Ennis. He was eager for a wife, but even so, had planned to take longer with things.

There were reasons for the rush, mostly on Nessie's father's end. In Ennis's posting, he had written that should the match result in marriage, he would send a flat sum back to the bride's family as a token of his gratitude. He named the sum in his handbill, and it was quite healthy. The daughter of a butcher who had far too many children to provide a decent dowry for any of the girls in his large brood, Nessie was promptly packed up and shipped out the very next morning, and word was sent by Pony Express that Nessie was already on her way. Ennis waited with apprehension, for he rather thought Nessie's father had jumped the gun and that this did not bode well. He'd expected some preliminary exchange of correspondence – and a photograph, of course.

But when the train came chugging into the Rocklin station and Nessie climbed down, the match was acceptable to Ennis, and Nessie stayed. She was a hard worker and a woman of few words. No one could have said whether or not she enjoyed the change of scenery when she made the move from Boston to California, for no one ever bothered to ask Nessie her feelings on the matter, and she hardly revealed such sentiments in idle prattle. She was a good deal younger than Ennis Thorn – a mere eighteen to his forty – but she behaved like an elderly matron. In a strange way, Ennis took to heeding her as though she were a kind of mother figure, and their relationship was curiously enriched by this arrangement.

Back in Ireland, Ennis's first wife, Liza, had been temperamental and a dreamer, leaving Ennis to play the part of the responsible provider. It was a role he'd chafed against, a role that had left him feeling suffocated – until, of course, he abandoned it altogether. For years, he assumed he was not cut from the kind of cloth that gave married life its appropriate shape. But married to Nessie, Ennis was the impulsive, impractical one by a mile, and he found he liked the contrast very much. As far as he was concerned, a thing wasn't worth doing if it wasn't worth hiding from Nessie. Surprisingly enough, the dynamic between them – a dynamic best described as that of disapproving schoolmarm and naughty pupil – nurtured an unexpected feeling in Ennis, and he found that despite his high jinks and regular philandering, he loved his wife with a strangely fierce, protective passion.

John Ennis Thorn was born on April twentieth, in the year 1877. It was a breech birth, and Nessie suffered terribly, almost to the point of death. The doctor wound up cutting her open and stitching her up – a last-ditch effort to save her life, but a rather haphazard, hastily enacted procedure even the doctor did not believe she would survive. She did survive, but only just barely.

Hearing his wife's screams and seeing her already frail form grow weaker sobered up a very drunk Ennis almost instantly. After John's birth, Ennis watched the small infant suckling at her pale breast with amazement, and never again touched his wife with carnal desire. Instead, he loved her just as fiercely, but from afar. It was an unspoken agreement between the two of them: from now on, Ennis would take his passion down to the ladies' boardinghouse in town, and there only. For her part, Nessie seemed to appreciate being left in peace. Her husband's 'loyalty' – the portions of it she prized, anyhow – was still hers, and hers alone. He revered her as his schoolmarm wife, and if he ever disobeyed her, he continued to take the trouble to do so behind her back. She was happy to rule the roost with her intense silence and let him entertain his mischief elsewhere. And entertain his mischief elsewhere he did, often gambling and spending hours and even entire nights in town while Nessie stayed home nursing the baby. She didn't mind. She enjoyed the quiet.

One night, Ennis surprised his wife and child by coming home earlier than usual – earlier than midnight, in any case – and burst through the front door in a swaying tangle of drunken legs and expletives. A huff of warm night air wafted in with him, carrying the scent of wet hay. Nessie and John looked up, stupefied. By then, John had grown into a toddler, chubby and sedate ('sedate' was a very fitting descriptor for the child – much more so than 'happy,' for, after all, it could be said he was a stoic baby). The pair of them sat before the fire, she with her knitting, he sluggishly toppling the towers of blocks his mother had laid out for him.

Right away, Nessie noticed that Ennis was drunker than usual and angry as a hornet. Ennis was always garrulous but rarely so angry. He was a man of mirth and merriment, a man with a special talent for avoiding the seriousness of life. And yet, when he wanted to, he could spew pure vitriol. Nessie said nothing; she simply put down her knitting and waited for him to speak, as was her habit.

'Goddamn cheats and thieves, all of 'em,' Ennis growled, swinging his fists through the air with deadly heft and all inclusive aim. 'That lousy Silas Northrup ain't got no morals . . . no morals at all, dammit . . .' He continued grumbling as he hit his head on a hat rack and caught his ankle against a bench that stood in the entryway. 'Dammit! Who put this here? I ain't given no one permission to rearrange the entire goddamn house!'

Nessie never asked a single question. Eventually, between hiccups, belches, and slurred curses, it came out that Ennis had been playing poker and lost big in a very unlucky hand. He often came home thoroughly drunk – Nessie was accustomed to this – but ordinarily he didn't turn up until one or two o'clock in the morning. Ennis had set a record for speed that evening. Here he was, and it was barely eight.

'Sonofabitch kept refilling my glass and raising the stakes,' Ennis grunted, 'the goddamn thief.'

Whether out of tolerance or indifference, Nessie let her husband rage and helped him off with his boots. After putting John to sleep, she helped her husband into the bed they shared.

'What did you bet?' Nessie broke her long silence to ask. There was no accusation in her voice, only a flat, affectless curiosity. She lay next to him, staring up vacantly at the ceiling, her hands folded neatly and pressed to her chest, over the quilt. There was a long pause.

'The western parcel,' Ennis finally answered. His words were frank, but his voice was deep and pained.

Ennis had originally purchased two adjacent plots of land, combining them to form his orchard and ranch, and so had two deeds that accounted for the whole of his property. He favored the western parcel – it was twice the size of the eastern parcel, the drainage was better, and the soil was richer – but he was smart enough to know he was a novice farmer, so Ennis had begun cultivating the eastern parcel first. He figured he could make all his mistakes on the eastern parcel, and as he expanded with more orchard trees and grazed more horses, he could turn that western parcel into a real prize piece of property. He even built his farmhouse on the eastern parcel, so as not to use up any of the land that contained the best soil.

Nessie took the loss with complacence, for she knew Ennis was possessive of any injury done to him, and this would fall into that category, even if it affected the household. A thing was only ever happening to him; she was not entitled to regard it as happening to her, too. She did not say, *At least we haven't lost the parcel that contains our home*, even if she might have thought it. She was wise enough to know her husband didn't care one bit about keeping the farmhouse – not at that moment, not in comparison to losing the western parcel. While with every passing year it grew more and more doubtful Ennis would ever get around to cultivating it, his plans for the plot of land nonetheless grew increasingly grandiose, and the western parcel possessed a certain abstract significance he'd come to depend upon. It represented his belief in the future, the idea that he'd staked his claim in California, that he was a great man who would leave his son a great legacy and that a region would be named after him – or, at the very least, a vital road.

Nessie braced herself for the days and weeks to come, for she knew Ennis would sleep fitfully that night, eventually waking with the sweats, a pounding head, and a ferocious, renewed temper. He was not likely to let this new grievance go anytime soon.

As fate would have it, Ennis Thorn lost his prized piece of land in a hand of poker that was almost an exact reversal of the hand that had won him the money to buy it in the first place. The man who'd won the deed to Ennis's land, Silas Northrup, had kept a careful tally of the glasses of whiskey Ennis had put down that evening. Moreover, Silas was reputed for keeping an ace up his sleeve. Whether or not Ennis's loss had been entirely fair, only

Silas could say, but either way, Silas knew better than to keep the land for himself; Ennis – once sober – would be furious.

Sure enough, the whole town got a good show once Ennis's hangover wore off the next day, when Ennis took to chasing Silas around in front of the general store, cursing up a storm and firing off his six-shooter. Deadly serious as Ennis was, it was nonetheless a comical sight, with skinny, lazy Silas even shimmying up a drainpipe, moving quicker than anyone had ever known Silas could move.

Ennis didn't catch Silas that day, or the day after, and the spectacle repeated itself several times – amusing and horrifying townspeople alike – until finally Silas was able to shout back his only defense: he'd sold the property to the first buyer he could find. Silas slipped away again, and this time, when Ennis tired, he got blind drunk again and staggered home. He prayed Silas had lied.

Less than a week after the poker game, Ennis spotted what appeared to be a Chinaman making camp on the western parcel, and knew immediately what had happened. His heart sank, becoming a leaded ball that dropped deep into some terrible recess in his intestines. But he also knew this was now his cross to bear alone. Ennis's appeals for justice had been turned away by the only judge in town, and then by every lawyer and civil court clerk for miles and miles around. No one wanted to get involved with a dispute that centered on a drunkard's foolish poker habits.

Ennis learned the name of his new neighbor – Kenichi Yamada – but nothing more. He didn't *care* to know more. In those early days, the neighbor, Yamada, called on the Thorn household exactly twice, hoping to introduce himself. But both times the young, smooth-faced Japanese man stepped gingerly onto the rickety wooden porch and rapped on the screen door, his knock went unanswered; Ennis refused to acknowledge him. He ordered Nessie to do the same and bade her to keep the baby quiet. It was bad enough Silas had stolen his land; now Ennis was forced to watch some young foreigner live on it and attempt to cultivate it.

In future years the foreigner, Kenichi Yamada, was not difficult to avoid. He proved himself a quiet man intent on leading a curiously lonely life, slowly and meticulously cultivating the land as his youth trickled away, harvest by harvest and year by year. To Ennis's irritation, Yamada did not plant apples, the sole crop Ennis had envisioned for his estate. He planted a then-unorthodox mixture of almonds, citrus, and plums.

By the time Yamada had fully planted and coaxed a complete yield out of Ennis's prized western parcel, Ennis's son, John Thorn, was a grown lad of ten or so. The two sat together on the porch of the Thorn ranch house in the evenings, and Ennis began to tell his son the great tales of his adventures. These entertaining yarns, inclusive of both fact and fiction, ranged from stories about Ennis's childhood back in Ireland, to his days following the wagon trail west, to his gambling and whoring in Nevada. (Ennis saw no reason to shield his boy from the rougher facts of life, much less the birds and the bees.)

Ennis's tales also included the infamous story of how he'd been betrayed by his friends and fellow gamblers, and more specifically how he'd been tricked by one enemy in particular – the immoral Silas Northrup – and ultimately been cheated out of the glorious western parcel. In Ennis's telling, certain details were altered. In his version, for instance, Silas Northrup had been in cahoots all along with the Jap who eventually stole the Thorns' land, and together Silas and the Jap had laced his whiskey with opium – he was *sure* of it.

Ennis's version of the story was certainly more colorful and entertaining than the factual account. He was Irish, after all, and knew how to instill sympathy in his listener.

In 1906, at the age of seventy, Ennis Thorn went to bed with a case of drunkard's pneumonia, and thereafter, never got out of bed again. He spent a month or so gasping and hacking away, day and night, at the terrible cough that would not leave his chest. Nessie dutifully propped every pillow in the house around her husband so that he might sleep in an upright position, but it was no use. Decades of hard living had left Ennis tired and run-down, and even as the pneumonia worsened, he demanded his flask be replenished and kept by his side at all times.

'It's medicinal,' he grunted, and winked, responding to the reproach that Nessie – consummately silent in her ways – never actually voiced.

Full of 'medicine,' he dosed off one afternoon while Nessie was outside pulling weeds in the little kitchen garden, and sighed his last rattling breath.

At that instant, and from that moment forward, the house fell silent: devoid of Ennis Thorn's terrible barking cough, devoid of his jolly banshee's laugh, devoid of his angry rants. Nessie and John – the latter, by then a twenty-nine-year-old man – were utterly alone in the world, left to run the ranch together in a mutually stoic silence.

John was an odd study in character. Neighbors and townspeople who were acquainted with the Thorns had come to think of him as Nessie Thorn's 'man-child'. Without Ennis as a catalyst to stimulate constant change, Nessie and John stagnated for a number of years and fell further into a state of arrested development. John ran the ranch and oversaw the orchard with a serious, competent air but had little interest in leaving the ranch or in pursuing adventures of his own, and Nessie was quite content to have it so. John's youthful years ticked by without much celebration or ceremony. He was thirty-six, a bachelor still living alone with his mother, when he finally got it in his head that maybe he ought to be married.

'It's time we had some help around here,' he stated simply on the day of his birthday. 'I'm thinking of taking a wife.'

Most mothers would assume this meant her son had a specific bride in mind, but Nessie Thorn knew better. She rocked calmly in her usual chair in the sitting room, working on a rather splendid example of the Ten Commandments in needlepoint.

'That Edith Sommerset is a nice young girl' was all she said in reply.

Conveniently forgetting the fact that she had once been one herself, Nessie harbored a secret fear of outsiders. She was afraid John would send away for a picture bride she wouldn't like, or that he would get sweet on some half squaw or worse. She'd been eyeing the local stock of pretty, docile, conventional girls and silently making her own selection for quite some time. Nessie's pick, Edith Sommerset, was seventeen to John's thirty-six. But she was also Irish, pale-haired, and freckle-faced. As far as Nessie was concerned, the girl had belonged on the ranch all along and only needed someone to teach her how to milk the cows and bake Nessie's signature shortbread in order to fulfill her role as a Thorn and as John's wife.

'Well . . . all right, then,' John replied to his mother in a matter-of-fact tone, and left the room. Nessie understood this meant she ought to ready the house for Edith. This had always been their way together – Nessie's and John's. John announced his intentions, and Nessie pointed him in the direction she preferred. They were a businesslike, taciturn pair, and had been ever since the two of them survived John's birth together.

Two weeks later, John Thorn and Edith Sommerset were married in a quiet ceremony in the little white-clapboard bungalow of a Catholic church up in Coloma. The priest, a man accustomed to a congregation full of unkempt miners who picked their noses and nodded off during services, was clearly delighted to marry the young couple. Before giving his blessing, he had only one question: would they baptize their children according to the Catholic faith? John gave his word they would, and the priest was appeased. Moments later, he pronounced the couple man and wife – married forever in the eyes of the Catholic Church.

Once home, Nessie diplomatically moved out of the master bedroom without a word, and John and Edith went about the business of starting a family.

To say they were successful in this pursuit is putting it mildly. Every year brought a new Thorn child for the better space of eleven years. A son came first; they named him Guy. He was followed by Marion, then Louis, then Otis . . . Gilbert, Lester, Carl, Ernest, Clyde, Rudolph, Franklin, and finally, little Ruth. John Thorn built onto the house accordingly, adding bedroom after bedroom with the scanty materials available to him on the ranch.

There was, of course, eventually an exchange for all this life.

The stock market crashed sometime just after Carl joined the family but before Ernest was born. John Thorn didn't think very much of this development at first: how could something that happened in New York make much difference to a simple farmer in California? Then, in the spring of 1930, Nessie was working on a piece of needlepoint when she suffered a sudden embolism, clenched her teeth, and died.

Nessie's death was like that piece of yarn that – with a small tug – unravels an entire sweater. As it turned out, in addition to betting away the western parcel, Ennis Thorn had accrued quite a lot of debt while he was still alive, borrowing against the farm, and Nessie had been holding that debt at bay, diligently robbing Peter to pay Paul with a persistent, steady hand. But in the wake of the Great Crash, her careful system had collapsed. The amount owed was substantial, and involved a partial mortgage of the property – a fact she'd kept hidden until her sudden death. If the Thorns could not pay, the ranch would soon fall into foreclosure.

This turn of events only meant one thing for John Thorn, and that, simply put, was that he could work as hard as he might for the rest of his life, and the best result he could hope to achieve was to hang on to what remained of the property and scrape by. In short, he and the rest of the Thorns were sentenced to a life of poverty.

What little traces of mirth John Thorn ever possessed died the day he learned his late mother's secret. He fought hard to keep the ranch from falling into foreclosure, but a certain resentment had set in for good. Just as in the days and weeks that followed Black Tuesday, there was no one who John Thorn might blame.

But then one day, while sitting on the porch with his eldest son, Guy Thorn, John's eyes fell on the dust being kicked up on the horizon, and a sudden realization occurred to him. *The Japs.* There it was: a single automobile belonging to what John Thorn now saw as a greedy, prosperous foreigner, driving along a lane in the distance, speeding toward a homestead that was stolen, on a parcel of land that did not truly belong to him.

'Damn Japs,' John muttered, loud enough for his son to hear. Guy startled, not expecting his father to say anything, let alone the words he heard now. Guy had been reclining on his elbows, and now he straightened up, attentive to his father's sudden proclamation.

'Damn Japs,' John Thorn repeated. 'Did I ever tell you the story about how those dirty Japs stole our land from my father?'

Guy shook his head, too intimidated and awed. His father rarely spoke, and he *never* told stories.

'Well, now . . .' John said. He began to repeat the words his father, Ennis, had spoken many times, and in that moment a strange thing happened: when

Ennis had told it, the story had merely been an Irishman's drunken yarn, but as John repeated it, it suddenly bore the ring of truth and the weight of fact. Such is often the way with family stories: they become more 'factual' with each repetition, with each generation further removed.

Either way, among the facts Guy Thorn learned that day was that it was the Yamadas' fault the Thorns were in such a state; it was the Yamadas' fault that they were not rich and prosperous; and that, because of Kenichi Yamada, the Thorn family never received the true bounty promised to them by California's gold hills.

Once learned, it proved a difficult lesson to unlearn.

20

EARL SHAW'S FLYING CIRCUS
SUTTER CREEK, CALIFORNIA, JUNE 8, 1940

'If they keep on like this, one of them's bound to break his neck,' Ava's mother commented.

'Hah – *both* of 'em will, is more like.'

Ava and her mother were standing in the middle of an empty, flat field, each of them with one hand cupped over her brow to shade her eyes as she stared up at the sky.

'They *are* awful fearless,' Cleo said, nodding her head and watching with wide eyes. 'And it does seem like more danger than it's worth.'

Louis and Harry were at it again. Even now, when they were merely practicing, the two boys couldn't resist competing. It was Harry who first upped the ante. From the time of their very first wing-walking adventure, Ava noticed that Harry was the better stuntman; you could see from the ground that he was more agile and more sure-footed – not that she would ever risk hurting Louis's feelings by saying so aloud. Harry had started the rivalry off when he danced on the wings in a jokey way. Soon he was doing push-ups on the wings, hanging off the side of one wing, even climbing down to the landing gear. Determined not to be outdone, Louis matched Harry trick for trick – though it was clear to Ava that Louis was enjoying the escalation far less than Harry.

Harry was a born daredevil, but Louis was determined to make himself one.

'I wonder what drives 'em to compete like that,' Cleo said. 'Some kind of powerful spite between them . . .'

'They used to be friends,' Ava commented.

Her mother looked at her, surprised.

'I wouldn't have suspected that. How do you know?'

Ava shrugged. 'Just something Louis mentioned.'

'My word,' Cleo murmured, staring up into the sky as the two biplanes made another low pass overhead. 'Well, there's certainly something more complicated than friendship between them now. I wonder what happened . . .'

Ava didn't reply. The two women continued to set up the place where the barnstorming act would camp for the night, pausing occasionally to glance nervously into the sky. *Fools will be fools.* Ava didn't want to watch, but there were moments when she felt powerless to look away.

While the competition between Louis and Harry struck Ava as reckless and unnecessary, Earl Shaw relished his good fortune. The stunts Louis and Harry did were so hair-raising that folks were beginning to talk. Word traveled on ahead of them as they moved from town to town, and all that gossip meant bigger crowds and more money in Earl's pocket than he'd ever seen before.

More money was a good thing – in some ways. Ava knew that when Earl was feeling kingly, he quickly set about spending. He also suddenly found his way into an awful lot of poker games. He drank more and, once drunk, grew moody and snappish with her mother.

What worried Ava most of all was Earl's growing nonchalance toward the law. So far, Louis and Harry hadn't asked why the flying circus didn't travel closer to the larger towns and cities – but of course Ava and all the others knew the reason. Ever since their run-in with the sheriff outside Los Angeles some years back, they all understood the necessary balance the circus needed to strike: make enough noise to turn a little profit, but not so much noise as to attract the eyes of the law.

But as Earl's wallet grew fatter and fatter, his sense of caution waned. They had traveled throughout the Sierra Nevada foothills, but soon they were circling in closer and closer to the city of Sacramento than they had ever dared to before. Ava was further shocked when Earl went so far as to have handbills printed up. *EARL SHAW'S INCREDIBLE FLYING CIRCUS IS PROUD TO INTRODUCE OUR ALL-NEW, SPECTACULAR, DEATH-DEFYING WING-WALKERS!!!* it shouted in large, heavy type at the top. The idea was, Earl explained, that Ava would post the handbills at each stop, and their crowds would easily triple in size.

'Isn't that awfully bold?' Ava asked, looking the handbills over with surprise.

'Bold? Bold brings us business!'

There'll be no passing ourselves off as crop dusters if the cops get ahold of that handbill, Ava thought, but bit her tongue. Earl Shaw was not a man who took kindly to criticism.

And so Louis and Harry continued to pursue their crazy stuntman competition, Ava posted handbills, and 'Earl Shaw's Incredible Flying Circus' grew into more of a spectacle than ever before. Earl was certainly right about one thing: the number of spectators they entertained quickly doubled, and then doubled again.

At least Earl's good mood meant he was not disposed to stingily complain about the flying circus's increased consumption of gasoline. It seemed to Ava that the two biplanes were constantly buzzing in the air now. Fetching more gasoline was becoming a constant occupation. Louis and Harry perpetually wanted to try out new stunts, and Buzz and Hutch were happy to oblige, their interest in aviation refreshed by the presence of the two young newcomers.

Ava was washing laundry with her mother early one morning when *Castor* and *Pollux* both came in for a landing. She hadn't seen them take off, but now, as the planes touched down on the dry yellow grass, Ava noticed something unusual: it appeared Louis and Harry were the ones doing the flying.

So, she thought, *Buzz and Hutch have been giving them lessons.*

She felt a twinge of something. Was it jealousy? The thought of flying terrified her, but it was starting to entice her a little bit, too. Like standing at the edge of a cliff and having that curiously strong inkling to jump.

She watched the four men tumble down from the biplanes, shouting and laughing and peeling off their caps and goggles. She could hear a little of what they were saying. She listened while pretending new interest in the washboard before her.

'Way to go, Eagle! I'd say you earned your wings!' Hutch said to Louis, clapping him on the back. 'You, too!' he added, clapping Harry on the back in turn.

Ava glanced up from the washboard and saw Louis and Harry exchange a rare, sheepish smile.

'Looks like you're taking pilot lessons from Buzz and Hutch,' Ava remarked later that day. She'd asked Louis to help her gather kindling for a fire, and he'd obliged, always eager to avail himself to Ava.

Louis's eyes lit up.

'That was Harry's idea,' he said. 'But . . . it seemed like the kind of chance that don't come along every day . . . so I figured, Why not?' He paused and summoned a nonchalant expression. 'We ain't learning anything fancy. Just the plain ol' basics of aviation.'

'I heard them calling you "Eagle",' she commented. 'What is that? Is that your new nickname?'

At this, Louis blushed. At the same time, a proud expression crept into his features.

'Aw, that's nothin', really. Buzz and Hutch insisted that all pilots had to have a call sign.'

Of course, Ava thought, *call signs*. 'And yours is 'Eagle'?' she asked.

He shrugged. 'With all that wing-walking business, Hutch said we ought to name ourselves after birds. Buzz laughed at that and said that if we *were* birds, we'd have to be two very different-lookin' birds, you know, on account of our nationalities . . .'

Ava saw where this was headed. 'So you're the American eagle?'

'I guess so.'

'And what is Harry?'

'Well, then they tried to think of a Jap bird, so . . . after a while, they started calling him "Crane".'

142

'"Eagle and Crane",' Ava repeated, frowning, suddenly lost in thought. 'And does . . . does that bother Harry much?'

Louis looked down at the ground and shrugged again. 'If it does, he don't let it show.'

'Sounds like Harry.'

'It's all in good fun. Buzz and Hutch don't mean anything by it. And anyway,' Louis continued, 'Harry *is* a Jap, after all.'

Something in Louis's tone troubled Ava.

'What's that supposed to mean?' she asked, frowning.

Louis looked at her, surprised.

'Nothing much,' he said. 'It's just a fact, ain't it? Harry's a Jap, no two ways about it.'

Ava didn't reply. She busied herself with gathering more kindling. Something still nagged at her about the tone of Louis's assessment, but she was hard-pressed to put her finger on what it was.

21

EARL SHAW'S FLYING CIRCUS
SACRAMENTO, CALIFORNIA, JUNE 16, 1940

As Earl grew bolder and bolder, the barnstorming troupe circled even closer to the city of Sacramento. Eventually, they came so close as to put up camp in Florin, a little town that brushed up against the very outskirts of Sacramento itself.

Florin turned out to be home to a sizable 'Japantown.' A large number of the Japanese residents owned land and made a living as strawberry farmers, and the biggest house of worship in town was a Buddhist temple.

As they strolled the small main street, Buzz teased Harry openly: 'Feel right at home here, eh?' Ava watched Harry's face, curious to know his reaction. But there was little written on his face to read; Harry's expression was calm and relaxed, but also stoic, indecipherable. One thing was plain, though: there was no jibe Buzz could make that Harry hadn't already heard.

They camped in Florin for several days, performing stunts and selling rides. Sometimes, in the late afternoons and evenings, Buzz and Hutch thumbed a ride into Sacramento, hankering for some entertainment.

'Say, why don't the two of you come along and have a beer with us this evening?' Buzz suggested to Louis and Harry after a day spent barnstorming for a packed crowd. 'Hutch knows a place where they won't give you any trouble about your age.'

Louis and Harry looked at each other, exchanging a slightly wary glance. They'd performed stunts together, they'd camped near each other, but both boys had carefully and purposely refrained from any kind of behavior that might be described as openly friendly.

Louis had always had the impression of the capital city as an incongruous mixture of farmers and politicians, denim coveralls and polka-dot bow ties, both groups constantly arguing over land and water rights. Though not much famed for its nightlife, it nonetheless promised to be livelier than any of the towns they'd traveled through over the past two months.

'I suppose I'd be tempted by a beer,' Harry replied, breaking the stand-off.

'Yeah, all right,' Louis agreed.

The four men changed into clean clothes and successfully thumbed a ride from a farmer headed into town in a large pickup truck. The bar Hutch had suggested turned out to be a floating barge on the river; getting to it required a boat. The farmer dropped them off in the old town, and they climbed down the steep embankment of the levy under the Tower Bridge. For fifty cents – a sum invented and negotiated on the spot – a local fisherman transported them in a small trawler upriver to the establishment in question.

Down that close to the water, a humid breeze cut the otherwise bone-dry Sacramento air. The river carried the gamy scent of thick silt, a fragrance of frog, and the musk of duck. Cattails and blackberry bushes knitted themselves together to form a border of dense underbrush all along the riverbanks. Stars began to emerge in the inky sky. Crickets chirped. Small bats began to appear like black cutouts against the glow of the rosy-purple twilight, making their strange, erratic, frenzied dashes through the air.

Louis stood at the port bow of the small vessel as it slowly prowled the river, watching the dull green water ripple away in tiny waves and swirl in eddies. He contemplated – with no small measure of disbelief – his new life, his new role as 'stuntman' in a flying circus. He'd been able to send some money home. His brother Guy had disapproved of Louis's decision to join the barnstorming group at first – especially when Guy learned Harry Yamada was involved – but he had softened up since, sending word that the money was appreciated, that it was actually helping. It was really incredible, when you took a step back to consider it all. Louis thought about what he would be doing if he were back home on the Thorn ranch.

But then, Louis already knew exactly what he'd be doing: his brother Guy would be ordering Louis around. Louis would either be completing chores or attempting repairs on their family's sadly run-down property – or else Louis would be sent to go pick in other people's orchards and farms. During most summers, all the Thorns took whatever work they could, harvesting whatever they could. They regularly hired themselves out to work in other families' orchards, pruning and harvesting as the seasons demanded. And no matter how diligently Louis worked – no matter how devotedly any of the Thorn children worked – the Thorn ranch still struggled. Guy would stalk around the property with his mouth set in an angry line, fretting gravely about the price of apples, about the price of milk and eggs, talking to their mother, Edith, in hushed tones, late at night – always, always warning her about the possibility of foreclosure.

Without the flying circus, life would have gone on like that. Probably forever.

Louis had to admit: if Harry hadn't begged Hutch to fly barrel rolls and a loop-the-loop during that first tourist flight, Buzz never would've offered to fly Louis through the same, and Louis never would have accepted. If Harry hadn't boldly announced his intentions to wing walk and dared Louis to follow suit – if Harry hadn't negotiated with Earl that the two of them go on getting paid to wing walk – Louis had to admit he wouldn't have tried half the things he'd tried if it weren't for Harry.

It was certainly something to think about.

When they reached the barge, the trawler pulled up to the landing and idled as the four of them, Louis and Harry, Buzz and Hutch, shuffled off the fishing boat and onto the floating dive bar. The establishment had no name. Louis was fairly certain it had served as a speakeasy during the nation's dry years. Now it was celebrating the legality of liquor, and was plenty wet. It also served the kinds of dishes most easily dredged up from the river – boiled crawdads and sautéed catfish – with wild onions and potatoes. As they boarded the barge they heard the twanging sounds of several guitars and a banjo – Dixieland jazz. It was, in short, a riverboat honky-tonk.

They stepped into the tin-sided building that rose from the middle of the barge and looked for a place to sit for a beer. Men sat around a single large, rectangular bar, in the middle of which stood a barkeep and cook tending to the patrons. A small band responsible for the music they'd heard drifting out over the river strummed away in the far corner. People looked up from their drinks as they entered the room.

As they stood there, Louis noticed Harry shuffling his feet with an agitated air. Louis realized the reason for Harry's nerves: as Louis looked around the room, he saw that every single face was white, and a large number of those faces were frowning in Harry's direction. This happened a lot wherever they went; Louis recalled the way the maître d' had scurried out to intercept Harry on the night Earl had taken them all out for a night on the town.

'Over there.' Hutch pointed to a cluster of empty seats on the far side of the bar.

They followed his lead. Once seated, Buzz waved the bartender over and ordered two shots of whiskey and four beers. The bartender was a balding, stringy-necked man with a pinched face. He slammed two shot glasses on the bar and filled them, then turned to tap the beers. Hutch and Buzz tossed the shots back while they waited. Finally, the bartender began to set out the foamy-headed, lukewarm beers on the countertop.

When he got to the fourth and last beer – Harry's – the bartender paused, held it up to his lips, and very deliberately expectorated a large wad of spit. Then he set it in front of Harry. A grotesque glob of yellowish mucus floated atop the beer's thick head of foam.

Hutch and Buzz hadn't seen. They were laughing and talking; Buzz was in the middle of complaining that there weren't enough girls in the joint.

Louis was shocked. He watched as Harry's jaw clenched and his face turned red. Harry's eyes were downcast and his mouth was set in a firm line as he pushed the beer glass away from him. Although Louis could plainly see Harry was furious, he realized Harry wasn't going to say anything. He would sit there all night, not drinking, the obscene insult perched quietly on the bar before him. He had likely endured worse.

Before he hardly knew what he was doing, Louis felt the impulse shoot through his arm. He reached for Harry's glass and picked it up.

'There seems to be something in my friend's beer,' Louis said to the bartender. 'I'll thank you to bring him another.'

He slammed the glass down on the countertop in front of the bartender. The amber liquid sloshed and suds ran down one side, but the glob of spit remained, still floating on the surface, looking a little like a rancid bit of runny egg yolk.

Hutch and Buzz jerked to attention, confused by Louis's abruptness.

'What's going on? What's happened?' Buzz asked.

'The bartender was just getting ready to pour Harry a fresh beer is all,' Louis said.

Hutch and Buzz peered between the bartender and the boys and glanced at Harry's untouched glass. Without needing to take a closer look at the contents, they immediately guessed what had just taken place.

'Good of him to accommodate,' Hutch said in a quiet, grave voice. The bartender understood this was not what Hutch had said at all; Hutch had issued a threat. There was a certain quality about Hutch that meant he could carry it off – something about Hutch's time driving cattle in Montana and flying for the British during the Great War that suggested he was a lonely, lethal man.

All four of them were now staring at the bartender with an expressionless intensity, waiting to see what the bartender might do. His eyes slid back and forth between all of them, from left to right and left again.

'Fine,' he said finally. He reached for a fresh glass, filled it slowly from the tap, and set it in front of Harry. Then, with a final grunt, he walked away, over to the other side of the bar, to wait on someone else.

They watched the bartender go. A few moments passed where no one said anything. All of them seemed to sense Harry's humiliation; all of them seemed to sense a remark of any variety would not be especially welcomed, nor would it be a comfort. Once a few moments had lapsed, Buzz lifted his glass in a perfunctory manner.

'Cheers, fellas!'

'Cheers,' they all murmured in response. Everyone clinked glasses. Buzz turned back to Hutch and the two of them resumed their conversation.

Louis and Harry sat side by side, staring off into the middle distance. The silence between them was only punctuated as they slurped at their beers, periodically wiping the foam from their upper lips.

'You didn't have to do that,' Harry said. 'Wasn't your business.'

'It didn't sit right with me,' Louis replied. 'I . . . couldn't abide it . . .'

Harry emitted a sound somewhere between a grunt and a chuckle.

'Must be nice to have a choice whether or not to abide it . . .' he said.

Louis thought about this and laughed a little.

'I guess I'm making it sound like I wasn't about to get my block knocked off,' Louis said. 'I'm pretty sure if Hutch and Buzz weren't here, that's exactly what would've happened.'

Harry smirked. He raised his glass.

'Well, here's to not abiding it . . . and to not getting your block knocked off,' he said.

The two of them clinked glasses again and drank.

Another moment passed in silence, then Harry said, 'You still collecting all those comic books?'

Louis looked at him, surprised.

'You remember that?'

'Sure,' Harry said. 'I remember you were crazy about *The Shadow* and *Dick Tracy*. You used to loan me all those detective stories.' He paused and gave a sober nod. 'I enjoyed all that stuff; I remember thinking it was awful neat . . .'

'What about you?' Louis replied. 'You used to pull off some pretty fancy magic tricks.'

The two young men smiled with the memory; as a boy, Harry had studied all the tricks of the greats – Houdini was by far his favorite – and he used to practice a handful of card tricks and even escape acts with Louis, showing him how each trick was done.

'You know,' Harry said now, 'I think I *finally* figured out how the Great Blackstone does that whole "floating lightbulb" business!' He chuckled.

'That so?' Louis asked.

Both boys laughed and took a sip of their beers, and, at Louis's prodding, Harry began to explain how the Great Blackstone was able to make electricity light up a bulb as it floated eerily through the air for an audience. When Hutch and Buzz ordered another round, Louis and Harry did, too. And, laughing and talking again about their old childhood enthusiasms, they even ordered another after that.

22

EARL SHAW'S FLYING CIRCUS
NAPA, CALIFORNIA, JUNE 28, 1940

Harry was relieved to be on friendlier speaking terms again with Louis Thorn. It took a lot of concentration to spend so many hours in another man's presence and not talk to him openly. Over the course of the past two months, they had hollered back and forth to each other while doing stunts or learning how to fly the two Stearman planes – but that was just what men did; they hazed their rivals. All banter ceased once Harry and Louis were down on the ground. And it was excruciatingly awkward to eat and sleep around a campfire – only a stone's throw away from each other – while trying to uphold a strict code of hostile silence.

Now something had eased between the two. Sometimes they joined in Hutch and Buzz's conversations in the evenings; sometimes they even carried on small talk of their own. One evening Louis even swapped a comic book for one of Harry's magician magazines as they read around the campfire. They still shouted insults at each other while stunting, zooming around high in the air, but more often than not, the insults were followed by a friendly laugh that suggested it was all in good fun.

The competition between them continued to escalate, but now, instead of feeling like they were bound by a bitter stand-off, there was a kind of mad joy to it all. The flying circus left the Sacramento area and pushed west, toward San Francisco. During a performance in Dixon, a good-sized crowd held its breath as Buzz piloted *Pollux* overhead while Harry shimmied down to the landing gear, hooked his legs over the bar between the two wheels, and hung upside down, waving his arms like a happy fool.

'Aww, for Christ's sake, Harry – why'd you have to go and do *that* for?!'
Louis shouted once they were back on the ground.

'You don't have to do everything I do, Thorn,' Harry replied, grinning.
'Nobody's making ya.'

Louis's only retort was to let out a chuff. They were both aware of Ava
standing nearby. Harry's eyes flicked in her direction.

'Don't look to me for a pat on the back,' she said. 'I already told you: I
think the pair of you are proof positive that bravery and idiocy sometimes go
hand in hand.'

She gave a toss of her jaunty red bob and walked away.

It was definitely less lonely for Harry now that Louis had let down his
guard around him, but as far as Ava was concerned, the jury was still out. It
was a shame, because Harry recognized something in Ava, a quality Harry bore
in common. They had both spent most of their lives as outsiders, although
each for different reasons.

The group drifted in the general direction of San Francisco, but before they got
quite there, they turned and headed north for a spell as they neared the San Pablo
Bay. They passed through Carneros, a sheepherding valley, and up along the Napa
Valley. The land grew increasingly picturesque. Rubbled, stony foothills laced with
the vibrant green of grapevines: they were in wine country. Prohibition had ended
more than six years earlier, and the region was thrumming with fresh energy.

They performed as they went along and Earl was in fine spirits, seeing the
number of curious locals who steadily turned up. By that point Harry and
Louis had worked out a routine that included a handful of stunts only the
professionals in Hollywood typically performed. People oohed and aahed and
eagerly lined up to purchase an airplane ride of their very own.

When they weren't wing walking for others, they were often practicing
the less-flashy basics of aviation. By the time the group reached Napa, Harry
and Louis had learned how to fly the biplanes with a level of competence that
meant Buzz and Hutch could allow them to fly short solo flights.

'That's how you really earn your wings, technically speaking,' Hutch
informed them. 'Flying solo!'

151

Solo flights made Harry feel freer than he ever had in all his life. Even short flights could be mesmerizingly peaceful, flying toward the horizon while watching the patchwork of land rolling far below unfurl like a never-ending quilt. When it came to solo flights, the irony was that it made him want to share the moment with another person.

Around that time, Harry had also begun a sort of game with Ava. It wasn't that she had grown any friendlier toward him but rather that Harry had discovered that Ava's stubborn streak meant she couldn't resist proving him wrong, even if it meant accepting a dare.

He began with little amusements, the kinds of pastimes easily found around farm towns. Despite her almost getting caught the day she'd tried to steal the book, Harry learned that Ava was actually pretty skilled in her sleight of hand – just as she'd claimed. She could pick a person's pocket without him ever feeling a thing. Harry began to challenge her to other tests of light thievery. Later he graduated to a wider variety of minor dares: sharpshooting bottles off a fence post, or holding a contest to see who could rope a steer. Challenging Ava to various dares didn't melt her stubborn, icy disposition any, but it was an amusing way to pass the time – Harry suspected, perhaps, for both of them.

But one morning Harry surprised himself when he blurted out an altogether unexpected dare. 'I bet you won't go up for a ride in *Pollux*,' he said as he helped her fill the biplane's tank with a heavy can of gasoline.

Ava's eyes widened. Then she tilted her head at Harry and her eyes narrowed with scrutiny. 'A ride? You mean . . . with you as the pilot?'

'Sure,' Harry said, shrugging. He grinned.

'Hah! Do you think I'm a fool?' She rolled her eyes.

'I think you're scared is what I think . . .'

Ava's eyes flashed. She held his gaze for a full minute.

'Fine,' she said, straightening her spine and standing up to full height. 'I will.'

Now it was Harry's turn to be taken off guard, and his eyes widened.

'You will? You'll go up with me?'

She stuck out her chin. 'I ain't backing down. But if you were just spoutin' off your mouth and didn't plan on going through with this . . . well . . . that's your business, I reckon, but it's not my fault.'

Harry felt his heart palpitate, a heavy lurching in his chest.

'No, no,' he said, on impulse. 'I'll take you up – if you're not too afraid.'

Ava stared at him, wide-eyed with defiance. Harry thought he saw a glimmer of something else in her eyes, too. Was that animal terror? It was too late to back out; he also sensed neither of them was about to shy away. He peered around to determine whether anyone else was listening to them.

'Well, all right,' Harry said, 'it's a deal.'

Ava nodded, but the color was quickly draining out of her face. Harry leaned in, confidential, his mind already working over the logistics.

'And unless you want a lot of fuss,' Harry said, 'I reckon we ought to figure out some way to go up together without anyone else knowin' . . .'

'Yes,' Ava agreed.

Their eyes locked. They both knew this endeavor – whatever it was – would have to be their secret.

'All right,' Harry said, taking command of the situation. He had a plan.

Harry was never nervous to fly – nothing about aviation frightened him – and yet, when he took off that morning, he was surprised to realize that there were butterflies in his stomach. Perhaps it was that he wasn't accustomed to telling lies; he had lied to Hutch and Buzz – and also to Louis, who had asked Harry where he was planning to fly.

Ava had lied as well. The sun had barely risen when she told her mother and Earl she was going to take a walk, maybe go to town. The truth was, she would need a comfortable head start in order to meet Harry somewhere far out of eyeshot of where they'd made camp.

'So early?' was Cleo's only question.

But nobody stopped either one of them. So off Ava went, on foot. And some time later, Harry fired up the engine of *Pollux* and taxied across the field, getting up to speed and taking to the sky. He flew for ten minutes or so – long enough to take him a few miles away from his takeoff point.

Landmarks were the easiest guides for a pilot to follow. There was a little river that dipped into the outskirts of the town of Napa, and they had mutually agreed that Ava should follow the river to a place Harry had glimpsed in previous flights – another flat, empty field.

Now, as he came upon the appointed spot, he felt the butterflies in his stomach again and knew beyond a doubt that it was not the act of flying, not even the guilt over the lies they'd both told; it was Ava herself. His heart and stomach gave a synchronous lurch as he spotted her from the air, her petite figure in trousers, her coppery hair glinting in the light. He circled, bringing the Stearman down lower and lower, managing to pull off a gentle landing. He hoped she hadn't been waiting long as he cut the engine.

'Are you ready?' he hollered, yanking off his goggles and climbing down so as to help her up.

He took one look at her face and had to laugh – a laugh of joy mixed with sympathetic angst: she looked every bit as nervous as he felt. Perhaps she looked even more so, for Harry noticed a grayish-green tint to her complexion. He saw she was carrying a small knapsack and tried to make a joke to lighten the mood.

'Say – whatcha got in there?' he asked. 'Brought your own parachute?'

But Ava, still looking a little green around the gills, refused to laugh.

'If only,' she replied.

'Don't worry,' he urged as she attempted a queasy smile. Somehow, in the past twenty-four hours, something had shifted between them, and they had become coconspirators. 'It's safe; I promise.'

Ava looked at him and took a breath. She had spent over five years watching airplanes zoom into the sky without ever journeying up once herself. Now she reached out a hand and accepted Harry's help into the cockpit to embark upon her very first flight.

23

Ava's heart was racing. She had half a mind to shout back to Harry to tell him she would be happy to eat crow; that she wanted to forfeit the dare entirely. But as the biplane began to bounce over the rutted field and the wind began to scream in her face, Ava's half-formed words were lost in the roaring commotion. Before she knew it, they were accelerating and the plane was lifting into the air.

It was a bizarre feeling, the way the biplane continued to lift once they were airborne – almost as if the plane were driving up the steep incline of a ramp, but so much smoother . . . It felt unnatural. Then, all at once: *Whoosh!* They were in the air, and the ground below was tugged away, and Ava felt a strange sense of split yearning: the part of her that longed to forever rise up, up, up, into the sky, and the part of her that felt the urgent need to stay on solid ground. It was exhilarating, and her heart was in her throat for every second of all of it.

'So, where would you like to go?' Harry hollered into the wind to where Ava sat in the seat before him.

Ava looked around, craning her neck and swiveling her head to inspect the ground below either side of the Stearman. It was astounding: she had cleaned the engine of this very plane, knew the contraption inside and out, yet never imagined seeing it like this, suspended over a seemingly miniature landscape down below.

'Show me . . . all of it!' was all she could think to reply.

'Roger!' Harry yelled back, and banked heavily to the right as Ava squealed with delighted shock.

Harry flew on and made the rounds of the most interesting local destinations he could think of, trying to show Ava all the landmarks he could find. Together they flew all the way to the southernmost end of the valley and back.

Eventually, Harry flew back toward the heart of Napa. But he didn't return Ava directly to their rendezvous point. Instead he flew on, passing it, and found a place to put the Stearman down in a clearing beside a pretty little lake. He circled, gestured to Ava, and brought the biplane in for a landing.

'I had a feeling you weren't going to take me straight back,' Ava commented once he had successfully put *Pollux* down on the ground and cut the engine.

Harry smiled sheepishly and helped her out of the cockpit.

'Oh, yeah?' he said as they clamored down and brushed themselves off. 'I guess you know everything,' he teased, but his voice was kind.

'I *do* know everything,' Ava joked back. 'And lucky for you, I know enough to bring along provisions.' She held up the knapsack she'd brought along, and surprised him by revealing its contents: sandwiches, a bunch of grapes, a flask filled with lemonade, and a blanket. All the ingredients of an impromptu picnic. Harry grinned, but at the same time something strange happened: his cheeks colored. Ava had seen Louis blush plenty of times, but never Harry. It had a disorienting effect on her, but more disorienting still was the realization that she was flattered.

He'd landed the plane in a flat, open expanse, and now they walked toward the little lake to seek out a better view of the water, some trees, perhaps a patch of shade.

'So?' Harry said once they had picked a spot and arranged themselves and the contents of the knapsack on the blanket. 'Was flying as scary as you thought it would be?'

'Yes . . .' Ava replied, '. . . and no.' She looked off into the distance, thinking of how to sum up her reaction. 'It *is* a little frightening, but maybe in the way that reminds you that you're alive.'

'Was that really the first time you've ever been up?'

She gazed at Harry for a moment and nodded solemnly. 'Way back, when Earl first hired Hutch and Buzz, they offered to take me up a few times, but Earl was always in a cheap mood – 'a waste of gasoline,' he said – and then, after a while . . . I just got comfortable with the idea of keeping my feet on the ground forever.'

'Well, that sounds awful boring.'

'I think the appeal was that it was *safe*,' Ava said, laughing.

'Hah – now you sound like Louis,' he joked.

'Hey, he's not here to defend himself,' Ava objected.

Harry nodded and waved his hands in surrender. 'You're right,' he chuckled. 'I suppose it's become a reflex. That's what Louis and I do: we heckle each other. It's all in good fun.'

Ava cocked her head. Over the past two months she had quizzed Louis plenty about Harry, but now she had an opportunity to ask questions the other way around.

'The two of you seem as though you've made friends again,' she commented.

Harry blinked at her, surprised. 'Louis told you we were friends before?'

Ava nodded. 'When you were kids.'

Harry looked thoughtful. 'It's true, we were,' he murmured. 'His friendship meant a lot to me back then. As a matter of fact . . .' He trailed off, then shook himself from his reverie and snapped back to attention. 'It's just a shame about . . . our families.'

'He mentioned there was a grievance,' Ava said.

Harry nodded. 'Oh, I know all about what the Thorns think of my family. Louis's grandfather, then his father, and now his older brother Guy – all of them – have been repeating those claims of thievery for so many years, everyone in town's heard them.' He paused. 'I wonder if the whole thing would've blown over by now if it wasn't for the fact that my family and I are Japanese.' He shrugged, but there was a bitter air settling over him. 'Easy enough in these parts to pile on anyone who looks a little different.'

'From what Louis has told me, it sounds like his family is pretty hard up,' Ava said. 'His brother works the whole family to the bone, but they can't seem to get ahead. Sometimes, being that poor and working hard . . . the only way it ever makes sense is if somebody stole away what should've been yours.' She paused, then added, 'Not that that makes it right.'

Harry appeared to consider her words as he took a bite of his sandwich and chewed.

'I know we're lucky,' he said. 'These past ten years or so hit everyone pretty hard. But we didn't make it through without a lot of hard work of our own. My father – he's an old man now, older than most fathers – he came over from Japan when he was very young, worked hard, and saved his whole life in order to give us what we have. He didn't *steal* anything from anyone.'

'I believe you,' Ava said. 'It's possible Louis even does, too. But he can't say so aloud – not without betraying his own blood. You must know that.'

Slowly, Harry nodded. 'I do.'

They sat quietly for a few minutes and their picnic continued more somberly, with nothing but the sound of the birds chirping and their own chewing for noise. Finally, Harry broke the silence and changed the subject by inquiring after the book he'd given Ava. Always happy to talk books, Ava began describing the mixed-up plot of *The Comedy of Errors*.

Harry tried to make sense of her retelling. 'And . . . neither knows he has an identical twin?'

'No!' Ava continued explaining all the humorous mishaps written into the plot of Shakespeare's play.

They circled back to the subject of Louis only once more, just as they were folding up the blanket to return to the biplane.

'I don't think we ought to tell anyone about . . . this,' Ava said. 'Not even Louis.'

Harry's hands on the blanket froze for the briefest of seconds, then continued along folding it as before.

'No,' he said quietly. 'You're right. We shouldn't. Not even Louis.'

They exchanged a look. They had said *not even Louis*. But both of them knew somehow it would be more accurate to say *especially not Louis*.

Though it was a warm day, Ava felt a little shiver pass over her arms. There was no reason to feel guilty, she scolded herself. She liked Louis plenty, and besides, she had never promised him anything.

24

THE YAMADAS
1860–1935

Kenichi Yamada of California was born Yamada Kenichi in 1860 in Osaka, Japan.

It was a peculiar time to be born in Japan, for at that time the nation had developed an idiosyncratic self-consciousness about itself as a sleepy backwater. Samurai families had ruled for centuries, but now the country wished to shake itself awake and compete with the West – or at least an influential portion of it did – and as the nation attempted to modernize, there were many challenges to the class system that ranked samurai, farmers, artisans, and merchants in descending order.

Kenichi's parents were one example of the new disruption between castes, as his mother descended from the Matsudaira, an old samurai clan, while his father's family owned the local rice mercantile in Osaka. The match had been arranged and approved by both families, of course, but represented a bargain that was familiar the whole world over: class in exchange for money.

Still, his parents seemed happy in their union together, and Kenichi's father taught Kenichi to stand tall, to take pride in the prosperity of the rice mercantile, and to be proud of his native city, Osaka, which was also known as 'the nation's kitchen.' His father's point of view was not considered typical among his countrymen. Sometimes they heard the cries of peddlers hailing from over their garden walls.

'Listen to that,' Kenichi's father would say. 'Your grandfather hollered those same cries and roamed the streets as a peddler when I was just a boy. Can you imagine?'

Kenichi tried to picture his paternal grandfather – by then a frail, elderly man – shouting in the streets, buying and selling rice.

'Many people disdain peddlers, but your grandfather worked very hard as a peddler . . . That is how we earned the mercantile we have now,' his father said. 'If the city is a heart, peddlers are the blood that make it pump. Never look down on anyone who works hard.'

Hard work had always been a Japanese value, but paying the same respect to a peddler as to a shogun was not. Yet Kenichi was an unorthodox child raised in an unorthodox household; he easily took his father's point of view on the subject for his own. As fate would have it, it was an outlook that would eventually serve him well in America.

One day, when Kenichi was ten years old, he made a discovery that steered him even further toward a nontraditional path. He was snooping around his mother's possessions when he came upon a delicately carved wooden box. He found it buried deep within a chest, keeping company with his mother's tea ceremony things. It was a Japanese puzzle box, and once he got it open, he saw that it contained a series of letters folded up in thick, rough, foreign-looking envelopes, all of them stamped with strange-looking postmarks. He read them without hesitation, as young children are wont to do with the private letters of adults, and determined that they were from an uncle he'd never met: his mother's brother, Haruto.

He brought the box to his mother, and when she finished scolding him for nosing about in her possessions, she sat down and told him the story of his uncle. Kenichi had never met his uncle Haruto for reasons too tangled and complex for his young mind to understand – in part due to his mother's marriage, but also in part due to Haruto's involvement in the Boshin War and the unusual travels that ultimately resulted. That was the next detail that grabbed Kenichi's attention: the letters were sent from a land an ocean away. His uncle had traveled all the way across the Pacific to America, to a place called California.

A year or so earlier, Haruto had joined a group of samurai-class families financed by Matsudaira Katamori as they set sail for San Francisco. The group landed in San Francisco on May 20, 1869. They did not linger in San Francisco very long. The group pushed onward, traveling east, through the Sacramento Valley and up into the foothills that stood at the other side, until finally they reached a place called Gold Hill, where they settled for a time. They had brought with them fifty thousand *kuwa* trees and six million tea seeds from Japan. Once they secured two hundred acres of land, they officially established what came to be known as the Wakamatsu Tea and Silk Farm Colony. It was the first Japanese colony of its kind in the so-called New World.

Kenichi was less interested in the historical details than he was in imagining his uncle roaming around an exotic, faraway country. He was riveted by his uncle's account of the journey, sailing into the San Francisco Bay and putting into port at the strange, hilly American city full of tall clapboard houses, saloons, theaters, opium dens – all of these structures populated by Western pioneers, Chinese laborers, and European gentlemen alike. In his letters, Haruto gave detailed descriptions of ship captains, merchants, painted women, and prospectors.

Haruto enthusiastically described his new life in his letters to his sister: he spent the days practicing his English, doing business at the trading posts with the old forty-niners, planting *kuwa* trees, coaxing silkworms into production with the mulberry leaves, and planning for the first-ever tea harvest. He wrote about the golden hills and black oaks, the orange iron tinge to the soil. He wrote about the dry, baking heat of the summer days and the icy rapids of the American River, which hosted agitated, lumbering bears hungry for salmon, and flowed with melted snow from the Sierra Nevada mountains. Kenichi's mother let him read the letters again and again, and Kenichi began to memorize the contents, *kanji* for *kanji*, until this place called California began to run in his veins.

'Where is Uncle Haruto now?' Kenichi asked his mother four years later. It had been some time since any new correspondence had arrived, and Kenichi still thought of his uncle from time to time, dreaming of his uncle's adventures.

Her face clouded.

'This was the last letter I received,' she said, pointing to a letter postmarked with the year 1871. Neither of them could know: the Wakamatsu colony had been short-lived, and its members had dispersed, some of them returning to Japan, even.

It didn't matter: Kenichi had set his sights on following in his uncle's footsteps. He'd set about learning everything he could about this new land, California. He'd even undertaken to learn English. His mother was vaguely alarmed, and Kenichi learned to hide the secret dreams he was nurturing.

By 1878, Kenichi was a grown man, ready to embark on his own adventure. He had worked all of his adolescent years at his father's mercantile exchange, buying and selling rice, saving his weekly pay, and making his plans in secret.

In 1879, he set sail for the California coast from Osaka Bay. The journey was long and terrible. Kenichi had never known the ocean could stretch on like that – endless mile after endless mile. There was something utterly vacant and lonely about that much sea; it was like being in a desert made of water. Perhaps it was for this reason that, once he arrived in San Francisco, Kenichi did not stay. San Francisco was a city surrounded by water, and after his tumultuous voyage across the Pacific, Kenichi craved dry land. He'd also fallen under the spell of his uncle's letters, which had only made him more certain he might like to try his hand at farming. To his peers who had grown up with him in Osaka, the very idea of Kenichi farming would have been laughable. He was a city boy; he may have bought and sold rice but he certainly had never farmed it. However, he could not be dissuaded. He pictured the rolling hills his uncle had described and found himself joining a wagon train out of San Francisco and into the foothills of the Sierra Nevada, disembarking at a town not far from the site of the now-disbanded Wakamatsu Tea and Silk Farm Colony.

Once off the wagon train, Kenichi felt certain he had found the place he was meant to stay, if only he could find some way to purchase a stake. He was in luck: when he inquired around town, he learned there was a young prospector eager to get a prime parcel of land off his hands. Of course, nobody told him about the poker games and bad blood between Silas Northrup and Ennis Thorn. When he happened upon Silas in the town tavern, he thought it merely a sign of his own good fortune that the young man was so desperate to sell him some land. Silas took him right away to see the land in question, and Kenichi surveyed the sloping hills and put his hands in the dirt to check the soil. He didn't have much experience, of course, but he'd studied books about agriculture back in Japan, and the books had told him what to look for. The soil was fertile, and the terrain appeared to have good drainage; it was just right for an orchard.

'Who owns the land in that direction?' Kenichi asked, pointing. He wanted to know who his future neighbors might be.

'The Thorns,' Silas answered. 'Man and his wife. Older folk. They got a son, too. It's all apples over there, mostly.'

'Apples?'

'Sure. They got a little pasture for the cattle, and an apple orchard on the property,' Silas answered. He did not add anything more, or continue on to say, *And this here land I'm selling you was a parcel belonging to Old Man Thorn that I took off him when he was too drunk to notice I had an ace hid up my sleeve . . .* Instead, he remained silent, staring at the hillside as Kenichi nodded in approval.

'An apple orchard,' Kenichi repeated.

Silas's lips moved in a slight grimace and he nodded. Just then, his eyes were drawn by a plume of dust rising in the air, far off in the distance. That would be Ennis Thorn's wagon, he thought, headed in the direction of the Thorn farmhouse. Silas didn't think it would be wise to linger much longer. There weren't any drainpipes to shimmy up out there in the open fields.

'Let's go back to town and talk it over down at the tavern,' Silas said, heading back in the direction of his horse.

'All right,' Kenichi agreed, already trying to think of the number he was willing to offer.

A few dusty miles later the two men found themselves seated at the bar counter. As Kenichi hoped to stay and make this region his new home, he wanted to establish himself as a good and moral citizen. He made Silas a very fair price, and Silas accepted. They toasted the exchange over two glasses of rye.

Kenichi could not believe he'd become a landowner so quickly. Now there was only the matter of making his plans for the property. Building a little campsite, hiring a few hands of help, and deciding what to grow. *Perhaps I ought to introduce myself to the neighbors*, Kenichi thought. He was still new to America and unsure what the appropriate decorum might be. Little did Kenichi know, in this particular situation, he'd be hard-pressed to discover any decorum that might impress Ennis Thorn. When Kenichi began to camp on his newly acquired land, there were only three Thorns living on the property adjacent, and none of them welcomed the sight of Kenichi's campfire in the evenings. The Thorns maintained an aloof distance from their new Japanese neighbor, establishing the relationship that would last for decades to come.

The years passed quickly. Kenichi Yamada matured from a young man into a middle-aged man. He had always assumed he would marry young. But when the first few years of his twenties passed and he had not gotten around to marrying, it did not seem so strange that another decade should pass, and then another. He was busy with plenty of hard work. The land he had bought was fruitful. Down at the growers' exchange and packing sheds that abutted the railroad tracks in town, he regularly sold almonds, plums, and satsumas – all for very favorable prices. He built the farmhouse and then – seeing it through a potential bride's eyes – expanded it, constantly improving it, bit by bit.

In the fall of 1916, Kenichi was finally ready for a bride, but at fifty-six he was afraid he'd waited too long, and that none would want him. The delay in marrying wasn't entirely intentional; it was largely due to the fact that Kenichi had been busy building up the orchards and ranch – he hadn't wanted to send back to Japan for a potential wife before everything was at its best, before everything was prosperous and ready. He was a dignified, proud man. He had insisted on making his own way in the world. His own parents had long since passed away, and Kenichi was cut off from any regular communication with Japan. Now he only had his land, his orchards, and his farmhouse to offer – and he wanted them to be perfect. The thought of asking a wife to move halfway around the world for anything less struck him as distasteful.

But now . . . could a fifty-six-year-old man successfully embark on marriage and a family so late in life?

Kenichi hoped the answer was yes. There were certainly examples, back in the old country, of samurai who'd served in battle so long that they didn't get around to taking a wife or fathering children until their fearsome samurai moustaches were already tinged with silver. But Kenichi was no samurai and no longer lived in the land where such legendary men ruled the history books.

Kenichi's inquiry was answered by a family named Miyamoto. Kenichi could write to their daughter, they said, and if what he wrote pleased her, he could send for her passage across the Pacific. The young woman in question, Shizue, was twenty-two years of age and had never been married. She was pretty enough but possessed 'a certain defect,' her family warned. Around the time Shizue turned sixteen, she had begun to suffer from terrible seizures that came and went without obvious provocation or warning. Kenichi understood what this meant: Shizue was an epileptic.

Her condition had taken a toll on Shizue's personality over the years. She had been a confident, friendly child. But suffering multiple embarrassing epileptic fits as a teenager had changed her. She had grown so that she was perpetually nervous and unable to conceal her condition. At tea ceremony, her hand shook so as to spill the tea. She could not answer simple questions without speaking in a flustered stammer. Shizue was awkward in a world that did not embrace awkwardness in any form. As things stood at that time, many matchmakers considered epilepsy a disfigurement, and her increasingly shy, nervous disposition only emphasized the fact of her affliction. The Miyamoto family was at pains to find Shizue a proper marital match. *Perhaps*, they thought, *our daughter is better suited to another continent. Perhaps, living among foreigners, she will not seem so strange or have to endure the daily embarrassments of being . . . the way she is.*

And so they gave their twenty-two-year-old daughter permission to exchange letters with Kenichi. He had, after all, guaranteed that he did not mind Shizue's condition, his property and fortune were sound, and he had further promised that whomever he took for a wife would have a life of comfort and security. It was not traditional for a man and woman to correspond before arranging a marriage, but clearly he was not a traditional man.

For his part, Kenichi insisted on exchanging letters because he wanted to know something about the mind of his future bride. He dreaded the thought of a young woman sailing halfway across the world because her parents forced her to, arriving on the orchards and hating her new life. Such an arrangement would pain his tired heart, after all his hard work and struggle to make a good life for himself in the New World.

I am much older than you, he wrote. *I do not know if you imagined marrying a man of my age.*

According to the traditions of courting, young women were obligated to point out their flaws, but it was uncommon for a man to do so. To point out his old age . . . perhaps she was supposed to be repulsed. However, Shizue was impressed by his sincerity.

I do not expect to fall in love with you, she wrote back, returning the favor of his honesty in kind. *If we married, I would only expect to make a shared life together that is prosperous and honorable.*

Kenichi was curiously comforted by these words. The sentiment was fair and true. He sent a large sum to her parents – more than enough for her passage to America, meeting the unspoken expectation. Shizue packed a small chest and prepared to make her departure. Her mind was made up. Even so, she was still as nervous as a sparrow. She wondered if this older man would truly want her for his wife in spite of her flighty nature. There was only one way to find out.

Then, while at sea, a curious thing happened. The ship sailed through a storm, and Shizue was tossed about like a ragdoll. She was sick often, throwing up into a tin pail, and utterly horrified as the ship listed so steeply from side to side, it felt as though it would certainly capsize. But something strange came over her during the worst of it: some sort of ironclad will took over her nervous body and steadied her. She was determined to make it to America, she realized. She was surprised to realize she was not apologetic for the unladylike intensity of her determination. A cool, collected calmness came over her. The nervous tremors in her hands ceased. Her breathing became even. When she spoke, her stammer was gone.

Shizue endured three weeks at sea. When she disembarked in California, the spring of 1917 was in full bloom and she was surprised to realize her new sense of calm was still with her. Somehow she understood it would forever be with her now. The ocean had tested her, distilled her, and washed away all the apologetic tics that had previously betrayed her.

Instead of sending a wagon or a train ticket, Kenichi met Shizue himself in San Francisco, so that he might personally escort her to the piece of property up in the California foothills that was to be her new home. Their rapport was instantly just as it had been in their letters: honest and simple; they harbored between the two of them a tacit understanding. It was a quiet journey, but peaceful. Kenichi brought Shizue back to the Yamada property, watching her face and carefully reevaluating his home as it must look through her eyes. Shizue stepped down from the buggy and gazed at the little white clapboard farmhouse cantilevered into the side of a foothill.

When a small smile of approval played on her lips, Kenichi just about felt his heart split at the seams like an overripe pomegranate.

They were married and settled into their life together. Shizue was surprised to sense love in Kenichi's heart – the kind of breathlessly optimistic, whole hearted love one might expect from a much younger man. He was also jolly, playful – a touch irreverent, even. Shizue was even further surprised when she woke up one morning and, listening to Kenichi humming cheerfully over his daily cup of strong American coffee, realized she had done the one thing she had dutifully informed him she wouldn't do: she had fallen in love with him, too.

And curiously, in America, Shizue finally became the good Japanese she never was back home. She was calm and graceful in all things – in the meticulous decoration and organization of the house, in the careful way she spoke and dressed, in the way she kept the old traditions, even arranging for a small teahouse and ancestral shrine to be added onto their existing home. Nonetheless, Shizue also embraced the new, and perhaps it might be said that her greatest grace was in blending the East with the West in harmonious balance. She knew adopting Western culture – at least to some degree – was important to her husband, who had struck out from Japan to make his home in California for a reason.

In those first weeks, as their mutual respect grew into genuine affection and then love, they began – shyly at first – to consummate their marriage. Shizue wondered if children would come; she waited anxiously every month with a mixture of excitement and fear to find out what her fate as a mother might be. Slowly, as each month passed and Shizue experienced the normal bleeding, the excitement and fear turned to puzzlement and then, bit by bit, a sort of silent, empty worry. Though her seizures had lessened, she was convinced her epilepsy was at the root of the problem. She visited the local doctor, but he could not tell her much, except that bearing children was a challenge for some women. Ironically, prior to this intersection in her life, Shizue had not thought about children – or the lack of them – very much. Now it was all she thought of.

She cried – never in front of her husband, never anywhere he could see – and, stony-faced once more, accepted her future as a barren woman. It was her fault, she was sure. She was being punished for her spectacular, inborn deficiency, and now her husband was being punished, too.

Weeks, months, and eventually years passed. Kenichi was anxiously awaiting a family, too, although he understood his wife's sensitivity enough to carefully conceal this desire. Kenichi's prime reason for eagerly wanting a family was to experience the miracle and blessing of a child, to pass along love and the fruits of his hard work to another living being. But Kenichi had a handful of more complicated reasons as well: he was not a US citizen, and neither he nor his wife was permitted to become a citizen under various anti-Oriental exclusion laws. This had never affected the Yamadas directly in the past, but as the state of California began passing more and more legislation aimed at ensuring aliens were not allowed to own property, Kenichi understood that everything he had worked so hard for was in jeopardy.

Other Chinese and Japanese families in the area were navigating their way around the potential legal pitfalls by transferring their holdings into the names of their children, who, having been born on American soil, instantly possessed the citizenship that had been barred to their parents. Kenichi knew their lives – his and his wife's – would be best secured if they could manage to have a child. But he also understood how wounded she was upon discovering their difficulty in conceiving.

A dedicated husband, he pretended to delight in Shizue alone, in the good company she provided.

There are many theories about the circumstances that best beget a child, and in the case of Kenichi and Shizue Yamada, it is certainly compelling that only when Kenichi had proved his love was unwavering, only when Shizue felt the pressure of the duty of motherhood fall from her shoulders, that they were finally blessed with a child. After almost three years of trying, Shizue's body ceased to bleed. She assumed it was a mistake, of course; her body was merely playing tricks on her. But the doctor who attended her – the same doctor who had condescendingly patted her hand and comforted her by telling her it was simply not possible for some women – confirmed the pregnancy.

Young Haruto was born in the autumn of 1920. The birth was not an easy transaction. First, the thing Shizue feared most – a seizure – sent her into early labor. Compounding this was the fact that the baby's neck was caught in the umbilical cord and it was only by some strange combination of coordinated actions on the part of all involved – Shizue, midwife, and baby – that he was not strangled. The second he breathed the air, unleashing the full power of his squalling lungs on a small, attentive audience, he was a miraculous joy to behold. They were so overcome at the moment of his birth – a moment Kenichi insisted on being present for – they forgot to count toes or demand to know the sex. *A boy*, they were later told, *a very healthy baby boy*. And then came the name: Haruto, after Kenichi's mysterious uncle. But as he would also be an American child, it would be 'Harry' for school, 'Harry' for his American friends. Although they could not know, this was indeed a fitting name for a baby who had, from a certain point of view, performed his first escape act and who would one day idolize the great Harry Houdini.

Kenichi was surprised to discover how much purpose he found in being a parent, especially given how long he had postponed this phase of his life. By the time of Haruto's birth, Kenichi had turned sixty and understood this made him an old father. Nevertheless, he was determined his son shouldn't suffer for it, and to his own gratification and surprise, a wave of fresh energy and enthusiasm sprang from some unknown well within him.

When Haruto grew into a toddler, Kenichi spent countless hours wandering the orchards with the boy perched atop his shoulders. As Haruto grew, they made a game together, joining in on the pruning and picking. The Yamada land was a wondrous playground for a small child; Haruto grew into an adventurous, outdoorsy boy. Some years later, when Haruto was going on nine years old, Kenichi and Shizue were blessed with a second child: a little girl. They named her Mai – a name that would be easily converted to 'Mae' by her American schoolmates. In spite of the age gap – or perhaps because of it – Haruto was exceptionally kind to his little sister, caring for her with a gentle, protective touch. As she grew bigger, Mai also roamed the property, helping and playing in the orchards. On an early school report, Mai was asked to name one of her favorite things, and the teacher would help her write out the words. She wrote, 'The smell of satsuma blossoms in Papa's orchard.' Kenichi took one look and knew in his heart that everything he had done, all of his work, had been so his daughter might write down that one sentence. It was worth it to him.

But Kenichi understood that, while their home made for a perfect haven for his two young children, the world beyond their property lines wouldn't always be so accommodating. He understood, too, that Haruto and Mai were not like him; they were *nisei* – second-generation Japanese in America – and would only call California home. The sounds of their American names, Harry and Mae, would eventually ring more familiar in their ears than Haruto and Mai. The Japanese words Kenichi and Shizue coaxed from their children's mouths were bound to quickly rust and decay. It was unlikely either child would ever set foot in Japan. Kenichi also knew that one day his children's assumptions – primarily the assumption that their identities as Americans was a given – might be shattered by others who might throw stones.

Of course, he could never have predicted the sharpness of the stones that would be thrown during war, or how thorough the shattering. Kenichi was more like his children than he knew. The land belonged to him, but he believed he belonged to it, too. They had adopted each other; this was how America constantly reshaped herself. A good citizen, a polite neighbor . . . Kenichi believed he was safe, and *home*.

25

NEWCASTLE, CALIFORNIA
SEPTEMBER 17, 1943

It's the nature of the friendship between those two boys that puzzles me,'
Agent Bonner says, shaking his head at Deputy Henderson and staring into
the giant amber eye of his beer glass. 'It's an awful big change: One minute
Louis Thorn and Harry Yamada are sworn enemies, and the next minute the
Yamadas trust Louis enough to sign over their land for safekeeping – the very
land that started their beef in the first place.'

The two men are perched on a pair of stools at the bar. To Agent Bonner's
relief, it is dim and cool inside the saloon, the damp air scented with a mixture
of barley and mildew. As promised, Deputy Henderson had shown Bonner
the way to Murphy's Saloon, and the agent was making good on his offer to
buy a round.

Bonner absently inspects his surroundings as they drink and talk.
Decorations in the saloon are spare and reassuringly free of a feminine touch.
Old newspaper clippings hang in cockeyed frames on the walls; the bulk of
the clippings themselves date back to the Gold Rush days, featuring local
prospectors who struck it rich. Laid out in haphazard fashion, they make
up a sporadic, lopsided mosaic of various shades of yellowing newspaper, a
conspicuous overuse of exclamation marks, and the occasional flash of a toothy
grin glimpsed through a wild man's beard. The only other adornments in the
saloon are posters urging folks to buy war bonds, a smattering of colorful
brewery advertisements, and a few now-defunct Anti-Saloon League signs and
handbills – no doubt displayed with a sense of humor.

'You ain't the first to puzzle over it, that's for sure,' Deputy Henderson replies now. 'There's been a lot of talk all over town.'

'Say, fellas,' comes a voice from behind the bar. 'Will you have another?'

Bonner glances at his glass and realizes it's already empty. A short, broad-shouldered man with a red complexion and dark, badly trimmed hair is looking at them with a stern expression that would be best described as a glare if it were not for the kindly crinkles around the man's eyes. The bartender flips a dishrag over his shoulder and leans on his elbows, waiting.

'I meant to ask: are you Joe Abbott?' Bonner inquires.

'I am. Will you have another?'

Bonner flicks his eyes in the direction of his companion. Henderson smiles awkwardly and looks away, scratching sheepishly at the scar of a healing pimple. It is clear that he is willing to drink as many as Bonner is willing to buy.

'Well, all right,' Bonner replies, after a pause. 'Suppose after one, a second tastes twice as nice.'

The bartender retrieves their glasses, places them under the taps, fills them with lukewarm beer, and picks up the wooden paddle used for slicing off the foamy heads.

'You say you're Joe Abbott?' Bonner repeats.

'I did. Who wants to know?' the bartender asks, shutting off the taps once the glasses are frothing over. He arches a wary eyebrow at the stranger.

'This here is Agent Bonner from the Federal Bureau of Investigation,' Deputy Henderson announces in an eager, important tone, thumbing in Bonner's direction.

Bonner nods in tacit greeting.

'Hmph,' Joe replies, unimpressed, slicing away the foam. Despite his show of indifference, his left eye begins to twitch ever so slightly, and it is clear he isn't saying the one thing he's thinking: *Why does 'Agent Bonner from the Federal Bureau of Investigation' know my name, and what does he want?*

'You read the headlines about how Harry and Old Man Yamada broke out of that camp up at Tule Lake, didn't you?' Henderson prompts.

'I did,' Joe replies.

'Well, that's why Agent Bonner's here: he was investigating their whereabouts.' Henderson pauses and looks thoughtful for a brief moment. 'Course, now it looks like there may be nothin' left to investigate,' he adds, 'since there ain't nobody to track down anymore.'

'What does that mean?' Joe asks in a flat voice, leery.

'Well, you seen the smoke yesterday, ain't you?' Henderson continues.

'Sure. Pretty certain everyone within forty miles or so caught sight of that. Heard there was some sort of accident.'

'It was an airplane crashing down.'

'That so?'

'Not only that, but it looks like them Yamada boys stole Louis Thorn's plane and was the ones to crash it.'

Joe Abbott frowns.

'I'm surprised you ain't heard all about it, Joe,' Henderson says. 'You working here at the bar, I'da thought you heard everythin' first.'

'I been sick,' Joe replies, clearly irked by the glee Henderson takes in gossiping. 'So you're telling me the Yamadas passed on?' he repeats. Joe's frown deepens, and Agent Bonner is interested to detect a flicker of surprised distress on the man's face.

'Yes,' Bonner answers. 'I'm sorry to be the bearer of bad news about your neighbors.'

Joe Abbott stiffens.

'They weren't *my* neighbors. I live here in town.'

'I just mean your fellow community members,' Bonner clarifies. He knows that, with the war on, even if Joe cared for the Yamadas, he won't want to give that impression. Bonner changes tack. 'But speaking of neighbors . . . mind if I ask you a few questions about the Yamadas' next-door neighbors?'

Joe blinks, bewildered by the shift in topic.

'The Thorn family?'

'Yes. Louis Thorn in particular.'

'All right,' he replies, his tone unfriendly. 'Shoot.'

'Louis Thorn says he was in here the other night, says he got into some kind of a fray . . . His whole face is busted up.'

'What's your question?'

173

'Can you verify that? Do you recall Louis Thorn getting into a bar fight here?'

Joe's eyes slide from Agent Bonner's face to Deputy Henderson's and back again.

'Sure,' Joe grunts finally, after a stoic silence. 'I remember that. Big scuffle, and for no good reason, too. Don't even know how it started, but lots of fellas joined in. I spent the rest of the night cleaning up their mess. But you know how it is. Boys'll be boys.'

The tension thickens as Joe Abbott and Agent Bonner lock eyes with each other. Another agent watching from the outside might have later scolded Bonner for the manner in which he asked Joe the question – serving it up to him on a plate instead of trying to trip him up. But Bonner sees everything he needs to know right there in Joe's uncomfortable expression.

'Say,' Deputy Henderson chimes in. 'Old Whitcomb keeps pointing out how you're real funny about Louis Thorn,' he continues, his eyes widening with fresh realization and the buzz of new gossip. 'You're thinking Louis Thorn might be a suspect in this crash?'

'I didn't say that,' Bonner replies. 'I only said Louis told me he got into a bar fight a few nights ago.'

'He did,' Joe Abbott affirms. With an air of finality, he grunts and reaches for the dishrag over his shoulder, wets it, and sets about scrubbing dirt off the wooden countertop – working his way down the bar and effectively ending his side of the conversation.

Bonner turns back to his beer and takes a long, deep sip, allowing the suds to wash over his upper lip. Eventually, he and Henderson carry on with their chitchat without Joe Abbott. They circle away from talk of the crash and the Yamadas to more benign topics as Bonner mulls over his case quietly to himself. He still can't prove Louis Thorn's bruises mean anything, but he is sure Thorn didn't acquire them four nights ago in the saloon where Bonner now sits. The truth is often complicated and requires some coaxing, but if there's one thing Bonner knows when he hears it, it's a bald-faced lie.

26

EARL SHAW'S FLYING CIRCUS
SONOMA, CALIFORNIA, JULY 4, 1940

By the Fourth of July, the barnstormers had made their way to the town of Sonoma. They secured a place to camp just north of the old Spanish mission, not far from the town's main square, and borrowed a nearby field for their flying circus act. On the actual day of the Fourth, there was to be an evening festival in the town square, complete with fireworks. Hutch, Buzz, Louis, and Harry performed their stunts during the early afternoon, hoping to beat the late-afternoon heat. Bubbling with holiday spirit, plenty of townsfolk were in the mood for a ride, and Earl made sure to herd every last one of them over to Ava to collect their money. Once Hutch and Buzz had given their last airplane rides of the day, the majority of the spectators ambled off to eat a late lunch and nap in the cool shade of their homes before the celebration that evening.

Hutch and Buzz made up their minds to have a beer in town at the Toscano Hotel, a place that looked as though nothing had changed since California's old stagecoach days. When Earl caught wind that the Toscano hosted a lively poker scene in the saloon downstairs, he decided to join his two pilots. Ava was left at the campsite with her mother. She had no idea where Louis and Harry had disappeared to.

'I heard there's going to be a dance in the town square tonight,' Ava's mother remarked.

'Yes,' Ava replied, 'Louis mentioned it . . .'

'Oh?' Cleo said, aiming a knowing smile at her daughter. 'Louis mentioned it?'

Ava squirmed. 'He did' was all she said in reply.

'You know, I believe he's sweet on you,' Cleo said, tickled.

Ava didn't care for the teasing but kept her mouth shut. The truth was, Louis had done more than just mention it, he had asked Ava if they might go together, and she had agreed. Now she felt nervous about the prospect of going to the dance with Louis. On some instinctive level, she sensed that the fact that she had said yes to Louis had something to do with the fact that she'd gone flying with Harry. *Nothing had happened*, she reminded herself. And yet she felt curiously guilty that she hadn't told anyone.

'Let's decide what you'll wear . . .' Cleo suggested.

Ava gave in and allowed her mother to help her wash up and pick out a dress.

A few hours later, as the sun drooped in the sky, a pleasant wind had begun to blow a little of the heat out of the Sonoma Valley. Ava stood outside, waiting for Louis to turn up. Her face was scrubbed, her shiny red bob was pinned in waves again, and she was wearing a light green dress her mother had insisted matched her eyes. As she waited, the jittery feeling from earlier returned again.

But her nerves vanished the second she saw Louis approaching the campsite. He was freshly bathed and dressed in a clean shirt and pressed trousers.

'Hello!' he called as he drew near.

He was grinning, and his smile instantly put Ava at ease. His bashfulness seemed tinged with a new hint of confidence as he looked at her with an admiring gaze.

'You look awful nice,' Louis said.

'Thank you,' she replied. 'You clean up all right, too.'

He offered his arm and she took it. They set off in the direction of town, but they had only taken ten steps or so when Ava glimpsed a second familiar figure coming up the road. Harry. What was he doing here? For some reason Ava hadn't expected Harry to return to the caravan before the big celebration in town. Now she saw he had been up to the same thing as Louis: he had bathed and was nicely attired with his hair neatly combed.

When Harry caught sight of Ava and Louis walking arm in arm, she saw him pause briefly in mid-stride. With a sinking feeling, Ava thought she understood why. But there was nothing else to do but to carry on, and so Harry did.

'Heading to the party in town, Harry?' Louis greeted him, seemingly oblivious.

Harry gave a stiff nod. Ava saw his jaw clench as he eyed the place where her hand rested in the crook of Louis's arm. 'Just thought I'd come see who else was going,' Harry said.

'Don't look so glum about it, Crane!' Louis teased. 'It's supposed to be a party, after all.'

Harry forced a smile. 'Truth is, I hadn't made up my mind. I might just stay in camp and get some rest.'

Ava was surprised he was bold enough to attempt the lie despite his neatly combed hair and pressed shirt and trousers.

'Aw, c'mon – it's bound to be fun!' Louis said. He glanced around and, seeing the opportunity for a joke, pointed to where Ava stood beside him. 'If you're worried that the two of you will get to fighting like cats and dogs like you always do, don't worry – I'll do my best to keep 'er dancing most of the night!'

Harry looked at Ava for a moment. He smiled, but Ava thought she noticed a discreetly bitter tinge. 'Well, that's a relief,' he said.

Just then, Ava's mother emerged from the caravan, dressed in a pretty white summer dress with fluttering sleeves, her hair shining in dark, glossy waves around her face and shoulders.

'Don't we all look smart!' Cleo called, joining the gathering group. 'Would you mind if I walked into town with the three of you? I think Earl's still there – Buzz and Hutch, too . . . I haven't seen any of the fellas all afternoon.'

They set off in the direction of town again, this time as a foursome. Louis led Ava on ahead, a bounce in his step. Harry politely offered Cleo his arm and they brought up the rear. Ava wasn't sure if she was imagining things, but she thought she felt a pair of angry eyes on her back.

Most of Sonoma was nestled around the main square. The old Spanish mission bordered the far corner of the north side, while a grand movie theater presided over the shops along the east side with a majestic façade. A sizable green park made up the heart of the square, with a pond, topiary, elms, redwoods, and the occasional palm tree. At the center sat the city hall – a two-story stone building with a clock tower, arched porticos, and a roofline that bore vague echoes of the Spanish mission that stood just over its shoulder.

At the northern end of the park, a brass band was playing a jaunty tune while a handful of couples jittered and twirled on a makeshift dance floor laid out on the lawn. The smell of hot dogs and corn on the cob filled the air. Dusk was settling in and Catherine wheels showered onlookers with sparks that glowed electric as they whirred and spun. Children dared one another to run through the bright fiery cascades, and shrieked with laughter.

'Can I buy ya something to eat?' Louis asked Ava as they neared the tables of food.

Stomachs grumbling, the whole group of them picked out a treat, with Louis paying for Ava and Harry paying for Cleo. Ava watched her mother smile courteously at Harry as she thanked him. She wondered . . . what did her mother see when she looked at Harry? If her mother thought Harry was the one sweet on Ava, and not Louis, would she giggle and tease Ava the same way?

They walked around for a good thirty minutes or so, taking in the scene as they ate, self-consciously wiping kernels of sweet corn and watermelon juice from their faces. As he had promised, Louis asked Ava to dance. Her eyes flicked briefly to Harry's face, but since walking into town Harry had refused to look at her.

'All right,' Ava agreed, and Louis took her hand.

Together, Louis and Ava danced a few unsophisticated fox-trots and even a jitterbug. Finally, Ava spotted the familiar shapes of Hutch and Buzz approaching the square. She and Louis took a dancing break to go say hello.

'Has anyone seen Earl?' Ava's mother asked, a slight wrinkle creeping into her forehead.

'Last I saw, he was still in the saloon in the Toscano,' Hutch drawled, tipping his hat politely to Ava's mother as though reporting to an Army sergeant.

'Don't worry about Earl,' Buzz said. 'He was up plenty of money last we saw him, so I expect he's happy as a clam, and not about to throw in his hand anytime soon . . . He'll be all right.'

Cleo didn't appear soothed by this information. Buzz frowned, but then his face suddenly brightened as he thought of something. He fished in his pocket, produced a small stick of some sort, and, with the help of his lighter, lit up a sparkler. He handed it to Ava's mother. 'Here ya are – Happy Independence Day!'

The wrinkle vanished from Cleo's forehead and she laughed as she accepted it, giggling with delight as the sparks shot out from her hand. She waved the sparkler around, making white, fiery shapes and letters in the inky darkness. Buzz fished out a few more sparklers and lit them up, handing them around.

'Somebody, ask me to dance,' Cleo said in a happy, breathless voice, wanting to sustain the feeling of good cheer once the sparklers had fizzled out. Buzz volunteered, spun her around once playfully, and led Cleo to the dance floor.

'We never seen *you* dance, Hutch,' Louis commented.

Hutch shook his head. 'And you ain't gonna. 'Fraid I dunno how. Never cared to learn.'

Louis was about to reply, when Ava spoke over him.

'We've never seen Harry dance, either,' she said in a flat voice.

'Say, that's true,' Louis said. He tipped his chin at Harry. 'You even know how to dance, Crane?'

'Sure I do,' Harry replied.

'Prove it,' Ava said. She surprised herself with the demand. Harry looked at her, perturbed and frowning, as though to say, *What are you doing?* But instead of backing down, Ava glared back at him and crossed her arms.

'I'd be happy to prove it, but I don't see a girl to ask,' Harry replied.

'I'm right here,' Ava said. 'I'm a girl.'

Harry looked at her but didn't say anything.

Ava felt her cheeks color with a mixture of anger and embarrassment. 'I *dare* you,' she added for good measure.

'I guess they're back to *that* old business again,' Louis said to Hutch. He shook his head and sighed as though burdened by the silly nature of their ridiculous contests, but there was a flicker of something else in it, too: a small shadow of suspicion.

Finally, Harry offered Ava his arm. They strode out to the dance floor and fell into a fox-trot. For the first minute or so they danced mechanically, and in silence. Ava worked up the courage to break the ice.

'Listen, Harry, I—'

'You might've told me,' Harry cut her off. He still sounded angry but spoke in a calm, even voice, as though confiding in her. 'I'd have understood.'

'Understood what?'

'About you and Louis.'

Ava struggled to reply. *Was* there something to tell Harry about her and Louis? She didn't know. She wanted to tell Harry what was on her mind, but it was all tangled up.

The fox-trot was ending. A new wave of music rose into the night air.

'A waltz!' Ava said. 'I'm awful at the waltz.'

'It's supposed to be the easiest.'

'Even so.' Ava shrugged.

She thought Harry might be done dancing with her, now that he'd risen to her challenge and proved himself capable. Instead, he gently offered his arms again and began to lead more carefully, making it easier for her to follow. Soon enough, Ava fell into the rhythm. Once or twice she found herself accidentally stepping on his foot.

'You're in too much of a rush,' Harry assessed.

'Says the man who can't wait to jump out of an airplane,' Ava replied, referring to Harry's recent proposal to add parachute jumps to their stunt routine.

'Fair point.' Harry gave a reluctant chuckle and they waltzed on. But as she became more competent and there was less to laugh about, an awkward quiet settled between them. Ava tried to think up some conversation. Her mind drifted from barnstorming stunts to magic tricks; Harry did both with the same panache and gusto. It was clear he loved both activities with a pure and vigorous passion.

'What is it about magic and magicians that you're so crazy about?' she asked in a friendly tone.

Harry shrugged. 'I guess it *is* kids' stuff. But a good magic trick is just like a good stunt.'

'How so?'

'Well, magic is all about how it's performed – whether the fellow has what it takes to pull it off, to dazzle an audience and make them believe they've just witnessed something impossible. And an *escape act* – like the kind Harry Houdini used to perform – is a feat of agility, strength, and smarts, all rolled into one.'

He had relaxed and his earlier grievance was forgotten. Harry seemed lighter now, dancing with Ava and talking about his favorite things.

'And then there are the stage illusions, of course,' he continued. 'Your average audience member believes he has seen real 'magic' – something utterly inexplicable – but a clever man knows it's all just a riddle, and if you have the patience and the smarts, you can puzzle it out. I like those, too – for the puzzle.'

Just then, Harry glimpsed something over Ava's shoulder and froze for a beat. He clenched his jaw and tried to get back into the rhythm. Ava twisted around to see what he was looking at. Around the perimeter of the dance floor, a gaggle of women had gathered. They were pointing and staring, whispering in one another's ears.

'Are they looking at *us*?' Ava asked, in disbelief.

'Yes,' Harry said. 'We can stop dancing if you want to. Probably should, as a matter of fact . . .'

'But . . . but they don't even *know* us!' Ava protested, indignant. 'What business is it of theirs?'

Harry sighed.

'I'm afraid it's the kind of thing that everyone makes his business, and always will be.'

He slowed to a stop.

'We oughta get back to the others. Besides, Louis will be anxious to dance with you again.'

Ava found herself sorry to end their waltz so abruptly. She wasn't ready to let go of Harry's shoulder as he pulled away, taking her elbow and gently steering her off the dance floor. Her mind groped wildly; there was something she wanted to say, if only her thoughts and words would take shape.

'Harry,' she began, hesitating. 'You'll take me up again, won't you?' He didn't reply right away, so she repeated her plea. 'We'll go flying together again, won't we?'

'Maybe Louis ought to take you,' he said in a quiet voice.

'I want *you* to take me,' she said. There was a sudden certainty in her tone. Harry halted as though he'd been shot, then looked at her. The expression on his face contained multitudes. She could make out confusion and anger, but she thought she glimpsed a hint of something else, too. In the next second the emotion was gone and his face had turned to stone again.

'Back so soon?' Louis called out to them, now that they were a short distance away. He had not taken his eyes off Ava and Harry for the entirety of their spin around the dance floor. The hesitation left Harry's body and he calmly finished escorting Ava back to their friends.

'Yes. It was all I could take,' Harry replied, hooking a thumb in Ava's direction. 'This one will clobber your toes if you're not careful.'

It was a joke, but Ava felt mildly stung. She was working on a sharp remark of her own when a young boy interrupted her. He ran up to them and tugged on Hutch's sleeve.

'Hey, mister,' the kid said, 'you're the one who came into the Toscano Hotel with the dark-haired fella with the slick moustache earlier, ain't ya?'

Hutch looked confused but realized the kid could only mean Earl.

'Yeah?' he said.

'He sent me to come getcha,' the kid reported. 'He told me to tell you . . . he's in *trouble* . . .'

By now the kid, a child of no more than eight or so, had everyone's attention. The group of them exchanged a wary look.

'Oh, dear,' Cleo murmured. The wrinkle on her brow reappeared.

'Well, we'd better go see . . .' Hutch announced, and they all walked in the direction of the saloon.

27

Earl Shaw was often lucky at cards, but – unlucky for Earl – he didn't always know how to quit while he was ahead. That night at the saloon inside the Toscano, after winning more money at poker than he ever had in his life, Earl proceeded to get tipsy. Once happily buzzing with a belly full of whiskey, he convinced himself his winning streak had surely not run its course. He began to bet more wildly, and as the night wore on, the players at the table changed; the middle-aged farmer who had lost a small fortune to Earl returned with a pair of thick-necked friends. Earl – by that point blurry with drink – paid little mind. When his winning streak gave way to the first few losses, Earl dug his heels in, irritable and eager to win it all back. His irritation grew as he continued to lose until finally it transformed into desperation, and before Earl knew it, he had not only lost all his winnings but had gambled away every last cent he was worth.

The terrible truth was, Earl had even bet away his livelihood. He had bet the planes with startling nonchalance, only to lose them in a single hand. He was drunk and was now trapped in a horrific nightmare. Sweating terribly, even in his stupor, he knew: he needed to send for help. Hutch was the last person he'd seen, the one to whom men usually listened. He promised the kid who'd been helping the barkeep all evening a dollar if he found Hutch and brought him.

When the group arrived, Hutch indeed did the talking. Inside the saloon, the room had acquired the stale atmosphere of a long night filled with numerous poker games. As Ava stood off to the side of the saloon with her mother, she noticed the wallpaper was stained and the room smelled like spilled beer.

'He placed them bets in good faith,' one of the thick-necked farmers argued, unmoved by Hutch's appeals to leave the airplanes out of it and call it a draw. 'He *can't* go back on them now just 'cause he don't feel like payin' up.'

The wiry, middle-aged man who'd originally lost to Earl stood up from where he sat at the table, angry. 'This fella was about to take me for all I'm worth, and you didn't see *me* whining about fairness!'

As they went back and forth, tensions rose and fists clenched. Ava felt her eyes nervously roving over the men's hips, looking to see who might have a gun. She said a quick prayer it wouldn't come to that.

Hutch continued in his negotiations, even-toned and steady. He talked the men down from demanding payment in the form of both planes to demanding one of the biplanes plus all the money the flying circus presently had in cash.

Ava saw Louis and Harry exchange a look, the silent protest plain on Louis's face. She knew Hutch was offering money that belonged to all of them, and Louis needed that money more than most, as he had been sending all of his shares back home to his family's ranch.

'Without at least one plane, we've got no act anymore,' Harry reminded Louis in a low, confidential tone. 'He's gotta do what he can to save at least one . . .'

The deal was struck, with the men insisting the money be paid immediately. The biplane they were owed they would collect in the morning, once they found a pilot of their own to fly it over to the winning man's property.

Earl kept a strongbox in his caravan and allowed the other members of the flying circus to stow their money and valuables in it – a necessary precaution when living life on the road. Hutch sent Ava to fetch the contents of the strongbox, and Louis and Harry accompanied her to keep her safe, just in case.

The three of them barely spoke as they ran this errand. Ava found herself full of mixed emotions: relief that the men wouldn't be taking *both* biplanes; pity for Hutch, Buzz, Louis, and Harry, who all looked deflated – Louis, in particular; and anger. Ava felt a terrible anger toward Earl for causing all of this to happen.

When they returned to the saloon, they gave every cent they had found in the strongbox to Hutch, who in turn handed the money over to the farmer. Everyone watched glumly as they counted the bills and coins.

'You're gettin' a deal, I'll have you know,' one of the farmer's friends said.

No, Ava thought. *Earl is.*

To heap injury upon insult, Earl was still too drunk to walk without stumbling and falling every few feet. Hutch and Buzz had to hook a shoulder under each of Earl's arms just to get him back to the campsite.

Later that same night, Earl snored inside the caravan as fireworks exploded in the sky. Hutch built a fire as the night's cool darkness settled around them and Ava's mother put on some hot cocoa.

The fireworks were quite pretty, brilliant bursts of green and red and white that pulsed in the sky like sporadic ethereal jellyfish. Ava, Harry, and Louis stared upward, abstractly admiring the show, but the mood had been irrevocably dampened. Buzz seemed bent on drinking his sorrows away. Hutch didn't even pretend interest in the fireworks; he lay down and promptly put his cowboy hat over his face in order to sleep.

'What'll we do now?' Louis muttered.

Harry shrugged. 'We'll have to come up with some way to do a decent stunt show using only one plane, I guess.'

'One plane instead of two also means half as many rides . . .' Louis pointed out.

'He's right,' Ava said, newly alert with the realization. 'What if we can't give as many rides as before? That's our bread and butter.'

'Maybe we can still sell the same amount; it'll just take us twice as long,' Harry said, clearly making an effort to retain some optimism.

They were quiet for a few moments. Far off in the distance, the sounds of festive hilarity could still be heard in the town square, and in the opposite direction a dog howled, perturbed by the explosions in the sky.

'My brother'll be sore,' Louis said, to no one in particular. He sighed. 'Guy works awful hard to keep things running on the ranch. He didn't approve of me runnin' off with this circus, especially not . . .' Louis hesitated, then continued: '. . . especially not once he learned I'd be spending time with Harry.' He looked down at the flames of the campfire, avoiding eye contact with the others. 'But things started to turn around between us once I started sending all that money home.'

Nobody said anything. Ava knew Hutch had just bailed out Earl with money that Louis couldn't afford to forfeit – not if he wanted to make good with his family. She felt a genuine pang for him, and a fresh wave of anger toward Earl.

'Now when I tell Guy I ain't got nothing to show for these past few weeks, he'll just say that's what I should've expected all along,' Louis concluded. 'That this is what I get for affiliatin' with the types of folks I done aligned myself with . . .'

They all knew: Louis didn't mean Earl, or transient air show types in general. Harry, if he was insulted, didn't show it. The three of them continued to sit around the campfire as the fireworks built up to a final frenzy of explosions, then petered out.

The next morning the farmer came to collect the rest of his winnings. He brought an old crop duster pilot with him, and together they took one of the biplanes, intent on flying it back to the farmer's own acreage.

Ava watched. It was both tragic and ironic that *Castor* and *Pollux* were named for twins, she thought, and now they would be separated. Unlike with her Shakespeare play, Ava could find little comedy about it. Of course – in the play, the comedy had resulted from an unexpected reunion. Ava feared there was little hope of that for their own twins.

A preliminary inspection of the two planes revealed they were in equal condition, so the farmer and the old crop duster pilot flipped a coin to decide which one to take. Ava found she was slightly relieved that they took *Castor*. If they had to take one, she guessed she was glad they had not taken *Pollux* – the plane Harry had taken her up in for the first flight of her life.

28

NEWCASTLE, CALIFORNIA
SEPTEMBER 19, 1943

Agent Bonner is certain of it now: he is being watched. Even alone in his room, he feels the prickle of eyes on him. During his first night in the boardinghouse, he thought he heard the sound of creaking outside his door. But now, on Sunday – his fourth night as a guest – he's sure he isn't imagining things. He's heard the creaking all too often and all too regularly.

Yet again he hears a soft rustling, the groan of a floorboard. He suspects it is his hostess, spying on him. Or, at the very least, straining to listen to his every cough and twitch. He can't imagine why she would spy on him, or what she wants, and yet he is sure she is.

Bonner has been restless all weekend, and Rosalind's behavior put him further on edge. Over dinner, he tested her by letting Sheriff Whitcomb's news about the punctured fuel line 'slip,' aiming to gauge her reaction. He watched her face closely and glimpsed surprise, alarm, and . . . something else he couldn't make out.

'Do you have any evidence to suggest *who* might've done such a thing?' she asked.

Bonner insinuated that he wasn't at liberty to say, and watched as she began nervously fingering the collar of her dress. Did Rosalind have an inkling who the culprit might be? Was she protecting someone? Or was she simply unsettled to think one of her neighbors *could* do such a thing? No one relished the idea of sharing her hometown with a murderer.

She didn't ask anything further and they finished the meal in silence.

Afterward, Rosalind dutifully cleared the dishes. Bonner retired to his room. Outside his window the light was slowly draining from the sky.

Now Bonner reclines on top of the neatly made bed with a pillow stuffed behind his neck, flipping through his notebook, rereading details about the case he has jotted down. Late Friday afternoon, the airplane mechanic they called in from Sacramento verified the business about the fuel line. Several questions remain: how was it cut? With what? And by whom?

Bonner turns his attention to the other evidence in the case, specifically the bodies of the men who perished in the crash. Kenichi Yamada's body was the less burned of the two and was positively identified by several people on the day of the crash. That much, at least, is straightforward. But even so, some curious details have emerged. Kenichi's body showed signs of faint bruising, and bruising suggests healing, even if the healing was brief. This in turn indicates Kenichi acquired his wounds – or some of them, at least – before the plane crash.

Bonner recalls the bruises he spotted on Louis Thorn's face when he went to his house on the day of the crash. Bonner is no expert, but the freshness of the bruises suggests the two men – Kenichi and Louis – acquired their injuries within the same general time frame. But why would Louis fight an old man? Even if Kenichi and Haruto Yamada had returned to their old property and confronted Louis Thorn and an argument erupted, it was far more likely that Louis would have had it out with Haruto – or 'Harry,' as everyone in town called him. How and why would the old man get directly involved in some kind of fistfight? Most troubling was a heavy contusion very near Kenichi's left temple; it looked as though he either fell down or someone dealt the elderly man a terrible blow to his head.

The other body – Harry's – was severely burned. This presents another puzzle. Harry's body suffered terrible fire damage, whereas Kenichi's body was only singed. They were sitting in separate cockpits, but the cockpits were not so far apart as to account for the unequal distribution of fire damage. If the suicide theory did, in fact, hold true, then it was almost as if Harry had doused himself in gasoline before taking off. Why would someone do that to himself? Then there was the question of Harry's uniform; while the body itself was charred, the uniform he was wearing was mostly singed in the manner that Kenichi's body was singed. The clothing should not have survived as well as it did.

Added to all of this is the fact that one of the two men had to have been well enough in mind and body to pilot the biplane's takeoff – airplanes didn't do that by themselves. All signs suggested that Harry Yamada had plotted a bizarre, pointless suicide, but a suicide nonetheless. And yet, Bonner can't stop thinking about the bruises on Louis Thorn's face or about Thorn's cagey reactions and transparent lies.

None of it makes any sense.

As Bonner flips through his notes, he hears the now-familiar creaking just outside his door. He freezes and suppresses his breath, listening. He feels his pulse quickening. Sure enough, the creaking comes again, and he is acutely aware of someone standing in the hall. The sound moves closer, and closer still. Is Rosalind thinking of opening the door this time? Bonner can hear her soft footfalls nervously shuffling this way and that, and swears he hears the meekest rattle of the doorknob moving under her hand. But ultimately the doorknob stops, and Bonner hears the soft groan of the floorboards as she takes one step away from the door. She has changed her mind.

Still holding his breath, Bonner finds he is oddly sorry to hear her go.

All at once, he leaps up, crosses the room, and reaches for the doorknob, yanking the door open. Just as he suspected, Rosalind stands only inches away from the doorway. She blinks in the abrupt light, startled and trapped.

'What do you want?' he asks gently.

To his surprise, she doesn't budge from where she stands. She only shakes her head. Her wide, surprised eyes never leave his. They are full of a strange, exquisite sadness.

He has an urge to touch her, to put his hands on her shoulders. It is an impulse of tenderness and reassurance, similar to the urge he had on that first day, when she showed him to his room and lingered as though she wanted something from him – some kind of comfort or kindness, or even simple attention. Now Bonner begins to reach toward her but he stops short when he notices she is dressed for bed: a white nightgown hangs on her body, and her shoulders are bare. Bonner shakes himself.

'What do you want?' he demands again, this time more forcefully. His voice surprises him, a near shout. 'Why are you watching me?'

Still no answer. She continues to blink. Her lips begin to move as though to speak, but no sound comes out. She is stymied, working to coax the words necessary to explain herself. To Bonner's discomfort, she begins to tremble, shaking as though he's abused her by shouting at her, demanding an explanation. She begins backing away, with tiny, mincing steps, down the hallway.

'I've heard you lurking outside my room,' Bonner says, a faint hint of exasperation creeping into his voice. 'I know you've been watching me. But I don't understand. I don't understand what you want. Why can't you tell me? What is it? What do you want?'

Rosalind suddenly halts in her retreat. Her entire body tenses, and she looks at him with a kind of heated glare. Bonner feels a strange sense of shame, as though *he* has been the one lurking outside *her* door, and now she is about to chastise him for it.

But everything changes in the space of a second. To Bonner's surprise, Rosalind lunges toward him. On instinct, Bonner feels his body ready itself for defense . . . until he realizes she is *not* attacking him. Her mouth is on his. Her skin is warm. He feels the breath moving through her body; within seconds it feels as though it is moving through his body, too.

As Bonner staggers backward, Rosalind staggers with him. Her hands fumble at his pants but never break their resolve. The two of them become a blur of tangled limbs.

Afterward, they lie together in Bonner's creaky double bed. Rosalind's dark curls rest in the crook of his armpit; her cheek is turned against his chest. Her eyes are open; he can feel her lashes periodically brushing against his skin.

Bonner has no idea what to make of this encounter. Mostly it was tender, but there was something almost anguished and violent in it, too. His thoughts roam the room, racing in a wide circle and returning to him again.

'How long . . .' Rosalind begins to say, but her voice catches in her throat and she gives a quick cough. Her voice has grown low and shy since their encounter. 'How long do you think you'll be in town for this investigation?' she asks.

The question hangs in the air. Under normal circumstances it would be an expected question, the kind of question a woman might ask a man she hopes to keep around – if Bonner could flatter himself to assume that's what Rosalind wants now: to prolong their time together. But Bonner also senses an unreadable element in the question's tone and delivery. Once again she seems less interested in Bonner himself and more interested in his investigation and the politics that orbit him.

'It depends,' he says, repeating his earlier response to the same question, 'on how much evidence I can turn up for my report.' He pauses. 'Someone has to account for the deaths of these two men,' he says, but as soon as the words leave his mouth, his gut tells him he wants this to be true, but it isn't.

Rosalind stiffens. She sits up with a restless air, holding the covers to her bare chest, looking around for her discarded nightgown. Bonner rolls over to his side and props his head up with one hand, frowning as he watches her. Her sudden agitation has him equally unsettled. He isn't entirely sure of what he wants – whether he wants her to stay or to go – but he doesn't like watching her move away from their warm huddle in the bed or watching her slip the thin white nightgown back over her head.

'I don't see *why*,' she replies to his assertion that someone had to account for the deaths of the Yamadas, her voice hard – angry, almost. 'American boys are dying all over the Pacific; why should we care about a couple of Japs who die here in a plane crash?'

Bonner studies Rosalind's face, taken aback by her sudden callousness. She returns his stare but does not soften. Her features are hard, her expression chilly. Bonner knows lots of folks feel that way nowadays. He is surprised, however; he didn't suspect his hostess belonged to their number.

Rosalind, now in her nightgown, stands beside the bed, holding Bonner's gaze as though deciding how much to tell him.

'If you ask me,' she says, 'I'm glad they're dead. Two less Japs to worry about.'

Her tone suggests she is finished with the conversation. With the ghost of her ugly remark still hanging in the air, she takes one more lingering look at his face – almost as if trying to memorize his features – then turns and leaves.

Agent Bonner stares at the floating white shape of her nightgown as she retreats through the doorway and down the hall. He doesn't bother to get up and close the door; he knows she will remain in her own bedroom, remote and distant, for the rest of the night. Whatever the interlude was to her, she is done with it – and him – for the time being.

After a minute, he lies back and stares at the ceiling, thinking, still disturbed by her hateful attitude toward the Japanese. She is hardly alone; hers is a popular viewpoint. *Two less Japs to worry about.* Even Reed probably would agree, even if he might phrase it more diplomatically. Bonner knows Reed has a knack for wrapping such sentiments up in the more respectable garb of patriotism.

It used to do the trick for Bonner – Reed's patriotic version of events, that is. But somewhere along the line, the rhetoric crumbled for Bonner. If Bonner was pressed to name a particular point that this happened, he would pick the day Jeanne Minami accosted him near the main entrance of the Manzanar Relocation Center.

In the years leading up to Pearl Harbor, Bonner and Reed and a handful of others led the FBI's efforts to monitor suspected Japanese spies. When it was discovered that a Japanese spy living in plain sight in Hawaii had sent critical messages through the consulate that led to the surprise attack, their work took on new importance and grew much more demanding. Suddenly, Bonner found himself knocking on countless Japanese-American doors, seizing suspicious contraband, and interviewing countless heads of household.

It was how he crossed paths with the Minami family. Fujio Minami owned a small fleet of fishing boats that he kept in the San Pedro Harbor, and lived with his family in the Japanese community on Terminal Island. When Executive Order 9066 was passed in February 1942, the FBI moved quickly to clear out this community, taking all first-generation Japanese into custody for questioning. Families of these men and other *nisei* were interned, and most of them were eventually brought to Manzanar.

Fujio Minami presented a problem for the FBI – his boats and fishing shack were outfitted with an extraordinary amount of high-powered shortwave radio equipment. He had also developed a pastime of reading about Japan's history of shoguns. He was old and his English was awful; he'd lived his whole life only speaking to other Japanese in his tight-knit community. When they asked him whom he wanted to win the war, he said, 'Japan.' Bonner wasn't entirely sure that the old man meant to say he wanted Japan to win. It seemed just as likely that Fujio thought the FBI was asking him to make a prediction based on his knowledge of Japan's military history, or perhaps was even reporting the winner of wars he'd learned about in school as a boy, as he sometimes added the names of various samurai clans, names that were lost on his interrogators. Either way, he continued to deliver the wrong answer, time and time again. The FBI promptly sent him off to a detention center in North Dakota to be kept under more rigorous watch.

Despite Fujio's poor English-speaking skills and lack of cultural assimilation, he had three very Americanized adult children: Fred, Jeanne, and Bill Minami. They had been born in America and been granted the citizenship that Fujio had all his life been denied. The oldest, Bill, was outraged to think his father was going to be sent to North Dakota and treated as a war criminal. When they interviewed Fred, asking him to explain away the abundance of radio equipment his father owned – 'He's a fisherman who can't afford to lose a boat' was all Fred would explain, shaking his head as though disgusted by their inability to grasp the obvious – he made it clear he did not intend to cooperate, and planned to start trouble.

'We'll protest,' Fred threatened. 'This is unconstitutional. You can put us in the camps, but we'll protest there, too. We have the right to free speech. You can't just shut us up.'

Fred was unusual. Almost all of the Japanese the FBI interviewed simply answered their questions and sat quietly, hoping for the whole ordeal to be over. Bonner found he had a certain measure of respect for Fred, for his demonstration of incensed behavior that was – ironically enough – most American of all. Bonner's peers did not see it the same way. Fred was in danger of being added to the growing list of enemies of the state, and shipped off to North Dakota himself.

Bonner took him aside and attempted to befriend the young man, who was only a year or two younger than Bonner himself. Bonner was sympathetic. He explained to Fred how difficult the FBI's job had become. He told Fred about Tadashi Morimura, the spy in Hawaii, how 'normal' he seemed, and how Japanese-Hawaiians had trusted him. They talked about the lives lost in Pearl Harbor, and Fred seemed every bit as grieved over the loss of American life as Bonner. By the end of one long chat in particular, Bonner had even managed to convince Fred to join the Army.

'I'm sure if you enlist, they'll ease off your father,' Bonner said. 'They're likely to send him home from North Dakota.'

Never mind that 'home' was now a camp in the desert surrounded by barbed wire; Fred was eager to see his father back with the rest of his family, healthy and unharmed.

'Are you sure?' Fred asked.

'I don't see why not,' Bonner replied. After he said it, he wasn't so sure, but Fred looked gratified, and Bonner was certain Fred Minami would not talk himself into worse trouble with the FBI

Fred signed up, and the last Bonner heard, Fred had been dispatched to Italy. He didn't give the matter much more thought – until FBI business brought him out to Manzanar one particularly fateful day. That day, as Bonner drove into the camp and got out of his car, a small ceremony was taking place near the main entrance. When he heard a lone bugler playing taps, he understood it was a ceremony to honor a fallen soldier.

He stood a short distance away to watch, curious to see how this long-standing American ritual would be conducted in one of the camps. Five families were lined up, seemingly at attention, while an Army officer delivered a folded flag into each family's hands. When the Army officer reached the fifth and final family, Bonner experienced a vague flicker of recognition. An older woman and her two adult children. He realized he was looking at what was left of the Minami family.

Before Bonner could react, he was recognized in return. Jeanne Minami, who had been standing quietly at her mother's side, looked up and spotted Bonner. All at once, her eyes filled with hatred and she began to run in his direction. Bonner was not at all prepared for the onslaught, the blows she rained down upon him as she screamed at him, 'You! You're the one! You lied to him! He enlisted because of *you*! You told him our father would be released! Now our father isn't here and my brother is dead!'

A camp guard peeled her off Bonner, dragging her back to where her startled mother still stood, holding the American flag folded into a tidy triangle. But Jeanne wasn't done. She freed herself from the guard's grip, knocked the flag from her mother's hands, and in one final shocking gesture spat on the flag where it lay in the dirt.

A gasp was heard all around. This was not the kind of behavior accepted by the Japanese community, camp or no camp. The guards at Manzanar asked whether Bonner wanted her sent to another facility – to Tule Lake, perhaps – but he said no. He didn't say so, but part of him felt Jeanne was right: he'd made Fred a false promise. He'd been almost callous in his casual reassurance, and now Fred's blood was on Bonner's hands.

After that incident, Jeanne's situation did not improve. The other evacuees – many of them still, by some miracle of faith, patriotic to America – remembered the image of her spitting on the flag. The older *issei* and younger *nisei* alike shunned her, and Jeanne became an outcast. When she was found trying to organize a protest with a small, unpopular group of rabble-rousers in the camp, the white guards, who had also taken deep offense to her outburst, did not hesitate to report her.

The last Bonner heard of her, she had been transferred from Manzanar to Tule Lake.

Bonner decided he'd had enough of fieldwork and put in a request for desk duty, which he knew he would be granted on account of its undesirability. He was still horrified by what had happened in Pearl Harbor, but he didn't know what to think anymore about Executive Order 9066. He wanted to sit in an office with only the paper version of Japanese evacuees around him. He felt he couldn't cause any further harm that way, and he'd still be doing his duty to America, to the FBI – and even to Reed, for that matter, who daily tried to force Bonner to agree that the Minami family was troubled and that for all they knew Old Man Minami might really be a spy after all.

Now, as he drifts off to sleep in his room in Rosalind MacFarlane's boardinghouse, the images in Bonner's brain begin to merge: Rosalind's disgusted face as she said *Two less Japs to worry about*, and Jeanne's face as she accused Bonner of deceiving and ultimately killing her brother. There is some quality both faces have in common, Bonner realizes – something that goes beyond simple anger. But as the faces continue to merge together, Bonner can't quite put his finger on the commonality he is sure exists that ties these two women. He is too tired, he decides, and allows himself to slip into the dark void that is, by contrast, a comfort.

29

EARL SHAW'S FLYING CIRCUS
SANTA ROSA, CALIFORNIA, JULY 13, 1940

They left Sonoma and moved a little north, camping on the outskirts of Santa Rosa. Despite losing one of their two biplanes, the barnstorming group nonetheless pressed on, determined to salvage the flying circus. Louis and Harry attempted to come up with a new stunt routine using only one plane, hoping that if they made it daring enough, they could attract as much attention as before. But Hutch and Buzz found themselves at a more awkward impasse. While no one mentioned it directly, everyone was acutely aware of the fact that a flying circus with only one biplane only needed one pilot.

Harry immediately proposed a solution for this dilemma: he wanted to attempt a car-to-airplane transfer.

'Not only will we need a steady pilot, but we'll need a steady driver,' he pointed out.

Buzz volunteered to drive, and the five of them – Buzz, Hutch, Ava, Harry, and Louis – tuned up Earl's old Model A. They tried the stunt out in a wide, flat field early one morning, before the summer heat thinned the air.

'Drive 'er at an even pace,' Hutch advised Buzz.

'Hah, easier said than done over these rutted fields. Here goes nothin'!'

Hutch took off in *Pollux*, circled, and came in for a low, slow flyover as Buzz drove along in tandem.

'*Now*, Eagle! Lower 'er down!'

Up in the air with Hutch, Louis threw down the ladder they'd made out of rope and wood from a hardware store. It unfurled with a clatter and trailed behind the Stearman like a strand of long hair blowing in the wind, the bottom rung five feet or so above the roof of the Model A.

'All right, Crane!' Buzz hollered. 'Time to fly!'

Harry climbed up out of the truck's bed, then onto the roof of the cab. He raised his hands in the air, ready to catch the ladder.

Watching from a distance, Ava held her breath.

'That boy is plumb crazy,' Cleo commented, likewise breathless and riveted.

'He's just trying to make up for Earl's loss,' Ava said.

'Hah – maybe, but that's not the whole of it, and you know it,' Cleo said. 'That boy's a born daredevil if there ever was one. Graceful, and never one drop of fear in him. He's got a real rare gift.'

Ava was surprised. She had never thought her mother paid Harry much mind, and she was curious to know more about her mother's opinion. But Cleo had already returned her gaze to the skies.

Just then, a hooting and hollering sounded. Ava looked back and saw that Harry had caught the ladder. Once it was clear that Harry'd gotten a grip on the lower rungs, Hutch pulled up on the stick and the Stearman lifted up, up, up, and away from the ground. For his part, Harry began to climb the ladder with easy, aerobatic gusto.

Ava realized: her mother was right. Harry was a natural. There was absolutely no fear in him. No fear at all.

Once they perfected their strategy and execution, their single-plane-stunt barnstorming show wasn't half-bad. Louis and Harry worked out a few additional stunts to include in their wing-walking routines, often performing simultaneously, one of them hanging off each wing.

But it was true that when it came time to sell rides, the flying circus wasn't able to take as many people up for scenic tours as they had previously. It simply took too long; during the extra time it took to take the same number of people up as before, many spectators changed their minds, wandered off to eat and socialize, and decided to give it a pass after all.

Earl in particular was frustrated by the futility of the situation. His remedy for the missing revenue was to change the way the circus did business – in particular, their patterns of travel and advertisement. Ava had already felt that Earl was throwing caution to the wind when he began printing handbills to draw more spectators. Now he had more handbills printed than ever before, and ordered them to be flagrantly plastered all over the main streets of every town they visited: *COME AND SEE EARL SHAW'S DEATH-DEFYING FLYING CIRCUS STUNT ACT!!!* the handbills shouted at passersby. He'd also discovered that the earlier they announced their arrival, the more people would venture out to see the show. Earl often sent Ava, Harry, and Louis on ahead to the next town to paste up handbills a week or so in advance of their performances there.

'Builds the suspense!' Earl insisted. 'Gives these poor farming families something exciting to look forward to!'

In addition to all this, they traveled closer and closer to San Francisco than they ever had before, and moved more slowly from town to town. Over the past few years, the flying circus had always kept brief engagements, moving on quickly and quietly. Now, as July gave way to August and finally September, Earl persuaded them to linger in the small towns that circled the San Francisco Bay, from the east side near Oakland, around to the little villages dotted around Marin County in the north and back again. They began to make a sort of familiar circuit, a horseshoe pattern around the bay.

'I dunno,' Hutch said, shaking his head. 'We oughta be keepin' our heads down in these parts . . . There's Navy folks near the bay, and we're cuttin' it awful close to the city now.'

'City folks pay more money!' Earl urged. 'They gossip to their neighbors and friends! After all, there are no riches in anonymity!'

In some ways Earl was right: attendance ticked up noticeably. The crowds grew thicker and thicker. Folks remembered them, even began chanting out demands for particular stunts. They had only one airplane, but by stirring up enough fuss, they were making a living again as July turned into August and then September.

30

EARL SHAW'S FLYING CIRCUS
SAN RAFAEL, CALIFORNIA, SEPTEMBER 29, 1940

Finally, toward the end of September, the barnstorming group moved closer than ever to San Francisco when they planned to perform throughout a series of little towns in Marin County – Fairfax, San Anselmo, and Larkspur. While preparing to put on a show in the little town of San Rafael, Harry had gotten so accustomed to the car-to-plane transfer he was yearning for a new thrill.

'What if . . . what if I got *back into* the car?' he asked the others.

'You mean do a transfer to the plane and then eventually climb down to the car?' Hutch asked.

'Sure,' Harry replied. 'It could be my entry and my exit from the stage, so to speak.' He paused and looked around at Hutch, Buzz, and Louis. Ava was only a short distance away, gathering dry weeds near their campsite for kindling, but she knew he was avoiding her glare. He already knew she hated everything to do with the car-to-plane transfer. *It was a terrible, harebrained idea*, she'd told him. *Too dangerous.*

Buzz shook his head and chuckled. 'Well, in order to reverse the transfer, Hutch and I would have to sync up again, and I'd have to drive *real* careful-like . . .'

'Can you do it?' Harry demanded.

Buzz whistled and shrugged. 'I can try. When do you want to take a swipe at it?'

'Today,' Harry replied.

'During today's *show*? After we've drawn a crowd? What if it goes pear-shaped?' Louis said, dismayed. 'You don't even want to practice it first?'

Harry shook his head. 'Let's do it!' he insisted. 'Why hide what we're up to from the audience? Let's tell 'em this is the first time we ever tried this one. They'll get a kick outta it! It'd be something unique!'

Ava was annoyed by Harry's cocky nonchalance. Of course, when Harry proposed his plan to Earl, Earl was thrilled and unequivocally all for it. They had come nearly full circle to the first bargain Harry had made with Ava's stepfather, the day he proclaimed he would wing walk, given the chance.

It was September in San Rafael, and therefore still warm, dry, and sunny, but Ava found herself even sweatier than one might expect as she watched the boys' barnstorming show that day. She knew she was holding her breath for the finale, when Harry was planning to climb back down the trailing rope ladder and into the open bed of the Model A. She had visions of him missing the truck and dropping onto the open field from a fast-moving airplane, only to break his legs.

Earl shouted his proud announcements to an only slightly less breathless audience: '*I assure you, ladies and gentlemen, this is the first time our stuntman has ever performed such a feat! Will it spell disaster? Or daring delight? Let us watch, and find out . . . !*'

Ava shielded her eyes, chewed her lip, and scrutinized the sky as Hutch swept in low over the Model A. The biplane was going much faster than the truck at first; Buzz jammed on the accelerator as he tried to keep pace. Ava winced to hear the roar of the engine. She knew the truck was an unreliable relic, hardly fit for Harry's stunt. Yet, with Buzz's determined handling, the Model A gave a hiccup and a spurt of sudden speed and shot forward.

Harry quickly crawled down to the bottom rung of the ladder, his weight making the whole thing flap more slowly but heavily, moving in deep waves through the air. Ava couldn't watch; she squeezed her eyes shut. A moment passed, and she opened them just in time to see Harry release the ladder. He leapt from where he gripped the rope, and *plop!* – he landed in the moving truck bed. Everyone in the audience cheered.

'*Aaaaaaand the daredevil lives to tell the tale, ladies and gentlemen!*' Earl cried. '*Let's hear a round of applause for our brave stuntman!*'

The cheering swelled to a crescendo.

'He dared to spit in the face of certain death, folks! Surely the least you can do is dare yourself to go up for a lovely, pleasant, scenic ride! That's right! Get all the satisfaction of a thrill, with none of the danger! Safest ride in town! Step right up, and give your money to Lovely Lofty Ava there! She'll get you on your way . . . !'

Ava sighed a huge breath of relief. She still found it annoying, however, that Harry was so utterly compelled to put his life on the line like that. She was grateful for Buzz's determined driving.

She had just made a mental note to remind Harry of his good luck in having Hutch for a pilot and Buzz for a driver, when Ava noticed a man in a dark suit approach Earl. The man stood out among all the other people gathered in the field due to that suit, which was much too dark and heavy for a hot Indian summer's day. Ava scanned the crowd and saw that a second man in a dark suit was not far behind. She squinted her eyes to watch and strained her ears to listen.

'You the owner of that biplane?' the first man demanded of Earl. He pointed in the sky, declining to introduce himself.

Earl wheeled about and looked the man over, clearly startled by the man's formal suit. 'Begging your pardon, sir – who wants to know?'

'The United States Department of Commerce,' the second man replied, catching up to his partner and chiming in. 'I assume you know your pilot is in violation of safety regulations, flying low like that, and performing stunts over a crowd?'

'We also need to see your licenses and your permit for public assembly,' the first man added.

Ava watched this exchange and read the truth in Earl's frown. She continued to strain to listen in on Earl's conversation but moved more slowly now, knowing she was selling rides that would never be given.

Earl had made a fatal mistake when he ignored Hutch's warning. He had gambled again; they *all* had, really. But more important: they had lost.

31

Earl had wanted to garner as much attention for the act as they possibly could. Unfortunately he had gotten the attention he craved, and then some. Catching the eye of the Department of Commerce in particular earned the flying circus a citation and a hefty fine. *Pollux*, the remaining biplane, was to be impounded until Earl could resolve the citation in court and pay the corresponding fine.

'Where are they taking *Pollux*?' Ava asked, watching as men came to collect the flying circus's remaining Stearman. The men were loading it onto a flat, wide trailer bed and chaining it down. They were going to transport the plane on the trailer bed, not fly it, Ava realized.

'Somewhere in San Francisco, I heard,' Louis replied. 'I guess . . . that's the end of our flying circus act . . .'

'Let's not get ahead of ourselves,' Harry argued. 'Earl can be pretty resourceful when he wants to. Maybe he'll think of something. Maybe he's even got something up his sleeve.'

'Hah, 'up his sleeve,'' Ava murmured. 'Speaking of that . . . I don't suppose you know a magic trick to make a disappearing airplane reappear?' It was a joke, but her heart was only half in it, and it came out sounding flat.

'Not yet,' Harry replied, straining to maintain a positive note. 'But I'm workin' on it.'

He had managed a jovial tone, but no one laughed. Together the three of them watched the Stearman being hauled away with a sick feeling, as though the biplane were a faithful old horse being sold to the glue factory.

Unsure what to do, the now-airplaneless barnstormers continued to travel together. Since the plane had been impounded in San Francisco, Earl insisted it would be best to remain nearby: by staying in the city, they would stand the best chance of getting the Stearman back. He convinced the group to cross the Golden Gate, promising to find 'inexpensive accommodations' for them.

Once over the bridge they headed to the wharf, circling around the Embarcadero, under and past the Bay Bridge, until they reached a gloomy stretch of industrial settlement along the shore of the bay that faced east. Across the water, the lights of Oakland glimmered, while all around them stevedores operated the great dry docks that hauled entire transoceanic liners and pan-Pacific cargo ships out of the water for repairs.

'There can't be a place to camp the caravan around *here*,' Ava complained quietly to her mother, but Cleo only put a finger to her lips and shook her head, not wanting to anger Earl. Despite the fact that he was the one to blame, Earl was the sort of creature who, when down and out, snapped unexpectedly, and with sharp teeth.

As they ventured farther into the industrial bowels of San Francisco, Earl claimed he knew a fellow, a longshoreman whose acquaintanceship Earl never bothered to explain. After asking around at the dry docks, he found the gentleman in question, and the longshoreman directed them to a disused warehouse.

'No one will bother ya there, and I'll even offer ya a discount,' the longshoreman said. He proceeded to accept a few greenbacks from Earl, behaving as though he owned the warehouse, though Ava was not entirely convinced this was the case.

However, the warehouse *was* empty, just as the longshoreman had guaranteed, and it had cost them even less than borrowing a farmer's field, so there was that. It was an enormous, echoing cavern of a place, large enough for them to park the caravan inside and even large enough for them to light an open fire without the hazard of smoke inhalation. Though huge, it was rickety, red with rust. It smelled of mildewed tarps, diesel, rotted wood, and putrefying kelp. The tin roof was riddled with holes; during the daytime, light shone in like a series of artificial stars.

Earl smiled and attempted a grand, conciliatory note.

'I realize it's hardly a fit place for a lady,' Earl said to Cleo, 'but if I can just buy some time to come up with a plan, I'm certain I'll have us out of here and back on the open road in no time . . .'

Hutch, Buzz, Louis, and Harry had it the worst. Sleeping inside a caravan parked in a damp warehouse was one thing. Sleeping on the packed dirt of the warehouse floor was another matter.

'Christ only knows what kinds of diseases these rats got. You two young'uns ought to put your bedrolls in the truck bed of the Model A and sleep there,' Hutch advised Louis and Harry, after noting the number of rats that skittered across the warehouse floor during their first night. A few days later, Buzz and Hutch began sleeping elsewhere, closer to the heart of the city's downtown. Buzz found he could usually charm his way into the warm beds of various ladies (and happily did so), while Hutch was content to board in the old rooming houses left over from the old forty-niner days.

Still, the group reconvened a few times a week, holding their breath for the moment when Earl might announce a definitive plan to get the Stearman back.

Unceremoniously, the day came and went for Earl to go down to the courthouse to address the citation the flying circus had been given.

Ava had assumed that Earl would remind everyone of the date and require the whole lot of them to go with him: Earl was always one for a loud parade cheering his name. At the very least, Ava thought Earl would demand her mother be at his side, as Earl typically instructed Cleo to dress to the nines whenever he thought it might help curry favor with those who mattered.

So it was a surprise to Ava when Earl didn't remind anyone of the date, and went alone. The only clue he'd even gone came at suppertime, when he stared into the campfire they'd built and muttered to Ava's mother,

'Can you believe . . . they wouldn't lower that fine one red cent . . .'

'What was that, dear?' Ava's mother asked, and Earl slowly, grudgingly described a visit to the courthouse as well as to several different bureaucratic offices dotted about the city. According to Earl, none of them would take pity on him or the plight of his flying circus.

Ava exchanged a look with both Louis and Harry. Sure enough, Earl had been absent all morning and afternoon, but no one had suspected he had been off seeing about official business. He had come back stinking of cigar smoke and cheap beer. Ava had simply assumed he'd been at a long day of his usual poker games.

Finally, a week or so later, the moment they were all waiting for arrived: Earl had hit upon a plan. He waited until they had all gathered: Ava and her mother, Louis and Harry, and Buzz and Hutch.

'I'm afraid the only solution to get the Stearman out of impound is to pool our money once again,' Earl announced, opaquely referring to the incident in Sonoma. Earl knew better than to bring it up too directly; he was hardly the hero of that episode, and he was, in short, asking for a donation to their group cause now.

'I dunno, Boss . . .' Hutch said. 'Do you really think that'll work? Will it be enough? And we'll have enough to get back out on the road? What's to stop 'em from keeping an eye out for us and issuing us another citation?'

'I'm afraid it's our only chance,' Earl answered. 'Unless you already have another job lined up?'

Hutch shook his head. Working as an instructor had never suited Hutch; he needed the open road. The only other job he'd settled into was driving cattle – but once the Depression hit, ranchers had all been too hard up to pay a decent wage anymore.

Earl saw his cue to continue. 'I took the liberty of counting what's in the strongbox,' he said, 'and it appears, between *all* of us, we have just enough to pay the impound fee . . .'

Louis raised an eyebrow at this. That *was* suspicious: what were the odds? 'I don't know,' he piped up, shaking his head. 'What if we hand over the money to the impound officers but they don't budge, or they claim it's not enough? Some of us *need* that money . . .'

Ava cast a sympathetic glance in Louis's direction. She knew the losses Louis had taken during their stay in Sonoma had caused some sort of row with his brother.

'It *does* seem like a gamble,' Hutch said. He cleared his throat and frowned – the sign that Hutch was about to consent to something. 'But, hell, I figure we'd better go all in with this thing. I'm in with my share.'

'I'm in, too,' Buzz said. He looked around and shrugged. 'Flying for this outfit has been the most fun a fella can have. Might as well try to turn every last stone to keep 'er going . . .'

The group was silent. Hutch and Buzz were in. Louis was on the fence. Now all heads swiveled in Harry's direction.

'Well, Crane?' Buzz prompted. 'Looks like you gotta cast your vote.'

Harry frowned, looking thoughtful. He glanced around the circle, from face to face. He paused for a moment when he got to Louis, a flicker of apology in his expression.

'I say we at least let Earl try,' Harry agreed in a quiet voice. 'If there's a chance we can get the plane back, well, then I guess the truth is, I want to know we tried.'

'That's the spirit!' Earl said.

Lower and more confidentially to Louis, Harry said, 'I don't want to put you in a pickle, Louis, but shouldn't we give it a chance? This is the best thing that's ever happened to us. I know you had plans for that money, but there never woulda been any money to keep in the first place if it weren't for Earl and Buzz and Hutch – and the planes, right?'

Louis said nothing. He only looked a little gray and defeated. He swallowed.

'Are you in, Eagle?' Buzz asked him directly.

Louis hesitated for a moment, then nodded.

32

It was decided that Earl would go to court to pay the fine; then – assuming he was given the all-clear – Hutch would go with Earl to the impound yard to reclaim *Pollux*. The rest of them would pack up their campsite and relocate to an agreed-upon location outside the city. Earl suggested an empty field they'd discovered outside the town of Petaluma. They had performed there earlier during the summer, and it had seemed to have no owner to claim it, so it would make for the perfect place to camp while awaiting Earl and Hutch's triumphant arrival.

'You'll need a head start,' Earl surmised. 'The five of you' – meaning Cleo, Ava, Buzz, Louis, and Harry – 'should go on ahead, and once we have the Stearman back, Hutch and I can zip right on up to join you.'

It seemed reasonable. Ava was nervous. She could tell Louis wasn't happy about any of it. But then . . . what choice did any of them have? Earl's way appeared to be the only way.

So the group did as Earl said: they set off, while Hutch and Earl stayed back.

'With any luck, we'll be along in two days,' Earl assured them. He kissed Ava's mother on the cheek with a terrible, loud smack. 'We'll come swooping in like a bird, my love, to save the day!'

They said a temporary goodbye to Earl and Hutch and headed north again, recrossing the majestic Golden Gate and puttering along the hilly highways in the direction of Petaluma. Soon enough, they found their way back to the empty field Earl had named. Its familiar features welcomed them, and they set about making camp.

'Don't worry too much about setting up the campsite,' Cleo advised everyone in a bright tone. 'Why, if all goes well, Earl and Hutch might be here as soon as tomorrow morning! We'll want to push on as soon as they join up, so don't unpack anything you don't want to pack back up!'

The next day came and went without ceremony, and there was no sign of the Stearman, Hutch, or Earl.

'I'm sure they're just finagling the details,' Buzz said, patting Cleo's hand. He sounded optimistic, but not entirely convinced. Ava raised an eyebrow at him, but Buzz was impervious. 'They'll be here soon.'

Another day passed with no sign of the plane or either man. And another, and yet still another.

'Do you think we've camped in the wrong field, and they don't know where to find us?' Cleo asked, anxious.

Ava wanted to say, *Perhaps*, but the lie got stuck in her throat.

Finally, five days and four nights into their stay outside of Petaluma, Ava glimpsed a figure steadily making its way along the dirt road toward them. When she recognized the familiar cowboy amble, she cried out.

'Hutch!' she cried. 'Everyone! Hutch is here!'

The awaiting group popped their heads up like a pack of curious prairie dogs, then dropped what they were each in the middle of doing and made their way toward Hutch as he approached.

Excited, Ava threw down the book she had been reading and stumbled to her feet. She was compelled to break into a trot, but before she could, a second thought overcame her, sobering her up. She surveyed the camp and saw Louis experience the same halt and hesitation. What was Hutch doing there alone, on foot?

'Oh, no . . .' Ava murmured. 'No . . . he wouldn't have . . .'

At the same time, a voice within her said, *Yes. He would.*

She cast a quick look around and saw Louis, also halting in his step, also plainly thinking what Ava was thinking. They locked eyes. A wave of mutual understanding passed between them. Everyone else had run on ahead. Ava and Louis brought up the rear. They walked side by side, close together. For the briefest of seconds, Ava felt Louis take her hand, and she gave it a heart-sickened squeeze.

'Got lucky – most of the time – tryin' to hitch my way up here,' Hutch said once they had gotten him water, two eggs, and a crust of bread. 'But that last stretch, I had to walk the whole way . . . I know all o' you been waitin' . . . Must've been somethin' awful, all that waitin' and wonderin' . . .'

Cleo bustled about, coping with her worried, distraught feelings by keeping busy. She automatically struck up a fire and hung a pot of coffee over the flames out of a mixture of instinct and habit. When it was ready, Hutch accepted a cup gratefully.

'Thank you,' he said. He took a deep sip and surveyed the faces all around him with apologetic caution. 'You might want to find a nip of something stronger yourselves for what I'm about to tell ya.'

'Just tell it to us straight,' Louis demanded. 'What happened with Earl? Where is he?'

'Well . . .' Hutch snorted. 'Where is he? That's an awful good question.'

Ava shook her head, knowing and incredulous all at the same time. 'You mean you don't know? At *all*?'

Hutch shrugged. 'He went off to pay that fine at the court, just like he said. Wanted to go alone, he said. I thought that was all right. But then a few hours went by and he never come back. More hours later and the sun went down and I ain't never heard a peep from him. I got to wonderin'. Well' – Hutch paused and sighed, the wind in his chest rattling like a tired animal – 'the next morning, still nothing. And the same for the afternoon. So I decided to start looking for him. I asked around, 'Where would a man go who has gotten this kinda citation and where would he pay his fine? Blah, blah, blah . . .' And, well, it turns out, the answer was . . . nowhere.'

'*Nowhere?*' Harry repeated, his eyebrows raised in scrutiny.

'Nowhere,' Hutch confirmed, nodding. 'At least, that's where Earl went.

I played detective a little, following Earl's footsteps around the city as best I could. Why, his citation was with the Department of Commerce; from all I could find out, it shoulda been a simple bureaucratic matter. But turns out there was a bigger problem keeping the Stearman in the impound. The more I dug around, I found the reason he couldn't get it out is on account of how he's been borrowing from the banks against that plane – against *both* the biplanes, as a matter of fact – even the one he ain't got no more, an' he started borrowin' almost from the first day the deed got transferred to his name. His version of what was happening with the Stearman was a lie. He weren't ever going to be able to get that plane outta the impound, not ever, not with all that money he owed. The Stearman ain't even in San Francisco no more: it's been moved to Sacramento, nearest the banks where he borrowed the most money, and from what I can tell, ain't no way anybody gonna give that plane back to Earl at any price.' Hutch paused, and considered. 'He got up that morning and said he was goin' to court, but he never done anything of the sort . . .'

The group around Hutch could not have been more wide-eyed if they had been a herd of deer surprised by the headlamps of a large truck.

'Well, then,' Ava said, her voice trembling with anger, 'tell us where you think Earl *did* go. It's perfectly obvious he's run off with the money, but do you have any clue at all where he might be?'

'None,' Hutch said, his voice sorrowful. 'But I got to pestering the folks at the records offices, and I'll tell ya what I found out about where he's *been* . . .'

They all listened as Hutch began to unravel the many aliases of the man they had known as Earl Shaw. It turned out he'd changed both his profession and his name a number of times over the years. 'Earl Sherman' had long ago been a schoolteacher in a small town outside Madison, Wisconsin, but had been run out of town when it was discovered he'd been skimming off the school treasury. A very different Earl – 'Earl Starelli' – had later surfaced in Chicago, where with his newly cultivated moustache he made a living as a door-to-door salesman for a life insurance company. There, too, Earl ran into some trouble when he was accused of selling policies he later never filed and pocketing the money. Earl's trail went cold for some time after that, but many years later grew hot again when Earl took the trouble to put in for a legal change of name and finally became 'Earl Shaw.' He had migrated a great distance from his Midwest origins by that point – all the way to New Mexico, Arizona, and California – and had joined a traveling carnival as a tonic salesman.

'I reckon you know the rest,' Hutch said, throwing an apologetic grimace in Cleo's direction. Ava turned to regard her mother. Cleo looked shaken and slightly pale . . . but, Ava noted, not surprised.

'I reckon we better go start lookin' for work elsewhere,' Buzz said.

Hutch nodded. 'Considering Earl not only left us with no airplane, an' made off with nearly everything we had, we shoulda started lookin' for other work weeks ago.'

'Will you . . . be all right?' Buzz asked Cleo.

She attempted a weak smile.

'We'll find a way.'

'What about you two? Eagle? Crane?' Buzz asked Louis and Harry.

Harry looked thoughtful. 'I suppose we'll go back home,' he said.

Louis said nothing. His expression had not changed since Hutch came ambling along the dirt road to find them and give them the news. Now, as the group's attention fell more directly on him, Ava noticed his temples and jaw flexing and realized he was livid.

'Louis?' Harry prodded, seemingly oblivious to Louis's quiet fury. 'I guess we'll go back home, won't we?'

Louis glared at Harry, and Ava got the distinct feeling that Louis was about to punch Harry in the nose. Suddenly, as though to subvert the impulse, he stood up and began storming off across the field. By now dusk had fallen, and Ava watched his shape disappearing into the waning light. She got up to hurry after him but realized she wasn't alone: Harry was alongside her, both of them intent on chasing Louis down.

Feeling the two of them close on his heels, Louis whirled around.

'*You!* I shouldn'ta listened to *you*,' he said, spitting his words at Harry. 'It ain't like you even needed that money; plenty more where that came from, as far as you're concerned. And if there ain't enough o' what you need, you'll just steal it from a neighbor, I suppose!' Louis turned away and his voice dropped to a mutter. Ava thought she could make out 'Just like the rest o' your back-stabbin' kind . . .' Alarmed, Ava glanced at Harry, but Harry didn't say anything.

'Louis,' Ava said, 'it's not Harry's fault this happened.'

But Louis was already stalking away again. This time Harry and Ava let him go and didn't follow.

The next morning they woke up to find Louis had packed up his belongings and left for good.

33

NEWCASTLE, CALIFORNIA
SEPTEMBER 20, 1943

Agent Bonner reaches up to knock on the now-familiar screen door of the former Yamada ranch house.

Over the weekend, it nagged at him: Cleo Shaw supposedly resided on the property – along with her daughter, Ava Brooks – and Bonner had not so much as laid eyes on the woman. He telephoned several times to arrange a meeting. At first, Bonner had the impression Louis Thorn was giving him the runaround. This only made Bonner more determined. After Bonner insinuated he would drop by unexpectedly, Louis relented, conferred with Ava and her mother, and appointed a time for Bonner to come to the house the following afternoon.

Bonner knocks again, and the screen door rattles in its frame. When the door behind it opens, he immediately glimpses a bob of red hair.

'Mother's in the front parlor,' Ava says to Bonner, in lieu of a formal greeting. She leans forward at the waist to push the screen door open for the agent. 'You can talk to her there if you need to interview her for your report. I've put some iced tea out.'

With an automatic hand, Bonner removes his fedora, and Ava leads the way to the sitting room where Bonner talked with Louis on the day of the crash. He sees a large glass pitcher of iced tea, along with four glasses, laid out on a tray on the coffee table. Four glasses: Bonner peers around the room and realizes both Louis and Ava intend to join him for this interview. It feels like they want to protect Ava's mother . . . but from what?

Bonner's eyes land on Cleo Shaw. His first observation is an obvious one: Cleo Shaw is strikingly beautiful, the kind of woman whom men whistle at in the streets. With her dark hair, red lips, and curvy figure, she looks a little like a screen siren. But on second glance Bonner notices other things: her fingernails are bitten to the quick and her hand quivers when she reaches for her glass of tea. When the ice cubes rattle a little too loudly against the glass, she thinks better of the gesture and returns the glass to the tray without taking a sip. What, Bonner thinks, could have possibly put this woman on edge in such a manner? He can't work out why or how she could be involved in the Yamadas' crash – unless, perhaps, it somehow affected her stay on the property.

'A pleasure to finally meet you, Mrs Shaw,' Bonner says now, bending over for a brief handshake. He sits down on the settee opposite hers. Ava sits next to her mother and Louis perches in a nearby straight chair.

'Pleasure,' she replies. 'But please call me Cleo.'

'That's right.' Bonner nods, taking out his notebook to make the interview official. 'Ava mentioned you're seeking a divorce from your husband . . . if it's not too indelicate of me to say.'

'No . . . it's fine,' Cleo replies. 'No offense taken. And I *do* want a divorce.'

'If only you can find him,' Bonner prompts.

At this, Cleo gives a tiny wince. 'Yes.'

'When was the last time you saw Earl?'

'Oh . . . I thought Ava had already told you that.'

'I did,' Ava confirms. Her tone is that of a watchdog.

'I've found it's often useful to ask the same questions of different witnesses. You'd be surprised how memories differ, and the truth is usually somewhere in between.'

'It's all right,' Cleo says. She touches her daughter's hand lightly. 'The agent is just doing his job.' She takes a breath and turns back to Bonner. 'The last time I saw Earl . . . well, it would have to be when Earl abandoned us almost three years ago. He got into quite a lot of debt and ran out on us, more or less . . .'

'That's around the same time your husband lost the second biplane?'

215

Cleo nods. 'It was impounded. He'd been taking loans out against the planes – real loans, from the banks and everything. I . . . well, I didn't know.'

'You must have been pretty near destitute at that point,' Bonner observes.

'I'd say we were.'

'And that's when the Yamadas took you in?'

Cleo throws a nervous look at Ava, but Bonner can't read its meaning.

'Yes,' she answers. 'We didn't stay here in the house or anything like that. But, yes . . . Mr Yamada was incredibly generous and welcomed us here on his property.'

'I believe your daughter mentioned you both live in a caravan of some sort?'

'Yes,' Cleo says, nodding. 'That caravan was our home while traveling around with the flying circus, and Mr Yamada allowed us to tow it here and to live on the property. He was so kind, and sympathetic . . . He paid us for our work in the orchards, and he and his wife let us use their kitchen and bathroom as we needed. They . . . they really saved us when we had nowhere to go . . .'

Bonner mulls this over. Something is amiss. Cleo Shaw sounds especially sincere in her gratitude, which makes him doubt his earlier theory: that she might've participated in sabotaging the Stearman to cause the crash that killed Kenichi and Harry Yamada. At the same time, Cleo Shaw's nervous demeanor, the way Ava and Louis hover around her, as though she were made of porcelain and might break . . . Things don't add up.

A stray thought occurs to Bonner.

'Would you mind if I took a look at your caravan?' he asks.

'Well, I, for one, would,' Ava interjects.

Bonner gives her a surprised look, full of new suspicion.

'It's an awfully small space, Agent Bonner,' Ava continues. 'You're essentially asking to see a couple of ladies' *bedrooms*.'

'Well, I don't mean to offend, but—'

But before Bonner can mount a proper defense, he is interrupted by the ringing of a telephone. The abrupt, shrill sound silences them all.

'I'll answer that,' Ava offers, a tight, close-lipped smile on her face. She crosses the sitting room toward the front hall. They can just see a glimpse of her back as she reaches into a little alcove and lifts the receiver.

'Hello?' she speaks into the phone. 'Yes . . . one moment, please.'

She turns back and leans her head into the room.

'It's for you,' she says.

Bonner realizes she means *him*. In a daze, Bonner rises and crosses over to where Ava stands in the front hall, holding the receiver out for him to take it.

'Hello?' he says. 'This is Agent Bonner.'

'*Bonner! I hoped we could find you there!*' an eager male voice says over the line. Bonner recognizes the vaguely adolescent timbre of Deputy Henderson. '*I was going to drive over but thought this might be quicker. Sheriff Whitcomb wants to talk to you here, in the office. There's been some important news regarding your case.*'

'What is it?'

'*He'd rather discuss it here,*' Henderson says. '*Anyway, if you could get down here as soon as possible . . .*'

34

THORN PROPERTY
NOVEMBER 17, 1940

For weeks, Louis received messages from Harry, all of which he ignored. He wasn't sure *why* Harry sent them – Louis had said some pretty awful things that day in Petaluma; nevertheless, Harry sent messages every which way he could. He sent them by mail. He sent his younger sister, Mae, to find Louis when he went to town. He had Joe, the bartender down at Murphy's Saloon, pass them along whenever Louis stopped in for a drink. Finally, Harry began hand-delivering them himself. He would turn up unannounced, knocking on the Thorns' front door – which caused a stir among the younger children, who had never seen a member of the 'mysterious Jap family' set foot on Thorn property.

Louis was still angry. He wasn't sorry he'd yelled at Harry. He was sorry, however, that he hadn't taken the time to say a proper goodbye to Ava. He wondered where she was and whether she and her mother were all right. Earl had certainly done them all a terrible turn, but Ava and her mother especially. They depended on Earl – Earl had always made certain of it. Louis wondered if Harry knew more than he did about Ava's whereabouts; he'd have to swallow his pride if he wanted to discover the answer to that one.

'Whatever that Jap wants from you, you best square it with him and keep him off our property,' Louis's older brother, Guy, warned in a quiet voice. 'It's an insult for him to be on our land, and if he keeps it up, I'll be forced to get my shotgun.'

The last letter Harry had dropped off – accepted at the front door by Louis's younger brother Clyde and swiftly passed along to Louis – had included an invitation for dinner at the Yamadas' home and named a date and time.

Louis took the letter out of the envelope, licked a pencil, and scribbled, *I'll be there but I ain't staying for supper. I'm only going to see what you want so we can be done with it. – L.*

He gave the letter back to Clyde and told him to take his brother Ernest and run the letter over to the Yamada house. The boys looked at Louis wide-eyed but were clearly burning with curiosity to see the neighboring acreage. Off they ran, and Louis had nothing else to do but wait for the appointed day.

Three days later, the time had come. Louis was on his way to the Yamadas' farmhouse when he stopped short, shocked by something he saw. Being that their acreage was adjacent, Louis had opted not to use the main road or the Yamadas' long dirt drive. Instead, he cut through the back side where the two properties connected, crossing the small stream where, so many years ago, he had once played in secret with Harry. Louis pushed those memories away; his heart was set on telling Harry to leave him in peace. After that, Louis never wanted to speak to him again.

But as he made his way through the Yamada orchards, past the barn, approaching the house from behind, something he glimpsed there brought him up short, stunned: Earl Shaw's caravan.

At first, Louis only froze, puzzled. Then, slowly, he advanced in the direction of the parked caravan and raised a tentative hand to knock. The door to the caravan flew open and there she was, looking surprisingly fresh and happy.

'Louis!' Ava smiled.

Louis only blinked. He took in the sight of Ava: her gleaming red hair, her shining eyes. And for the third time since Louis had met her, she was wearing a dress.

'What are you doing here?' he blurted out.

'Well, nice to see you, too,' she replied in a playful, sarcastic tone.

'Hello, Louis,' came another voice. Cleo Shaw emerged and, exiting the caravan, turned to her daughter. 'Good to see you again. Ava? I think it's time we ought to go up to the house now.'

'Of course.'

Louis realized the obvious: Ava and her mother were living in the caravan on the Yamada property, and they had *all* been invited to dinner. Cleo walked on ahead, leaving the two young people behind to chat.

'Why . . . why didn't Harry tell me sooner?' he asked as he and Ava walked in the direction of the house.

'I asked him not to. I wanted it to be a surprise,' Ava said.

'Well, you sure got that part right,' Louis said.

Once they'd walked up the hill to the house, Harry's little sister, Mae, was waiting for them at the back door, plainly excited. She ushered them inside and ran off to alert her older brother. Louis faltered when he saw Harry – overcome by a fresh wave of resentment and anger – but Harry only smiled and shook his head. He did not bring up the business in Petaluma, or the rude refusal Louis had scribbled in reply to Harry's note – *I ain't staying for supper* . . . Instead, Harry waved an arm in the direction of his father.

'I'd like to introduce my father, Kenichi Yamada. *Otōsan*, this is my friend Louis – who I've been telling you about.'

Louis took in the sight of Harry's father and instantly felt cowed: Kenichi was quite old and, while not a large man, carried a sort of large, graceful presence about him. Louis was suddenly aware of the fact that he was in another man's house.

'Welcome,' Kenichi said, and shook Louis's hand with a grip that was at once both friendly and firm.

Harry and Kenichi showed them all to the dining room, and Shizue began to fill the table with dish after dish of food. It was meant to be a celebratory meal, and between not knowing what else to cook and eschewing anything traditionally Japanese in honor of her non-Japanese guests, she had settled on foods one might expect at a Christmas or Thanksgiving feast. There was roast goose and stuffed turkey, corn on the cob and mashed potatoes, string beans and cranberry sauce. Louis hadn't planned on staying, but when Kenichi pulled out a chair for him, his body silently obeyed. After everyone was seated, dishes began to change hands as Louis looked on in a daze.

'Smells delicious,' Ava said.

'Thank you so much for having us,' Cleo added.

Shizue Yamada pressed her lips together in a quiet, Mona Lisa smile, and gave a small bow of her head.

'I am happy to have you both here,' Kenichi Yamada said now, raising his glass to Ava and to Cleo. 'And I am very pleased to have you, Louis, here at my table.'

The last traces of Louis's plan to hurry back to the Thorn ranch evaporated. Kenichi raised a glass and so did everyone else, respectfully honoring his toast.

Later, over the main course, Kenichi brought up the flying circus to Louis. 'It is a shame. I was very sad when I received the news it had come to an end. I was there that day you and my son went for your first wing-walking expedition! So brave, both of you – you made it look easy!'

'Harry does,' Louis said in a moment of sober honesty, curiously moved to discover that instead of disapproving of the barnstorming act, Kenichi Yamada was actually quite proud of his son. 'Harry's the one who makes it look easy. I just try to keep up.'

Kenichi beamed, his elderly face shining with joy, and Louis was again touched to see a father so proud. Life in the Yamada house was clearly different than life in the Thorn household.

'I'm a little surprised,' Louis admitted. 'You were all in favor of Harry attempting stunts on an airplane?'

'I was not,' Shizue volunteered. She smiled that same enigmatic smile. 'But I was outvoted.'

'I voted for Harry to perform stunts!' Mae proudly announced.

The whole table laughed. Then Kenichi turned serious.

'Harry has explained, but I'm not sure I understand . . . May I ask? What has become of the airplanes?'

'Earl gambled the first away,' Ava spoke up to answer. 'I'm afraid we don't know where it is now. And the other, well . . . it turned out Earl had been borrowing money against both planes, so the one we still know about, at least, has been repossessed as collateral.'

'Ah . . . I see,' Kenichi said, nodding. 'So for now it belongs to the bank . . .'

'Yes.' Ava nodded. 'The last we heard, it will go up for bank auction . . . in Sacramento sometime next month, I believe.'

Louis and Harry exchanged a look. The blame Louis had heaped upon Harry was momentarily forgotten, and it was a look of shared empathy, both of them still disappointed to think of the Stearman that had brought them together and was now forever gone. The look was observed by Kenichi, who was seated near his son.

Bank auction. Kenichi began to ponder the situation.

He raised his glass again, this time toasting the impressive splendor of their air show, despite its brief run.

After the dinner dishes had been cleared and dessert had been served and cleared away, Louis caught a glimpse of the grandfather clock in the Yamadas' front parlor and realized with a start that he'd better be getting home. He thanked his host and hostess, said his farewells, and promised Ava he would pay her another visit soon. The last person he spoke to was Harry, who saw him out to the porch alone. Louis hesitated before leaving.

'I know it wasn't your fault,' Louis said finally.

'Well, that makes two of us, then,' Harry replied, the tone of his voice only half-joking.

'It makes things awful hard on me,' Louis said, 'us being . . . friends.' He had trouble groping his way to the last word – 'friends' – but as he said it he knew that's what they were again.

'I reckon I know that, too,' Harry said quietly. He understood that Louis was referring to the reaction he had to endure from the Thorn family.

They said good night, and Louis walked into the darkness and cricket song, finding his way back to the Thorn property the same way he'd come.

When Louis arrived home, he saw a light on in the kitchen. His older brother, Guy, was waiting up for him. Louis had half a mind to pretend he hadn't noticed the light and go straight to bed. But loyalty prevailed, and besides, he knew that wouldn't be the end of it anyway.

'You were gone an awful long time,' Guy commented as Louis entered the kitchen.

Louis did not answer right away. He rummaged around in the icebox and eventually settled on a glass of cold buttermilk. He took a sip, the icy sour tang strangely comforting as he tried to find the right words — words that wouldn't set Guy off.

'It wasn't . . . it wasn't what I thought . . . I went there to square things with Harry, but . . . but the Yamadas invited me to dinner,' he said.

'That so? Have a nice time?'

'Suppose so,' Louis replied, now guarded.

'I thought that now the flying circus business was all done, you wouldn't be spending time with them anymore,' Guy said.

Louis noticed an ashtray full of discarded butts in front of Guy. Not only had his brother taken up smoking again, he had evidently been sitting there for quite some time.

'I have business with them. And besides . . . Harry is my friend,' Louis said, boldly repeating the word he'd used earlier.

'Your *friend*?'

The wooden chair legs screeched as Guy stood up. Louis's eyes flicked in his brother's direction, slightly frightened, mostly alert. Guy leaned toward Louis; his anger was plain.

'We'll see about that,' Guy said. 'Time tells all.'

Louis did not reply, and Guy left the room, with no other utterance on the matter.

35

YAMADA PROPERTY
DECEMBER 13, 1940

Kenichi Yamada rose early that morning. He spent the predawn hours with his wife, discussing matters over hot tea. Although Shizue was an elegant mastermind when it came to avoiding the appearance of directly contradicting her husband, she nonetheless had a way of making her disapproval clear. Ordinarily, Kenichi came around to his wife's opinions. She was wise and practical, and he was happy to defer to her judgment. But on this particular occasion he was intent on winning her over to his side. Shizue listened to her husband as he tried to persuade her, and she had to admit it was touching to see how happy it made her husband to make their son happy. Her daughter was bright, her son was brave, and her husband was tremendously kind: what fault could Shizue find with any of that? She was grateful.

Which was why, when Kenichi returned shortly after taking a stroll in the orchards to watch the sunrise and announced his decision to drive down into Sacramento, Shizue only really pantomimed her disapproval, not quite convinced of it herself.

For his part, Kenichi swore he saw his wife smiling quietly to herself as she prepared *oyakodon*, a hearty dish of chicken and eggs over rice, for breakfast.

'Haruto,' he said once his son had risen from bed, 'I'd like you and your sister, Mai, to come with us to Sacramento today.'

'All right,' Harry agreed, raising a still-sleepy hand to smooth his rumpled hair. 'Why today, *Otōsan*?'

'There is an auction, and I would like your advice about an appropriate price,' his father answered.

Harry grunted. He was certain his father meant to bid on a prize bull or a herd of milk cows . . . and Harry had made it his business to never let such matters be his business. He would be terrible at giving advice on this front. His sister, Mae, would be better, in fact. But of course he would go anywhere his father wished him present.

When they drove into Sacramento, they did not drive south of the city, to the open fields where all the farmers' auctions took place. Instead they drove to the heart of town, and Harry followed his father into a building next to the capital.

'I don't understand,' Harry said. 'What are we doing here?'

Mae giggled. Harry turned to her with surprise. He had been too distracted to notice that Mae was clad in a very nice dress and wearing her favorite patent-leather shoes. In fact, as Harry looked around now, he realized all of his family members were nicely attired.

'Do *you* know what we're doing here?' he said now to Mae.

'Perhaps,' she said, and gave another giggle.

'You said you wished to bid on something up for auction,' Harry said to his father in Japanese.

'That is true,' Kenichi agreed. He exchanged a knowing look with his wife, Shizue.

Harry blinked and looked around. They were walking down a long, echoing hall of a large building with clerical offices on one side and what appeared to be a series of small courtrooms along the other. Kenichi led his family, then paused and looked down at a slip of paper in his hand. Harry recognized the Japanese character for the numeral 5 and realized they were looking for courtroom five. Kenichi glanced again at the number over the doorway, touched his bow tie once to ensure it was straight, and entered.

Inside, an auction was already in progress, the auctioneer using the judge's bench and gavel to facilitate the transaction. The Yamada family quietly took a seat in the back.

'All right! The next property item up for auction is . . .'

It was a house. Harry realized they were at a bank auction. His father hadn't come to Sacramento to bid on livestock for the ranch; he'd come for something else.

'*Otōsan*,' Harry whispered, shaking his head. 'I can't let you—'

'*Shhhh!*' his mother snapped at him.

Surprised, Harry immediately shut his mouth. It was not his mother's way to shush people. Ordinarily she restrained herself from scolding; her manner of ruling the roost was silent and stony – she could level a grown man with a look – but she never shushed.

Despite her having done exactly just that now, she was not looking at Harry as he glanced at her in surprise. Her eyes were fixed on the front of the courtroom, where a man propped a large card on a picture stand that displayed the name of the item up for auction. He shuffled through the oversize cards now and put a new one up. Harry saw that it contained an enlarged black-and-white photograph. He squinted at the grainy image.

A biplane, with lettering on the side that read *POLLUX*.

'The next item up for auction is a Stearman Model 75 biplane,' the auctioneer announced. 'Well maintained and in good condition. Opening bid will begin at eight hundred dollars.'

The auctioneer cleared his throat.

'Let's begin. Do I have eight hundred dollars?'

'Eight hundred,' Kenichi said, tersely raising his hand.

'Eight-fifty!' someone else called out.

'Nine hundred!'

'Nine-fifty,' Kenichi spoke up again.

The bidding went all the way up to twelve-fifty. Harry wanted to say something but didn't know what. *One thousand two hundred and fifty dollars!* You could nearly buy a house for that much. And the bidding was still going; who knew where the price would land?

'*Otōsan* . . . what are we going to do with a plane?'

'The same thing you were doing before,' Kenichi replied in a matter-of-fact tone. 'However, you will do it *legally*,' he added. 'I have spoken to

226

a lawyer. There are ways. But we will need permits, and money to lease proper venues . . .'

Harry was awed by his father, and somewhat dumbstruck. As Kenichi spoke, he continued to raise his hand periodically as the auction went on.

'You will want to collaborate with your friend Louis, I assume,' Kenichi said. He gave Harry a sidelong look and a little smile. 'I have noticed: together you are very competitive, but also quite happy and creative, too – a winning combination.'

Kenichi raised his hand again. After several more minutes, he was the only bidder left. The gavel fell, its hammer strike echoing throughout the room.

'You will be responsible for collecting the airplane and transporting it from the county impound, Mr Yamada,' the clerk droned, minutes later, as the paperwork was being filled out. He pronounced it *Yaw-may-duh*. 'I trust you have the means to do so?'

Kenichi looked at his son.

'Yes,' Harry answered, still pinching himself. 'We can arrange for that.'

36

MURPHY'S SALOON
FEBRUARY 28, 1941

It took some time to locate Buzz and Hutch and successfully wire each of them a message. Eventually, Louis and Harry were able to track them down: Buzz had picked up charter work in Oakland, and Hutch had gone to stay with some old Army buddies in Portland, Oregon, while he decided what to do next. Harry invited the two pilots to Newcastle, and Harry's father paid for a pair of train tickets. Puzzled yet curious, Buzz and Hutch both made the trip.

The five of them gathered in a back booth in Murphy's Saloon: Louis, Harry, Buzz, Hutch, and Ava. Cleo remained behind on the Yamada property, learning to prune fruit trees. Her mother was happy, Ava realized. Cleo, for all her glamour, loved working in the orchards. She should've been a farmer's wife all along.

The remaining former members of the flying circus sat in the dark gloom of the bar, arrayed about a sticky wooden tabletop. It was afternoon, but the only sunlight in the establishment came from a series of small windows cut into the walls just under the eaves, making their faces glow in an almost eerie manner.

'All right, fellas,' Hutch said, once they had settled in. 'You boys got us down here. Wanna tell us what this is all about?'

'We were able to get *Pollux* back,' Harry said.

'Well, Harry's father was,' Louis corrected, a stickler for the details.

'We're getting a barnstorming act together,' Harry continued. 'A new one, a *real* one . . . bona fide and legal . . . without Earl.'

'It'll be different,' Louis said. He cleared his throat. 'No more living off chump change from taking poor farmers and their families up for tourist rides.'

'I don't get it,' Hutch said. He appeared interested yet wore a frown. 'How will you make your money?'

Louis and Harry exchanged a look.

'We've been talking,' Harry continued, 'and Louis has some ideas for more of a true spectacle. We've been talking about putting on a straight stunt show.'

'A stunt show?' Hutch repeated.

'Yeah . . . it's kind of a themed variety act of sorts.'

Buzz raised an eyebrow. Both pilots looked confused but intrigued.

Harry turned to his friend. 'Louis?' he prompted.

Louis cleared his throat. He produced a notebook he'd been nervously clutching and placed it on the table.

'All right,' he said. 'Well, to start with, you oughta know we won't be doing this in any old farmer's field. The law says we gotta use official airstrips, which we can lease for a price. The good news about that is now we can charge our spectators for a seat in the bleachers just to watch.'

'Instead of making our money on individual tourist rides,' Harry said, 'we'll be selling tickets to see our act, more like . . . well, more like a *show*. Like a tented circus, or something you would ordinarily pay to go see.'

'Who's going to pay just to watch us monkey around with one airplane?' Buzz asked. 'One airplane ain't much, and folks don't go nuts for airplanes like they used to.'

'Louis might just have an answer to that,' Harry said, and nodded at his friend to continue.

'To really draw the crowds,' Louis said, a tinge of nervous embarrassment in his voice, 'what I've been thinking is that we need to put together something *unique* . . .'

Inside the pages of his notebook, Louis had diligently sketched out a hodgepodge of influences: he'd dissected and diagrammed several comic-book heroes, with special emphasis on flying ones such as Superman or Flash Gordon, who traveled in a rocket ship. He'd mapped out legendary performances by the Flying Wallendas and other famous circus acrobats and finally, with Harry's help, he'd broken down and analyzed a number of Harry Houdini's most celebrated escape acts.

'What we're gonna do,' Louis said, hesitantly at first, 'is some of . . . well, some of *all* of this.'

''Fraid I don't follow,' Hutch said, staring at Louis's handmade illustrations.

'Well, all of these, they all tell a story, they all give their audiences a thrill of danger,' Louis replied. He glanced at Harry. 'They pull off something that *should* be impossible and make them puzzle over a magic trick.'

As Louis continued to talk, his embarrassment was overcome with enthusiasm. He went on to explain that they were going to make it a themed show and wear costumes – the new name of the barnstorming act was to be Eagle & Crane. The act involved an airplane *and* an automobile, which Hutch and Buzz – if they signed on – would keep in constant motion throughout the show. Meanwhile, Louis and Harry, dressed in costumes inspired by Louis's comic-book heroes, would perform on the wings as 'Eagle' and 'Crane'. There was a loose narrative – a battle between good and evil – but really the true spectacle was in the colorful nature of the costumes, in the choreography, and in the story.

He tapped his pencil on one page of the notebook.

'We want to include the automobile–airplane transfer we been doing,' Louis said. 'But we also want to try some other things we ain't tried yet, too: parachute jumps and more stunt aerobatics in general . . .'

Buzz and Hutch both raised their eyebrows with surprise but looked interested as they nodded and made a closer study of Louis's sketches and schematics.

'And,' Louis said with an air of show-stopping finality, 'we'll end each performance with one last trick . . .'

'Oh?' Buzz prodded.

'A sort of tribute to the Great Houdini, really,' Harry explained. 'Louis and I been talking about a way to combine all our favorite things, our areas of expertise. Just look at what he's come up with . . .'

Louis flipped the page in his notebook to reveal a detailed diagram of the planned feat. Hutch and Buzz leaned in for a better look. Together, they studied the elaborate sketch. Hutch stroked his chin, his eyebrows raised with an even mixture of dubiousness and awe. They gathered from the details in the drawing that one of the two young men would be rigged up in a straitjacket and dangled upside down from the landing gear, whereupon the Stearman would fly in low circles for the audience while the man performed his escape.

'I sent away for the straitjacket and it arrived last week,' Louis said proudly. He grinned at Harry. 'We've been practicing a little already how to escape it – on the ground, that is.'

Buzz gave a low-pitched whistle.

'Awfully ambitious of you, fellas,' he said. 'This is the kinda stuff Hollywood stuntmen do. Are you up for it, Harry?'

A flicker of a frown passed over Louis's face. He knew Buzz had directed the comment at Harry because he'd assumed that 'Crane' would be doing all the most perilous stunts. It was true, but nonetheless the assumption nagged at Louis.

'I think we're up for it. Right, Louis?' Harry said.

Louis nodded. He and Harry resumed their detailed explanation of how the show would go: they had decided it would be carefully choreographed and scripted. They needed to hire a good announcer to take care of the latter part. Ava would ask her mother, Cleo, to sew some costumes.

Buzz, Hutch, and Ava all listened and looked on and asked encouraging questions, but Buzz's comment had subtly brought into the open an unspoken truth. He had stated aloud what all of them already knew: that Harry was by far the better stuntman. Louis could sketch and dream and plan all he liked, but Harry was the true daredevil; Eagle & Crane needed Harry. Without Harry, Louis never would have stepped foot upon a single airplane wing.

37

NEWCASTLE, CALIFORNIA
SEPTEMBER 20, 1943

'There was opium in his body,' Sheriff Whitcomb says, almost as soon as Agent Bonner steps through the door. He delivers the news with a characteristic grunt. 'The coroner did as you requested and took some of his blood – Kenichi, the elderly Jap's, that is. Sent it to that laboratory all the way down in Los Angeles. They wired with the results. Didn't want to deliver the news over the telephone. I got the details of what was wired right here.'

'Opium?'

Bonner stands frozen in the middle of the sheriff's office, still holding his hat in his hand. He'd been about to hang it on the coatrack when Sheriff Whitcomb temporarily paralyzed him with the unexpected news.

'Opium?' Bonner repeats again.

'That's what I said.'

'How much opium?'

'Enough to kill a horse, according to the coroner,' Whitcomb says, grunting again. He hands Bonner the transcription of the results that had come over the wire.

'Opium . . . Is that common around these parts?' Bonner asks, reading and rereading the scanty details. 'Easy to acquire?'

Whitcomb shrugs.

'Some folks keep a little around for toothaches and such. The pharmacist two towns over sells a tea plenty of women like. Helps with insomnia, I suppose.'

'Makes sense the Yamadas would be good and stocked, don't it? Everybody knows Chinamen love to smoke opium,' Henderson chimes in. 'Out of those long Oriental pipes they got.'

Bonner doesn't make the effort to point out the inaccuracies of this statement, and even Whitcomb shakes his head like a weary parent too tired to correct a boisterous, misguided child.

'We ain't seen opium dens in these parts since the gold-mining days, to be honest,' Whitcomb says to Bonner in a stern, confidential tone, as though to set the FBI agent straight.

'Even so . . . Chinamen *are* Chinamen, ain't they – even if they're Japs,' Henderson persists.

Whitcomb and Bonner have no reply for this; they stare at Henderson, both of them with blank, unamused faces. Bonner shakes himself, still trying to work the puzzle out aloud.

'But the high dosage . . . it doesn't make any sense . . .'

So much opium! Were Harry and Mr Yamada suicide pilots after all? And Harry had to have been flying the plane – during the moment they took off, at least. Planes could not take off without a pilot who knew what he was doing, of this Bonner is certain. Could a person ingest that much opium in midair?

'The other body,' Bonner continues, tracing out his thoughts, 'did they find opium in the second body as well?'

Whitcomb shakes his head.

'Can't say. It was too burned-up for anybody to tell, really. The coroner couldn't get much off it to send to the lab boys in Los Angeles, and they reported back they couldn't make heads nor tails of what they *did* send.'

'So . . . just because Kenichi Yamada tested for opium doesn't mean Harry Yamada necessarily ingested any,' Bonner reflects aloud. 'It would make more sense, given the fact that Harry had to have piloted the plane. Perhaps it was a . . . a . . . kindness to his father? A suicide pact, but one that spared his father the pain?'

Sheriff Whitcomb's mouth twitches irritably. It is plain he doesn't care for all this speculation, making wild guesses about what dead people did and did not do and why. A plane crashed. There was opium in at least one of the bodies. Fine. Sometimes people did strange things and you couldn't account for it.

Oblivious to Whitcomb's fresh annoyance, Bonner moves across the room, back to the empty secretary's desk, staring at the lab results as if in a trance. Without asking for permission this time, Bonner sinks into Irene's vacant chair, further unmindful of Whitcomb's disapproving grunt. Some time passes as Bonner ruminates in silence. Finally, more questions come to him and he pipes up again, breaking the quiet thrum in the room.

'Say, Louis and Harry and that flying circus of theirs . . . the one they started on their own after the first one folded . . . was that operation successful? Know if they turned a profit?'

Yet another grunt from Whitcomb. 'I reckon that's their business,' the sheriff says.

'I'd say it looked like they were doing pretty okay,' Deputy Henderson chimes in. 'Their act sure got an awful lot of attention. Eventually, they even had that Hollywood producer offering to make 'em rich and famous.'

Bonner's head snaps to attention.

'Hollywood producer?'

'Louis said that fizzled and came to nothing,' Whitcomb reminds his deputy.

Henderson shrugs.

'Well, maybe it did,' he replies, 'but they only got themselves to blame. I know for a *fact* they got a bona fide offer to be in a Hollywood picture. They stood to make some *real* money, get some fame in the whole deal. Louis told his brother Ernest, and Ernest . . . well, Ernest is the kind of fella who can't help himself; he's always gotta run his mouth . . . ya know?'

'What happened?' Bonner asks. 'Why didn't it take?'

'I heard one – or maybe both of 'em – decided to back out.'

'That doesn't make any sense,' Bonner mumbles, more to himself than anything else.

'Who knows?' Henderson continues. 'Maybe it was that girl they were both chasing – Ava what's-her-name – who talked them out of it. They were funny about her, both of them, I reckon.'

'I don't understand why the two of you are on about Ava Brooks or Hollywood or any of the rest of it,' Whitcomb abruptly snaps from across the room. 'I'll thank you to both shut your traps and not spread idle gossip about

234

the good folks of this town unless you know something I don't know and can prove it.'

Bonner falls silent. Whitcomb is right: Bonner can't prove anything – yet. But, given the new information he's just acquired – the opium, the alleged Hollywood offer that didn't pan out – Bonner knows one thing: he certainly has more questions.

38

THE INCREDIBLE EAGLE & CRANE
BARNSTORMING SPECTACLE
SACRAMENTO, CALIFORNIA, MAY 3, 1941

They practiced all spring. It was slow going at first. Louis and Harry had to learn how to move in their costumes, and the stunts they were now attempting were significantly more complicated, not to mention more dangerous. There were a few near misses that terrified Ava at the time. Later the fellas ribbed each other and laughed about their brushes with death as Ava shook her head in disapproval and rolled her eyes.

'Say, Harry,' Buzz teased in the bar one evening after Harry had nearly fallen to his demise that afternoon, 'someone oughta have told you: those wings on your costume are just for show! I'd stick with the plane or at least a parachute if I was you.'

While they practiced and perfected their choreography, Ava set about making arrangements to rent out a string of airfields throughout the state, setting up a tour for their show. Most of the bookings required payment in advance. She was nervous, handing over Mr Yamada's money on the expectation that they would be able to fill the stands with spectators.

'I sure hope we can get folks to buy tickets,' Ava muttered to herself as she studied the growing list of costs.

'Spread the rumor someone might die – or, better yet, that someone already *did* die – and we'll have no problem filling seats,' Harry joked. 'Folks can be awful morbid.'

'Keep practicing with that reckless attitude of yours, and it won't have to be a rumor,' Ava warned.

They exchanged a look – half-joking, half-serious. Surely, Ava thought, Harry knew by now that he had the power to worry her.

In addition to booking airfields, Ava was also in charge of hiring the show's final touch: an announcer. According to Louis, it would be the announcer who gave the show life, who transformed the action into a *story*, and who compelled the audience to feel like they were following a radio program or watching a picture show. Eventually, a man in Auburn answered their ad: a part-time auctioneer named Bob Howard, a sweaty, pink-faced man whose voice seemed to boom directly from the pit of his enormous belly. He wasn't handsome, but what Bob lacked in appearance he more than made up for in the charismatic appeal of his announcing voice. It turned out he had a talent for memorizing lines, too. He began to practice with them while Ava supervised, and by their second day he had the whole show down pat.

It began to look and sound like an actual *spectacle*, Ava thought. She felt herself grow hopeful.

The time for Eagle & Crane's big premiere finally arrived on a bright spring day in Sacramento. Luckily, the airfield was already fenced and contained ample bleachers. Ava recruited her mother's help to sell tickets, popcorn, and lemonade. Ava kept a careful count of bodies as they paid and entered.

It was not as many as Ava had hoped, but it was a decent enough mass of folks to qualify as a crowd. There was a genuine current of electric excitement in the air when the show finally began.

'*Ladies and gentlemen!*' Bob hollered into a megaphone in suave, energetic tones. '*What you are about to witness today is no casual, commonplace air show! I assure you, the performance you are about to see is unlike anything you have ever heard of! These are no crop dusters, no farmers with a simple hobby! What you are about to witness is a harrowing, death-defying battle between good and evil! Watch as two ancient gods of the sky slug it out! Half-man, half-bird, these superhumans will test their strength against each other . . . only one may reign supreme! Please, ladies and gentlemen, turn your eyes now to the sky and let us hear some applause as we welcome . . . the spectacular . . . the amazing . . . the incredible EAGLE & CRANE!!!*'

At that point, Hutch piloted the Stearman so it swooped down low over the top of the crowd while Louis and Harry stood, one of them on each wing, their arms outstretched. Louis's costume was white and blue, with a hood and mask that was patterned after an American bald eagle. Harry's costume was white and black with a bit of red, and a hood and mask patterned after a red-crowned crane. Both costumes were draped with 'wings' that hung from their arms, from their shoulders to their elbows, almost like a pair of truncated capes that otherwise might belong to a comic-book hero. The hoods were snug, like normal aviators' caps, but came down to form masks over the top halves of their faces, with holes for their eyes, and the noses of each costume tailored to resemble birds' beaks.

Admittedly, the costumes and all the extra fuss had a somewhat silly, juvenile aura about them. But this was quickly undercut as Eagle & Crane launched into their first stunt, which was a violent, terrifying mock fight. They danced back and forth across the plane, climbing from one wing to the other, pretending to antagonize each other.

Of course, as Crane, Harry was obliged to play the bad guy. They knew their audiences were bound to be mainly white folk, and most spectators would side with Louis, with his face full of freckles, costumed as an all-American eagle; they identified with him too closely to see him fail. When it came to the Eagle & Crane equation, both Louis and Harry understood it was Eagle who must always, always win.

As the more villainous one, Crane attacked Eagle first, of course, and the whole crowd gasped as Eagle took a terrible punch, windmilled his arms, and rose up on his tiptoes, nearly 'falling' to his death. Then it was Crane's turn to take a punch and nearly fall. The sum effect of this very real-looking fight ultimately hushed the onlookers and quieted any skepticism or ridicule that otherwise might have ensued on account of their gaudy pageantry.

Next, Hutch flew another low pass over the crowd as Louis and Harry climbed up onto the upper wings. They took turns doing further stunts. They did handstands; they hung on and waved their arms dramatically as Hutch flew the Stearman through a series of barrel rolls; they braced themselves against a special metal scaffolding (installed for specifically this purpose) as

Hutch flew a grand loop-the-loop. There were more choreographed fights and feats of strength; they did push-ups and pull-ups and dared each other via pantomime to dangle off various parts of the biplane.

Eventually, as Hutch was flying so high the two barnstormers were barely discernible, Eagle was able to get the upper hand, and during the struggle the villainous Crane fell from the plane and came plummeting down from the sky.

Everyone gasped. Several women screamed.

Harry's parachute would open at the perfect time – just at the point where a frightened audience had grown certain the macabre action was real and that they were witnessing a horrifying accident.

'*Aaaaaand it looks like the evil Crane is getting a-way, ladies and gentlemen!*... *What's that? Oh dear! He's vowing to take revenge against our noble Eagle!*'

Harry, having landed, gathered up his parachute and shook his fist in the air at Hutch and Louis as they flew on without him. A hearty round of boos sounded in the stands, the audience having quickly recovered from its scare and ready to participate again.

'*Careful, folks! Crane is a dastardly character! Who knows what diabolical plans the evil Crane has in store for us all!*'

Harry shook his fist at the crowd. More booing.

Next, Buzz zoomed up in the shiny red Ford Deluxe convertible that Kenichi Yamada had purchased for this very purpose, and Harry leapt into the open passenger seat. He pointed one finger into the sky after Hutch's now-distant plane, as if to say, *Follow that Eagle!* Hutch made a turn and came in for another pass. Buzz revved the car's engine and charged toward the approaching airplane, then spun the car around using the handbrake and hit the gas again, furiously shifting and trying to keep up as now the plane and the car were running parallel to each other.

Hutch's plane was trailing a rope ladder. It flapped behind the Stearman as he put the plane down low to the ground.

'*Looks like the fight between Eagle & Crane isn't over just yet, folks! I can see Crane aims to get back aboard that plane!*' Bob bellowed. '*Will he make it?*'

Crane caught hold of the ladder and proceeded to climb out of the convertible, upward into the sky, as the Stearman lifted higher and higher and the car broke away, leaving them to it and turning and driving again back toward its origin.

Once back aboard the Stearman, Crane began a second fistfight with Eagle. After a good five to ten minutes of many harrowing close calls, Eagle finally vanquished Crane, knocked him out, and 'imprisoned' him, buckling him into the straitjacket. Harry was then lowered down by his ankles, and strapped to the landing gear, so that he dangled upside down. Hutch buzzed low and circled as Eagle celebrated his victory. All eyes remained on Crane, who was making his escape, and a great gasp went up from the crowd as Harry pulled the straitjacket completely off and let it drop to the ground below.

Just as Crane successfully freed himself and struggled to right himself, the Stearman began to fly out of sight – implying, of course, a sequel.

'*What a show, folks! So many questions remain . . . Will Eagle vanquish Crane a second time? Or will the dastardly Crane get the better of our hero? You'll have to visit us a second time for all those answers and more!*'

Forty-five minutes had elapsed. Hutch flew back over the crowd to perform a few final aviation stunts, and the show reached its conclusion. The crowd was small, but the applause was ample. Spectators chattered to one another as they gathered their things. It was almost as though a thrilling, action-packed radio show had come to life!

'Tell all your friends about it!' Ava hollered, over and over, as the audience shuffled back toward their parked cars.

39

THE INCREDIBLE EAGLE & CRANE
BARNSTORMING SPECTACLE
MONTEREY, CALIFORNIA, AUGUST 15, 1941

For the most part, Eagle & Crane was a success. Its colorful, costumed pageantry appealed to children, while the very real peril of the daredevil stunts Louis and Harry attempted kept the adults gasping, almost hoping to see an accident, and then breathing a sigh of relief when they didn't. Their first few crowds did exactly what Ava hoped: they gossiped about it to friends and neighbors.

It was a different sort of operation than Earl's flying circus had been. Ava kept a very organized schedule of where they were performing. Each stop offered a proper airfield, where they typically performed two or three times over the course of a weekend. Their crowds were no longer the impromptu product of kicking up a fuss in the sky over this or that small farming town; now they were entirely reliant on advertising. Ava commissioned Louis to draw up his most colorful representations of Eagle & Crane in action, and had bright, glossy posters printed up.

Louis was happy to accommodate and proud to have helped create their new, unusual barnstorming act. However, he was anxious about the fact that they were slow to see the kinds of profits he'd imagined. According to Ava, performing Eagle & Crane was expensive: there was the cost of the airfields, the expense of the costumes and props, the price of printing up posters and placing advertisements . . . the list went on. The price to ensure you could fill an airfield full of paying spectators was steep, and consequently the show's profits were sluggish at first.

Unfortunately for Louis, he'd gotten ahead of himself during the winter months he and Harry had spent designing the act and coming up with new stunts. He knew his brother Guy would not approve of any of it – of Louis barnstorming again, or of Louis continuing to fraternize with their hated neighbors – and Louis had managed to keep his meetings with Harry a secret. But when it came time to put on their first performance and later to ship out with the act, there was no more hiding it; he had to come clean with Guy. As expected, Guy was not pleased. Louis was needed around the ranch, Guy said, and if Louis insisted on running off with another flying circus – this one *directly* owned by the Yamadas, no less – then maybe Louis oughtn't bother coming back to the ranch at all. Louis figured maybe he could change Guy's mind when he started sending more money back home than ever before. By that point, Louis had gotten swept up in the excitement of imagining Eagle & Crane as a runaway success, making money hand over fist, and dazzling all.

They were starting to gather some good-sized crowds, but they weren't nearly at the level of fame Louis had allowed himself to fantasize about, and nowhere near as rich as he'd dreamed. The winds of fortunes would have to change, or else Louis would have to find some other way to make amends with Guy.

They were busy that summer. They began performing shows in early May and had plans to continue all the way through September. Ava had booked air shows for them all over the state: down south in Lancaster and Riverside . . . then up north, near the border of Nevada, in Grass Valley and Truckee, then west again to the Salinas Valley, where they played Hollister and Watsonville. The most recent stop was an airfield near the Monterey Peninsula.

After they performed a weekend full of shows, Buzz and Hutch decided to take a couple of days to try the local deep-sea fishing. Ava thought it might be a good idea for Louis, Harry, and her to spend some time by the seashore.

'We've all worked so hard to get the show up and running, we've earned a little holiday, I'd say,' Ava argued. 'Superheroes or not, even Eagle & Crane have to rest sometime.'

They explored the three little towns the peninsula had to offer: Monterey with its wharf and cannery full of fishermen roaming about in bib overalls, the charming walk along the shallow cliffs of Pacific Grove with its pretty

Victorian houses, and the surprisingly quaint, English-looking village of Carmel. It was cold and foggy in the mornings, sunny and pleasant in the afternoons. The sandy beach in Carmel was surprisingly white, and the water shocking turquoise. The water's enticing color almost made Ava want to swim in it – if a dip of her toe hadn't warned her of its brutal chill.

The air smelled of cypress, redwoods, and eucalyptus. The dunes along the beach were dotted with manzanita, coastal sage, and a variety of sprawling ice plant that seemed to erupt in a fountain of brilliant purple flowers. As they toured around, they saw otters playing in Christmas-colored kelp, and pods of whales visible from shore with the naked eye. It was beautiful there – more beautiful than any place Louis had ever seen.

On their last day there, Ava announced that she had a plan. She disappeared that morning, but not before making Louis and Harry promise to meet her around one o'clock that afternoon.

When she came back, she was driving the convertible coupe they used for the car-to-plane transfer stunt in their show.

'You fellas comin'?' she hollered as she pulled up to where the group had been camping quietly in the woods.

'She's driving?' Louis said to Harry as they walked toward the open car.

'I wouldn't try talking her out of it if I were you,' Harry advised, exchanging a smile with Louis.

'Where's our destination?' was all Louis said as he and Harry piled into the car.

'You'll see. Hold on to your hats, boys, if you'd like to keep them!'

She hit the accelerator and they sped away. Ava steered the car south, onto the curving, treacherous coastal highway, Highway One. It was a winding, exciting, breathtaking road, vast and full of surprises but mainly devoid of people. Big Sur – or *El Grande Sur*, as the Spanish missionaries had named it – the great, rugged landscape lay south of Monterey and Carmel.

Ava alternately punched the accelerator and brake, picking her way along the frighteningly steep cliffs, each twist and turn of asphalt offering a glimpse of yet another tiny, eerily pristine beach nestled between the ominous-looking jutting rocks down below.

Finally, Ava pulled off the highway into a dirt turnout surrounded by a wooded area and put the car in park. She cut the engine and scrambled out of the vehicle.

'Someone fetch up that picnic basket tucked in the rumble seat, would you?' she called, staring into the thick underbrush and cypress trees as though searching for something. She took off at a brisk pace. They followed with the basket as requested, hiking along a little path to a rocky outcropping.

'There!' Ava shouted, pointing to a small cabin perched at the farthest point.

'That? That looks abandoned,' Louis commented.

It was a wooden structure with a little stone chimney, the whole of it somehow anchored by stilts to the rocks. The wood was dark and wet, perpetually soaked by salt spray and sea fog. Electric-yellow and rusty-red lichen bloomed in asymmetrical patterns; the roof was made of shale and polka-dotted with several years' worth of birds' nests.

They drew nearer.

'You saw this earlier?' Louis pressed Ava. 'From . . . an earlier drive?'

Ava didn't answer.

'When did you have the time to drive the coast?' Louis wanted to know. For the slimmest of seconds, he thought he saw Harry give Ava a look that he couldn't quite read. But Ava seemed wholly distracted by the dilapidated cabin.

'You're right, Louis,' Ava mused. 'I think it *is* abandoned.'

Louis frowned.

'Look, though.' Harry pointed to where rusty iron bars anchored the cabin's stilts to the giant basalt boulders beneath it. 'Someone took all the trouble to do that.' He continued to indicate the cabin's unusual foundation.

'I love it,' Ava murmured. 'It's a ramshackle Frankenstein of a thing.'

'You *would* love it,' Louis said. 'I doubt it's safe to go inside.'

'Only one way to find out,' Ava said with a gleam in her eyes.

Now Louis's frown deepened. 'Ava, don't—' Louis started to complain, but Ava had already scampered out of earshot, leaping from rock to rock, quickly advancing upon the cabin. She approached the front door, tried the latch, and disappeared inside.

'I guess we're going in,' Harry laughed.

Harry followed Ava, and Louis – grudgingly – followed Harry.

It was mostly empty inside. There were a couple of forgotten wooden chairs with broken backs, and in one corner, an empty mattress frame with no mattress. Louis and Harry watched as Ava poked around cupboards filled with cobwebs. Inside were a few tins of soup and sardines and a packet of molding crackers. There were two large, shuttered windows on either side of the fireplace. Ava undid the latches on the shutters – the mystery architect had deemed glass panes unnecessary – and pushed them open. The wooden shutters groaned on rusty hinges to reveal a magnificent view of the Pacific Ocean at its most rugged and feral.

'Holy moly,' was all Ava said in an awed voice. She spun around. 'Why did anyone ever leave this place?' she asked rhetorically. But Louis thought he could come up with a few answers.

'Picnic time,' she announced brightly, whirling around. She took the basket from Harry, who had been holding it all the while.

One by one, she produced item after item. Her choices represented all the foods the region was locally famous for: crabs from the Monterey wharf, artichokes from Castroville, a skinny loaf of bread and a stick of butter from a general store in Carmel. She spread a blanket on the floor and reached into the basket again to bring out some tin cups and plates. At Ava's direction, Harry fussed with the fireplace to get the flue open and started a fire to warm the artichokes, the butter, and the bread.

'That stuff wasn't terribly expensive, but I have to confess, I did splurge a little when I got . . . this!' Louis and Harry both raised their eyebrows in surprised appreciation as she produced a bottle of champagne.

'Louis?' Ava nudged, handing him the bottle. Louis took it and obediently worked to loosen the cork from the neck. Too late, the cork sprang away with a loud *pop!*

'Quick! Quick!' Ava said, hurrying cups into their hands and gesturing for Louis to pour as best he could.

They tucked into the feast Ava had laid before them. The crab was delicious – fresher than anything Louis had ever eaten. Out the two giant open windows, the Pacific steadily roared.

'You know,' Ava mused, 'we've never actually toasted it.'

'Toasted what?' Louis asked.

'Eagle & Crane.'

'Easy enough to remedy,' Harry said. 'To Eagle & Crane!'

They raised their tin cups and clinked.

'It's a good show,' Ava said once they had all taken a long sip.

'It is,' Harry agreed.

'What's the matter, Louis?' Ava said, noticing the faraway look in his eyes. 'Aren't you proud of it? The costumes, the routines . . . So much of it was your design, I would think you'd be proud!'

Louis nodded quietly. He hesitated and decided to come out with the matter that had been nagging him since they'd begun the show earlier that summer. 'I just . . . well . . . I'd hoped we'd make more profit . . . I'd been hoping to send some home, make up with my older brother . . .'

'I think we still will,' Harry said. 'I have this feeling . . . this feeling that Eagle & Crane is going to catch the attention of someone or something . . . *big*,' he added, the happy-go-lucky arrogance back in his voice.

Louis gazed at Harry. It struck him that optimism came much more easily to those who didn't need it so desperately.

'Well . . . I hope so . . .' Louis replied. He raised his cup. 'I'll drink to *that*.'

They clinked cups a second time. Guzzling so much champagne in such a short time was beginning to make all three of them feel a little warm and fuzzy.

'I love this place,' Ava said dreamily, glancing around at the run-down shack. 'I'd stay here forever if I could.'

'Doesn't seem like there's any proprietor around to run you off,' Harry joked.

Louis looked between the two of them as they laughed, and an odd feeling came over him. His mind drifted back to the questions he'd asked Ava earlier – the questions she'd ignored, about how and when she'd glimpsed the abandoned cabin in the first place. It wasn't visible from the road. It was the sort of thing you could only see from a boat . . . or . . . *an airplane*. A small suspicion began to form in Louis's mind.

But, seeing Ava's face shine with happiness as they sat picnicking in the derelict cabin, he pushed his suspicion off for another day.

40

THE INCREDIBLE EAGLE & CRANE
BARNSTORMING SPECTACLE
OJAI, CALIFORNIA, SEPTEMBER 14, 1941

Almost exactly one month later, Harry's prediction came true. Around that time they had moved south, putting on their air show in airfields in Santa Maria, Solvang, and Santa Barbara. Word had begun to catch on about their show, and a reporter from a small local newspaper even wrote a little feature about Eagle & Crane. THE COMIC BOOK COME TO LIFE, the headline declared. But it was while they were performing at an airfield near the sunny town of Ojai that Louis and Harry had an unexpected encounter that suggested their show had caught the attention of 'someone *big*,' as Harry had phrased it.

They had arrived a few days earlier at the little idyllic inland town, with its golden sunsets and its citrus groves and horse ranchers. Ojai was an appealing place, with mountains that rose high and jagged in the distance and a little colonial Spanish downtown. They had a three-day engagement there, and it was on the third and final day that the strange and unexpected event occurred.

With the barnstorming act concluded, the audience was taking its time shuffling away, milling around and socializing. Louis and Harry were still in their costumes but had set about packing their props away, when a skinny young man approached. He was dressed like an office errand boy and removed a newsboy cap to reveal hair so red he might've been Ava's twin. He squinted into the sun as he drew near, wiping his brow with the back of his hand.

'Howdy, fellas,' he said, addressing Louis chiefly. 'May I have a word?'

Louis tried to size him up. The young man was about seventeen or thereabouts – close to Ava's age – but he was tall and thin as a rail; his limbs were that particular sort of gangly that favors youth best. He was clutching one of the programs Ava handed out to people as she sold tickets. Louis had sketched up a sort of comic-book-style depiction of Eagle & Crane performing a few of their stunts and tricks, and every few towns Ava had copies printed – simple black ink on the cheapest paper they could find, a kind of yellowish-white newspaper.

It's a way to get folks to remember Eagle & Crane, she had argued. *We want people to pass along the name. If we're lucky, some of them'll even pass along their programs to their friends . . .*

Now there was a stranger standing before them, clutching one of those programs with a slightly anxious expression. He was not unkempt per se, but there was something distinctly hungry-looking about him. He was the picture of raw ambition: a scrappy young man who'd grown up playing kick-the-can in the streets but now worked as a clerk's assistant.

Maybe he wants an autograph, Louis thought, flattered. But then, more soberly, he considered, *Or a job as a stuntman . . .*

'I work for Buster Farrow,' the young man said now, clearing his throat and establishing a surprisingly businesslike air.

Louis and Harry blinked stupidly, saying nothing.

'I'm his *third assistant*,' the kid added, as though this new fact cleared things up. It was clear they were meant to be impressed. The young man's head swiveled from face to face, reading the lack of comprehension that was written there.

'*Buster Farrow?*' he demanded, shocked. 'Buster Farrow, the movie producer?'

'Oh,' Louis murmured. The name was *vaguely* familiar.

'Owner of three newspapers and Hollywood's *richest* movie mogul?'

He waited. Nothing.

'Look, anyway,' the kid finally continued, shaking off his incredulity at Louis and Harry's ignorance. 'See here, fellas, you can give yourselves a good pat on the back, because Buster Farrow has heard about your show. He sent me to come find you two.'

'I'm not sure I understand,' Harry said. '*Why* has he sent you to come find us?'

The young man sighed as though burdened by unfathomable exasperation.

'*Because* . . . he's interested in your stuntman act,' he said.

Louis and Harry continued to blink, their faces blank.

'He wants to make arrangements to shoot some footage!' the young man exclaimed, sarcastically rapping on the side of his head with his knuckles to underscore the thick-skulled nature of his present audience. 'You know . . . shoot some footage? Screen a reel? See if there's anything there?'

'Anything there for what?' Harry asked.

'Why . . . to cast you as stuntmen!' The young man grinned but instantly relented, forfeiting a fraction of his enthusiasm. 'He's looking to make a new movie, something action-packed, and he's gonna need one or two good stuntmen. He wants to put on a one-night-only event that showcases the best in the biz and see how they screen so he can make a decision.'

The young man was clearly tickled with the impressive nature of his own tidings. He paused and waited for all that he had said to sink in.

'So?' he pressed. 'Are you interested?'

He reached into his pocket and produced a business card.

'All you gotta do is telephone this number here.' He pointed. 'Tell 'em who you are and Farrow's first assistant will explain all about how they want to get this thing on film.'

His hand remained outstretched, the card still waiting.

'Hey – snap out of it, eh? Are you interested, fellas?'

Louis and Harry found themselves every bit as tongue-tied and confused as when the conversation had first begun.

'What am I saying?' the young man chuckled. 'Of *course* you're interested.' He reached out to Louis as though to slip the business card into a breast pocket, but flailed briefly when he realized Louis was attired in a costume and therefore *had* no breast pocket. Awkwardly, the young man tucked the card into the neck of Louis's costume and gave it a smug pat. 'Of *course* you're interested . . .'

His mission completed, he turned, preparing to depart. Thinking better of the situation, he twisted around and pointed to himself with one finger.

'Remember – the *third* assistant!' he hollered, reminding them with such pride, it made one wonder exactly how many assistants Buster Farrow had in total. 'Tell 'em Reggie sent ya!' the kid added, and was gone.

41

NEWCASTLE, CALIFORNIA
SEPTEMBER 20, 1943

That night, as Bonner waits for sleep, his mysterious hostess comes to him again. She had given no sign over dinner that this would be her intention, and yet, when he hears her soft footsteps, he is somehow expectant, not at all surprised.

He had retired to bed two hours earlier and had lain awake, restless, on the mattress, mulling over his case – in particular, Sheriff Whitcomb's revelation of opium in Kenichi Yamada's system, and Deputy Henderson's gossip that Louis and Harry had attracted a possible offer to perform their stunts in Hollywood. As he mulled, the night drifted in through the open window, bearing the scent of damp oak leaves.

This time there are no groaning floorboards, no feeling of being watched. He simply hears Rosalind's feet approaching without stealth, and watches the doorknob turn. She lets herself into the room and silently crosses to the bed. With one efficient gesture, she strips her nightgown off, over her head, and crawls under the sheets beside Bonner's own warm body.

They don't speak throughout the entire interlude. They reach for each other with plain understanding, limbs moving without apology, hands and mouths advancing frankly to what each wants. Bonner notices that while Rosalind's movements are sure and steady, he nonetheless detects a kind of tremor beneath her skin, a flutter deep within her chest that is more than a simple heartbeat. And there is that look in her eyes again: a frantic, tortured look that suggests the transaction between them is far more complicated than Bonner can comprehend.

His own mind races. She is a stranger to him; he has never met a respectable woman who behaves as she does. Her motivations are opaque, confusing. Will people in town find out? And what will happen if they do? Will he have caused her shame? What will, say, Sheriff Whitcomb think of her, or him? Bonner can't help but wonder.

He has never been the type to visit whorehouses or bed strangers. He is rarely so free with himself, but there is a quality about Rosalind – a dark, intense melancholy – that makes him feel blameless, makes what they are doing feel curiously necessary, free from filthier connotations.

After their bodies are spent, she allows him to hold her again, as she did the last time – albeit briefly. He stares up at the ceiling, where his mind finally strikes upon a piece of the riddle. Once he sees it, it seems obvious.

'You're grieving for someone,' Bonner says now in a low voice, breaking the silence between them.

Rosalind's body tenses but does not move. A matter of minutes goes by. Bonner almost begins to believe he never spoke at all. He shifts so as to get a better view of Rosalind's eyes, but the configuration of their tangled bodies makes this awkward, impossible. He waits, but can't tell whether she ever intends to acknowledge him. Soon enough, however, he gets his answer.

When he reaches a hand to gently touch her face, her cheek is wet with tears.

42

'*It's time to wrap it up.*'

Bonner is on the telephone again with his supervisor, Reed. According to Deputy Henderson, Reed phoned the sheriff's office a few times, trying to track down his field agent. Reluctantly, Bonner called to check in.

'*It's over, Bonner. Time to wrap up your investigation,*' Reed repeats. '*You've been up there for five days. You ought to have everything you need for your report by now.*'

'I can't.' Bonner hears a frog in his voice and coughs to clear it. 'Sir, I'm not done yet. I'm still following up on a couple of leads,' he protests. 'Besides the evidence suggesting someone may have tampered with the airplane's fuel line, I just found out there was opium in Kenichi Yamada's blood – a lethal amount.'

'*Oh, I know all about that, Bonner – you had them send a blood draw all the way down to the lab in Los Angeles . . . Who do you think gets the bill for that?*'

'It seemed necessary, sir.'

'*Necessary for what?*'

'To determine what killed the two Yamada men,' Bonner replies. He almost says, *To determine if it was murder*, but stops himself, realizing this is the wrong tack to take – exactly what Reed doesn't want him looking into. 'To determine if someone engineered that airplane crash,' he says, shifting course slightly to emphasize the insinuation of a terrorist plot.

'*First you were thinking a sabotaged fuel line, now you're thinking opium poisoning?*'

'Maybe . . . a combination of both . . .' Bonner tries to keep a neutral, persuasive tone.

'*All right, Bonner . . . here's my take on that, as your supervisor . . . There's a war on. We got plenty to do just monitoring the living Japs; we don't need to spend weeks investigating a couple of dead ones.*'

'They were internees in a federal facility,' Bonner stammers. 'That makes it federal business.'

'*Maybe so, but I'd just as soon hand it over to local law enforcement,*' Reed replies. '*Like I said, dead Japs don't pose a national security threat; live ones do. You haven't been able to find anything on the Yamadas concerning treason or a plot to do harm against Americans – certainly nothing that might continue to be a threat now that they are deceased; you said so yourself. If it's a murder case, the local sheriff can investigate.*'

Hearing Reed's words, Bonner feels as though he has been winded. It takes him a moment to catch his breath.

'But, sir . . . he won't,' Bonner says quietly into the receiver, throwing a cautious look in Sheriff Whitcomb's direction to determine whether he's listening.

'*Well, that's his business, then,*' Reed replies. '*Local cops have local reasons for doing what they do.*'

'Wait – sir,' Bonner begins to plead. 'There are still some things I'd like to follow up on. Just give me a couple more days to tie up loose ends.'

Pondering what this will entail, Bonner silently decides he will confront Louis Thorn, once and for all.

'*If this is about you atoning for the Minami family, Bonner, I'm warning you: you'd better nip that in the bud. The FBI is not going to cater to your guilty conscience. We're in the business of protecting America for Americans, not playing Sherlock Holmes for the Jap community. I hope that's clear.*'

'It is,' Bonner says. 'And I'm telling you, this has nothing to do with the Minami family.' It is a lie. It was relatively true when Bonner first requested the case: back then, all Bonner wanted was to get a look at Newcastle, at the Thorns. But as soon as the biplane fell out of the sky, the case had become something else for Bonner, and the Minami family – who he had been able to push to the outskirts of his thoughts for weeks at a time – has circled in closer and closer to his consciousness.

On the other end of the line, Reed sighs.

'Just a couple of days . . .' Bonner repeats.

'*Fine,*' he says, '*but I'm only giving you through Friday – which means no per diem to stay the weekend, mind you; I want you driving out of there Friday night. Get what you need for your report and wrap it up. And be prepared to hand off whatever you find to the sheriff. Come Monday morning, I expect you back in the San Francisco office, bright and early.*'

'Understood, sir.'

Bonner hangs up the phone, grateful but not altogether relieved.

43

HOLLYWOOD, CALIFORNIA
OCTOBER 3, 1941

Louis, Harry, and Ava were so awestruck they hardly knew where they were. Champagne coupes clinked in the air all around them. None of them had ever been to a Hollywood screening, let alone one with such lavish pomp and circumstance.

Once they stepped from the chauffeured car the studio had sent for them, they were lost in a swell of bodies clad in evening gowns and tuxedos, milling about outside the theater. Velvet ropes created an aisle and there was plush red carpet underfoot, covering every inch of sidewalk for almost a full block. It was as though a party had turned itself inside out, as though the theater – a stark white adobe building styled to look like a hacienda or maybe a great palace in Spain – had opened its mouth and its sumptuous ruby interior had spilled out onto the surrounding pavement.

Outside the main entrance, a showgirl in a shimmery dress stepped up onto a riser and struggled to lift a bottle nearly half her size, eventually managing to pour it over a pyramid of glasses stacked three feet high atop a table. Her arms quivered, betraying the perfectly lipsticked smile she beamed throughout her struggle. Onlookers cheered as golden suds slipped down the champagne fountain and the pyramid of glasses began to fill up, brimming over and filling each successive tier below. More coupes clinked.

Photographers' lightbulbs flashed and popped, and magnesium sparks showered the dark with spectacular brilliance. Doll-eyed women, most of them minor starlets, wiggled up the crimson swath of carpet, sipping champagne, speaking a few words into the radio announcer's giant silver microphone, turning and waving before disappearing between the dark curtains that flanked the theater's entrance. The majority of these beauties were escorted by various Hollywood types: producers, directors, leading men, oil barons, eccentrics – even the occasional European aristocrat. Ava couldn't help but notice that a great number of the starlets wore hats with veils pulled down over only one eye, or else had their hair pinned to one side, occasionally festooned with a flower tucked over the exposed ear, each of them with their blond, brunette, or red smooth-brushed curls spilling over one shoulder like a liquid wave of silk. They reminded Ava of her mother's efforts to imitate an earlier generation of starlets in what already felt like a lifetime ago, living in that little bungalow in Santa Monica.

A SELECT ENGAGEMENT, the marquee above the theater read.

'I still feel like there's been some kind of mix-up,' Louis breathed in disbelief.

'*Shhh*,' Harry hissed, 'or they'll catch on and give us the boot.' He winked.

'HELLO THERE!' came a jovial roaring voice. They turned to see Buster Farrow. He was a large bear of a man, well over six feet, with graying hair and very pale blue eyes. His face was slightly red and he was puffing prodigiously on a cigar. 'Boys, boys – my boys!' he repeated, his cheeks shining as he smiled. 'Welcome! We are honored to have you here!'

The event was technically an 'exhibition' – a screening of several different stuntmen plying their trade, all of them motorcyclists and wing-walkers and the like. Buster Farrow had – with the help of his assistants, of course (it turned out there were nine) – rounded up all of the daredevil acts that had recently caught Farrow's eye and commissioned ten minutes or so of film to be shot of each. Then he'd had the footage all cut together, with black title cards to introduce each stunt act, and a sound reel laid in for good effect. It was a slapdash job, but it was good enough for a single screening. The idea was to call it a 'special event,' but, more important, Farrow wanted to screen the different stunt acts together to see how a Hollywood audience reacted to them. He liked everyone who his studio employed to constantly compete; it kept the overhead low and the profits up.

Farrow pumped Louis's and Harry's hands and welcomed them inside the theater.

'And who do we have here?' he asked, noticing Ava for the first time. He towered over her, leering a little at her pretty mouth and lithe figure; but when he got to her décolletage – or lack thereof – his interest waned.

Ava fought the urge to roll her eyes at him.

'Only one date between the two of you?' Farrow joked.

'This is Ava Brooks,' Louis explained. 'She's . . . well, she helps us run our act. She does the books for our barnstorming spectacle.'

'I'm here as their manager,' Ava said in a matter-of-fact voice.

Farrow raised an eyebrow.

'Oh-ho! *Manager*, is it?' His lips twisted into a jovial, bemused grin. 'I guess I'd better be on the lookout for this one, eh, boys?'

This time Ava openly rolled her eyes at Farrow, but Farrow took no notice, herding them all into the theater instead.

'If you'll pardon me, I ought to say hello to some of the other stars and their, ahem, *managers* . . .' Farrow winked at Louis and Harry, still ignoring Ava. 'Enjoy the show, fellas! Nothing like seeing yourself on that silver screen, I hear. We'll talk afterward!'

With that, he shuffled off to clap some other, brawnier stuntmen on the back in greeting.

'He's not going to offer us a movie contract,' Louis said. 'He thinks we're small fry. Besides, he already got the footage he wanted for free.'

'You don't know that,' Harry insisted. He turned to Ava. 'What do you think?'

'I think that man doesn't do anything that isn't in his best interest,' she replied. 'And in some ways that's encouraging: there is the slightest chance that in this case his interest runs parallel to ours.' She looked at Louis and Harry. 'You're talented – both of you,' she said. 'I wouldn't be surprised if Eagle & Crane steals the show tonight,' she predicted.

Unaccustomed to the sound of blatant compliments spilling from Ava's lips, Louis and Harry were surprised into silence. More trays of champagne were being passed around them as they lingered in the lobby; one whizzed quite close to Ava's shoulder and she turned to lift a pair of glasses, offering them to Louis and Harry.

'Cheers,' she said, flashing them a rare grin.

The beautiful people around them continued to mill about until, at last, a bell rang, the signal for the audience to take their seats. Everyone in the lobby made a quick move to shuffle into the theater, and the three of them followed, sinking into their seats just as the lights went down. A curtain opened and a projector flickered to life. There were no advertisements, no newsreels. A hush settled over the theater.

'*THROUGHOUT THE HISTORY OF TIME,*' boomed the narrator's voice, '*MANKIND HAS DARED TO PERFORM FEATS OF BRAVERY, PUSHING HIS LIMITS FURTHER AND FURTHER . . . NOW MODERN TECHNOLOGY HAS ALLOWED TRUE DAREDEVILS TO GO FURTHER THAN EVER BEFORE, HIGHER, AND FASTER THAN WAS ONCE THOUGHT POSSIBLE! LADIES AND GENTLEMEN, LET'S DELVE DEEP AND TAKE A CLOSER LOOK AT THE GREATEST LIVING STUNTMEN OF OUR DAY!!!*'

Out the corner of her eye, Ava observed both Louis and Harry watching the footage very carefully as the movie progressed. The other stuntmen were profiled first; Eagle & Crane turned out to be last on the reel. They watched the other performances with rapt attention, nonetheless agonizing to see *Eagle & Crane* turn up on-screen. Louis and Harry both held their breath as the black title card announcing their act finally appeared and the screen flickered to life with their own grainy black-and-white shapes performing various tricks.

The cameraman had done a pretty good job capturing their various stunts: you could even make out a little bit what the storyline was behind their choreography. Ava knew that would make Louis proud; he'd come up with the idea to *have* a story in the first place, and had even drawn it out like one of his comic books. For the purposes of the exhibition, their forty-five-or-so-minute act had been compressed down into twelve minutes. This gave it an additional impression of exhilarating, nonstop action.

When their act concluded, their familiar Stearman – piloted by Hutch –

flew off into the sunset in a parting shot, and the theater lights came up. The audience began to cheer and applaud as though they had just witnessed a live performance. It was clear that Eagle & Crane was the finale, the favorite. Ava looked to Louis and Harry, who were grinning madly and blushing at the same time, as though overcome with a strange sense of embarrassment mingled with pride.

'So, boys,' Farrow called to them, leaning over the aisle and grinning in his tuxedo, 'whaddaya say I take you fellas out for a late supper and we talk about your future?'

'I dunno . . . you better ask our manager,' Harry replied.

Louis elbowed him, but Ava only gazed at Harry, rolling her eyes. It was a different kind of eye roll than the one she'd given Farrow earlier. Harry could be cocky and ridiculous sometimes, and for that she was grateful.

44

The city of Los Angeles projected a rare combination of enervation and harmony that night. The sun had long since set, but the evening was warm and balmy, laced with only the slightest hint of Pacific chill. The wildfires that usually haunted the mountains during that time of year were dormant, the Santa Ana winds at peace.

Buster Farrow decided to take the two prospective stuntmen he hoped to sign – along with the red-haired girl who called herself their 'manager' – to the Cocoanut Grove, the popular nightclub in the Ambassador Hotel. He could see they were impressed from the moment the car pulled up to the stately hotel. Inside, what looked like a cavernous Moroccan palace was filled with tall palm trees, nightclub tables dimly lit with red lamps, glamorously dressed patrons, and cigarette smoke. A man in a tuxedo and a woman in a slinky gown were performing a duet onstage, dancing and singing as an impressive twenty-piece orchestra played in the background.

The maître d' recognized Farrow immediately and ushered him to a prime table near the stage, lifting away a sign that read RESERVED with a discreet, white-gloved hand. It was immediately clear to Louis and Harry that Buster Farrow was a habitué, an important man who had waiters and maître d's all over town 'hold a regular table' for him at all the most fashionable establishments.

They sat for a while making small talk. The waiter who had showed them to their seats returned and poured them all a round of champagne without Farrow saying a word. For Farrow himself, the waiter set out a snifter of brandy and a fresh cigar. Onstage, various performers came and went. Every so often a showgirl finished her act and passed through the sea of tables. Farrow pulled an occasional blonde or brunette into his lap. Even sitting down, he was a bear of a man, and the girls got lost in his lap. He teased them and they swatted playfully and pretended to laugh with gay glee until they could wriggle free.

Finally, after at least thirty or forty minutes of Louis and Harry biting their nails while Farrow misbehaved as though all of Los Angeles were his fraternity and he was the president, it seemed the producer was ready to get down to business.

'So here's the thing, boys – are you listening?' Farrow said, jabbing a heavy finger against the white tablecloth with surprising force and an imperious air, as though he were banging a gavel. 'I can make you both stars. You heard me right: not just "stuntmen" – *stars*! *Headliners*! The two of you: the main attraction! That is, I can make Eagle & Crane a star act!'

'With all due respect, Eagle & Crane already is a star act,' Ava reminded him in a friendly voice. 'If they weren't, why else would they be sitting here with you?'

'No.' Farrow shook his head at Ava and turned back to Louis and Harry. His pale, almost colorless eyes flashed. 'See, now, there's the rub: you fellas don't know what you have. What you have is *local celebrity*. Don't go confusing local celebrity with *true stardom*. That's a rookie mistake when it comes to Hollywood. A girl wins the local beauty pageant back home in Nowheresville, Iowa, and thinks naturally someone will give a hoot about her title here in Los Angeles, only to find out how little it means. No; I'm offering you something on a far grander scale than you can probably even imagine right now.'

Farrow's words hit their mark. 'Small fry' – that was the phrase Louis had used while worrying aloud. Buster Farrow had just confirmed it in no uncertain terms.

'All right. I guess I'd say we're pretty interested,' Louis admitted.

'What do you propose?' Harry asked.

'I propose a feature film,' Farrow said. 'We'll use the characters you've created to tell a fresh story, and we'll pack it with action, of course, to make use of your talents! Picture your names up in lights!'

'That sounds good to me,' Louis said, the grin on his face turning outright goofy with enthusiasm.

'Of course, we *will* have to rework the act a bit, fix a few of the major problems . . .'

'What problems?' Ava asked.

Farrow looked at her, acknowledging her question, but stubbornly directed his answer back to Louis and Harry.

'Well, right now, as it stands . . . it's all out of whack. I mean, you have the villain doing all the best stunts! The audience wants to root for the Eagle character – the wholesome, all-American one, you know? He needs to show he is more powerful than Crane. There's a reason most villains are portrayed as cowards, ya understand? If you keep on the way you are, I shouldn't be surprised if your audience decided to root for the villain instead; the way you fellas have it, he comes out looking like the brave one! You're sending the audience a mixed message . . .'

'Okay, sure,' Harry said. 'So you want Louis to do more of the showstopper stunts?'

'Not necessarily, kid,' Farrow said, snapping his fingers. 'We just need to have *Eagle* doing all the fancy stunts – ya got me?'

Louis, Harry, and Ava stared at the producer, puzzled. But before any of them had the opportunity to speak, Buster Farrow cut back in.

'Don't worry,' he said, 'I get it: the Jap loves doing the reckless bits. Okay, sure – that's all fine and well. I don't need Louis to do the risky stuff . . . We just need to be *strategic* about things.'

'Strategic?' Ava asked, her eyes narrowed.

'Yeah, sure. If you fellas like to keep your arrangement how it is, we just need to shoot plenty of shots of Louis's *face*, and then put Harry here in the Eagle costume to get the actual stunts on film.'

'But . . . but . . . isn't that . . .' Louis stuttered and blinked.

'A *lie*?' Harry finished the question for his friend.

Buster Farrow eyed Harry with surprise, looking him over from head to toe. The kid was handsome, Farrow observed; it was a shame the kid was an Oriental, otherwise Farrow could ditch the freckle-faced kid and make this one his only star. But Farrow read the newspapers. Invading China, shaking hands with Hitler – Japs weren't exactly popular nowadays.

A lie, the kid had said. Farrow erupted with a soft belly laugh.

'That's *Hollywood*, son,' he replied. Amused, he regarded both young men, so somber, so serious. Were they serious with this earnest Boy Scout business? 'The magic is in the story, my friends,' he continued. 'That's how Hollywood works, that's what we sell, that's what we *do*!'

He set about toasting a fresh cigar the waiter had set out for him, clipping it and holding it steady as the flame licked the edges.

'Look, I've seen you fellas perform. It's clear we'll need Harry to pull off certain stunts,' Farrow said. 'I've watched the film closely; he makes it look better anyway. My assistants have written up a list of who'll do what, and that'll go into the contract.'

Farrow continued. He decided to come out with it and be direct with the boys, but at the same time he knew enough to switch to an easier, more casual voice.

'It's clear that we can't very well have a Jap parading around as the front man, eh? He's very talented, but you, Louis, are obviously much better suited to be the *face* of this hero act. You get it, right? The audience wants Eagle to triumph; they want Eagle to be an all-American sort of hero, ya see? What I'm saying here, now – tonight – is that I'm offering you fellas a joint contract. Work it out however you want. But Eagle needs to rule the show when it comes to stunt work, and when he takes his mask off, he needs to look like *that*.' He pointed to Louis's freckled face.

'The writers, well, they'll refine your script, and it'll still be a battle between Eagle & Crane, good and evil, blah-blah-blah. But the stunts – my point is, nobody has to know which one of you is in the Eagle costume – not from far away, at least.'

He paused and extracted a business card and a fountain pen from his inside jacket pocket.

'And,' he said, arching an eyebrow at the two young men sitting before him, 'as far as compensation, this is what I'm prepared to offer you.'

He wrote a number on the back of the card and slid it across the table.

Neither moved to pick it up. Finally, Ava reached her hand out and lifted the card so all three of them could read it. She struggled to hide her surprise but found her eyes widening in spite of herself.

'*Each*,' Farrow added.

Now it was Louis and Harry's turn to stare at the number goggle-eyed.

Buster Farrow lit his perfectly toasted cigar and puffed at it, getting it to draw. Silence greeted him from all sides of the table.

'Look,' he said, 'maybe you want this Hollywood contract, and maybe you don't. You'd be a pair of fools not to, but I've seen plenty of fools in my day.'

Ava cleared her throat.

'If we understand you correctly, Mr Farrow,' she said, 'the contract you're offering is a joint one: they both have to sign for it to be valid, and it specifies that in certain instances Louis is to play the face of Eagle while Harry performs Eagle's stunts?'

'Precisely,' Farrow said, pulling his cigar out of his mouth to point at Ava directly. '*She* gets it,' he said in an approving tone.

'Indeed,' Ava murmured. She peered at Louis and Harry, wondering which was likely more deeply insulted. No one spoke for several minutes. Onstage, the orchestra boomed and wailed with the happy, frenetic sounds of a big-band number.

'Look, boys,' Farrow said with an air of finality, 'I don't need you to gimme an answer right away. While you make up your minds, we'll put you up in style and I'll have my people keep you entertained!'

He snapped his fingers again.

'As a matter of fact, I'd like to have you up to my house in Santa Barbara this weekend. I'm throwing a little party and I'd like to introduce you fellas to some other folks in the movie business.'

'A party?' Louis echoed, a little dazed by the barrage of information Farrow had just dumped on all of them.

'Yes! A party! You'll stay the weekend! Bring your little manager along.' He sent a condescending wink in Ava's direction. 'You'll all have a *grand* time!' He hit Louis on the shoulder, and the mood shifted yet again. Buster Farrow was done with them, for now.

'Now, if you'll excuse me . . .' Farrow stood up from the table and, leaning over with his big bear posture, shook Louis's and Harry's hands in turn. 'It's been a pleasure, fellas. Think about everything I said. One of my assistants will send a car for you to bring you up to Santa Barbara.' As his lips continued to shape the last of his words, his eyes were already wandering from the table. It was clear he intended to chase showgirls for the remainder of the evening.

'Oh!' Ava called after the producer, remembering. 'Mr Farrow?'

He stopped and turned around.

'What about Buzz and Hutch?'

'Who?' Mr Farrow asked. 'Oh – those your pilots?'

'Yes,' Ava replied. 'About the contract: does the contract you mentioned include provisions for them as well?'

'We can use 'em and pay 'em by the day, if it makes you fellas more comfortable, but I got plenty of pilots just as good. It's unique stuntmen I need! That's who the contract is for.'

With that, Buster Farrow strode away, his cigar gripped between yellow teeth.

'We were offered a Hollywood contract – that's something,' Louis said as they watched Farrow walk away.

'Or *half* of one,' Harry grunted.

'That *was* a little insulting, I guess,' Louis admitted. Being told that one of them was cut out to play only the body of Eagle, and the other cut out to play only the face . . , Ava glanced between them and inferred the answer to her earlier unasked question: Harry seemed to be the one taking it more personally.

Louis shrugged. 'I could maybe see past that if you can, Harry. I mean, it's a *Hollywood contract*, and worth an awful lot of money.'

Harry didn't say anything.

'But Buzz and Hutch,' Ava reminded Louis. 'They aren't part of the official contract. They might feel a little left out in the cold.'

'Farrow said he'd hire them if we wanted,' Louis replied.

'He said 'pay them by the day,'' Ava countered, shaking her head. 'Doesn't sound too good.'

'We don't know that for certain,' Louis insisted. He hooked a finger under the bow tie around his neck and tugged. It was obvious how badly he wanted the contract, and the awkwardness of his desire was thickening the air around them all. Ava suspected it had something to do with the multi-digit number Buster Farrow had scribbled on that slip of paper moments earlier.

'What do you think about all this, Harry?' Ava asked. In truth, she couldn't completely blame Louis. Now she looked to Harry.

'I don't know,' Harry murmured softly, shaking his head. 'Tonight reminded me a little of that first dinner we had with Earl.'

'Well, see? That turned out all right . . .' Louis said.

Ava snorted. 'That depends an awful lot on your definition of "all right".'

'It brought us all together.'

Ava looked at Harry. He shrugged.

'That part's true enough,' Harry said.

'Let's think about it,' Louis said. 'Like we promised.'

Harry nodded.

45

The next day, Louis, Harry, and Ava were chauffeured from Los Angeles north to Santa Barbara. They rode along the coastal route the whole way up. The drive took hours, but the ride was scenic.

Ava noticed straightaway: their new Hollywood prospects had put the three of them in very different moods. Louis was over the moon, drunk with happiness, and ready to sign on the dotted line. Ava was cautious, leery. She wanted to know more about Farrow's terms and get him to include Buzz and Hutch in the contract. Harry was quiet as a stone, a stoic yet thoughtful expression on his face.

They reached Buster Farrow's weekend house a little past three. But here the word 'house' was not quite adequate, for the structure they encountered as they pulled into the long private drive revealed itself to be an enormous Italianate mansion with a plunging cliff-side view of the Pacific Ocean. The lawns leading up to the stone veranda that encircled the entrance were vast and emerald green. A narrow, rectangular, and vaguely Arabic-looking fountain ran the length of it all, a stripe of watery oasis that started from a tall scalloped stone dish on the veranda and flowed in terraced steps down the sloping hill, cutting through the lawn like a long turquoise tongue unfurling. Italian cypresses stood at attention, and the topiary struck such perfect, tidy poses it looked as though every shrub was trimmed by a gardener on the hour. Bougainvillea climbed the mansion's ochre-colored walls, a riotous fuchsia flame that snaked around the countless arches and porticos.

Louis, Harry, and Ava stepped from their car and blinked in the glaring brilliance of it all. The day was balmy and mild; the ocean beyond twinkled as though someone had spilled a thousand golden coins upon its blue, blue surface. The air was scented with jasmine and orange blossoms.

Inside the marble foyer, a butler brought them a tray of drinks and directed them each to a room for changing and freshening up. Ava allowed herself to be escorted away by a maid. She gave Louis and Harry a little wave as the staircase branched in opposite directions.

'Early festivities begin at five o'clock,' the butler informed them. 'Mr Farrow asks that you wear evening attire.'

In each of their rooms, Farrow had arranged for a set of new clothes to be laid out on the bed: a pair of white summer suits for Louis and Harry, a silvery slip of a dress for Ava.

'Well, you two sure look like a pair of leading men,' Ava commented when they reconvened downstairs at five o'clock. It was meant as both a joke and a compliment, but as soon as the remark was out of Ava's mouth, it reminded them all of Farrow's complicated movie offer.

'I suppose that was his point in picking those suits out,' she added more soberly. They hadn't decided if they would accept the offer – they had hardly discussed it – but Ava realized that just by being in Farrow's house, they were inching closer and closer to acceptance, whether they liked it or not.

Farrow's party guests had already begun to arrive. Glamorous, swan-necked women drifted in through the front door, were each handed a coupe of champagne, and floated through the house and out to the garden. Elegant white-haired men mingled in clusters, laughing and trading stock tips, their voices echoing against the marble walls of the mansion's hallways. Here and there a famous leading man or silky-haired starlet arrived with much to-do, air-kissing and introducing the grim-faced guardians at their elbows. Louis recognized a few of them from last night at Farrow's red-carpet screening.

'There you are!' boomed a familiar voice. The three young friends turned and saw the tall, broad-shouldered figure of Buster Farrow approaching. 'Come, come!' he commanded. 'I'd like for you to meet some folks,' he said, ushering them toward a pair of open French doors. 'Out in the garden.'

The back garden was even more impressive than the front. Another impossibly green lawn sloped toward the horizon, whereupon it plunged dramatically downward to reveal a beach just below. The shallows glowed turquoise. Colorful flowers burst into the air from every angle: from pots and urns, from trellis arches and romantic gazebos. Somewhere a live band was playing jazz. Louis turned his head to locate the source and saw that a pair of tennis courts had been outfitted with a polished wooden dance floor, a sea of tables covered in elegant white silk tablecloths bordered the outskirts.

'Over there.' Farrow pointed to one of the tables. It was larger than all the other tables around it, and half occupied by ten or so men and women, dressed in varying degrees of glamour. He herded the three of them over and they all settled into the vacant seats.

'Now,' Farrow said, making introductions, 'you remember my two cameramen from your shoot last month, don't you?' He gestured to two of the less fancily attired gentlemen at the table.

'Good to see you again,' one of the cameramen said, nodding.

'And this here is Mr Cecil Bauer,' Farrow said, patting a bespectacled gentleman on the shoulder. 'If you two sign with me, he'll be the director for your feature film.'

Louis's eyes went wide and he scrambled to shake Mr Bauer's hand. Harry shook, too, but with more reserve. Ava frowned.

'I didn't realize you'd already picked out a director,' she said to Farrow. 'Isn't it a little early for that?'

'Why, that's how Hollywood works!' Farrow said, waving a relaxed hand. 'So many moving parts to every picture; best to line them up and get things into motion as early as possible.'

He continued with his introductions. There was a scriptwriter, a cinematographer, a soundman, and several beautiful actresses. ('Why, Eagle *must* rescue a damsel or two in distress! The audience will expect it!' Farrow roared.)

'And, finally, here you have the best pilot in all the business, 'Firefly' Clancy!'

Ava stiffened, surprised. 'I thought you said we could bring in our own pilots?'

Again Farrow waved a hand, but it was becoming clear he was growing irritated with Ava's presence.

'Yes, yes,' he said. 'We can certainly *talk* about that option, if you insist. But as these boys are aviators themselves, I thought at the very least they'd like to meet one of Hollywood's most famous stunt pilots!'

The evening carried on in the same manner. Food was periodically brought to their table and cleared away, while champagne was regularly replenished in a steady stream. Some couples got up to take a spin on the dance floor; others drifted over to take their seats at Farrow's table.

At one point, the cinematographer's wife – a gaunt yet glamorous women with dyed red hair – said in a confidential tone, 'My husband tells me you do some sort of scripted air show with a hero and a villain . . .'

'That's right.' Louis nodded.

'I see,' said the cinematographer's wife. 'I assume you play the hero and the Chinaman plays the villain?'

'I'm Japanese, as a matter of fact,' Harry said.

'Oh!' the woman exclaimed, briefly clutching her chest as though surprised to hear Harry speak. She had clearly mistaken his silence for an inability to speak English. 'Oh,' she said, recovering herself, 'Japanese. Well – that works just as well for a good villain, doesn't it?'

Harry smiled, but Ava noticed a trace of sadness in it.

'I suppose it does.'

The woman leaned in over the table and dropped back into a confidential tone. 'I did so love *The Mask of Fu Manchu* – positively terrifying!' She shivered as though to demonstrate the chills the film had given her.

As the sun dipped lower and the hours wore on, Ava noticed the two boys growing more and more divided in spirit. Harry was becoming more reserved, while Louis glowed with an excited, newfound optimism. The problem, Ava knew, was that they both had to decide to sign Farrow's contract together – or not. And, to Ava's surprise, it looked to her like Harry was leaning toward not.

She bit her lip and glanced at Louis, who seemed impervious to Harry's discomfort. Perhaps it would be best to pull him aside and warn him not to get too carried away. She leaned over and tapped Louis on the shoulder.

'Would you mind taking a little walk with me?'

Louis looked flattered and pleased. 'A walk? You sure you wouldn't like to dance?'

'No, but a walk would be lovely, if you don't mind.'

'Well, all right.'

They set off in a slow stroll and made a wide turn of the grounds. They kept walking until they ceased to pass any more fellow party guests. They kept walking until the tinkle of glassware and the laughter and the band music were all muted to a low, faraway din.

At the end of a red-brick path they spotted a gazebo overlooking the ocean. The structure was cantilevered over the edge of a small cliff, affording an incredible view. Ava steered them toward it.

'I woulda thought you'd be afraid of this,' Louis said as they stepped out onto the precariously perched gazebo.

'Oh?' Ava replied, absentmindedly. Looking down at the wooden floor, she could see skinny stripes of ocean far below, peeking up at her from between gaps in the planks. It was a long drop to the water. The sound of crashing waves rose up to fill the air all around them. But Ava was lost in thought, trying to come up with a way to break it to Louis gently that there was a chance Harry might not sign.

'Yeah,' Louis said. 'Afraid of heights, ain't ya?' He paused and studied her face. Ava got the impression he was almost suspicious of something and was testing her somehow. 'That's why you never been up in the Stearman, right?'

Ava's heart skipped a quick beat. Louis couldn't possibly know about her flights with Harry, could he? But there was no time to wonder about that now. She decided to change the subject.

'Listen, Louis,' Ava said, 'that picture deal . . . you know it isn't exactly straightforward. I mean, weren't you a bit insulted last night when Farrow said he wanted Harry to wear your costume and do your stunts, but for you to be the face?'

Louis shrugged. 'Sure I was. Any man worth his salt would be insulted. But I don't know . . . it's still the opportunity of a lifetime. We'd be fools to walk away, and frankly, I can't afford to.'

Ava was slightly subdued by this. She understood Louis's financial need, and the rift between him and his family.

'And besides,' Louis continued, 'Harry and I are in it together. I'm sure he's partly insulted, too. But we can laugh together about it – all the way to the bank, I expect.'

Ava saw her opportunity. 'Well, that's just it, Louis,' she said. 'I can tell Harry is bothered by a lot of things about this deal . . . and perhaps a lot more bothered than you are.'

'Did he tell you that?'

'No . . . I can just . . . tell.'

'Well, don't worry about Harry. He's a smart, practical fella. He's used to this. It's nothin' new to him. He knows perfectly well he's a Jap, and he's sharp enough to understand this is just how the world works.'

Ava shook her head. 'I don't know, Louis.'

'Well, good thing *I* do.'

Ava's mouth clamped shut. She realized that no matter what she said, Louis was not going to listen to her. Maybe she was wrong about Harry's feelings, anyway. She felt sure, though, that she wasn't. She felt a fresh wave of sympathy for Louis, wondering how he'd ever face his brother Guy if the Hollywood contract didn't go through.

She reached for Louis's hand. He had worked so hard. So many of the show's ideas were his. There was something she wanted to say to him, but she wasn't quite sure how to phrase it.

Before Ava knew it, Louis was kissing her. She was surprised. Down below, the waves crashed against the rocks, a thunderous uproar in her ears, adding to her feeling of dizzy disorientation. Not knowing what else to do, Ava kissed him back.

Ava was certain Harry knew about their kiss almost the instant they returned to the table. Louis was terrible at hiding his feelings or keeping a secret. Since the kiss he'd grown downright jubilant. He left a vaguely possessive arm lingering on the back of Ava's chair. He insisted she take a spin on the dance floor with him a couple of times.

Ava met Harry's knowing gaze and cringed, but Harry said nothing. It was a wonderful, terrible evening, and Ava felt the night was steadily spinning toward some sort of disastrous conclusion.

Her suspicions were confirmed a few hours later. The garden had been transformed into an enchanted wood, with paper lanterns hanging from all the trees and candles guttering in the ocean breeze. The ocean itself had become a black void far off in the distance, the steady roar of waves the only reminder of its now-faceless presence.

Buster Farrow had wandered away from their table, milling around with the other guests, dancing with a few young aspiring starlets. Puffing away on yet another cigar, he now came back around to check on his prospective stuntmen, a signature trail of heavy, sickly-sweet smoke drifting behind him.

'I swear to ya, boys,' he said, clapping Louis and Harry on the backs, 'I can't tell you how excited I am to have you star in my next picture! You boys are something special! Audiences go *nuts* for real stunts, and you oughta see the cameras they have these days. The ones we used for the screen test footage are nothing in comparison! These new cameras capture the action like you wouldn't believe!'

Louis grinned. He was about to reply, when Harry cleared his throat and spoke first.

'I've been thinking about things, Mr Farrow . . .' Harry began. Ava admired his bravery while at the same time bracing herself for what she knew was coming. 'I've been really mulling it all over . . .'

Farrow frowned.

'I hope you've come to the conclusion that you'll never get a better offer than this!' he prompted.

'With all due respect,' Harry said, 'and I certainly don't wish to offend you . . . but the arrangement you described . . .' Harry hesitated, then plunged forward. 'It just doesn't sit right with me.'

Farrow's sizable eyebrows shot into the air.

'Are you saying what I think you're saying?' he demanded. 'You're turning the contract down?'

'Speaking for myself,' Harry replied, 'I am.'

Farrow was taken aback. His jaw went slack, revealing a set of curiously long, British-looking teeth. His complexion flushed red with anger. Then, after no more than five seconds ticked by, the shock and anger passed almost as quickly as they had arrived. Farrow's mouth closed. The red drained from his skin like ink going down a drain, and he forced a smile.

'Suit yourself, son,' he said. He shook his head as though at a naughty pupil he couldn't be bothered to discipline anymore. There was an insinuation of disposal in his voice. 'I assure you, it's your loss – both of you.' His eyes moved briefly to Louis, as though to dismiss him, too. 'But suit yourself . . . We'll move on to our backup choice.'

Farrow walked away, back into the endlessly milling bodies of the party.

Harry turned to his friend, who so far had not uttered a word.

'I'm sorry, Louis,' Harry said.

All three fell silent. Ava looked between the two friends.

The expression on Louis's face was colder and blacker than anything she had ever seen.

46

NEWCASTLE, CALIFORNIA
SEPTEMBER 23, 1943

Bonner is back in the front parlor of the Yamada house for what he believes will be one last visit. The time has come for Bonner to be more direct. It is already Thursday, and if he hopes to make one last attempt to squeeze any answer out of Louis Thorn, it is time to lay his cards on the table.

'What can we help you with this time?' Ava asks in a deceptively pleasant voice. She pours some tea in a pretty porcelain cup for him – hot tea instead of iced, as it is still morning, and the afternoon heat hasn't set in just yet. Bonner already knows: she would rather he go.

It is Bonner, Ava, and Louis today; according to Ava, Cleo Shaw is busy working in the orchards. Bonner doesn't insist that they fetch her. He turned up at the Yamada doorstep unannounced, and it is Louis Thorn whom he really wants to speak to, anyway. He clears his throat and decides to ease into it, to bring up the things he's heard about their Hollywood business and see what kind of reaction it gets.

'We haven't talked much about your barnstorming act,' Bonner says now, 'at least, not the newer one you organized after Earl Shaw was no longer part of the operation . . . Eagle & Crane, was it?'

Ava and Louis exchange a quick flicker of a look.

'Yes,' Louis replies. 'That was the name.'

'Named for the two costumed personas you and Harry portrayed, is that correct?'

'Yes. You already know all this,' Louis says. 'I told you all that on the day of the crash.'

'That's right,' Bonner agrees. He taps a pencil against the open page of his reporter's notebook. 'I wrote it all down right here.' He licks his thumb and flips a page. 'I don't mean to be insensitive. I only need to ask a few more questions about the barnstorming act itself.'

'You still need to know more about Eagle & Crane?' Louis sounds puzzled.

Bonner nods. 'More specifically, I need to inquire about the relative success of the show.'

'Its success?'

'Would you say it was a financial success?'

Louis and Ava appear slightly unnerved.

Louis shrugs. 'We were able to draw folks out to the airstrip, get them to buy air show tickets . . . but it was a more expensive show than we'd ever done, so the profits . . . well, they were just okay, I reckon.'

Bonner smiles and affirms this with an easy nod. He is ready to prod Louis with the next round of questions. He flips a notebook page and pretends to look at it.

'Something else I meant to ask about . . . Deputy Henderson informed me that Eagle & Crane had attracted the attention of Hollywood – that it got an offer from some sort of big-time producer.'

Neither Louis nor Ava says anything, so Bonner presses on.

'I tried to dig around as best I could and came up with a name – a *big* name, as a matter of fact.'

'Oh?' Ava says.

'Yes. Buster Farrow. That's the name I heard. I heard he was interested in offering you boys a nice Hollywood contract to make a feature film based on your Eagle & Crane act, full of your stunt work.'

'That didn't come to nothin',' Louis says.

From the tone of Louis's voice, Bonner knows he's hit a nerve.

'Was it you or Harry who killed the deal?' Bonner asks point-blank.

'Beg pardon?'

'Farrow made the offer, and it's clear that one or both of you declined,' Bonner states. 'So, which way around was it?'

Louis doesn't say anything. Bonner looks at Ava, but she is looking at

Louis, a worried expression on her face. Bonner knows he's guessed correctly, and Ava's expression is as close to confirmation as he's going to get.

'That must've made you pretty mad,' he says now.

Louis won't look at him or reply. He only stares down at the Yamadas' rug.

'What was your relationship with Harry like after he lost you the Hollywood offer?' Bonner asks, and at this, suddenly Louis snaps back to life.

'He didn't "lose me" anything,' Louis replies, irritated. 'It . . . it just wasn't meant to be.'

'All right,' Bonner relents, trying to reintroduce a friendly tone to his voice. 'How about business after that? Did Eagle & Crane carry on with regular performances?'

Louis shrugs.

'It was close enough to the end of the season anyhow,' he says. 'We weren't some anonymous traveling circus anymore; we were running a bona fide air show. The idea was always to put the Stearman away during the wet months – November, December, January – and then take 'er out again when the weather dried up in the spring.'

'So you remained in contact with Harry?' Bonner asks. 'Your relationship remained friendly, even after he turned down Buster Farrow's offer?'

Louis shrugs again. 'I suppose.'

'We all went back home,' Ava said. 'We went back to work in the orchards and on the ranches. Things . . . things blew over.'

Bonner notices as Ava throws a nervous look in Louis's direction, as if silently asking him to confirm that was indeed the way of things.

'What was the amount Buster Farrow proposed to pay you, Mr Thorn?'

'Beg your pardon?'

'How much money would you have made if you and Harry had signed the Hollywood contract?'

It is plain that Louis understands the accusation Bonner is making. He stares at Bonner, and for a fleeting moment Bonner believes he discerns a flash of quiet anger ripple over the young man's brow. But then Louis's expression changes again, and the anger appears to subside. His body goes limp and he shakes his head.

'It doesn't matter. We never would have gotten it anyway.'

'And why is that?' Bonner asks.

'*The war*,' Ava interjects. Her voice bold, she looks Bonner squarely in the eye. 'The war,' she repeats, as though to emphasize the obtuse nature of Bonner's question.

Pearl Harbor. She means Pearl Harbor. It was always fated to come up; now here it is.

'The Hollywood deal would've been pretty good, like you say,' Louis says now, explaining in a quiet, measured tone. 'But even if Harry *had* signed on, it wouldn't have mattered. We weren't supposed to film until spring, and then, what happened in Hawaii . . . it changed everything.'

Bonner mulls this over for a minute. It didn't prove Louis's innocence, but Ava and Louis do have a point about the timing: Harry turned down the offer in October, and Pearl Harbor happened in December.

'The war changed everything,' Louis repeats. 'And once everything changed, there was nothing we could do to change it back.'

47

US DECLARES WAR, PACIFIC BATTLE WIDENS
UNITY IN CONGRESS

THE PRESIDENT'S MESSAGE

Following is the text of President Roosevelt's war message to Congress as recorded by The New York Times from a broadcast:

Mr Vice President, Mr Speaker, members of the Senate and the House of Representatives:

Yesterday, Dec. 7, 1941 - a date which will live in infamy – the United States of America was suddenly and deliberately attacked by naval and air forces of the empire of Japan.

The United States was at peace with that nation, and, at the solicitation of Japan, was still in conversation with its government and its Emperor looking toward the maintenance of peace in the Pacific.

Indeed, one hour after Japanese air squadrons had commenced bombing in the American island of Oahu the Japanese Ambassador to the United States delivered to our Secretary of State a formal reply to a recent American message. And, while this reply stated that it seemed useless to continue the existing diplomatic negotiations, it contained no threat or hint of war or of armed attack.

It will be recorded that the distance of Hawaii from Japan makes it obvious that the attack was deliberately planned many days or even weeks ago. During the intervening time the Japanese Government has deliberately sought to deceive the United States by false statements and expressions of hope for continued peace.

The attack yesterday on the Hawaiian Islands has caused severe damage to American naval and military forces. I regret to tell you that very many American lives have been lost. In addition, American ships have been reported torpedoed on the high seas between San Francisco and Honolulu.

Yesterday the Japanese Government also launched an attack against Malaya.

Last night Japanese forces attacked Hong Kong.

Last night Japanese forces attacked Guam.

Last night Japanese forces attacked the Philippine Islands.

Last night the Japanese attacked Wake Island.

And this morning the Japanese attacked Midway Island.

Japan has therefore undertaken a surprise offensive extending throughout the Pacific area. The facts of yesterday and today speak for themselves. The people of the United States have already formed their opinions and well understand the implications to the very life and safety of our nation.

As Commander in Chief of the Army and Navy I have directed that all measures be taken for our defense, that always will our whole nation remember the character of the onslaught against us.

No matter how long it may take us to overcome this premeditated invasion, the American people, in their righteous might, will win through to absolute victory.

I believe that I interpret the will of the Congress and of the people when I assert that we will not only defend ourselves to the uttermost but will make it very certain that this form of treachery shall never again endanger us.

Hostilities exist. There is no blinking at the fact that our people, our territory and our interests are in grave danger.

With confidence in our armed forces, with the unbounding determination of our people, we will gain the inevitable triumph. So help us God.

I ask that the Congress declare that since the unprovoked and dastardly attack by Japan on Sunday, Dec. 7, 1941, a state of war has existed between the United States and the Japanese Empire.

48

YAMADA AND THORN PROPERTIES
DECEMBER 7, 1941

The radio squawked all day and well into the night, like some terrible shrieking war bird. Earlier that morning, Mae had settled in to help her mother darn a pile of winter socks that had inconveniently sprouted holes. She'd switched on the radio, hoping to listen to a bit of big band or perhaps a radio soap opera. The two of them were the first to hear the news. Shizue ran outside to find her husband and son. When Harry heard, he ran to fetch Ava and Cleo from their caravan.

All six of them now sat in a semicircle around the radio as though around a bonfire. The radio crackled and popped; disembodied male voices shouted in excited, jittery stage voices; nothing seemed real. The attacks had been intentional and terrifying. It was estimated that at least two thousand American servicemen, nurses, and even a number of civilians were dead, and that they perished never having had a chance to defend themselves on that sleepy Sunday morning. The radio reported atrocity after atrocity, the mounting statistics of ships downed and people wounded or dead, descriptions of the horror and confusion that had been reported at the scene. There was much speculation about how President Roosevelt and Congress would respond.

They'd spent all day like that: huddled, listening. By evening the details had been picked over and there was little fresh news added to the broadcast; one announcer replaced another, and then another replaced him, and all had begun to repeat most of the information on a kind of endless loop.

'What will happen now?' Shizue asked quietly as the radio continued to squawk. She fixed her eyes on her husband.

'War,' Kenichi replied somberly. 'War will happen.'

'What will that mean for us?'

Kenichi shook his head. He tried to give her a reassuring smile but a shadow fell across his features, accentuating his advanced years.

'I don't know,' he said. 'But we will not be harmed. This is America. America is made up of many things, including many Japanese. We are not alone in this country. America is part of us, and we are part of it now. The government's leaders will not look at us as they do their enemy.'

It sounded right to everybody: Kenichi, Shizue, Harry, Mae – even to Cleo and Ava. It sounded *right*, and yet it did not sound quite true. Kenichi was speaking of the America as America *wanted* to be, not as America was.

Instinctually, they all knew: after the attack on Pearl Harbor, the American people would be full of anger and fear. The nation would run on these two fuels for quite some time and behave accordingly.

Sitting on opposite sides of the room, Ava and Harry exchanged a very worried, knowing look.

The scene at the Thorn household was similar, but with the additional noise and commotion that goes hand in hand with additional children. Edith Thorn and most of her older children were clustered around their old Philco Cathedral, listening intently, grappling with the unreal terror of the events, and trying to guess what the future now held. Marion sat listening while trying to occupy a distractible five-year-old Ruthie. Otis, having just turned eighteen, was already chattering excitedly about joining up, while Edith scolded him to drop the idea at once. Gil, Lester, and Carl all sat listening intently, intimidated by the gravity of the situation but also secretly glad they had been given a temporary reprieve from their daily chores on the ranch. Ernest and Clyde were listening, too, but also taking turns punching each other as hard as they could in the arm. Frank and Rudy – six and seven, respectively – knew it sounded bad but couldn't understand why the adults were being so boring nonetheless. They chased each other around in a boisterous game of tag until Edith caught Rudy by the ear and sent them outside. When they returned hours later, they were so exhausted they fell asleep on the floor in front of the wood-burning stove like a pair of puppies. Edith was too distracted to prepare much in the way of meals that day; dinner wound up being eggs and bacon eaten in the sitting room while continuing listening to the radio broadcast.

On the subject of what this attack meant for the United States, Guy Thorn was of course the most knowledgeable. He religiously read the newspapers every day. Louis had listened to Guy enough to know that Guy had months ago become convinced that America was destined to enter the war sooner or later.

'I would've guessed Europe,' he said, 'but all over the Pacific the Japanese been up to no good, too. It's obvious we ain't gonna sit it out anymore. We *can't*.'

Guy sat leaning forward, nearest the radio, listening intently. Beside him was his sweetheart, Lindy – a girl whose grandmother ran the boardinghouse in town, and whom Guy had courted ever since the two of them were sixteen. It was plain to everyone that Lindy adored Guy, and now, seeing how furious Guy was over the broadcast, Lindy appeared three times more distressed. She smoothed her dark brown curls nervously, and periodically reached for Guy's hand for reassurance.

'Those goddamn sneaky Japs,' Guy said angrily, shaking his head. 'I'm only surprised our own government let it happen like this. I bet none of our sailors even knew what hit 'em . . .' He continued shaking his head as a funny expression wormed its way over his lips, twisting them in anger and disgust.

Louis shivered to think of it: those men aboard their Navy ships, resting one minute and sinking to the bottom of the harbor floor the next – trapped, drowning, likely clawing like animals for a surface they would never again see. It was an ugly picture, and, like many ugly pictures, once you imagined seeing it, you couldn't stop seeing it. To attack like that . . . the only thing to conclude was that Japan – and the Japanese – were a ruthless, vicious people.

As though reading his brother's mind, Guy broke into Louis's meditative state. 'What do you think of your friends next door *now?*'

It was a statement, not a question. Since the garden party at Buster Farrow's Santa Barbara estate, Guy's opinion of the Yamadas had regressed to its previous vitriolic state. Louis felt it was his own fault: in Hollywood, in his state of excitement, Louis had sent a cable to Guy telling him the figure Buster

Farrow had offered. He'd made it sound like a done deal. He never should have done any of that – Ava had warned him against it – but he could hardly take it back now. When Louis had come home a few days after sending that cable, his tail between his legs and none the richer, Guy's anger and disgust was written on his face. *If you lie down with dogs*, Guy had said to Louis, *don't expect to get anything but fleas.*

'The Yamadas aren't like the Japs that did this,' Louis murmured now, after a moment's pause. He was mad at Harry – this time he had plenty of reason to be – but even so, Harry's family didn't have anything to do with Pearl Harbor.

Guy looked at him but said nothing.

'The Yamadas aren't to blame for this,' he insisted.

Although . . . as the radio broadcast droned on and on, Louis wondered just how much he truly meant it.

49

YAMADA PROPERTY
DECEMBER 15, 1941

A group of four agents came unannounced, knocking very early, dressed in suits, their mouths drawn and their brows furrowed. There was no true sunrise that morning, only a dim glow in the gloomy December sky, flat and gray. For a little over an hour, the men rifled the house, emptying drawers and making a mess, while the entire Yamada family waited patiently in the sitting room. Shizue watched as the agents unplugged and carried away their family radio, along with a box of family photographs, decorative scrolls, and a large number of old letters from her family back in Japan. *Enemy contraband.* Shizue knew that was what they were looking to find; she couldn't imagine why this might include her daughter Mai's baby portrait or old photos of Shizue's aunts back in Japan, dressed in full *kimono.* The world had gone mad overnight.

When their search was concluded, the agents insisted Kenichi and Haruto go with them to be interviewed. They declined to name the location, and the Yamadas knew better than to ask.

'Don't worry. We will be back soon,' Kenichi said to Shizue in an incredibly calm voice, as though he were running into town for a bag of grain or some kerosene. He pulled on a weatherproof jacket that hung from a hook by the front door and smiled serenely, though he knew exactly where he was being taken.

Shizue nodded, but did not believe him. And sure enough, the hours ticked by with no sign of their return, and the long wait began.

* * *

'Where have Mr Yamada and Harry gone?' Ava asked a little later, noticing their coats missing from the pegs by the front door.

She'd spent the morning with her mother, doing chores on the back property. Under ordinary circumstances, Ava didn't set foot in the Yamada house very often; she and her mother were grateful to be staying on their property and wanted to give the family their privacy. But when Ava had returned from the far side of the acreage, making her way past the barn and the house, she had noticed an awful lot of fresh tire treads in the dirt. Ava thought perhaps she'd ask Harry about it.

Now, as Shizue tried to answer Ava's question, she pressed her lips together and shook her head as though trying to shake the explanation loose. Her eyes turned glassy.

'He said not to worry . . . that they will be back soon . . .' was all she could muster, repeating the words her husband had spoken to her a few hours earlier.

Ava didn't need to ask anything more. She comprehended exactly what had happened. They'd all been on edge, ever since all the newspapers exploded with news about Pearl Harbor a week or so ago. America was at war with Japan; everyone – even folks in town who'd known them for years – had begun looking at the Yamadas differently.

'Would you like me and my mother to sit with you . . . maybe keep you company while you wait?' Ava asked, hesitant, sympathetic. There was something else mixed into Ava's concern – a shiver of wild panic, something to do with her feelings for Harry – but she pushed it aside. It was enough to focus on offering consolation to the woman standing before her.

'No,' Shizue replied. There was certainty in her voice. 'I'm sure they will return soon. Thank you,' she said with an air of finality.

Ava nodded respectfully and quietly let herself out the kitchen door again. She went to find her mother, and together they began to wait and worry a small distance away from the house, in their little caravan.

'They can't keep them,' Cleo reasoned. 'They haven't done anything wrong. They can't keep them if they haven't done anything wrong.'

Ava did not answer, wishing her mother was right for once.

* * *

287

Afternoon eased into evening, eventually the winter light faded from the sky, and Kenichi and Haruto were not back. Shizue stared out the kitchen window, which pointed to the road beyond, pretending to do dishes. Finally, when all the dishes were done and put away and Shizue could pretend no longer, she simply remained standing, staring out the window, gripping the edge of the empty sink with no guile or subterfuge. When her daughter prodded her, she refused to move to the sitting room, where she might be more comfortable, and which offered the same view.

'Why have those men taken *Tōsan* and *Onīchan* away?' Mai asked. 'What do they want with them?'

'They want to determine where their loyalty lies,' Shizue answered, wearing a vacant expression, her lips seeming to move independent of the rest of her face.

Mai frowned. The way her mother said it, it sounded like loyalty was something you could misplace, like a bone their dog had buried in the garden and couldn't find again.

'I don't understand,' Mai said, shaking her head. 'Their loyalty is here, in this home . . . with us . . . isn't it?'

'Yes,' Shizue replied, her voice hollow and distant. 'Their loyalty remains here, on this land. But those men will want to know if their loyalty lies with America.'

'Well? Isn't this land *America*?' Mai demanded. She pointed out the window at the land that surrounded the farmhouse. 'Isn't this all America?'

Shizue's head jerked. Her eyes suddenly flicked from the window to her daughter's face. Mai was thirteen. A teenager now; a girl no longer.

'Yes,' Shizue answered. 'But it is also our land, and we are Japanese.'

'I've never even been to Japan,' Mai said.

Her daughter was American, Shizue realized, and so only had access to that exclusively one-sided porthole that looked out onto the world and was peculiar to all Americans. Through such a porthole – and perhaps ironically – Mai could not glimpse herself as other Americans saw her. Shizue did not know how to explain the panicked fears that would dictate the circumstances of their future now, the belief that America's Japanese

288

population was not as horrified by Pearl Harbor as the rest of America was; that all Japanese, no matter how far from 'home', were secretly glad. It was an ugly belief, born of hatred and fear.

Still angry and confused, Mai gazed back into her mother's delicately shaped face and large, lovely eyes. She had never seen her mother look so sad.

'I've never even been to Japan . . .' Mai repeated softly.

Shizue's eyes lingered on Mai for a moment.

'It is not so simple,' she said. She turned back to look out the window as a solitary tear rolled down one cheek.

Finally, after nearly twenty-four hours had passed and it was once again early dawn, Shizue heard an automobile coming up the drive. She was trembling as her eyes searched beyond the windowpane for signs of what was imminent, part hopeful her husband and son were coming home, part terrified that the men in suits were coming to take her and her daughter away now, too.

But Shizue was in luck: Kenichi and Haruto had been questioned and released. Other Japanese-American men who had been rounded up for interrogation were not so lucky; many were accused of conspiring against the United States, of secretly radioing boats off the coast of California, of hoarding resources, or of outright plots of terrorism. If the accusation could be made to stick – no matter how flimsy the allegations – the men being questioned swiftly found themselves on a bus to a detainment center in Bismarck, North Dakota. It was nothing short of a miracle that Kenichi and Haruto had not joined these men, as owning an airplane in and of itself presented a threat. The wild argument *could* be made that Kenichi and Haruto were conducting some kind of aerial surveillance. But as it turned out, the Yamadas' saving grace was that neither Kenichi nor Shizue remained in touch with any of their relatives back in Japan. Kenichi was an old man; his parents had long since passed away, and Shizue's ties had faded letter by letter, until it became clear that she was never returning to Japan. This lack of traceable communication was enough for the FBI to let them go . . . for now. There was a second consideration, too, Kenichi said – involving the ownership of the Stearman – but he would explain later.

When Kenichi walked through the front door, he looked tired, rumpled, and bleary-eyed. Shizue wept with a mixture of joy to see them again, and a fresh tinge of fear to see that – written on her husband's face – something had permanently changed. The flame of bright optimism that perpetually flickered in Kenichi's eyes had been dampened, and knowing her husband as well as she did, Shizue knew that was not easy to do. She only hoped it had not been snuffed out completely.

'America has changed for us,' Harry's father said later that evening, after Harry's mother had successfully forced them both to eat a bowl of hot *sōmen*, wheat-flour noodles. 'They say it is always changing, and I have always known this to be true. But not all changes are good, and I fear this change is too big for us to survive.'

At his father's use of the word 'survive' – *ikinokoru* – Harry noticed his mother's alarmed expression. Harry's father immediately attempted to correct his phrasing.

'I don't mean they intend to kill us,' he corrected himself. He sighed. 'I don't know what I mean.'

'Whatever else you mean, you mean we will lose our home and our land,' his mother concluded in a frank voice. 'All the things you've worked so hard to earn.'

Harry's father answered with a firm nod of his head. 'It is not unreasonable to expect so, yes,' he said. 'Already they announced their intention to confiscate the Stearman.'

'When do they plan to collect the Stearman and take it to their impound?' Harry's mother asked.

Harry perked up, listening now. The first thing he'd done since returning home was to tell Ava he was back; he knew she had likely heard and was worried. But after a brief reunion with her to let her know he was okay – neither injured nor under arrest – Harry had retreated to the house to spend some time with his now-exhausted family. After walking in the door, he had sat slumped on the sofa, tired, dirty, and depressed. He had always known he would never *look* quite like what people expected the 'all-American boy' to look like – his brush with Hollywood had certainly reminded him of that – but America was the only home he had ever known. He had always *felt* that, deep down in his bones, he was American. Now he wasn't so sure. The confusion drained him, made him lethargic.

But at the mention of the Stearman, Harry sat up and wiped the sand from his eyes. He was all ears. His father glanced at him from out the corner of his eye.

'They have no plan to collect it,' he answered.

'What?'

'I told them I do not own it, so they cannot take away from me what is not legally in my possession in the first place.'

'*Otōsan* . . . why did you tell them that?' Harry demanded. His mind was swirling. Why had his father told the FBI such a lie? It only ensured the Stearman's confiscation, and now they would find themselves in deeper trouble for lying to the government.

'Because it is true,' his father replied.

'I don't understand . . .'

'I signed the title to the Stearman over to Louis Thorn last week,' his father said. 'It was the next morning, after . . .' His voice trailed off, but the words 'Pearl Harbor' hung in the air nonetheless. 'I didn't want to wait too long. It seemed the wisest course of action. And now I am glad I did not wait,' he finished, curtly nodding.

Harry's jaw dropped.

'You did . . . you did *what*? You *gave* the Stearman to *Louis*?'

'In legal title, yes. It was the only way,' his father replied. 'If I hadn't, it would belong to the government right now.'

This was true, but . . . but . . .

'But what about Ava? Or her mother? Why Louis?'

'Though she cannot locate him, Mrs Shaw is still married to Earl Shaw, and that might present complications,' his father explained in a tired, patient voice. 'Earl Shaw is not a man to be trusted. And Ava . . . Ava is seventeen . . . not yet eighteen. That might cause complications also. Louis was the best hope to keep the Stearman safe. The only hope.'

The head-splitting confusion Harry had experienced all day and all night grew even thicker. Why was he so upset to learn that his father had appointed Louis the legal owner of the Stearman?

'Louis Thorn is an honorable young man,' his father continued, as though reading his son's thoughts. 'He says he will keep the Stearman safe, and see that it comes back into our possession, if and when there is an appropriate time.'

'Yes, *Otōsan*,' Harry replied, rote, limp.

They were all exhausted – all four of them. They sat around the kitchen table now, eating hot soup and noodles, aching for a measure of comfort. But Harry's father, sensing his son's swirling feelings, sat up, focused.

'Listen to me, Haruto,' he commanded.

Harry was caught off guard, surprised to hear his father's voice so forceful all of a sudden.

'I believe your friend Louis is a man of honor,' his father said. Then he paused, as though considering carefully. 'Or, at the very least, he wants to be a man of honor and is on his way. None of our lives will be simple during these coming years. You must trust in me, as I trust in him.'

He reached for Harry's hand where it lay on the kitchen table but wound up gripping Harry's wrist – it was an extremely uncharacteristic gesture for Kenichi – and gave it a squeeze.

'Yes, *Otōsan*,' Harry said. 'I understand.'

He bowed his head before his father. Kenichi gave one final, definitive squeeze and released Harry's wrist. Then he turned his attention to the cup of hot tea Harry's mother was pouring for him.

50

YAMADA PROPERTY
APRIL 30, 1942

The Yamadas might have moved east. Other Japanese families were packing up, selling their land, and heading to Chicago or New York. The prices these families received for the sale of their homes and land were ridiculously low, an example of the banks' greed and the government's callous indifference. Kenichi Yamada had enough saved to weather such gouging. But every time he contemplated moving his family eastward, he could not imagine it. He was eighty-one years old and had spent sixty-two years of life on that land, in those orchards. He could not imagine leaving. The Yamadas stayed.

There was hope – for a little while, at least – that the whole business would blow over, that the war would be over quickly, or that the question of Japanese-American loyalty would be settled once the government determined the notion of spies was far-fetched, ridiculous. For a few months, this hope kept Japanese Americans working and living as they normally would. But it was not to last.

Ava was the first to glimpse one of the signs, coming upon it while she was running errands in town.

INSTRUCTIONS TO ALL PERSONS OF JAPANESE ANCESTRY, the signs read. *All Japanese persons, both alien and non-alien, will be evacuated from the above designated area by 12:00 o'clock noon Wednesday, May 6, 1942.*

Ava was carrying two bottles of sarsaparilla in a brown paper grocery bag. Sarsaparilla was Harry's favorite – she'd teased him several times over about his corny taste – and when she caught sight of the first sign, she dropped the bag, breaking both bottles. She didn't move, seemingly frozen as a moment passed. In a daze, she looked down at her wet shoes, covered now in irregular shards of glass and brown-tinged liquid, watching the sarsaparilla drain away into the cracks in the wooden boardwalk outside the general store.

The date named on the handbill – that was only a week from the current date. They were giving Japanese families *one week*.

Without knowing quite what she was doing, Ava found herself suddenly running. She clambered back into Earl's old Model A, shifting it into gear and wrangling the steering wheel, gunning the motor and flying over potholes as she headed out of town. The truck raced up the Yamadas' drive, all the way to just below the house, at which point the sound of screaming brakes rang out, echoing throughout the surrounding orchards.

'Harry!' she yelled, seeing him atop a ladder that leaned against the Yamada farmhouse. Spring had sprung, and there was no better time to do the chores that had been put off all winter. Harry was cleaning the gutters, a good son doing the jobs he didn't want his parents attempting.

'Ava?' he called back, somewhat puzzled and alarmed. He climbed down from the ladder. 'What is it?'

She charged up the wooden stairs to the porch and rushed toward him, out of breath. He opened his arms as though to catch her, wondering if she was sick or injured. She was in some kind of frenzied state, pale and sweating. But before she made it to his embrace, Ava abruptly drew up short. They had never touched each other – not like that. The one time they'd danced together was the closest they'd ever come, and it had been polite, procedural. She stood and stared at him instead; she had no idea what she wanted to say.

'What?' he repeated. 'What's the matter?'

'We could leave,' she blurted out.

He looked at her, wordless, baffled.

'I would go with you,' she impulsively added. She heard it aloud at the same time he did, heard how it sounded. She drew a breath and suddenly looked shy. 'If you wanted.'

Harry gave her one of his lopsided smiles. 'Oh, yeah? You would go with me?' His tone was friendly, joking. 'Where are we goin'?'

She realized that he didn't understand.

'We could go east, away from all this,' she said, trying to be clearer. 'I heard it's better back East for . . . for . . .'

All at once, Harry realized the word Ava wasn't saying was 'Japanese.' His grin vanished and he swallowed as though he had just been given a sip of something bitter. He gave a slight shake of his head and clenched his jaw.

'What's happened?' he asked in a low, flat voice.

He knew from the look on her face that things had just gotten worse. His father had warned that they might. They'd heard rumors that evacuation orders had already been given to people in San Francisco and Los Angeles. Harry was suddenly very tired. The fact that he didn't know how to feel wasn't relevant, because he remembered his interrogation with the FBI all too well, and in remembering it his heart went cold. He couldn't feel anything.

'We knew in February this might happen,' Kenichi said.

Once his son had passed along the news, Kenichi knew what must be done. He had called everyone together – his wife, son, and daughter . . . Cleo and Ava . . . and Louis Thorn, from the neighboring property. It was Louis in particular who Kenichi wished to speak to now.

'We knew this might happen,' Kenichi repeated, 'when they issued the order.'

Executive Order 9066. It was the official United States executive order signed by President Roosevelt on February 19, 1942, authorizing the relocation of Japanese Americans to internment camps.

'Perhaps it would have been wise to leave California, to leave the – what do they call it? – the Western Military Zone,' Kenichi continued, 'but the truth is . . .' He paused, looked around at the faces of his family and at the faces of the people he hoped were their true friends. 'The truth is, this is our home, our only home. How could we leave?'

Harry suddenly felt very angry. He clenched his teeth and nodded.

'But now the choice has been taken away from us; we must leave. Which is why we need to appeal again to you, Louis,' Kenichi said, turning to gaze at the young man. 'Just as we did with the Stearman.'

Louis blinked, staggered by the news.

'You signed the Stearman over to my name to protect it,' he said, slowly comprehending.

'Yes,' said Kenichi, 'and now I would like to ask to do the same as concerns our house and our land.'

'You . . . you want to sign them over to *me*?' Louis stammered. Louis appeared rattled by this request, and Kenichi knew why.

'The land is technically in Haruto's name,' Kenichi continued, 'as I am *issei* and he is *nisei* – born here, a citizen. We were obliged to transfer the deed into his name shortly after he was born.'

This was news to his son. Harry looked at his father in surprise.

'If you agree to help us, Louis,' Kenichi said, 'you will have to sign, and Haruto will have to sign – all in the presence of a notary. I have already had the paperwork drawn up. I'm sorry for the rush, but we will have to be swift about this to make certain it is legal. Once we enter those camps . . . we will lose many of our legal rights, and a belated transaction could be invalidated.'

Kenichi was done speaking. Silence invaded the room as everybody pondered the gravity of the situation. No one discussed what was expected of Louis – that, quite naturally, he was expected to hold the land and the house, but return both to the Yamadas if and when they were allowed to resume their old lives. Kenichi felt that to state this directly – to remind him they wanted it all returned – would be to insult Louis Thorn's honor. You did not ask a man for a favor so large as this and insinuate that you did not trust him.

'I . . .' Louis said, trying to muster an answer. 'This is a lot to chew on.'

'I understand,' Kenichi said.

'I oughta at least sleep on it . . .' Louis peered into Kenichi's face in earnest. 'Is it all right if I sleep on it and tell you my answer tomorrow?'

The tension in Kenichi's face tightened slightly, but only Harry noticed as Kenichi's right temple twitched. He saw the look on his father's face as the reality of the situation sunk in: Louis was their only hope.

'Of course,' Kenichi said. 'Of course. We thank you for considering doing our family this service. It is a lot to ask, and I am humbled by your listening to my request.'

51

'Do you trust him?'

Harry and Ava were alone. After Louis had gone home, Kenichi, Shizue, and Mae had gone to bed, while Cleo retired to the caravan. Harry and Ava were taking a walk together. It was a chilly, damp night, and they trudged through the woods until they were standing beside a little streambed. The water glittered eerily silver in the moonlight, while everything else around them was reduced to flat black shadows. They were sitting on an old tree stump together when Ava broke the silence.

'Even if he signs . . . do you trust him?' she repeated.

'Louis?' Harry asked, needlessly. 'Absolutely,' he answered in a knee-jerk reaction. Then, after a brief pause, 'I don't know,' he said, relenting. 'I think I do.'

'He needed the money he didn't get from that Hollywood business. He . . . might blame you for that.'

'He does,' Harry confirmed. 'But he's been working hard to be the bigger man.'

'His family has poisoned him against you,' Ava continued quietly. She shook her head. 'Over a lot of years.'

Harry didn't say anything.

Sitting side by side, they both peered into the dark woods that lay before them, the scent of wet oak leaves thick on the night air. The scene was peaceful, but somehow the stillness was only adding to Ava's feelings of panic. She couldn't lose Harry; she'd only just discovered how she felt about him. Meeting both of them at the same time – Louis and Harry – had confused things. Ava genuinely liked Louis – she felt at ease around him – and it was clear from the start how much he admired her. Ava felt grateful, and perhaps even somewhat protective of Louis's sensitive heart. Harry, on the other hand, had done nothing but tease her, contradict her, and challenge her at first. He could make her angry like no one else could. She thought she could barely tolerate him.

But then . . . they'd gone up for a flight, and several more after that, until Ava found herself counting the days in between. Harry had a funny way about him; in private, he never showed off. He also never belittled Ava in any way, treating her like a shrinking violet or a girl to be courted. Instead, he insisted she handle the stick herself, then slowly but surely taught her how to take off and land the Stearman. When Earl abandoned them, Harry drove the Model A and caravan straight to his family's property, reassuring Ava they would be welcome and safe there.

Ava found herself thinking about those flights – and about Harry – when they were not together. And yet, despite all the time they'd secretly spent together, Harry had never indicated that his newfound friendliness went any further – not since the day Ava had agreed to go on Louis's arm to the town dance in Sonoma. If tension cropped up between Ava and Harry, Harry changed the subject to Louis, a habit that left Ava confused and half-convinced she did love Louis after all.

But the confusion she'd felt had evaporated the second she glimpsed the evacuation notice pasted up on the general store in town. In that moment, as the sarsaparilla bottles clattered to the ground and smashed to pieces, Ava suddenly knew: it was Harry she couldn't live without. She cared for Louis – she cared for Louis deeply – but as a friend.

Now she wanted to set the record straight, to get it all out in the open. Harry might tell her he didn't want her – he probably would, Ava thought – but it didn't matter, so long as he stopped trying to fob her off on Louis. If he tried to do that one more time, Ava was sure she would scream.

She mulled over how to begin, staring at the shimmering silver surface of the creek.

'I kissed him,' she finally said. 'Louis, I mean.'

Harry didn't say anything.

'At Farrow's party,' Ava added. 'He kissed me . . . and I . . . I suppose I kissed him back.'

'I know,' Harry said quietly.

'But you *don't* know,' Ava replied, her voice firm.

'It's all right,' Harry said.

'It's *all right*?'

He pressed on. 'Louis is kind and decent, he's—'

'Not you.'

Ava felt Harry's body jolt with surprise as she said the words. *Not you.*

'The kiss didn't mean anything, Harry,' she continued, intent on driving her point home. 'And I realize the reason it didn't mean anything is because Louis is not you. Haven't you ever thought about . . . us?'

'No.' He shook his head.

Ava had braced herself for this, but even so, watching him shake his head now, she felt the early sting of rejection.

'You deserve someone who is more . . . like yourself . . .' Harry was floundering for words now. 'Someone who is . . .'

'What?' she demanded.

'Someone who isn't about to be detained in a camp somewhere,' Harry answered. 'Louis will be here for you.'

'But I'd rather *you* were,' Ava said. 'Do you understand? I don't want Louis, I don't *choose* Louis. I choose you.'

Harry was silent. Ava rose to her feet, angry.

'Dammit, Harry, you're brave about everything else in life – why not about this?'

He stood and faced her. Their expressions were lost in the dark, but he seemed angry, too, Ava thought – though why, she could not comprehend.

'What on earth do you think I *want* to do? Don't you understand letting you go *is* being brave?'

It didn't make sense. Ava was annoyed. She let out a huge sigh of exasperation and turned to go. But as she did, she felt Harry's hand on her arm, suddenly turning her back around. He kissed her, and she kissed him back. It was a very different kiss from the one she'd shared with Louis.

Standing in the trees some distance away, Louis watched them, a silent witness. He bristled as he watched their two bodies come together. He'd been restless, thinking matters over, and taken a walk in the wooded area at the border of the Thorn and Yamada properties, drawn to the old childhood meeting spot he'd shared with Harry. He'd planned to sit and think things over, perhaps remind himself of their friendship – old and new.

And now, here Harry was. But not alone. Louis stood there, frozen, unable to take a step closer. Unable to make his presence known. He had seen and heard things. All of them things he could neither unsee nor unhear.

Eventually, Harry and Ava walked back in the direction of the Yamada homestead. Louis remained, still as a statue. When nearly a half hour passed without a single sign of another human being, Louis began to move again. He turned on his heel and walked in the opposite direction – back in the direction of the Thorn farmhouse and everything it represented.

52

Early the next morning, Louis Thorn made his way up the dirt road that led to the Yamadas' farmhouse, approaching their residence via the official route instead of cutting through the woods. A gentle dawn broke in the sky above, painting the clouds in pastels, and Louis moved with purpose and determination.

He had made up his mind.

Shizue Yamada answered the door when he knocked. She pushed the screen door open, slightly surprised by Louis Thorn's presence on her porch at such an early hour. Neither of them spoke, but after a fleeting moment Shizue understood the young man wished to see her husband. She pushed the screen door open even further, giving Louis the signal to enter. Once inside, Louis crossed to the fireplace mantel and remained standing, waiting. His body language made it plain that he didn't intend to stay long and that he didn't intend to sit down. Shizue went to fetch her husband.

Less than a minute later, Kenichi Yamada appeared in the sitting room. He understood his young neighbor had arrived at a decision with regard to his request and was ready to give him an answer. The expression on Louis's face was not encouraging. Kenichi coughed, clearing some of the morning's congestion from his throat.

'Good morning,' Kenichi greeted the young man.

Louis nodded. He, too, coughed.

'I've made up my mind,' Louis reported, with no further preamble.

'I see,' said Kenichi. He braced himself for bad news. He looked at Louis, studying the face of his son's best friend. Your average Caucasian boy, sandy-haired and blue-eyed. Kenichi had observed that Louis was often myopic in his view of the world but occasionally magnanimous with his sympathies once he raised his head and really saw the world around him. But Louis did not look particularly magnanimous that morning. Did this young man understand the power he held? It was a given that he understood what the Yamadas had to lose and gain. Did he understand the implications of it all?

'I'll sign,' Louis said.

Kenichi blinked. From the expression on the boy's face, he'd been bracing himself for a different answer.

'I'll sign what you need,' Louis restated.

Kenichi gathered his composure.

'I cannot thank you enough,' he said. 'My *family* cannot thank you enough.' Though he knew perfectly well the act meant nothing to Louis, Kenichi bowed, purely on instinct. It was a deep, sincere bow – a significant gesture coming from a man so advanced in his years, to bow so deeply to a young person.

'How soon can we get this done?' Louis asked abruptly, before Kenichi had quite finished bending at the waist.

Louis's interruption, his terseness, his tone, bothered Kenichi somewhat. It was distant, cold . . . but there was something else, too. There was anger in Louis's voice. It seemed a perplexing contrast to Louis's gracious gesture to act as their guardian.

'I have the papers already drawn up,' Kenichi said, repeating the information he had given Louis the day before. 'It is only a matter of signing before a notary. We can visit the notary at your convenience.'

Louis nodded. His eyes bore a faraway, distracted look.

'I'll be in town around three o'clock today,' he said. 'If that suits.'

'I will tell Haruto,' Kenichi said, nodding. He bowed again – a smaller, slighter bow.

'Good,' Louis said. He turned to go.

'Wouldn't you like to see him?' Kenichi said, surprised.

'I'll see him this afternoon' was all Louis said in reply. He continued on his way and let himself out the front door.

Kenichi watched the young man go. Louis had agreed to sign and legally take ownership of all that the Yamada family possessed. That ought to have been a relief to Kenichi, a ray of hope in the darkness that was America's manic political climate. Instead, Kenichi felt unsettled and on edge. Something was not quite right; something in Louis Thorn's demeanor was not reassuring. Kenichi knew there were reasons not to trust the boy. He had hoped none of them would ultimately dictate the boy's actions. The day before, Kenichi was confident his hopes were not misplaced. Now something had changed.

'Was that Louis who was just here?' Haruto asked, coming into the sitting room and pulling aside the curtain in order to peer outside. He quickly made out the familiar figure of his best friend retreating into the distance. It was plain that Haruto had only just woken up. His hair was rumpled and his eyes were not quite open, groggy with sleep.

'Yes,' Kenichi answered.

'What did he say?' Haruto asked.

'He said he would sign as guardian of our property,' Kenichi replied.

'That's good of him, right?' Haruto said, but already his voice was a little weaker, his resolve less sure. 'Why didn't he stick around? Didn't he want to talk to me? Why didn't you or *Okāsan* wake me?'

Kenichi only stared out the window to where he could see Louis Thorn's shape growing smaller as it disappeared down the drive. He put a hand on his son's shoulder.

'He said he would meet us at the notary at three o'clock today,' Kenichi said, hoping his voice conveyed reassurance.

His son frowned, and looked from Kenichi's face to the window. 'You mean . . . he only wanted to set up a time to sign?' he asked.

'Yes, Haruto,' Kenichi said. 'It is most generous of him. We owe him a debt, to be sure.'

'Yes . . .' Haruto murmured. 'I guess so.'

His son glanced again out the window, but already the familiar shape of his son's friend had vanished.

53

At first, Ava refused to drive Earl's old Model A truck, which would ultimately bring Harry, his sister, Mae, and their mother and father to the designated pickup location. It was plain she thought she was making a righteous stand in her refusal, that she was somehow sticking up for Harry and the Yamadas by being unhelpful. It was misguided, perhaps, but endearing.

'You know we can't drive ourselves,' Harry said. 'No automobiles are allowed in the camps; we have to leave it all here.'

Ava didn't answer.

'We'll just ask your mother, then,' Harry said. He laughed as though he'd gotten the last word or won some sort of staring contest.

'All right. Fine,' Ava agreed.

In the end, they all went together to see the Yamada family off: Ava; her mother, Cleo . . . and Louis, too, when he finally turned up of his own accord.

The Yamadas had packed carefully but assembled near the curb in front of a local Methodist church. (*How ironic*, Ava thought, *that the government had designated churches as the sites of so many pickup points*.) The Yamadas looked strangely disorganized, lost . . . Centuries of proud family history and decades of Kenichi Yamada's dedicated labor had been transformed into a hurried jumble of embarrassment, with the ultimate result that they looked like a pack of hobos.

All over America, Japanese families stood on the curbs at other bus stops, their trunks and suitcases lined up, looking overstuffed and straining. The men and women and children looked a little overstuffed, too, having bundled themselves up with as many layers of clothing as they could stand, so as to be able to transport as much as possible. This would not have been so inconvenient in March and April, but by May the weather had turned unseasonably warm, and the expressions on people's faces betrayed their discomfort.

'Do you have your list?' an Army soldier in uniform demanded.

Kenichi handed it over. They had been instructed that the head of each household was to do all the talking, all the paperwork, all the accounting for what was being toted along with them to the camps. The government intended to interact with as few individuals as possible, and the Army soldiers assigned to direct them could not be expected to attend to distressed women and crying children.

The soldier took the list and, with a group of his peers, checked the Yamadas' baggage. It was mostly all clothes, pots and pans, toiletries. After the FBI's initial visit, the Yamadas had obediently turned in everything that had been declared contraband, the sorts of things a spy might be expected to have: radios, cameras, and so forth.

'All clear here,' the soldier declared, pounding the topmost suitcase on the Yamadas' pile with his fist in approval. They moved on to the next family lined up along the curb.

Each family was assigned a number. Evacuation tags were tied to everything. There were quite a few families; over the decades, a large number of Japanese had settled into the areas surrounding Loomis, Penryn, and Newcastle. The farmland had been perfect for growing plums and mandarins. 'The fruit basket of the nation,' folks called it. Like the Yamadas, the *issei* – the first generation – had immigrated years earlier, and the majority of their children had been born on American soil, where they grew up playing baseball and speaking English far better than Japanese. Of course, none of that mattered now. As far as the Army was concerned, they were all Japanese, period.

'All right! LOAD UP!' the soldier who had inspected their luggage hollered. They had finished checking all the families off their list.

In other parts of the nation, Greyhound buses and school buses had been commissioned to pick up and transport the Japanese to the internment camps.

In the smaller, more rural areas, like Newcastle, the government sent military trucks instead of buses, making the rounds of all the ranch towns. Evacuees rode in the back, in the drab, olive-green darkness of the covered cargo beds, as the trucks bumped along, kicking up a terrible cloud of dust behind them.

'They mean for you to ride in there?' Ava gasped and murmured in disbelief. 'Like . . . Army cargo?'

A shadow of fear darkened Mae's eyes. She turned pale, and her face squirmed as though she was fighting back tears.

'Hey . . . no . . .' Harry tried to soothe his sister. 'It's gonna be all right.' He put his arms around his kid sister and hugged her to his chest. Over the top of Mae's head, he shot Ava a scolding look. She bit her lip and scowled. She knew she would aid the Yamadas in their departure best by being quiet, but she couldn't help herself. It was all too outrageous, too unjust – all of it.

Louis, meanwhile, had appeared stoic up until that point. Days earlier, he had signed the paperwork to take ownership of the Yamada property and all of the Yamadas' remaining possessions. All of them had noticed his cold demeanor; none of them had commented on it. Louis had promised to say goodbye on the day of their departure, and now he was there, making good on his word, but he had arrived separately and had strode up with his hands in his pockets, looking detached.

However, seeing the evacuation labels dangling from the Yamadas' luggage and from the Yamadas themselves – they had been requested to tie the same labels bearing their family number to their coats – Louis's expression softened for the first time in a week. A small wrinkle of worry crept into his brow as he peered at the Army trucks.

The soldiers were urging the evacuees to hurry up now.

Everyone said goodbye. Ava and her mother hugged and kissed each member of the Yamada family, with Kenichi and Shizue looking particularly surprised and stiff by these unexpected embraces. Louis shook hands.

When he got to Kenichi Yamada, Louis paused. He stood up straight, placed his hands against the sides of his legs, and bowed respectfully from the waist. Harry watched in surprise. In that moment, he felt certain his father had made a wise decision entrusting Louis Thorn with all they ever had. *It will be all right*, Harry thought. Although he had repeated this phrase aloud several times since hearing about the evacuation order, it was the first time Harry had genuinely said it to himself and meant it.

The Yamadas shuffled into a line of people loading into the back of one of the trucks. They climbed up and took a seat on one of the benches within, clutching their suitcases in their laps. When the motor started up and the truck began to pull away, Ava and her mother waved.

It looked as though the Yamadas waved back, but it was difficult to be sure. It was a sunny day out and they were lost in the darkness of the truck's canopy. Ava squinted and convinced herself she saw a hand moving, a flash of light in the gloom, but then a dust cloud rose up behind the truck and in a single swirl, and they were gone.

54

TULE LAKE, CALIFORNIA
MAY 20, 1942

The Army truck that picked up the Yamadas on the morning of May 6 brought them first to the Sacramento Assembly Center, a place otherwise known as Camp Kohler. There was little there; it had been used for years as a camp for migrant workers, outfitted – as nearly all migrant workers' camps are – with the most Spartan of accommodations. Japanese families were packed into a series of shacks with others. Toilets were outhouses. Showers were nonexistent. They heard there were worse assembly centers: in the Bay Area and down near Los Angeles, for instance, Japanese families had been gathered at racetracks whose operations had been temporarily suspended. Rumor had it that the families in those facilities were sleeping in actual horse stalls.

At the assembly center just outside Sacramento, days passed as the Yamadas were asked to fill out more paperwork, until it was decided that they would be sent from the Roseville rail station up to the Tule Lake Relocation Center, where, supposedly, resources had been set aside for the internees, and more permanent lodging was waiting for them. This same decision was made about the majority of Japanese Americans who passed through Camp Kohler, but some were sent down to Manzanar in Southern California, and still others were rumored to have been sent as far away as Arkansas. All things considered, the Yamadas felt grateful to stay in California, assuming it was best not to be sent so far away from home that they might never return to Newcastle. They had pinned all their hopes on Louis Thorn, and they wanted very much to return.

A train took them north to Tule Lake, then a bus brought them from the

308

station to the camp. Everyone held their breath, hoping this new, presumably more permanent camp would be a significant improvement over the poor facilities at the assembly centers they'd had to endure. Mae pressed her nose against the glass of the bus window, her eyes searching for anything familiar, but the land was strange to her. Its wide, flat, dry landscape was punctuated by several faraway buttes, giving the impression of an alien planet. There wasn't much out there in the way of towns, of civilization. Perhaps that was the point: to keep them away from anything important, anything they might spy on or sabotage or think to bomb. Mae let out a grunt and a chuckle – not a chuckle of joy but a small, sarcastic, precociously bitter chuckle – to think of herself, a young girl, being so powerful as to merit being quarantined from her town, her school, her home. It was ridiculous, and would be funny if it didn't also make her sick to her stomach.

'What's tickling you, Chicken Legs?' Harry asked, elbowing her gently in the ribs.

Mae shrugged, rolling her lips into a tight line.

'C'mon,' Harry urged, smiling. 'You can tell me. It's okay to laugh. We don't have to pretend this is all some big funeral. We have to laugh sometime.'

Mae shook her head, but after a moment she gave in.

'It's only that I didn't understand until now.'

'Understand what?'

'They're afraid of us.'

The easy smile vanished from Harry's face. He sometimes forgot how old Mae was now.

'Yes,' he said. 'They're afraid of us.'

He winced as the words left his lips. It looked like something sharp pierced his chest as he said it.

'But Ava's not afraid of us.'

'No,' Harry replied. 'She's too smart.' He paused, and a glimmer of his previous smile returned. 'And too mean. She knows better than to be afraid of us.'

'And Louis,' Mae went on, insisting. 'Louis isn't afraid of us.'

Harry's face went blank for the slenderest of seconds, then he shook his head.

'No,' he said. 'I don't think Louis is afraid of us. I think he means to help us.'

309

'So if our neighbors aren't afraid of us, why must we be sent away, all the way out here?'

'I suppose it's the neighbors of our neighbors . . . and their neighbors, too, who don't know us and don't trust us,' Harry said.

They fell silent, both somberly entranced by the scenery outside the window as the bus drove onto the property that was to be their new home. It was a dry, flat, dusty patch of earth. Wooden barracks had been erected – hastily, from the looks of them – and stood in rows in eerily generic likeness.

Harry noticed there was no fence around the camp, no gate, and, noting this, he felt a sense of relief. Of course, he could not know: the fences, gates, and barbed wire would be added soon enough.

A heavy haze of dust swirled around the bus long after it had rolled to a stop. The Yamadas followed the shuffling mass of people off the bus and were herded over to a series of tables, where the contents of their luggage were rifled yet again, and they were assigned a block number, a figure that was scribbled onto the end of the family number they'd already been given.

'Where do we go?' Harry's mother, who was confused by the camp's numbering system and layout, kept repeating to his father.

'Follow Haruto,' he replied, resigning himself to his own confusion. Harry could see it in his father's eyes: for the first time in his eighty-one years, his father felt truly old. It broke Harry's heart to see such a young spirit show its first splinters.

The four of them successfully located their new home. It was not an encouraging discovery. The barrack they were assigned had been carelessly slapped together and bore the marks of shoddy craftsmanship: irregular gaps showed between the pine planks, and no effort had been made to weatherproof this most basic of bungalows.

There was also another family already inside. Harry introduced himself and learned they were to share the single rectangular room with this family, the Akimotos, from Los Angeles. A mother, two teenage daughters, and an adult son. They had lived on the coast and owned a fishing boat until it had been confiscated by the government. They would have been in Manzanar, they said, if not for the fishing boat, for the trouble it had brought them. Tule Lake, they told Harry, was a more serious place to be; Manzanar was better somehow. The father was not with them; after some vague, embarrassed discussion, Harry came to understand that Mr Akimoto had been detained somehow at another camp somewhere in North Dakota.

Everyone moved politely around the barrack, their footsteps echoing terribly on the plank floor, revealing the hollow space just beneath. The two families worked together to string up a sheet to divide the room and to create a sense of dignity and privacy. It was hardly enough to reclaim either, but it helped.

Somewhere in the distance, a bell clanged.

'What's that?' Harry asked his new roommates.

'The dinner bell,' Bill Akimoto replied. 'You can follow us to the mess hall, if you want. It's a little bit of a walk.'

Harry thanked him, and the four Yamadas followed the Akimotos to the other side of the camp. Along the way, Harry and Mae took in the scene. The landscape was dismal. The camp was built on a dry lake bed, and the earth beneath their feet looked hard and parched, riddled with cracks. Dust got everywhere. Mae rubbed at her eyes where a tiny boulder of hard sand had already accumulated and solidified. There was a constant hum of commotion and chatter, a whole village of people trying to get a toehold in their new environment. It reminded Mae of the time she kicked over an anthill, and – wondering if that was how the Caucasian authorities saw her and her family – she suddenly felt disgusted, but also very small and ashamed.

The barracks were nearly all identical; the public toilets – which none of the Yamadas had set eyes on yet – were located at the end of each row and gave off an odor so foul, to breathe it in made one's eyes cross slightly. Later, when Mae and Shizue went to use the facilities, they were horrified to discover the toilets themselves were unpartitioned, with those who used them on display for all to see. As a little girl, Mae had had bad dreams like that; she never thought such unpleasant dreams would – or could – come true.

They arrived at the mess hall. It was loud and crowded, with a long line that stretched out the main door.

'You'll have to be issued a mess kit first,' Bill Akimoto said, continuing to be helpful and pointing to a second line full of new arrivals. 'It's your job to clean it and keep track of it.' Bill appeared to be close to Harry's own age.

The Yamadas did as instructed and waited to be handed an Army regulation mess kit, which included a shallow tin bowl and a flimsy fork and knife. (The latter, Mae was soon to discover, made everything taste a little like pennies and nickels.) Then they rejoined the first line to retrieve some food.

It was, to be frank, rather wretched fare. Everything came from a can – Spam and Vienna sausage, canned beans, canned corn, canned fruit. The only thing not from a can was an enormous vat of rice that had been so overcooked it had turned to mush; the rice scooped up from the bottom was burned. This, then, explained the hideously offensive aroma emanating from the latrines.

Harry caught the look on his kid sister's face. She looked tired. He thought maybe she would feel better if she sat down.

'We can play a game,' he said, nudging her.

She looked at him. She knew he was trying to sound casual and upbeat. Harry glanced around, then thought of something and reached into his back pocket for his handkerchief. It was a white handkerchief and he draped it over his arm like a dapper waiter. He bowed deeply at the waist.

'We can play restaurant,' he said. 'You sit, and I'll bring your food to you.' He did a funny little shuffle and pretended to twirl an imaginary Frenchman's moustache.

Mae glared at him, annoyed he might presume she would be so easily placated with a child's game. She was not a child anymore.

'That won't make it taste any better,' she replied flatly.

Harry glanced at the food that was being scooped up and distributed in ugly, gelatinous mounds. He sighed.

'Hmm, you're right.' He held up his mess kit and draped the handkerchief temporarily over the top, performing a sleight of hand. The mess kit magically vanished.

Mae arched an eyebrow.

'Just like my appetite,' she said.

Harry laughed.

'Fair enough, kid. Me, too.'

55

NEWCASTLE, CALIFORNIA
SEPTEMBER 23, 1943

'And you ran the orchards for the Yamadas, in their absence, with every intention of legally returning everything – the house, the land, their cars, the biplane – assuming they would be released one day?' Bonner asks. He is still in the front parlor of the Yamadas' former house, asking Louis and Ava questions.

'Yes,' Louis answers now.

'That's mighty generous of you.'

Louis doesn't say anything.

'I'm sure you must've had to put up with some criticism for that,' Bonner comments. 'Not a whole lot of folks around these parts are very sympathetic to the Japanese.'

Louis gives a half nod and shrugs.

'Only natural.'

'And from what I understand,' Bonner continues, 'your family might've had their criticisms, too.'

'I suppose I caught some grief from my brother Guy.'

'Guy Thorn?'

'Yes,' Louis affirms, declining to elaborate.

Bonner notices Louis's eyes flick to the mantel over the fireplace. On instinct, Bonner stands up and crosses the room. His gaze lands on a framed portrait. He picks it up.

'This him?' Bonner asks. 'This your brother Guy?'

Louis's jaw clenches, a sign that he doesn't appreciate Bonner touching the photograph, but he nods.

Bonner takes a look at the man in the photo, noticing the uniform straightaway. 'A Navy man,' he remarks, and Louis nods again. But then, as Bonner looks at the man's face, he is startled by something he sees there. He squints to get a better look, scrutinizing the man's features, taking in his height, his stance.

'You see it, too, don't you?' Ava pipes up to ask. 'Uncanny, almost.'

Bonner blinks, wide-eyed and as unsettled as any man might be upon realizing he has a doppelgänger in the world. He shakes himself and tries to recover. He sets the photograph back down and clears his throat.

'Yes . . . well . . .' Bonner says now. 'That is something.' He sits back down. He has forgotten his train of thought, the path of questioning he was in the midst of pursuing. He tries to get the conversation back on track.

'You said your brother Guy gave you grief?'

Louis nods.

'What kind of grief?'

'Well . . . just . . . he never liked the Yamadas. He felt the way our father felt – and how our grandfather before him felt. He said . . . he said if I gave this land back to the Yamadas, then I would be a traitor.'

'Looks like you don't have to make that choice anymore.'

Louis and Ava stare at Bonner, caught off guard by the abrupt gall of it.

'Awful lucky,' Bonner presses, 'in some ways . . .'

'Our friends *died*,' Ava says, openly fuming. 'There is nothing *lucky* about it.'

'I didn't mean to offend,' Bonner apologizes.

'You did,' Ava replies, refusing his apology. Bonner can't tell whether she means *You did offend us* or *You did intend the offense.*

Bonner glances at his watch and realizes they've been at it for over half an hour, and while Bonner has grown more and more direct in his questioning, he has yet to make his final move: to lay out all the evidence that gave Louis Thorn motive and to dare the young man to deny it. He makes up his mind to try to maneuver Louis outside and confront him alone. He wants to see Louis's raw expression when he confronts him,

314

and knows Ava is too smart to let that happen; she'll intervene in the conversation in some way. Bonner flips his notebook shut and tucks it back into his inside jacket pocket.

'I ought to be going,' he says. 'But would you walk me to my automobile, Mr Thorn? I'd like a word with you alone, if you don't mind.'

Ava's face lights up with a mixture of panic and outrage. It is clear she senses what Bonner is up to, but can't think of an appropriate way to object.

'All right,' Louis says reluctantly, standing and following Bonner to the door.

Ava watches them go, frowning, her complexion turning pink with frustration. Bonner places his fedora on his head and politely tips it at her, then steps through the front door. Louis follows him, and they descend the long, steep flight of wooden porch stairs.

Bonner parked the Bureau car some distance away from the house on purpose, at the bottom of the hill, near the edge of the almond orchards. They walk in silence for a few minutes. Finally, Bonner speaks.

'I think you know the question I need to ask you; it's the one question I've never directly asked,' Bonner says.

Louis neither looks surprised nor comments. It is as if he has been expecting Bonner's direct approach, so Bonner gets on with it.

'Did you have anything at all to do with that crash?'

Louis shakes his head. 'No,' he says. 'It looked to me like an accident. And I was standing right there with you at the time,' he says, reminding Bonner of the morning they stood together on the Yamadas' porch, staring dumbfounded at the sky.

Bonner hesitates for a moment, then makes up his mind once and for all. It is a gamble, but he knows he's out of chances.

'Well . . . that's where you're wrong, as a matter of fact,' he says. 'It wasn't an accident.'

Louis frowns.

'What do you mean?'

'We *know* it wasn't an accident,' Bonner repeats, watching Louis's expressions closely. 'And the reason we know that is because somebody cut the fuel line.'

Louis's rhythmic stride hits a tiny hitch, but he carries on after the brief hesitation, playing it cool.

'That so?'

'Yes,' Bonner replies. 'Somebody tampered with the plane's engine.' He pauses for emphasis. 'Somebody *wanted* that biplane to crash.'

'I'll admit, it did seem strange,' Louis says, 'the way the engine cut out like that. I'd wondered.'

'Not to mention how the plane plummeted,' Bonner reminds him, still steering the conversation.

'That, too,' Louis agrees. 'But I still can't account for that part.'

Bonner pauses a moment before springing his next trap.

'I can,' he says.

Louis looks at him, and a slight twitch appears in the line of his mouth. By now they've reached Bonner's car and come to a stop before the driver's-side door. Bonner takes his time before delivering the news, taking careful account of the tiny expressions flickering just under the surface of Louis's stoic face.

'The coroner found an enormous level of opium in Kenichi Yamada's system,' Bonner says.

Louis only shakes his head, his brow furrowed with confusion. Either he is acting, or else . . . or else he truly knows nothing. Bonner studies him closely.

'Yes,' Bonner repeats. 'Opium. A significant amount.'

'In Kenichi Yamada's body?'

'That's right.'

'What about Harry?'

'His body was too burned up for us to test,' Bonner answers. 'But that much opium . . . there's no way it was accidental. It had to have been administered somehow. We at the Bureau don't jump to conclusions, but you can understand from an investigator's unofficial point of view that the opium, plus the fuel line . . . it doesn't look very innocent.'

'I know what you're accusing me of, and I ain't done it,' Louis says. 'You don't understand. I would trade places with him if I could . . .' He trails off, as though a shocking thought has just occurred to him. There's a funny look on his face, his jaw slightly dropped. Bonner has been hoping for a raw reaction but can't tell what exactly this reaction means.

'You said yourself,' Bonner continues, 'you didn't think Harry would do injury to himself or his father.'

'No . . .' Louis murmurs in agreement, looking distracted, lost in thought.

'As far as I can tell, Louis, you had the most reason to be harboring a grudge against Harry. You certainly had access to the biplane's engine. And we both know you stood to gain the most from the Yamadas' deaths.'

Louis doesn't answer. He appears to still be lost in thought, his eyes moving as though doing some kind of math problem in his head. But for some reason Bonner gets the impression that he isn't focused on the FBI agent's accusation. He certainly doesn't look outraged or offended, just thoughtful. Then, all at once, a sharp focus snaps into Louis's eyes. His head suddenly jerks in the direction of the house.

'Wait—' Bonner begins to say, but it is too late. Something has Louis jumpy, spooked. Before Bonner can get out another word, Louis turns to go, and in a near run hurries back in the direction of the house, taking the long staircase up to the porch two stairs at a time. Bonner stands powerless for a moment, uncertain how to make heads or tails of the interview. He'd laid all his cards on the table and wound up right back where he started.

56

YAMADA PROPERTY
MAY 31, 1942

At first it was strange – being in the Yamada house without the Yamadas themselves.

'Why don't you move inside?' Louis complained to Ava. 'There are empty beds – empty rooms, even! It doesn't make any sense, you and your mother sleeping outside in that rat trap of a caravan when better bunks have freed up in here.'

Ava dropped the bag of chicken feed she was lugging to the shed and looked at him in disgust.

'*Freed up?*' Ava repeated back to him. 'Is *that* how you think of it?'

'No,' he insisted, but then stopped short. He picked up the feedbag and carried it for her. 'Forget it,' he mumbled.

He was embarrassed to admit as much to Ava, but the truth was Louis found himself deeply uncomfortable in the Yamadas' house without the Yamadas – like he was a criminal squatting on someone else's property. He didn't dare sleep in Mr and Mrs Yamada's bed. The first night, he slept on the floor of the sitting room, huddled under blankets he'd brought over from the Thorn household. Slowly he worked his way to Harry's room, to Harry's childhood twin mattress. He felt fairly comfortable there. The room contained Harry's old things – things from as far back as the time of their first friendship: posters of Houdini, even a model airplane Louis had built and shyly given his friend. Who'd have guessed how fitting that gift would one day be?

The rest of the house still gave Louis pause, though. He found he was afraid to sit on the furniture in the sitting room, afraid to open the drawers in the kitchen – afraid, even, to open the medicine cabinet in the bathroom one morning when Louis had cut himself and needed something for the wound. Perhaps 'afraid' was the wrong word; it was more like that strange feeling that comes with trespassing, a feeling of holding one's breath. Louis jumped each time he thought he heard an automobile come up the drive, as if the Yamadas were coming home and he'd been caught.

Louis wondered if he would feel the same if not for the very specific and complicated ties between the Thorns and the Yamadas. He wondered – not aloud, of course – if he would feel as deeply uncomfortable if there wasn't a part of him that sometimes contemplated what it would be like to *keep* the Yamada property, to not give it back. He wondered if Ava didn't look disgusted with him for exactly the right reasons.

His older brother, Guy, certainly had his own opinions on Louis's role as guardian of the Yamada estate.

'As far as I'm concerned,' Guy said, 'that property has been returned to its rightful owners. Father would roll over in his grave if he thought you'd just hand it back over to those Japs.'

'Well, then,' Louis replied in a calm, quiet voice, 'I guess Father's rolling over in his grave, then. I promised I would give it back to Mr Yamada, and I intend to keep my word.'

'Then you're a traitor, and a bigger fool than I thought you were,' Guy said.

After that, Louis's trips 'home' to the Thorn ranch grew increasingly infrequent.

One day, however, Louis was specifically summoned to the Thorn ranch. His younger brother Clyde was dispatched to fetch him. Surprised, Louis blinked down into the earnest blue eyes of his little brother as he stood on the Yamadas' front porch. Ever since Louis had begun living on the Yamada property, none of his brothers or sisters had come calling. Louis suspected that Guy had forbade it.

'Mama said I was to come get ya.'

'Now?'

It was a Sunday, a lazy day. Louis had figured there'd be no rush.

'She said the sooner I could get you to come over, the better,' Clyde said.

'Anyone hurt?'

Clyde shook his head. 'Just . . . come.'

'All right,' Louis agreed, puzzled by this strangely urgent yet vague request. He reached inside the entryway for where his hat hung on a hook. It was a hot day out, and the sun was directly overhead.

Together the two brothers walked the distance from the Yamada farmhouse to the Thorn household. They arrived sticky, dusty, and thirsty.

As they entered the little clapboard house by letting themselves in through the kitchen door, the only thing on Louis's mind was the need for a tall glass of water. If he was being honest, he was a little nervous to see Guy again; the last time Louis had seen his brother, Guy had made it clear – yet again – that he was not pleased with Louis.

Now, as Louis walked through the door, he immediately saw Guy sitting at the breakfast table along with his girl, Lindy, and their mother, Edith. For a fleeting moment, Louis wondered if the news was something to do with Guy and Lindy. Guy had told Louis he intended to propose; perhaps this was to be a celebration party.

But this notion evaporated as quickly as it had come. Louis's brow furrowed when he noticed that Lindy's face looked downcast and his mother was quietly sobbing. Across the table, Guy held her hand, his jaw clenched as though enduring something taxing. But it was what Guy was wearing that finally caught Louis's attention above all else: a uniform.

Louis froze.

After Pearl Harbor, Louis had expected that some of his brothers might enlist, but not Guy. Guy was too essential to the Thorn ranch. He had been the head of the household ever since their father died, and for some of the younger Thorn children, he was the only father figure any of them had ever known. But Louis also knew that after Pearl Harbor, Guy couldn't stop talking about the war. He memorized every detail of every newspaper and radio report. He had opinions about tactical strategies and got himself good and worked up talking about patriotism.

Louis stared at his brother, dressed in full Navy uniform. The last they'd seen each other, Guy had called Louis a traitor and told him to stay off the Thorn property. Louis didn't expect a warm reception, and he didn't get one.

'What are *you* doing here?' Guy demanded, his voice an unfriendly grunt.

'I asked Clyde to send for him,' Edith Thorn explained, mopping her face with a soiled handkerchief. 'I thought he might talk some sense into you.'

Guy stood up abruptly. The kitchen chair made a scraping sound against the weather-beaten wooden floor. '*Him* talk sense? I think you got that backward,' he said, indignant.

'What in the hell are you doing, Guy?' Louis asked.

'*Language!*' Edith snapped. Louis repressed an urge to roll his eyes. They all knew their mother couldn't be bothered to police their language anywhere but church. It was too chaotic in the Thorn house: there were too many boys; as a harried widow, she was outnumbered. She only really came down hard on the two girls, Marion and Ruth, about their manners. It mattered when it came to girls, she figured.

'Who's going to run things here on the ranch?' Louis demanded.

'Ma will,' Guy answered. 'And Marion and Otis.'

'I thought . . . I thought . . .' Louis looked at Lindy, sitting at the table. He stood debating how much to say, when he noticed a ring. The proposal must've already happened during Louis's absence. 'I thought you were getting married?'

'We're planning on marrying when I get back,' Guy answered stiffly. 'Hopefully there'll be more money then. Her grandmother left Lindy that old house by the railroad tracks; Lindy's going to take in boarders while I'm gone.'

Louis blinked, still overwhelmed. 'When . . . when do you ship out?'

'Today,' Guy replied. 'I gotta report to San Francisco by tomorrow morning.'

'And you're going to—'

'*Japan*,' Guy said, firm in his resolve. 'Or the Pacific, at least.'

Louis didn't know what to say.

'I guess you'll get to kill some Japs there,' he said. 'That'll make you happy.'

Guy looked at him, aware that Louis meant it, but inclined his head in a serious, solitary nod. 'I'm happy to do my duty for our country,' he said. His voice was so full of conviction, Louis felt impressed in spite of himself. 'Hell,'

Guy said, shaking his head now. 'It's your duty, too. It's this whole nation's duty.' He paused, and looked his younger brother over from head to toe. 'But I suppose you'd rather stay here and play babysitter to some Jap family's property – property they done *stole* in the first place, to boot.'

'If you won't let him talk you out of this foolishness,' Edith snapped at Guy, 'then at least you'll say goodbye in proper fashion. You're *brothers*.'

Guy and Louis looked at each other, neither of them yielding.

'I've said everything I have to say to him,' Guy said. 'If he won't admit that those Japs next door are our enemies, then he might as well be my enemy, too.' He looked at Louis. 'I hope you think about that.'

'What if you're . . . you're . . . killed?' Edith said, making one last attempt to reconcile her children.

Guy shrugged. 'I got nothing else to say. I'd have more respect for you if you did something useful – like enlisting yourself – but I can already tell, you ain't gonna do anything of the sort.' He gave Louis one last look. 'You're a coward and a traitor. So I don't give a damn about you bein' here to see me off.'

He turned and stalked out of the room.

'Guy—' Lindy said, following him.

Edith's eyes flooded with a fresh wave of tears. She tipped her forehead down to her clasped hands on the table, then, after a moment, raised her head and looked up.

'He doesn't mean it,' she said. 'I know he needed to see you, that he *wants* to say goodbye . . .'

'No.' Louis shook his head. 'He means it.'

Edith only looked at him.

'He means well . . . but he also means every word he says,' Louis added with an air of finality. He paused, and without having gotten the glass of water he had been dying for, let himself back out the kitchen door.

Ava noticed that Louis seemed upset after visiting his family, but she knew enough about what made Louis tick to wait several days before asking what might be troubling him.

'Guy enlisted' was all Louis said when Ava finally asked.

Ava knew Louis and his brother had argued over Louis's involvement with the Yamadas. She also knew Louis looked up to Guy. Whatever had happened, Louis seemed angry with Guy, but he also seemed sad, too. A month or so later, Ava – who rarely set foot inside the Yamada house, where Louis was now sleeping – noticed a framed photograph had appeared on the mantel of the Yamadas' fireplace. To her knowledge, Guy had gone off to the Pacific theater to fight the Japanese. It was strange and slightly unsettling to think of his photograph now displayed in the Yamadas' house, and what that meant to all parties involved. But then, the world was getting to be a pretty strange place. Ava said nothing more to Louis on the subject. She worked hard on the orchards, thinking all the time of the Yamadas, and – if she were being honest – of Harry in particular.

The days passed. Before she knew it, summer had come and gone, the light grew honeyed and leaned in sideways, and autumn was upon them.

57

TULE LAKE, CALIFORNIA
OCTOBER 31, 1942

Rain shower from mountain
quietly soaking
barbed wire fence.

– SUIKO MATSUSHITA

When the Yamadas arrived in late May, the muddy land that surrounded the Tule Lake Relocation Center had already baked into dry clay, and soon afterward the season transformed into a hot summer of dry dust and ash. By October, the ash had turned to mud again. Fences were erected around the camp, and Harry saw that his relief at not seeing fences when they first arrived had been foolish. It had only ever been a matter of time.

Of course, when you got down to it, the barbed-wire fences were somewhat absurd. There was no place for the internees to go, for there was nothing for miles around.

They were offered jobs – *offered*, the government repeated the word often, emphasizing the difference between *offered* and *assigned*. Most of the jobs involved intensive physical labor and paid less than the poorest migrant workers' wages back home. Despite this unappealing combination, the majority of internees accepted some form of employment anyway. They were restless and bored; they needed some semblance of the lives they had known before internment, and regular work had certainly been part of that.

Camp officials put Japanese men and women to work either producing goods for the war effort or coaxing vegetables from the dry earth all around the camp. Harry and his father decided to volunteer for the latter, assuming their experience on the ranch would prove useful. They found themselves having to learn everything all over again: the only crops grown at Tule Lake were potatoes, wheat, and onions. These were not crops that Kenichi or Harry knew, let alone knew well. But little by little they learned alongside their fellow internees. Soon the camp had established a steady yield, and Japanese-American agriculture proved it had earned its reputation for good reason. The soil, mostly volcanic, was actually not terrible. It was irrigation that presented the largest challenge. The summer months were so dry that everything died. The earth baked back into hard clay.

After the Yamadas' first experience in the mess hall, the food did not improve much, and camp food turned out to be problematic for the Yamadas in more ways than one. No one except perhaps Shizue herself understood how diligently she'd been managing her epilepsy with good nutrition . . . until the camps. Over the years, on the ranch, she had been able to keep the handful of seizures Shizue was *not* able to avoid from her children – more or less. She had been proud of this fact, of the way she had been able to hide her illness. The episodes had been minor events compared to the seizures she'd experienced in Japan. Often she suffered a minor attack in silence – or, when she could not conceal her affliction, Kenichi knew what to do and was able to help her.

But all of that changed in the Tule Lake camp, where their food consisted mostly of starch, and sleeping through the night was a luxury. Shizue's health deteriorated rapidly. The first seizure, a terrible one, happened in the morning, two weeks after the Yamadas had moved into the shack that was to be their home. Shizue was removing a pot of boiling water from the small camp stove they had set up to serve as a makeshift kitchenette. Her head tipped downward and, staring into the flickering flame of the camp stove as she lifted the pot, she felt the old sensations come over her.

She felt her body grow rigid and a curtain drop over her senses.

Mae was the only one to see her mother suddenly stiffen like a board and did not understand at first what was happening. It looked as though a lightning bolt had shot through her mother's body, and seconds later her mother's body went rigid, her eyes rolled back in her head, and Shizue keeled over – almost as though someone had flipped an electrical switch. Mae screamed as her mother hit the ground, the pot of hot water cascading down as it left the safe grip of her mother's tea-towel-wrapped hand.

Her father and brother came running.

'Turn her on her side!' Kenichi commanded, and the three of them scrambled to accomplish this. Kenichi felt in his wife's mouth for food or any other kind of obstruction and, satisfied, made certain she was breathing.

'Should I fetch someone?' Mae asked, recovering from the shock.

'No time,' Kenichi replied. 'Haruto,' he barked in an uncharacteristically authoritative tone. 'We'll carry her to the infirmary.'

Harry nodded. Together they lifted Shizue's limp body. Harry took most of the weight; Kenichi was quite elderly, but Harry also understood his father's need to help carry his own wife, to keep the contact of touch between them. Harry realized he had never seen his father look so worried.

At the infirmary, Shizue regained consciousness. The nurse tended to Shizue's burns. The water had scalded her arm badly, but the nurse assured her that it would heal.

'Camp stoves aren't really allowed, you know, and you shouldn't be boiling water in your barracks if you're accident-prone,' the nurse scolded, clucking her tongue. Her tone was friendly yet firm, the same as a kindly schoolteacher.

Kenichi recoiled.

'My wife is *not* accident-prone,' he corrected the nurse. 'She had a seizure.'

Harry flinched inwardly to hear his father's faint Japanese accent – an accent Harry had never paid much mind to before.

'Well, I don't see any evidence of that,' the nurse drawled, her tone still friendly but now tinged with a hint of condescension. 'Low blood sugar is what I see. A simple glass of orange juice ought to fix you right up!' She smiled. The nurse had tended to Shizue's wounds after Shizue had already come to, so Kenichi guessed that perhaps the nurse simply did not understand.

'No. It was a seizure. She has had them all her life,' Kenichi insisted.

'Well, if that's true, then she certainly should have developed a technique for managing them,' the nurse replied. It was plain the nurse still did not believe Shizue was anything other than thin and clumsy. 'Has she seen a doctor for them?'

'Yes,' Kenichi replied. 'Is there a doctor here we may see?'

'Oh.' The nurse's cheerful face fell. She wasn't offering. The poor Japanese fellow had gotten himself confused. 'No,' she replied, 'I'm afraid the doctor comes twice a month, and today is not one of his days.' She paused. 'I just meant has she seen a doctor in the past?'

'Yes.'

'Good.' The nurse relaxed and smiled. 'Then whatever his advice was, I'm sure it was sound. If she's always had seizures, like you say, then it's nothing curable, and it's a question of proper management.'

Shizue had not spoken during their entire exchange, and the nurse said these last words, 'proper management,' with slow, deliberate articulation, as though the nurse wasn't entirely certain Shizue spoke English.

The seizure scared them all, but they didn't discuss it. Kenichi and Harry continued to toil in the fields, Mae attended the makeshift school that had been organized for the internees' children. After she recovered, Shizue took a job sewing bandages for the troops. She wasn't particularly chatty herself, but she liked to hear the other women gossiping over their needles and sewing machines.

And then there was communication with the outside world. They were allowed to get mail, and postal service – while slow – was often the only connection between the camp and the rest of America. Of course, there were plenty of subtle reminders that even these communications were under scrutiny. Envelopes arrived already opened, letters often had various sentences and paragraphs blacked out – sometimes even the idlest comments on food or the weather. This was especially when they contained correspondence between internees and Japanese friends or family members assigned to other camps. The hysterical notion prevailed that the entire Japanese-American population was entirely made up of spies lying in wait.

'Who's that from?' Mae asked one day, glimpsing her brother with a letter.

'Ava,' he replied. 'It's to all of us . . . or Father, really. She's been keeping us updated as to how the ranch is doing, how the orchards are faring . . .'

Mae frowned.

'If it's from Ava, why don't you look more pleased?'

Harry blinked, not sure what his sister was getting at, not sure how to respond. Mae giggled.

'C'mon. It's obvious that you love her,' Mae said now.

Harry made a face.

'I never said anything along those lines.'

'You didn't have to,' Mae said. 'So why aren't you happier to have a letter from her?' Mae squinted at Harry as though looking for an answer. 'Oh!' she gasped, her face lighting up with sudden comprehension. 'Is it that you wanted to hear from Louis?'

Harry didn't say anything. Mae understood she had hit upon an unexpected truth.

'When was the last time Louis wrote?' Mae asked.

'He hasn't.'

'At all?'

Harry shook his head, and with that, he turned on his heel and walked out of the bungalow they shared with the Akimotos.

58

YAMADA PROPERTY
NOVEMBER 30, 1942

Louis was at odds with himself, rattling around on the Yamadas' property, and especially when he found himself alone in their house. Summer had come and gone, and autumn had begun to leave a telltale frost on the ground first thing in the mornings. He had remained loyal to the Yamadas by working hard in the orchards and on the ranch, but he couldn't bring himself to write to the family, and especially not to Harry. He heard their news through Ava, who exchanged letters with Harry and Mae and sent little care packages to all of the Yamada family members. Lately, the care packages had included homemade scarves and quilts; evidently it was cold at Tule Lake, and they had no heat.

Louis had registered for the draft but hadn't been called up – yet. The truth was, Louis couldn't get his brother Guy's last words to him out of his head: *I'd have more respect for you if you did something useful – like enlisting yourself – but I can already tell, you ain't gonna do anything of the sort.* Louis wouldn't have minded fighting in France or Italy; the adolescent boy within him who still loved comic books knew all the best heroes fought the Nazis. But if he was sent to the Pacific, he wasn't sure how he'd feel. Or perhaps he knew he would feel too much. He was so damn angry at Harry. And he also felt a little sick to his stomach when he pictured the things Ava told him about in Harry's letters: the Yamadas living behind barbed wire, in a shack with tarpaper for walls, white guards looking on from watchtowers, prepared to shoot anyone who tried to escape. Picturing it made Louis feel something, too – something less easy and straightforward than anger.

And so Louis found himself working and waiting, wondering what his role might eventually be in this war.

Then, one day, it came to him as he was sitting on the Yamadas' front porch. He was gazing out over the property as the sun was setting, and his eyes fell upon the airplane hangar off in the distance. Louis realized: he had his pilot's license. And he wasn't just some old crop duster; Hutch and Buzz had trained him to perform some of the trickiest maneuvers they knew. Louis might in fact be considered an experienced pilot.

He knew there was an airfield in Lincoln where the US Army Air Force trained pilots. He woke up early the next morning and signed up to work as a civilian pilot, training new recruits. Glad to have his help, they put him to work the very next week.

Louis quickly discovered he enjoyed teaching young men to fly, to earn their wings. Harry had always been the better stuntman; Louis had always been acutely – and sometimes painfully – aware of that fact. But now it dawned on Louis that he was a damned good pilot and a natural teacher. He had a helpful way of explaining piloting procedures to the recruits, of breaking the whole business down into a series of logical steps, of instilling confidence in even the most nervous young man.

It was gratifying to finally feel truly *good* at something.

Of course, it was not a profession that came without its own fraught complications. Late at night, sometimes, Louis wondered where his former pupils might be and how they might be faring. He wondered how many of them were still alive. And he thought, too, of the enemy soldiers and civilians they possibly had killed. The majority of his students were dispatched to the Pacific, to fight the Japanese. What would Harry – or any of the Yamadas, really – think of that? Had Ava told them what Louis was doing with his time now? Louis wanted to ask Ava exactly what she wrote in all those letters she scribbled to Harry; she wrote one almost every day.

Louis wanted to ask her, but he didn't dare.

'Move into the house,' he continued to urge Ava. 'The Yamadas wouldn't mind; I'm sure of it.'

He was urging again one evening when Ava had come inside to deposit fresh groceries in the icebox. Ava shook her head. 'It isn't that I think they would mind.' She looked at Louis, holding him in a long, meaningful stare. 'When was the last time you wrote to any of the Yamadas?' she asked.

Louis didn't say anything.

'I don't need to live here in the house to know, Louis: Harry writes to you every single day. I see you putting the envelopes in the china cupboard. Do you even bother to open them?'

Louis still didn't answer, but it didn't matter. Ava stopped waiting for a reply. She dismissed him with a sigh and turned to go. Suddenly, Louis felt a ripple of hot anger welling up. He couldn't tell who he was angriest with anymore – Harry, Ava, or maybe even himself, for allowing himself to seem so small and petty. A meanness sprang up in his heart.

'You're never gonna be able to make a life with him,' Louis blurted out. 'He's a Jap.'

Ava froze. Louis realized he was waiting for her to say something. He wanted her to look embarrassed or deny she loved Harry. But she only stood there, silent and glaring.

'He's a Jap,' he repeated, frustrated. 'You *know* that, don't you?'

She continued to glare at him until finally Louis had to look away.

Ava didn't answer. Louis watched her go and heard the back door to the kitchen slam shut with a loud bang.

59

NEWCASTLE, CALIFORNIA
SEPTEMBER 23, 1943

When he arrives back at the boardinghouse, Bonner finds a bundle of brown parchment tied up with string waiting for him on the entry hall table: miscellaneous documents forwarded over from the sheriff's office. Deputy Henderson likely dropped them off and Rosalind left them here. Bonner recognizes the hand of Sheriff Whitcomb in the thoughtful delivery, too – the sheriff's not-so-subtle way of suggesting Bonner work the case from some location other than Whitcomb's office from here on out.

Bonner takes the bundle upstairs, unwraps it, and begins laying out each item on the bed. The majority of the documents are items sent from the Yamadas' barracks in the Tule Lake Relocation Center. There are keepsakes, letters, and other documents. There are photographs, too, of the Yamada family throughout the years. And a photograph that includes Louis and Harry, along with all the members of the barnstorming act from the time when it was still 'Earl Shaw's Flying Circus.'

Bonner sets the image apart from the others and stares intently at it. He picks out Harry on the far left, standing next to Louis. Next is Ava . . . and then the two men he guessed were the circus's original pilots, Buzz and Hutch. Earl Shaw is in the shot, too, standing on the far right, dressed in a colorful red-and-black suit, as though he were the ringleader of a more traditional circus. In the photo, Earl has one arm around his wife, Cleo, the other angled in the air as though to showcase the two biplanes parked behind them. Bonner can read *CASTOR* painted in gold lettering on one plane, and *POLLUX* on the other. While everyone in the photograph is smiling, it seems to Bonner that there is a suggestion in their expressions and postures signifying a shared dislike of Earl, which lends the photograph a slightly amusing air.

After staring at the photograph for several minutes, Bonner slips it back into a file folder and returns his attention to the other photographs and documents. He reaches for the folder that contains all the Yamadas' official records: birth certificates, internment papers . . . death certificates, too.

As Bonner looks these over, contemplating all the tragedy the Yamada family has had to endure, he begins to reconsider the possibility that the crash was an act of suicide after all. There were plenty of reasons Kenichi and Harry would be tempted to die by their own hands. Perhaps Louis's strange, abrupt reaction – as though something had clicked in his brain – and the faint traces of guilt Bonner was sure he'd detected in Louis's demeanor were merely the grief any man feels upon discovering his friend has chosen death over life. Could that be the truth of the matter all along? Throughout the entire investigation, Bonner had been so focused on Louis Thorn – Was he capable of murder? Did he ever really intend to return that land? What sort of people were the Thorns, anyway? – that Bonner neglected to really delve into the Yamadas' experience and whether or not it would make sense for Kenichi and Harry to have a role in the crash after all.

Bonner realizes he didn't want to know that much about the Yamadas' time in the camps because he did not want to have to imagine their struggle or dwell on their pain.

Now, looking at one document, letter, and photograph at a time, Bonner allows himself to let it all in: the Yamadas' lives in internment; the hardship, humiliation, and grief they had to put up with; the reasons Harry and Kenichi might have decided on death during those last moments, soaring high in the air.

60

TULE LAKE, CALIFORNIA
FEBRUARY 11, 1943

When she was young and newly married, Shizue Yamada had harbored one fear above all others: that she would be unable to bear children. Once she was pregnant, that fear transformed itself into the fear that her epilepsy would jeopardize the baby – that a seizure would cause a miscarriage or a terrible birth defect. Shizue felt nauseated at the very thought – not of an impaired child, but of the guilt she would suffer knowing she was to blame for the child's deformity.

In the years after her children were born, her primary fear went through another transformation. Shizue buried it deep within her own heart, perhaps believing if she never named it and told no one about it, it would have no power over her.

She watched her first child, Haruto, closely, and when he passed through adolescence without showing any signs of her affliction, she breathed a sigh of relief. It had been during her teen years when she had the first seizure; the doctors had told her the disease almost always made itself known then. The day Haruto turned twenty, Shizue had only one thought in her head: *Healthy – my son is healthy!* She began to relax. Mai was still growing but showing every sign of following in Haruto's footsteps. Little Mai was healthy and hearty, if a little unruly.

So when the Yamada family was shuttled off to Tule Lake, Shizue developed a subconscious confidence in her children, and believed they would easily manage to endure camp conditions, unpleasant as they were.

* * *

When Mai had her first seizure, Shizue was horrified. She was certain the reason her daughter was suffering was her fault. She had let down her guard, growing complacent, and the fates had pounced on her daughter while Shizue's back was turned.

The first seizure was mild; Shizue hadn't witnessed it and Haruto had reported it, so she had only his description to rely upon.

'We were sitting outside, Mae was eating an apple, and her face suddenly went slack,' Haruto said. 'I think she sort of passed out there for a second or two. Or maybe not. I don't know. Her eyes were open but not seeing, moving strangely . . . I was speaking to her and she wasn't responding. She doesn't remember any of it now.'

Shizue's heart lurched and a sudden chill gripped her body. She knew all too well what had happened.

'But it's nothing . . . right, Ma?' Haruto asked. His voice indicated that he, too, was unconvinced of the event's insignificance.

'Yes,' Shizue said, trying to keep her voice calm.

That afternoon Shizue went to the infirmary and demanded to see a doctor. Two weeks later, after she had made a proper pest of herself, the nurse finally relented and she was able to talk to an elderly man in a white lab coat who was, he claimed, only a part-time government employee and otherwise ran a small family practice across the border in Oregon.

'There are medications,' Shizue insisted, 'that would help my daughter get through these episodes.'

'Anti-seizure medication?' The doctor frowned.

'Yes.'

'That's complicated stuff. I'm afraid we don't have access to those drugs here,' he said. 'And anyway, it's expensive.'

'She needs it,' Shizue continued to insist.

'I'm sorry. We can't provide you with such things.'

'But . . . how can that be? If it is a necessity . . .'

'Those medications are *luxuries*,' the doctor corrected her. His tone had turned snippy. 'There are quite a lot of people in *need* these days: think of our American soldiers, all the things *those* boys need nowadays, and all because your countryman General Tojo took it upon himself to attack innocent people.'

He dragged the syllables out, spitting out the name 'Tojo' while an ugly sneer moved across his face. Shizue was taken aback. She abruptly realized just how little help she could expect from the doctor standing before her. Without another word, she gathered her things and left.

From that moment, Shizue carried a ball of dread in the pit of her stomach. And it was just as she feared: after her daughter's first seizure, the episodes increased in frequency. What was worse, however, was the fact that they increased in *intensity* until Mai was suffering from terrible, convulsing seizures that were unlike any Shizue herself had ever experienced.

Shizue found a man in the camp who tried the old *kampo* art of placing needles on the body, and for a time it seemed to help – until it didn't. The man shook his head, apologetic. 'There are herbs, but even if your husband can afford them, they'll never let me get my hands on everything I need in here. They are convinced we're all cooking up bombs.' Mai's seizures eventually returned.

The worst was when one happened in the middle of the schoolroom, in front of other children. Mai was mortified and began to withdraw into herself. Shizue anguished as her daughter grew more introverted. Mai smiled less and less as summer approached, and the heat made it all worse; Mai's laughter dried up along with the rainfall. She reminded Shizue of herself back in Japan, when Shizue thought of herself as nothing but a freak and a failure. Now her daughter was an exile among the exiled. And Shizue could do nothing.

This wounded Shizue in a way she had always feared, a way that went far deeper – and, she was sure, she deserved. Shizue was highly adept at blaming herself for anything that pained her children, and now she was convinced she had poisoned her own daughter by passing along her epilepsy. Every day Mai suffered, Shizue took another portion of guilt and blame into her heart, as though her heart were a stomach and she were consuming a never-ending sickly cake. She wanted her family to know she would never forgive herself for the pain she had passed along to her child. As it would turn out, she was too skilled in this manner.

Shizue had just returned from stitching bandages at the camp's community workshop. When she walked in and saw Mai, she knew exactly what had happened. Mai was draped awkwardly across the bed – not Mai's own bed, but the bed Shizue shared with her husband. She wouldn't lie there on purpose, Shizue knew. But there Mai was, facedown, her head turned to the side, her eyes open, her tongue covering her teeth in a strange manner.

She had suffered a terrible seizure, alone in their horrible single-room bungalow. Books were knocked off a makeshift shelf and a chair was turned over; it looked as though she had thrashed about quite a bit, convulsing violently before choking on her own tongue, her complexion turning blue from a lack of oxygen.

Thirty minutes passed where Shizue did not dare to move or speak. She barely drew breath.

At first, all she could think was *I must be thankful I am the one to find her now, not one of the Akimotos.*

The Akimotos were fine enough people. That was not the issue. But, being fine people, they did not deserve the horror and shock of finding a dead body in their home, any more than Mai deserved the dishonor of having her lifeless corpse discovered by virtual strangers.

Shizue stood there, memorizing her daughter's vacant eyes, until eventually Shizue's body began to react to the pain. She could not stop herself; she began to wail. She wailed like a wild creature, alarming people around their barracks. Still wailing, Shizue curled her own body around her daughter's on the bed. Together they made a forlorn sort of snail shell, tears soiling the bed like a wet snail's trail. Internees poked their heads into the bungalow to see what was wrong. Eventually, Haruto came walking along, puzzled to see a small throng of people gathered as he returned home.

'Oh, God,' Haruto exclaimed when he broke through the crowd around the open door and found his mother and sister. He tried to say more but his voice broke. Among her son's unique attributes was a bold lack of fear, but

Shizue remembered hearing his voice that day and thinking, *Finally, in my fearless son's voice . . . there is fear there . . .* All those times she had wanted Haruto to have the good sense to be afraid of things as a child – for his own safety, so he wouldn't touch the hot stove or try to swim in the river when the current was dangerous – his voice had never adopted a single tremor of fear. Now that it had, she was sorry to hear it.

Kenichi, too, when he came home, immediately went into shock. He had always understood that the US government would likely take his land, his possessions – perhaps even his freedom to speak his mind. But he had never considered that the government might cost him either of his children. He stood there in disbelief as his wife and son mourned his lifeless daughter.

'It was too much,' Shizue lamented. 'This life, the poor nutrition, her adolescence . . . I knew it would come, this storm . . . I asked for medicine but they refused . . . they refused to give us any . . .'

'Shhhh.' Her husband tried to comfort her. With an anguished heart of his own, he had alerted the camp officials at the infirmary. After thirty minutes or so, they responded by sending men with a stretcher.

They took Mae away. For a while it was strange to Harry, who, despite having seen the body, caught himself perpetually expecting his little sister to come back, to come bouncing in from playing outside. Even the camp guards seemed apologetic. Kenichi was able to arrange for cremation and an urn. Friends they had made in the camp suggested they hold a small funeral service, but Kenichi refused. 'We will take her home, where she belongs,' he insisted. No one pointed out the fraught nature of his words. Where did any of them belong anymore? They were strangers in their own country. Who knew what had become of the houses they'd raised their children in?

Shizue was never the same after that. Her own seizures grew worse, a fact that was perhaps a relief to her: she felt she took comfort in the notion of punishment. When she realized this latter fact about herself, she knew what she must do if she ever hoped for relief.

* * *

It ought to have been shocking. But one month later, when Kenichi came into the bungalow to find his wife hanging from the rickety, hastily thrown-up beam that ran through their barracks as the structure's main support, his heart was deeply aggrieved but he was not surprised. There was a note. A simple apology, a prayer for forgiveness, the brushstrokes steady and elegant, written in beautiful *kanji*.

61

27. *Are you willing to serve in the Armed Forces of the United States to combat duty, whenever ordered?*

_____ *(yes)* _____ *(no)*

28. *Will you swear unqualified allegiance to the United States of America and faithfully defend the United States from any or all attack by foreign or domestic forces, and forswear any form of allegiance or obedience to the Japanese emperor, or any other foreign government, power, or organization?*

_____ *(yes)* _____ *(no)*

— From the War Relocation Authority
Application for Leave Clearance

Yamada Kenichi's life had never made so much sense as it did that afternoon he had brought a young woman named Miyamoto Shizue of Kyoto, Japan, to his orchard in Newcastle, California, and watched as she set her eyes for the very first time on the charming white clapboard farmhouse he'd built. In that moment, as he saw her face light up with a smile at the sight of the farmhouse, everything Kenichi had ever done – all his adventures immigrating to a faraway land, all of his hard work, all of his dedication and discipline – all took on a sudden, potent new meaning. Everything he had done, he had done for the sake of the gentle soul of the young woman standing before him, and for the beautiful family they would have together.

Kenichi had lost his daughter in a manner he never would have expected. He had worked all his life to build up the sort of security that meant young Mai would always have proper care and medicine – only to lose her the way a pauper would: terribly afflicted, having no access to a doctor or drugs, no cures, Eastern or Western. And then, to watch his cherished wife torture herself over the tragedy, until Shizue could not take it . . . Kenichi had entered a hell beyond anything his imagination could have ever built.

Both had died in the space of a month and a half. Several more months had passed in the wake of these dual tragedies, but the sharpness never quite came back into Kenichi's eyes. He seemed lost, purposeless . . . He sat for hours in a chair staring out into the flat, ugly landscape that lay beyond the camp's barbed-wire fences, not quite seeing anything at all.

So perhaps it was for this reason that, when given a loyalty oath sometime in March, only weeks after his wife's violent death, Kenichi – dwelling in a blur of anguish, grief, and anger – answered those two critical questions 'No' and 'No.'

'*Otōsan*,' Harry murmured, after his father told him what he had inadvertently done.

'It was an accident,' Kenichi pointed out. 'I believe it was.' He paused and then looked up at his son with wide, blinking eyes – like a small child answering to a parent. 'It was an accident, wasn't it?' Kenichi said, as though Harry knew how to riddle out Kenichi's own intentions.

'We had agreed, in order to stay together, we would both answer "Yes" and "Yes",' Harry reminded his father.

Men who answered 'No' and 'No' – they were actually called 'No-Nos' – were moved to the isolation center near the Tule Lake camp, or else to an Army fort, to be treated like POWs. Rumor had it these men were destined to be deported back to Japan.

'You answered "Yes-Yes"?' Kenichi asked his son.

'I kept to our agreement,' Harry replied. It hadn't been easy – an irony, given that when the war first started, Harry would have happily gone to war as an American soldier. But the camp – the things that had happened to his mother and sister – had altered his resolve on this matter forever. Now there was a significant part of him that very much wanted to answer 'No-No'. There was a significant part of him that wanted to tell the whole nation to go to hell and give every camp guard he saw the middle finger. There were activists in the camp, too – men who held not-so-secret meetings and lobbied to organize demonstrations against their 'captors'. These men had declared that anyone who answered 'Yes-Yes' was an *inu* – a dog. Deep inside his heart, Harry had begun to agree.

But he understood all too well: he was all his father had left, and vice versa. And if he was being honest with himself, he hoped to see Ava again someday. He hoped to see Louis, too, even though Louis had proven a questionable friend and refused to write to him. So Harry and Kenichi had talked it over and agreed: they would both answer 'Yes-Yes.' They would be dogs, but they would be dogs together.

'I believe I was confused,' Kenichi said now, trying to explain his spontaneous 'No-No' answer. 'One question was: would I be willing to go to war as a soldier? And I could only think: *I am an old man; what does it matter? Who could possibly want me as a soldier in the first place?*

'*Otōsan*, we discussed this . . . They would not have sent you. It was only a question . . . a hypothetical question, in your case.'

'But not in your case,' Kenichi said, his voice grave. He had a point. It was *not* a hypothetical question in Harry's case. He was healthy, strong . . . just the right age.

'We would have been separated anyway, I am sure of it,' Kenichi concluded. He sighed. 'Dishonesty requires effort. I am too old. I answered 'No-No' because I am tired and that is the truth.'

Harry was silent. There was a tremor of angry defeat in his father's voice that had never been there before.

'It is not that I do not love America,' Kenichi said. '*This* is my country – America; not these disgusting filthy camps that have murdered my wife and daughter. But would I go to war and take up arms against other Japanese?

Even if my age did not make that idea absurd, the answer is no, I would *not*. A child cannot take the knife his father gives him and plunge it into his mother's heart. That is not the way of things. The child is both his parents, and only waits – and weeps – while his mother and father fight.'

Harry was silent for a moment. He had heard his father say as much before, he understood the weight of the words. When he finally replied, he only said, 'What will come next will be difficult.'

His father looked at him. A sad, bitter ghost of a smile turned the corners of his mouth.

'What has come so far has been difficult.'

'True enough,' Harry replied.

When the news came, it was no surprise to Harry. They learned Kenichi would be moved to the isolation center, just as Harry feared, and Harry would not be allowed to visit his father, who was now considered an enemy of the state.

Months passed in utter loneliness. Eventually, however, Kenichi's predictions about the implications of Harry's 'Yes-Yes' answer proved right: in August, Harry was called up for the draft. There was a fair amount of paperwork and bureaucracy, a physical exam. By then it was September, and he was scheduled to ship out to basic training on the thirteenth of the month.

A change was in the air, and Harry had made up his mind.

62

YAMADA PROPERTY
SEPTEMBER 13, 1943

Louis knew something was wrong by the look on Ava's face when she came and found him, and insisted he come with her to the barn.

'What's the matter?' he asked, thinking one of the animals had taken sick.

'Just hurry,' she demanded, refusing to answer. She strode ahead of him in a near run, moving so fast that when they came up out of the orchards and the barn's roof came into view, Louis found himself relieved to see that the barn was not on fire. He hurried to keep pace with her. Just before the barn door she drew up short and turned around to face him with a serious expression.

'I told them you would keep this quiet,' she said.

Louis only looked at her in confusion.

'I promised them you would. They're trusting you.'

'Who are?'

'Harry and Mr Yamada.'

Louis started.

'They're *here?*'

She nodded. 'They broke out of that horrible camp. Well, Harry did. He put on his Army uniform and made as though he were leaving for basic training, and then found Mr Yamada and snuck him out.'

Louis was staggered. He didn't understand half of what Ava had just said. He stared at the barn door, trying to wrap his mind around the fact that the Yamadas were inside.

'Harry's . . . in the Army?' was all he managed to blurt out.

'You would know as much if you ever bothered to read any of his letters or write to him the way you promised you would,' she replied.

Louis frowned, annoyed by Ava's efforts to shame him. Of course, she didn't know the reason Louis found it difficult to write, or what she herself had to do with it. After she'd told him about the deaths of Mae and Shizue, he had wanted to write . . . but by then too much time had passed. It felt so awkward; he had not known where to begin.

'Look,' Ava said now, 'I promised them they could trust you. Was I wrong?'

'No,' Louis replied.

Ava sighed and pulled the barn door open, and Louis followed her inside.

Once his eyes had adjusted to the dim light of the barn, sure enough, there they were: Harry and Mr Yamada. No one spoke right away; the only sound was the idle rustling of the horses, occasionally stamping their hooves or nickering. Harry and Mr Yamada were sitting in the hay in an empty horse stall. They looked tired. *From their journey?* Louis wondered. It was not as if they could hop on a train or thumb a ride in a car; they must've had to make the trek on foot. Kenichi Yamada looked particularly drained and thinner than Louis remembered. The thought of Kenichi's age prompted Louis to finally find his tongue.

'Is . . . is Mr Yamada all right?' Louis asked, breaking the silence with a halting voice.

'I am fine,' Kenichi replied. He nodded his head politely.

'What . . . what are you two doing here?'

'What do you think?' Harry replied in a flat voice.

'Won't they come looking for you?'

'I imagine they will.'

'Harry, you'll be in serious trouble,' Louis said. Vaguely panicked, he looked at Ava. 'We *all* will be.'

'Those camps . . .' Harry shook his head, looking down at the ground. '. . . aren't suitable for animals. I couldn't leave my father there and go off to war thousands of miles away to fight for the government that . . .' He faltered. '. . . has done what this government has done,' he finished.

Louis understood what Harry meant but was *not* saying, and relented.

'I was sorry about Mae and about your mother,' Louis said now, in a quieter voice.

Kenichi perked up, his face inscribed with fresh concern. 'Did you bring them, Haruto?' he asked his son in Japanese. Harry nodded somberly.

Louis and Ava looked on with puzzlement as Harry reached into a knapsack. When they saw the two small urns, they caught on.

'We will find a place for these when the time is right,' Harry said to his father, apologetic.

'The two of you will have to stay hidden as well,' Ava said. The sight of the urns had turned the content of Harry's letters into a terrible reality. The government had put Mae and Shizue in a camp with barbed wire and watchtowers, and now they were dead. A quiet wave of anguish, anger, and panic went through her. But for now she was resolved to address the matter of protecting the living. She turned to Harry and Kenichi.

'You can stay in the caravan. I'm sorry it's not in better condition, but I don't think it'll be safe for you in the house – at least, not for a few weeks. Louis is right: the government *will* send someone to look for you. They'll come here, and I doubt they'll announce themselves before they decide to drop in.'

'No . . . that makes sense.' Harry nodded. Ava looked at Kenichi in particular. He looked so tired, so defeated.

'You deserve to be back in your own home, but that will have to wait.'

Kenichi shook his head. 'Do not apologize. Your plan is wise, and we are grateful for your help in hiding us.'

'I'll tell my mother – you can trust her, too – and we'll pack up some things and maybe bring a few things down from the house to make you both more comfortable.'

There was a pause.

'Louis?' Harry said. 'You haven't agreed.'

'Yes,' Louis said. 'Of course. It's fine.'

Numb and dazed, he left the barn and walked back into the orchards – *their* orchards, he reminded himself: the Yamadas' orchards. All of it was theirs.

63

Two days passed. Louis was uneasy. He periodically checked on Mr Yamada out in the caravan and worried that the old man never looked as strong as he once had. Louis and Harry danced around each other, awkward as ever. From a distance, Louis also watched Harry and Ava talking and laughing – the two of them careful never to touch, never to acknowledge the secret affection between them that Louis had already witnessed, and this annoyed Louis. Harry never brought up the letters he'd written to Louis or asked Louis why he hadn't written back. The chip on Louis's shoulder had not gone away, but now it was wedged under the tremendous weight of all the terrible tragedy the Yamadas had been through.

From the moment Harry and Mr Yamada had turned up in the barn, a pair of runaways from the camp, Louis had been holding his breath, waiting for someone in a position of authority to accost him, accuse him of harboring two treasonous fugitives, and even perhaps arrest Louis for aiding and abetting. He waited for something to happen, but nothing did . . . until an even more unexpected event occurred.

It was a Wednesday, a weekday. Louis was at the airfield in Lincoln, training pilots. Around eleven in the morning, Louis had already taken two flyboys up, and was preparing to take a third, when the boy who ran errands for the airfield's on-duty commanding officer came scurrying out across the tarmac, waving his arms.

'Major Comstock wants to see ya!' the boy hollered.

'Can it wait?'

The boy shook his head. 'I don't think so. He looked pretty sour-faced when he sent me to get you just now.'

Louis bit his lip, suddenly nervous. As he walked in the direction of the major's office, he felt the collar of his shirt grow damp with a prickly cold sweat. This was it – he was certain – but what had he expected? What had Ava, or Harry, or any of them expected, really? It had always been only a question of time before the Yamadas got caught.

When Louis got to Comstock's office, the major was seated at his desk with a somber expression on his face. A bottle of whiskey was sitting in plain view on the desktop along with two glasses. It was the two glasses that caught Louis's attention: surely Comstock wasn't about to pour him a drink? Pilots weren't allowed to drink during training hours, and he doubted Comstock wanted to offer him a drink before interrogating him about the Yamadas.

As Louis entered, Comstock reached for the bottle and poured.

'Here,' the major said in a gruff voice.

Louis didn't move right away. He regarded the glass in Comstock's outstretched hand with puzzlement.

'Drink,' Comstock commanded.

'It's only eleven o'clock,' Louis said, hesitantly accepting the glass if only to alleviate Comstock's waiting arm.

'Doesn't matter,' Comstock replied.

'But . . . the rest of today's lessons . . . I can't take fellas up with whiskey on my breath. I doubt the military would approve of that.'

'You're not going up for the rest of the day.'

Louis's blood ran cold and the sweat prickled the hairs of his neck again. So . . . he *was* about to be reprimanded. Louis braced himself. A shiver of shame went through him as he imagined the news getting back to his brother Guy. *Louis Thorn, fired by the military for harboring enemy fugitives.* Would there be jail time, to boot? Poor Guy. At every turn, Louis had proved a perpetual disappointment in Guy's eyes.

But then Comstock stymied him again when he said, 'Just drink up. I insist. Trust me: it will help.'

Louis looked dubiously at the glassful of Comstock's cheap, faintly murky whiskey and, after a second more of hesitation, tossed it back.

'All right,' Louis said. 'Now, may I ask, sir: help what?'

He put the glass down. Comstock immediately reached to refill it.

'We received this,' he said, and pushed a thin slip of telegram paper across the desk.

Louis read it, blinked stupidly, and read it again.

'Someone will have delivered a telegram to your mother,' Comstock explained. 'But since the military knew where to find you, I guess they figured it would be a courtesy to pass along the news here, too. Best not to wait with this kinda news, in my experience.' Comstock looked at Louis, his jowls drooping with sympathy, and said, 'I'm sorry, son.'

THE NAVY DEPARTMENT DEEPLY REGRETS TO INFORM YOU THAT GUY DONAGHUE THORN SEAMAN FIRST CLASS USN WAS KILLED IN ACTION IN THE PERFORMANCE OF HIS DUTY AND IN SERVICE OF HIS COUNTRY, TWELVE SEPTEMBER IN THE GILBERT ISLANDS. THE DEPARTMENT EXTENDS TO YOU ITS SINCEREST SYMPATHY IN YOUR GREAT LOSS . . .

The color drained out of the room.

Louis didn't entirely remember what happened next. He thought he recalled drinking another glass or two of Comstock's whiskey. At some point he got up and shook Comstock's hand; Comstock was sending him home for the day. He wanted to know if Louis could drive. Louis assured him he could. Comstock wanted to have the errand boy drive but the boy was too young anyhow. Comstock said something Louis couldn't quite hear – something like *Don't worry, I'll see to it myself you get some bereavement. Now . . . you're sure ya all right to drive, son?*

It was a bumpy, blurry ride, and Comstock's whiskey had started to kick in. Louis drove automatically to the Yamada property, not thinking. As he pulled up the Yamadas' drive, it suddenly occurred to him that he ought to go to the Thorn ranch, that he ought to go and see his mother and give her the news as gently as possible, but then he remembered what Comstock had said about a telegram going directly to her. It was just as well; he was not ready to see her face. He knew something had changed in his family – that now there would always be a *before Guy died* and an *after Guy died*, and Louis was a little drunk, besides.

He trudged on leaden legs, stumbling slightly, toward the house. But when he reached the top of the porch stairs, his brain seized upon the idea of his friends. He changed course and followed the wraparound porch toward the other side, in the direction of the barn, and, more important, in the direction of the caravan. But before Louis got quite there, he stopped cold.

Harry. Harry was *Japanese.* Japanese – just like the men who had probably murdered his brother Guy. Could Louis stand the sight of Harry just now? His stomach turned. He was aware of the fact that he hadn't cried. He had a vague memory of Comstock commending him on his stoicism.

Attaboy, Thorn – a stiff upper lip, that's the way to go . . .

Louis wasn't at all sure what might happen when that stiff upper lip crumbled. He changed his mind about seeking out his friends and decided to go back to the farmhouse. He needed to lie down, close his eyes. Maybe he could still wake up and discover it had all been a terrible dream. If only.

Louis let himself in through the back door in the kitchen. He thought briefly that he heard a stirring in the house.

'Ava?' Louis called, wondering if she had come inside to fetch something. No one answered. He realized he was home early, of course, and here it was the middle of the afternoon. Ava was likely outside, somewhere in the orchards, working. And Harry . . . Harry was meant to be hiding in the caravan, keeping out of sight.

But then Louis heard the sound again. The sound of voices . . . strange . . . muffled . . . He followed the sound to Mae's room. Louis saw Mae's favorite things scattered around as though someone had been making an inventory: a doll she'd loved to tatters as a child, a ribbon she'd won for raising a prize heifer, poems she'd scribbled, butterfly wings she'd collected and pinned to a board, the little watercolors she'd painted while trying to take lessons from her mother. In a flash, Louis realized how it had happened – how Harry had come into the house to mourn his sister, how he and Ava had gone slowly, patiently, reverently, through Mae's things. How Ava had comforted Harry. How they found each other again.

Perhaps Louis had always known they were in love, even before he caught a glimpse of them kissing by the stream that ran through the woods, but nothing could have prepared Louis for the feeling of seeing them now. A rush of black, blinding emotion flooded over him.

In the minute or two that Louis stood there, too stunned to react, Harry moved to politely shield Ava. He managed to get his trousers on in one swift, deft movement. Louis had a brief urge to vomit.

'*You son of a bitch*' was all Louis could get out. It felt like his lungs were being squeezed in a vise.

When Harry looked at Louis, surprised to hear his friend use the expletive, Louis suddenly absorbed the details of Harry's face and felt a sudden and acute hatred. Remembering Guy, a fresh charge of white-hot anger coursed through Louis's veins. Suddenly, Harry didn't look like Harry to Louis anymore; all Louis could see when he looked at Harry was: *Japanese*.

He had to get out of there; something unfamiliar – something terrible – was percolating in the darkest chambers of Louis's heart. He turned back around and left the house through the back door in the kitchen. He heard Harry jogging behind him to catch up, Harry's bare feet stamping the earth somewhere over his shoulder. Louis hadn't gone out the front door and didn't trust himself to get in the car, anyway. He dove into a row of plum trees, hoping to lose Harry in the orchard.

It was no use.

'Wait! Louis! Wait!'

Harry caught him up and as he touched Louis's shoulder, something came over Louis. He spun around and punched Harry as hard as he could, square across the jaw. The blow landed with tremendous force. Louis had never been much of a fighter, but something about the betrayal, the anger, the blind hatred he felt, had bestowed upon him preternatural strength. Harry fell to the ground, bleeding.

'*You son of a bitch*' was all Louis could say. He felt himself shaking his head. He kept repeating it, over and over. For some reason they were the only words that would come to his lips.

The next thing he knew, he and Harry were tumbling on the ground between the row of trees in the orchard, trampling the tall yellow grass that had sprung up there over the course of spring and summer. He caught a few blows to the face and landed a few more himself. It got so he couldn't tell whose blood was whose, all of it warm and stinking of iron.

'Harry! Louis!' Ava had managed to exit the house. She was trying to pull them apart. Several times she narrowly missed being punched herself.

Then, all at once, something snapped in Louis. He stopped in mid-swing and retracted his arm. He got off of Harry and got to his feet.

As soon as he felt Louis's body release, Harry did not try to continue the fight. He and Ava looked on, surprised, as Louis stamped in the direction of the Yamada house, bound for the back door.

Louis disappeared. Harry and Ava exchanged a look. Harry sat up and she knelt down to examine his injuries. But then both of their heads snapped in the direction of the back door as it swung open again – violently, with so much force it slapped the outside wall and the whole house shuddered.

Louis had returned, and he had a gun – a military pistol that one of the Air Corps officers he'd trained had given him as a gift. Ava's and Harry's eyes widened with terror to see it. Louis emitted a bizarre, low, guttural cry and charged toward Harry. Ava, who did not ordinarily scream at all, screamed at the top of her lungs.

Only Harry remained silent. He stared into his friend's red face, watching Louis's nostrils flare like a bull's as he breathed. Louis closed the distance between them in record time. The gun was now pressed to Harry's forehead.

'Louis!' Ava shrieked. 'Louis! *Stop!*'

He flicked his eyes in her direction for the briefest of intervals, and in that second Ava only saw a terrifying blackness there. She understood he did not intend to stop. She screamed and threw herself between the two young men.

'STOP!'

It was not Ava's voice. Nor was it Harry's. It came from behind Louis.

When he looked and saw the small figure of Kenichi Yamada standing there, Louis suddenly got ahold of himself. There in Mr Yamada's eyes was the dull flint of grave disappointment. The invisible wave of hatred crested into shame and broke over his head, drenching him in the reality of what he'd been about to do.

'Louis,' Ava said more softly, now that his arm had slackened and he'd lowered the gun. 'Louis . . .'

'Don't' was all he could say, flinching away from her hand. He felt Harry's eyes on him.

When he looked at his friend, Louis saw that Harry knew everything – knew what Louis had been about to do, what Louis was very likely *capable* of doing. Ashamed, Louis threw the pistol in the tall grass and stalked away into the orchard as fast as his legs could carry him.

64

Louis was gone. He had stormed off, leaving a bloody Harry in the orchard and a discarded pistol tossed onto a nest of dry weeds. Ava picked the gun up carefully. Then she and Kenichi helped Harry back to the caravan, which was parked on the back side of the hill, just below the house. By then, Ava's mother had heard the commotion and come running.

'What's going on?' Cleo asked. The bucket of chicken feed still clutched in her hand suggested she had been tending to the hens in the coop.

'Louis . . .' Ava began, unsure how to phrase what had just taken place. 'Louis and Harry got into a fight.'

Cleo observed the cuts and bruises on Harry's face.

'That looks serious,' she said. 'Maybe he ought to rest inside the house?'

Much like her daughter, Cleo had felt funny about moving into the Yamadas' bedrooms while the Yamadas themselves slept outside, in the run-down caravan Earl Shaw had left behind. Ava understood, and now Harry was injured: he should have the comfort of his own home, his own bed. But Ava shook her head.

'We have to keep him hidden,' she said. 'No one has come looking for Harry and Mr Yamada yet, but they will – and very likely soon, now.'

Ava had been doing constant mental calculations. Harry and his father had run away more than forty-eight hours earlier; by now it must be obvious to authorities that Harry had done more than just gone AWOL: he had helped his father – a Japanese who had answered 'No-No' on his loyalty

354

oath, no less – break out and the two had absconded together. Who would come looking for the two escaped internees? The US Army? The FBI? Or would they dispatch someone local, like Sheriff Whitcomb? Ava knew it would be useful to have an idea who to be on the lookout for, but it was impossible to guess. From the caravan, at least you could see the house – you could see if someone came calling and, with any luck, sneak out to hide in the orchards. Everyone had agreed Ava's plan was a good plan, mostly because it was the *only* plan.

Inside the caravan, they helped Harry onto one of the straw mattresses perched atop the pair of wooden bunks built into the sides. Cleo hurried about, fetching iodine and some bandages, and together Cleo and Ava began tending to his wounds. Ava knew that Harry had simply let Louis give him a beating, allowing Louis to do his worst out of a sense of guilt. He hadn't defended himself or fought back as much as he could have. Louis's anger proved surprisingly powerful, leaving Harry badly hurt now.

'Do you think Louis will come back?' Cleo asked, still surprised the two boys had gotten into such a violent fight.

Ava pressed her lips in a fine line. 'He was hurt, too, but not as badly. I think he'll go somewhere to cool down, lick his wounds.'

'It appears Haruto will heal, given some rest,' Kenichi observed, looking over the two women's shoulders as they worked.

'Yes,' Ava agreed. 'I think he *might* have some bruised ribs . . . but I can't be sure. We could fetch a doctor . . .'

'No,' Harry growled from the bunk. 'They'll just haul my father back to that godforsaken place. Or worse.'

The four of them sunk back into a busy silence. Harry closed his eyes as Ava and Cleo continued to bandage him up. Everything felt peaceful for a moment – which was perhaps why none of them was prepared for what happened next.

No one heard the sound of footsteps on the caravan stairs – the door was open – so the intruder entered without notice. When he spoke, they all jumped at the sound of his abrupt, booming voice.

'Well, now . . . what the hell have we got here? After all this time . . . I hadn't taken you and your daughter for a pair of Jap lovers, my dear . . .'

Cleo's blood ran cold as she recognized her husband's voice. She spun around and there he was: Earl Shaw, standing in the doorway, as plain as day.

65

NEWCASTLE, CALIFORNIA
SEPTEMBER 23, 1943

The floorboards creak, announcing Rosalind MacFarlane's presence in the hall. The door to Bonner's room is open. The privacy between them has long since melted away, rendering itself a useless, unnecessary pretense. Bonner does not need to look up to know she is standing in the doorway, watching him sift through the Yamadas' photographs, documents, certificates, and letters . . .

'You believe Louis Thorn did it,' Bonner says to Rosalind now.

She doesn't answer.

'You believe Louis Thorn sabotaged that biplane, and on purpose,' he repeats. He looks up at her. Her face remains expressionless. She shrugs.

'I don't see why it matters.'

Bonner finally understands Rosalind a little – understands a little more about why she feels the way she does about the Yamadas. When he first encountered her, she was an inscrutable mystery, one that perplexed him more and more as she threw her body at him, then angrily pushed him away and held him at arm's length.

But then he'd glimpsed the framed photograph sitting on the mantel at the Yamadas' former farmhouse. Now it was clear that Louis had placed that photograph there, next to the radio, where he could listen to war broadcasts and think about his brother Guy Thorn. When Bonner first saw the photo, he noticed the Navy uniform but seconds later was entirely distracted by the likeness: Guy Thorn looked so much like Bonner himself, it had left Bonner completely disoriented for several minutes.

It wasn't until his conversation with Louis was over, and Bonner was driving away from the Yamada house, that he realized he hadn't thought to ask Louis the obvious question: was his brother still alive? As he drove along the dusty country roads, all the pieces began to come together for Bonner: Guy Thorn had died in the Pacific. When Rosalind 'Lindy' MacFarlane looked at Bonner, she saw her dead fiancé. The mystery of his landlady's curiously hot-and-cold heart was revealed.

Bonner hears her now, coming into the room, padding closer to the bed with a soft tread. She is not there for his body this time – he understands that much, too. In fact, she is more than ready for him to pack his bags and go. Now she inches closer to the bed to peer at the array of documents and photographs there. The softness leaves her face, and her eyes narrow.

'You really hate them, don't you?' Bonner says. It is more an observation than a question, but Rosalind replies anyway.

'Guy did,' she says, meaning the Yamadas specifically. 'I never cared before.' She takes a deep breath and lets out a shuddering sigh. 'Now I hate all of them.' She no longer means the Yamadas; she means the Japanese. 'How could I not?' she challenges Bonner.

'He died in the Pacific,' Bonner says. Again it is an observation, but this time Bonner wants to know if he's guessed correctly.

'He was *killed* in the Pacific,' Rosalind corrects him. '*Killed in action,*' she says, echoing the language of what was likely the official telegram.

As if to confirm Bonner's thoughts, Rosalind pulls a flimsy piece of folded telegram paper from her apron. 'Edith Thorn let me keep it,' she says flatly. Her gaze drifts off, out the window, as if she might glimpse the horizon of the ocean at a distance, even though they are at least a hundred miles inland.

'We were engaged to be married,' Rosalind murmurs now. 'But he couldn't stand what had happened in Pearl Harbor.' She blinks as though in a trance. 'He promised he would be back, and he was the sort of man who was very serious about his promises; he didn't make them easily.' She stops, and an unflattering spasm of pain crosses her features. 'If I'm being honest, I *knew* he wasn't coming back . . . We heard the broadcasts, we all knew . . .'

'I'm sorry,' Bonner says, uncomfortable to have dredged up all this pain for her. Not knowing what else to do, he reaches a hand out to pat her shoulder. She recoils from him as though he has burned her.

'Stay away from me,' she hisses.

Bonner looks at her in wonderment, taken aback. Her body and face are tensed, disfigured with anger and hate. He repeats the blunt realization that began their conversation.

'You believe Louis Thorn saw his opportunity to take revenge . . . and took it,' Bonner says.

Rosalind glares at him.

'*If* that were true,' she says finally, 'I would hardly blame him.' She pauses, and adds, 'In fact, I would shake his hand.'

And with that, she turns and leaves Bonner's room. Bonner still plans to spend one final night there. But already he knows she will not return; she has visited him in his room for the last time.

66

The next day, Bonner sits and stares into his beer in contemplation, his eyes vacant. It is Friday, and his per diem has run out. It is no use telephoning Reed and begging for more time; Bonner already knows what Reed will say.

Earlier that afternoon, Bonner checked out from the boardinghouse. His goodbye with Rosalind was curt, formal. Bonner stopped in to say goodbye to Whitcomb and Henderson, too, even though he is sure Whitcomb would've been fine – more than fine – if Bonner had just found his way out of town with no goodbyes. That was the funny thing: Bonner was having trouble finding his way out of town, period. He spent the afternoon wandering around, wondering if there was something about the town, and about Louis and Harry, that he had missed. Eventually, as the sun began to set, he decided to stop in at the local tavern, to go over the case one last time. The bartender – the same Joe Abbott he'd spoken with previously – was hardly welcoming, but Bonner didn't care. After tapping a beer for Bonner, Joe retreated to the opposite end of the bar, intent on ignoring the FBI agent.

Joe's show of neglect suits Bonner just fine. He wants the respite in order to think.

As he stares at the case files and takes a sip of his beer, he recalls his exchange with Rosalind the night before. He saw it in her face: she was *certain* Louis Thorn had sabotaged the biplane, that Thorn had essentially murdered Harry and Kenichi Yamada. Remembering the almost gleeful, satisfied look of

360

vengeance on her face, Bonner shudders. To live with that much hate, Bonner thinks, is not living at all.

The question that remains, of course, is whether Louis Thorn is living with that much hate, too. Bonner can't make up his mind about Louis – whether or not Louis is capable of murdering his best friend. Louis's reaction when Bonner accused him directly left Bonner unsettled, and certainly undecided. The only thing Bonner knows for certain is that Louis is hiding something.

Bonner sighs, and stares again at the pile of evidence laid out on the bar. His eyes fall upon the bundle of family letters. He's made his way through most of them. Now there are only a handful left to read, all from Ava, letters that arrived at the camp days after Harry and Kenichi had gone AWOL, days after there was anyone there to receive them. The camp authorities collected them and mailed them on to the FBI

Bonner picks up one of the final letters and slides a finger along the envelope, ripping it open, and taps the letter free. He unfolds it and smoothes it rather carelessly on the bar with his hands.

My Dearest Houdini, it begins in a jokey tone. But as Bonner reads on, he discovers the letter is a love letter of sorts. He's wondered about the ties between Harry, Ava, and Louis all along, and now Bonner has hit upon one solid piece of the puzzle. *So Ava loved Harry*, he thinks. It wasn't criminal to love a Jap, not in a court of law in California, at least. However, Ava's feelings for Harry only add more motive to the case against Louis Thorn.

But then, as Bonner continues to read Ava's letter, he suddenly stops and flinches. He starts again from the beginning, reading the whole letter over again. *Could this be true?* It doesn't make sense, and it means that Ava lied – or had she? Bonner tries to remember. No. It was Louis who spoke *for* her. Which meant either Louis lied or else didn't even know he was lying . . . It was Ava's secret.

Bonner taps his fingers and chews the inside of his cheek in agitation. A theory begins to form in his brain. *How did he overlook the possibility?* He takes a sip of beer, wipes the foam from his upper lip, and makes an abrupt scramble for the attaché case lying on the barstool beside him. Digging through it, he finds the photograph he seeks and pulls it out for a better look. He has to be sure.

He stares at the photograph, scrutinizing it, taking careful account of all the clues. And of course they are so obvious once Bonner sees them, once he is really looking with his eyes open. The entire barnstorming troupe grins back at him: Earl Shaw with his black hair and dapper suit, his hand clamped possessively around Cleo Shaw's waist; Ava and Louis; the two pilots, Buzz and Hutch; and – finally – Harry standing at the opposite end, counterbalancing Earl somehow, both of them approximately the same height and weight. Behind the group, the two biplanes, and the words CASTOR and POLLUX painted in shining, proud, gold letters.

'Jesus,' Bonner mutters. He rubs his eyes and looks again. *It was in front of me this whole time*, he thinks. 'Houdini,' he grunts, a combination of flabbergasted, impressed, and annoyed. He shakes his head. 'Houdini,' he repeats, 'eat your heart out.'

In the next second he becomes a flurry of motion. He grabs up the letters and the photograph and shoves the entire wad clumsily back into his attaché case. He throws several greenbacks down on the bar and races out the saloon door, leaving Joe Abbott looking after him, frowning and scratching his head.

Eventually, Joe crosses back to where the agent was sitting and scoops up the bills. As he tosses what remains of Bonner's warm beer down the drain with a dismissive shake of his wrist, it makes a satisfying *splat.*

67

YAMADA PROPERTY
SEPTEMBER 16, 1943

'We have to all agree,' Ava said. 'No one will ever know about this.'

She poked the fire that was burning in the oil drum with a stick. It was so late, it was now early. The first hint of dawn had begun to glow, eerie and blue, in the eastern horizon. It was only a very slight glow, but it alarmed Ava nonetheless. She was worried they were running out of time.

They were all so stunned, it had taken them a while to get a grip on their senses, to figure out what to do, and then there was Kenichi – *poor Kenichi*.

Three of them now stood in a circle, watching the barrel burn: Ava, her mother, and Harry. Harry stood slightly slumped, still injured from his earlier fight with Louis, his spirit now broken even further by everything that had happened since. Something rustled in the bushes nearby. They all jumped and looked but saw nothing.

'A chipmunk,' Ava diagnosed.

She poked the contents of the barrel again. The fire was getting too hot for them to stand so close, the heat was radiating in waves, and it was beginning to feel like an oven. *Good*, she thought. *We need it to get as hot as we can get it.* When she was sure no one would be able to identify the remains, she would douse the barrel with water, and that had to happen before the sun came up, otherwise the white smoke of the fire being extinguished might catch folks' attention. There could be no questions about what they had done. There could be no questions about what they were about to do.

It was not their fault – none of them. Earl Shaw had always had bad timing and a knack for trouble. After he disappeared, Ava had tried to help her mother track him down. All Cleo wanted was a divorce, but looking for Earl proved difficult – and expensive. The shoddy private investigator they hired traced Earl's steps to the Southwest but said the trail went cold near the Mexican border. After stealing the flying circus members' money, he managed to rack up even more debt borrowing from loan sharks. For all they knew, said the private investigator, Earl might be hiding from his creditors in Mexico, biding his time and possibly even changing his name yet again. After a few months, Cleo and Ava stopped looking for him. It seemed he would stay gone forever.

Of course, there were times when they occasionally looked over their shoulders – not only Cleo and Ava but the rest of the barnstorming troupe, too: Louis, Harry, Buzz, and Hutch. If Earl caught wind of the fact that they'd banded together and resurrected the barnstorming act – if he heard the rumor that Eagle & Crane was successful and had even caught Hollywood's attention – well, then there was a good chance he might come back to try to stake a claim.

And, sure enough, Earl had done just that – right when Cleo and Ava both had let their guard down and forgotten all about him.

After they'd all recovered from the shock of seeing Earl standing there inside the caravan, Ava noticed two things. One: from the looks of him, Earl seemed more down on his luck than usual. And two: he reeked of moonshine.

'Lookit, you sorry thieves . . . Thought you were gonna steal my flying circus and put on shows without me, eh?' he slurred, confirming Ava's fears. 'This here is my goddamn caravan, and you been getting rich offa my goddamn plane, my goddamn pilots and stuntmen!

'The way I figure it, you owe me my cut,' Earl continued to rage. ''S'all I want, just my cut! Now . . . if these Japs gimme what I'm due, then there ain't got to be any trouble, and I'll be on my way . . .'

It was Kenichi who accidentally set Earl off. He chuckled – a small, almost lighthearted chuckle. It struck Kenichi as absurd that after everything his family had been through, after everything they had lost – material, physical, and spiritual – this white con man might think they were holding out, that they were secretly hoarding some kind of riches, when the truth was, they had been systematically stripped of everything, including their dignity. It was an unintentional laugh, the maniacal laugh of a man still grieving his wife and daughter.

'Think that's funny, you old Jap?' Earl growled. He whirled on Kenichi, fists flying. Harry was still laid out flat on the straw mattress farther inside the caravan. There was an iron crowbar propped near the doorway that they had used to bar the caravan doors whenever Earl parked the caravan overnight in less-reputable areas. Cleo and Ava had continued to keep it there, forgetting about it, mostly. But now Earl knew all too well where to find it. Before anyone could stop him, he picked up the crowbar and brought it down hard upon Kenichi's skull. Harry was off his bunk in a flash, but before he could reach his father a flurry of motion plunged the room into stunned chaos.

The terrible *CRACK* of the crowbar meeting Kenichi's skull was quickly eclipsed by a louder, more earsplitting *BANG!*

For a long, terrible moment, Ava and Harry couldn't figure out what had just happened. Then they recalled: the pistol. Ava had picked up the pistol Louis had dropped in the orchard and carried it back to the caravan, where she had set it down on the table.

All heads turned in the direction of Cleo Shaw. She stood with her back against the wall of the caravan, a terrified expression on her face, the gun trembling in her hands.

Earl lay in a heap on the floor. The bullet had caught him smack in the chest.

No one dared to move until Kenichi broke the silence, groaning nearby.

'Oh, God!'

With Ava and Cleo's help, Harry lifted his father onto the bunk and tried to get a better look at the wound. It was bad – mortally bad. It was very likely that Earl had fractured the older man's skull. Kenichi's eyes were open and his lips hissed as though trying to speak.

'We *have* to get him to a doctor,' Ava said in an urgent voice.

Still moving painfully, Harry began to lift his father into his arms, ready to transport Kenichi anywhere that promised salvation.

'No . . .' Kenichi managed to form the word with his lips. 'I am already done with that. They will punish Harry and they will take me back . . .' He fought to open his eyes and look at his son. 'There is no medicine for us . . .' he said.

'But, *Otōsan*, you're hurt too badly—'

'Let me die.'

The moment the words touched air, they haunted the caravan. No one spoke. Harry felt a small, excruciating stab.

'Let me die, Haruto.'

Harry was still half holding his father as though he couldn't decide whether to rush him to a doctor or let him be. His eyes were dry and steady, but his mouth trembled.

'*Please*,' Kenichi added with an air of finality.

Harry relaxed his arms, letting his father lie back again. Ava came over and propped pillows behind Kenichi's head, and Cleo – still with quaking hands – did the same. With no further discussion they agreed to obey Kenichi's wishes.

Earl had blown in like a vicious wind. Now a vacuous feeling invaded the caravan, taking the place of the tremendous chaos Earl had caused. Earl was definitely dead; no one touched his body where it lay on the floor. All eyes were on Kenichi. Everyone was filled with quiet distress at the prospect of witnessing the old man's passing.

It was, however, more difficult than simply deciding to let him sink into a dignified slumber. Kenichi was gravely injured, but he did not die immediately. It soon became clear he was in tremendous pain. He began to moan.

'I have opium,' Harry said finally in a quiet voice. 'I got some from a man in the camp . . . a lot of it, actually. If something happened to us and we didn't want to go back to the camp, there was always this . . .'

He produced a packet from his inside jacket pocket.

'We could boil it with water,' he said in a somber voice.

Ava took the packet, but Cleo was too quick.

'I'll do it,' Cleo said firmly. 'You keep him comfortable.'

Cleo set about making a thick, syrupy tea.

'It will be quick,' she said when it was ready.

Kenichi's body was still in the caravan, hours after his final moments.

They had propped him up on the straw mattress and Harry had helped him take long, steady sips from a tin mug. He slipped away into unconsciousness, an angelic expression on his face. Harry gripped Ava's hand. After an hour of ragged breathing, Kenichi gave one long, last, sibilant exhale, and it felt as if a spirit was truly passing, moving from the caravan, making its way out into the gentle California night air.

Earl was another matter.

It was Ava who had ultimately devised their plan. She took a long look at Earl. Then her eyes swept around the caravan and happened to land on the book Harry had given her: Shakespeare's play, *The Comedy of Errors*. She thought of the names of their two original biplanes, *Castor* and *Pollux*: the solution was already all around them, she realized. She looked at Harry – Harry, the *magician* – and the idea came to her. *The ultimate escape act.*

The first step was to char the body, making it unrecognizable. They loaded Earl into an oil drum and doused him in kerosene. Ava insisted they remove his clothes first. *Nothing identifying on his person*, she said. *We ought to wrench his teeth out if we can . . .*

When she explained the rest of her plan, Harry protested. It was too much risk for her. But Ava insisted. She was taking charge again, just as she had taken charge when Harry and Kenichi had shown up back on their old property, having broken out of the internment camp.

She had a plan, and they would follow it.

68

After leaving the Yamada orchards, Louis Thorn walked into town and promptly got drunker. At Murphy's Saloon, Joe Abbott took pity on him, glimpsing the fresh bruises on Louis's face and guessing the boy was likely full of piss and vinegar on account of his brother being killed in the Pacific. Word traveled fast, and by that time the whole town knew Edith Thorn had received a telegram earlier that day. The Thorn children were simply too numerous for anything in their family to remain secret for longer than an hour. Full of sympathy and patriotism, Joe had gotten Louis good and tanked up, then let him snooze in a corner of the bar until four o'clock in the morning, when Joe roused him with a cup of coffee and told the poor fellow he was obligated to lock up.

Now a very hungover Louis retraced his earlier walk, trudging in the direction of the Yamada ranch. He hardly knew what he wanted to say to them, but he needed to go back and see Harry, see Ava . . . and, if nothing else, knew he needed to go back and clear out his things.

He arrived just as dawn was breaking. It was a hazy day, a day made overcast by all the agricultural activity in the area, the farmers all burning their fields in the valley. There was a terrible charred scent on the breeze. The sunrise was intensely bloody, then all the color drained out of the sky, replaced by a dull gray. It was just as well: what little sunshine there was only gave Louis a splitting headache.

'Hello?' he called out as he entered the Yamada house. He didn't necessarily expect to see Harry or Mr Yamada – he knew Ava would want to keep them hidden out in the caravan, per her plan – but Louis assumed Cleo and Ava had slept inside, even after Louis's awful scuffle with Harry. He was surprised to find absolutely nobody at home.

Feeling lonely, he switched on the radio. It had become his ritual to listen to the war bulletins every day. Remembering Guy, he reached out to switch it off, but hesitated and decided to leave it on. It was nice to pretend, if only for a minute or two. The radio quivered with excitement and gave off a curiously reassuring noisy squawk, as though it were promising the end of the war in one ultimate blaze of glory.

Louis felt nature calling and went into the bathroom. Once there, he caught sight of himself in the mirror and let out a shocked grunt, followed by an exhausted laugh. Dirt was caked over the cuts and bruises on his face, his left eye sported a shiner, and he displayed all the obvious signs of a terrible hangover. On top of all that, he needed a shave.

It was something to do. He turned on the hot-water tap, took out some shaving soap, splashed water on his face, and lathered up. He had gotten through half of his shave when he heard a truck sputtering up the drive and, soon after, heavy boots on the wooden stairs leading up to the Yamada porch.

Still only half-shaven, his undershirt dirty and his suspenders hanging at his hips, Louis went out to see who was at the door. He recognized the shapes of Sheriff Whitcomb and Deputy Henderson through the window, coming up the stairs. There was a third man, too – a man Louis didn't know. He squinted and was startled almost to the point of nausea to notice the man bore a striking similarity to his brother Guy.

Louis's stomach twisted, suddenly remembering it all: the fact that Guy was dead, the fact that he had nearly shot Harry in the head, the fact that he was, technically, still harboring two escaped Japanese internees on property that was his in legal name . . .

The men neared the top of the stairs, arriving at the front porch. Louis took a deep breath and pushed through the screen door. It closed with a slap behind him.

'May I help you fellas?'

Only minutes later Louis Thorn watched in disbelief as the Stearman puttered out of gas, stalled, and plunged from the sky.

69

NEWCASTLE, CALIFORNIA
SEPTEMBER 24, 1943

Having finally put the pieces together, Agent Bonner hurries out of Murphy's Saloon and immediately jumps into the Bureau car parked out front, intent on racing over to the former Yamada residence as quickly as he possibly can. It is nighttime but not completely dark; the moon is full. It casts a ghostly silver glow over everything and cuts clear black shadows onto the ground of every structure, creature, and leaf. As Bonner pulls up the drive, he spots a single plume of smoke rising into the air. It, too, catches the moon's light, undulating white, silver, and black as it rises up to the heavens in a column.

On instinct, Bonner knows the plume is Louis Thorn's doing.

He kills the engine and steps out of the car. He can smell the burning. He does not bother approaching the house and knocking on the front door. Instead, he walks around the farmhouse to the source of the smoke, a short distance behind the barn. He wonders if he might find Louis and Ava together – and possibly Cleo Shaw, too. But when he rounds the corner of the barn, he sees only a single figure standing vigil over the flames that are steadily consuming the old wooden caravan.

'Agent Bonner,' Louis greets him.

Louis has his back to the FBI agent, but it is plain he knows exactly who it is without having to turn around.

'Where is Miss Brooks?' Bonner asks. He stands beside Louis. Together they stare into the flames. The fire crackles as though it is breaking down the bones of the caravan – presumably the site of two deaths: Earl Shaw's and Kenichi Yamada's. There is something else in the flames, too, something that has been thrown in more recently than the rest of the burning mass. Bonner can just barely make out a letter, rapidly curling into blackened tar, and something else – perhaps a parachute.

'She's gone,' Louis says, answering Bonner's question. 'She left with her mother.'

'I suppose you don't know where she's gone or when she's coming back,' Bonner says.

'Don't reckon she *is* coming back.'

Bonner points to the items burning in the caravan. 'And I'm guessing she wrote a letter exonerating you . . . She left the parachute she used and explained how she did it.'

I figured it out before then, Louis thinks quietly to himself.

'You didn't know she had learned how to fly the Stearman.'

'I should've figured Harry had been taking her up,' Louis answers, his voice far away, thoughtful. In the flickering light Bonner thinks he sees a shudder of pain cross Louis's face.

'But they kept it a secret from you,' Bonner replies, recalling the letter he has just read, sitting at the bar – a personal love letter from Ava to Harry. In it, she confessed some of her fondest memories together, and Bonner was surprised to learn that Ava – who was supposedly afraid of flying – not only trusted Harry enough to go up with him, she also learned to fly herself.

'They kept a lot of things secret from me,' Louis says now.

Bonner looks at Louis's face more closely and cocks his head. 'Are you glad or disappointed to know that Harry is still alive?'

Bonner's brain worked hard to put together the rest of it, but it came down to that photograph. The names painted in gold lettering on the two biplanes in the background, CASTOR and POLLUX: the twins. When he remembered an old astronomy lesson – the constellation Castor and Pollux, the two famous twins that made up Gemini – it unlocked something in Bonner's brain. So did seeing Earl and Harry standing on either side, both of them about the same height and weight, both of them with black hair – not that the hair mattered so much; they had singed most of that away when they burned the body. They had still taken a huge risk, nonetheless. The coroner examined

371

Kenichi Yamada's body but hadn't done much with the charred mess believed to be Harry Yamada's body. Bonner knew a closer examination from a more seasoned coroner might have revealed the body's racial identity – it possibly still could, although he also knew that was unlikely. In devising her plan, Ava counted on everyone to assume the second body was Harry's. Moreover, she relied on the notion that no one would care enough about the deaths of two Japanese men to probe very deeply. She had been right about that: Bonner thought about his last conversation with Reed, and the order he'd been given to close the case without further ado.

Bonner guessed that Cleo Shaw had been the one to pull the trigger on Earl, and that accounted for why she was so jittery, so fragile and on edge. She had shot her husband – in self-defense possibly, but still, it was bound to shake a woman up.

Bonner's mind lined up the rest of it. He'd had the bruises all wrong, but that was only because he'd been shown the wrong two sets of bruises: the ones on Louis's face and the ones on Kenichi's corpse. He'd assumed they'd gotten into a scuffle together, but that was utterly foolish. He knew now: the bruises on Louis's face had come from a fight with Harry. Kenichi's bruises had come from Earl.

And then there was Ava, who supposedly did not know how to fly the Stearman. Her letter to Harry – a letter he never had the privilege to read – was full of reminiscences of secret flying lessons. When her mother shot Earl, and Kenichi died, Ava knew exactly what she could do about it.

He had to admire her boldness – not only to mastermind the body switch, but also to pull it off. She had guts.

'Are you glad, or disappointed, to know that Harry is still alive?' Bonner repeats his question.

'I don't know what you're talking about,' Louis says, his voice firm.

Bonner looks at Louis and smiles with quiet respect.

'I wondered,' Bonner remarks. 'I wondered if you would protect them – both of them. I guess now I have my answer.'

Louis doesn't say anything.

For a long time, both men stand together in silence, watching the caravan burn. Louis's eyes fall on the parachute. He hadn't really *needed* to burn that . . . it wasn't proof of anything, really. But the parachute had always belonged with the plane, and now they were all united in fire.

Louis wonders which of them had used it. *Ava*, he thinks. *It must have been Ava*. She would have insisted Harry not be anywhere near the crash, which would inevitably draw more attention from law enforcement. Besides, Harry was not in top form; Louis thought he'd felt some ribs crack when he attacked Harry the night before. Louis's shame deepens when he remembers the fight. He knows Harry held back, restrained himself, let Louis rage.

No; it had to have been Ava who'd flown the Stearman with its fuel line punctured. She was small enough and light enough to fit in the cockpit with the bodies loaded up. Just as dawn was breaking and the plane was nearly out of gas, she must've parachuted away, leaving the biplane flying at a high altitude, eventually to putter and run out of fuel and crash. She was lucky no one saw her. Louis tries to imagine the moment she jumped, the courage it demanded. He has always known Ava was strong, even belligerent in the face of fear, but even so, he is impressed.

'What will you do?' Louis asks Bonner.

'You mean, will I send the FBI out looking for Haruto Yamada?' Bonner asks.

Louis doesn't speak at first, then nods.

'No,' Bonner says. He lets out a sigh, and as he does, a pressure lifts from his shoulders. 'My supervisor ordered me to close this case, and that's what I intend to do.'

Louis turns to Bonner. In the firelight, their faces are mirrors – one half in shadow, one half glowing with the orange flames of the fire. But it is more than that. They bear the similarity of brothers.

'Why?' Louis finally asks.

'When I first took this case, I only came here because I wanted to meet you. I didn't know anything about the Yamadas. I only noticed the name of the town, and your last name, Thorn. I figured, in the worst case – if you'd taken it upon yourself to hide some Japs, I'd help you by turning a blind eye.'

Louis starts in surprise. 'I don't understand,' he says.

Bonner looks at him. 'There's a reason your brother Guy and I might look alike,' he says, turning to take in the sight of the foothills in the moonlight. 'My grandmother grew up here.'

Louis doesn't speak, and Bonner can see he is struggling to make sense of it all.

'She didn't talk about it much,' Bonner adds, 'on account of the fact that her family hit a rough patch, and she fell into awful poverty here. She wound up working in a . . . well, shall we say, house of ill repute.' Bonner waits a beat. 'She moved to San Francisco to have her son – my father. Much later in life, when he asked, the only things she told him was the name of the town where he'd been conceived, and the name of his father: Ennis Thorn.'

'We share a grandfather . . .' Louis murmurs. It is not entirely crazy to think such a thing is possible, but it is a fact that, in his wildest dreams, he never would've guessed.

'Yes,' Bonner answers quietly. Louis mulls this over. Finally he speaks.

'You have no idea what it was like, every time you came around asking questions, the fact that you look . . .' His throat catches and he pauses. 'It was like having my brother's dead ghost haunting me,' he finishes. His voice is frank, without a hint of melodrama.

'This case became something else for me, too,' Bonner says. He considers explaining – confessing, really – about the Minami family, about how it changed the way he felt about the camps, about the Yamadas, and about how badly he needed to know whether Louis had sabotaged that plane. But he realizes it doesn't matter; Louis already feels the weight of these things. So instead Bonner simply stands beside Louis. Together they watch the caravan burn.

'You'll really leave Harry alone?' Louis ventures, the first direct acknowledgment of the fact that Harry is still alive.

Bonner shrugs. 'No one cared much about Haruto Yamada's death,' he says. 'I won't concern the government with what remains of his life.'

They stand staring at the flames a little while longer. Finally, Bonner shoves his hands in his pockets and shakes his head. He walks away, heading back in the direction of his car. No handshake, no farewell. Louis knows Bonner is not coming back, that they will likely never see each other again. He hears the car engine starting up and shifting into gear, and then Bonner leaves, taking the ghost that has been haunting Louis along with him.

Dawn glows in the sky – not red, but a surreal, pure greenish blue. The sun will be up soon.

Satisfied, Louis goes to the well, fills a bucket, and begins to pour water on the fire, until slowly the charred remains of the caravan begin to let off a distinct hiss.

70

Two weeks pass, and the time for Guy Thorn's memorial service arrives. It is a memorial service and not a funeral because there is no body, no coffin to inter. The Thorn family has been informed: Guy's remains will be buried alongside other sailors killed in action, in a marked grave in an American cemetery in Manila. The Navy has assured them that it is a very honorable place to be buried. Louis's mother, Edith, had to ask Louis to help her look up Manila on a map. When her finger found the distant island nation of the Philippines, she began to cry.

'He's so far away,' she said, weeping softly.

'We'll make a place for him here,' Louis replied. 'We'll make a place out near the orchards – the spot where Guy liked to stand and oversee picking season.'

He proceeded to have a marble marker made. The marker was expensive, and Louis had to dip into profits from the Yamadas' orchards to pay for it. He felt funny about it at first, but as more days pass, so does the funny feeling. In a war filled with so many tragedies, it is difficult to think the dead would begrudge anything that might help to alleviate the suffering of the living. And in remembering the kindness of Kenichi Yamada, Louis remembers that the man did not have a resentful or uncharitable bone in his body.

On the morning of the memorial, Louis wakes up and puts on his nicest clothes. Then he walks the familiar route from the Yamadas' old farmhouse over to the Thorn property. It's a crisp, sunny October day and the Thorns' apple orchard glows with the brilliant colors of turning leaves. Louis wishes Guy could be there to see it.

The service itself is brief and to the point – the way Guy would've wanted it. Though there is nothing to bury, they dig a hole nonetheless and fill it with mementos. Lindy MacFarlane adds hers last, and as she drops the simple gold ring Guy gave her in the hole, Louis can see the embers of anger still smoldering in her face. Louis recognizes her anger instantly, because it is the same fiery fury that followed him like a shadow in the days after he was informed of Guy's death.

The local undertaker, who regularly arranges such things with a stonecutter up in Auburn, handled the marker Louis commissioned, having it chiseled and delivered. Louis is surprised to see the undertaker at Guy's memorial – but then, most of the town of Newcastle and nearly half of the towns of Penryn and Loomis have turned up, too. Guy was well known and, despite his stern, overworked demeanor, was also well liked by most folks. But after the service, the undertaker approaches Louis, and Louis learns the undertaker has a secondary mission to address as well.

'It's about the Yamada boys,' the undertaker says. 'After the autopsy, the bodies were cremated. I've got 'em now, but Sheriff Whitcomb says I'm to hand the ashes off to you, seein' as how there's paperwork naming you the executor of anythin' they got left . . .' The undertaker trails off, plainly embarrassed. Louis can't tell if the undertaker's embarrassment is due to the fact that he's discussing the remains of two Japs at the funeral of a serviceman killed by the Japanese, or if he's simply humiliated to be saddled with ashes that have been essentially orphaned at his funeral parlor.

'I'll pick them up tomorrow,' Louis says quietly.

The undertaker looks relieved.

The next day, Louis fulfills his promise. The undertaker hands over two cheap-looking wooden boxes. The boxes are significantly smaller than Louis expected, but then, Louis immediately realizes how foolish it was to have any expectations at all. He thanks the undertaker and takes the two boxes back to the former Yamada ranch.

Once there, he hardly knows what else to do with the ashes. He winds up taking the two boxes inside and placing them on the mantel. He doesn't know why he does this, except for an abstract idea that funeral urns belong on a mantel. Cremation is exotic to him; everyone Louis has ever known has gone into the ground. And besides, the wooden boxes are not proper urns, anyway.

He sits down and stares at the boxes, musing on how out of place they look. One box is stamped YAMADA, KENICHI. The other, YAMADA, HARUTO. The box with Kenichi's ashes sends a numb pang to his heart; it is difficult to think of calm, rooted Kenichi – after the years of work he had put into the soil of his farm and orchards – as having been transformed into something that might now blow away in a gust of wind. Louis sits with a quiet apology in his heart. It is a big apology to carry, because it is bigger than himself. It is an apology for his family's grudge against the Yamadas, an apology for the ugly spirit of a nation that put Kenichi and his family in a camp – an apology from Louis, too, for doing nothing to stop any of it.

Louis sits and meditates on Kenichi's ashes. But then Louis's eyes move to the second box, and the second name, and they stumble. He reads the name again and then again, pondering. The box says HARUTO, but of course it is not Harry inside the box, Louis realizes. Louis has known this since the day Bonner confronted him, when Louis put it all together. Ava has confirmed everything in her note.

Louis did his duty, burning the caravan and all the evidence it contained.

But now Louis realizes he hasn't allowed himself to fully absorb the larger truth: *Harry is alive.* And, contemplating this now, Louis realizes something even more significant: the immense relief he feels. The *gratitude.*

The pain Louis feels over Guy's death, the hurt he feels over the fact that Ava chose Harry for her lover, the grudge he has all his life been expected to inherit – all of these can exist, and still none of them completely cancel out the relief Louis feels to know his friend is still alive. Perhaps, even, they cannot completely snuff out the small but resilient flame of hope Louis feels that he may someday see his friend, even joke and smile again.

He looks again at the boxes. What to do with them? Louis feels sure that Kenichi Yamada's ashes belong on the Yamada property. He remembers the two urns, still hidden out in the barn. *We will find a place for these when the time is right,* Harry promised his father. Louis realizes Harry has both new and unfinished business with the dead.

The other box, though – what will any of them ever do with that? Louis rises to his feet and lifts the second box from the mantel.

A fake Harry in place of the real one. As Louis stares at the box in his hands, the faintest hint of a smile creeps into the line of his lips. He has to admire the feat they've pulled off: it is the ultimate magic trick.

But now Louis decides to see if there isn't a little more magic left in the exchange – one more turn to the trick. This last reveal is only meant for the three of them: Louis, Ava, and Harry.

He takes the box out to the Ford coupe, secures it in the trunk, and proceeds to load the car up for a short road trip. He will only be gone for a few days, he decides. Just long enough to make amends. Just long enough, he hopes, to make one last exchange: the fake Harry for the real.

As days turn into weeks, Ava tells herself not to get her hopes up. Louis might not want to forgive them. Or he might forgive them but not want to find them.

The one thing she does know for certain: he knows *where* to find them. She didn't dare write it in the letter she left for Louis – in case the letter was found by someone else – but she knows all Louis has to do is think for a moment and the answer will come to him.

By then, Cleo, Ava, and Harry have gone to work sweeping out the cabin, trying to weatherproof it, make it livable. Ava makes trip after trip up the coast in the Model A. She retrieves bedrolls and blankets, food and toiletries. Afterward, they are careful to roll the truck a short distance along the footpath and cover it with tree branches and brush.

The days that followed the crash were hell for Ava. She had sent Harry on ahead, but he had to travel on foot and keep himself hidden. Every day the FBI agent's presence delayed her departure, she worried that Harry might run out of supplies. And her mother was a nervous wreck, biting her nails all the time and reliving what had happened with Earl. Finally, when Ava could take it no longer, she loaded her mother into the Model A and went to join

Harry. She left a letter confessing that she'd been the one to sabotage the plane but leaving out the part that Harry was still alive. The letter would exonerate Louis if he needed it. Ava wasn't willing to risk the rest.

She was sorry she hadn't told Louis the whole truth all along. He'd looked so angry that afternoon he'd fought with Harry. There was a moment Ava thought for sure Louis was going to kill him.

'Be patient,' Harry tells Ava, whenever she wonders aloud if Louis will ever come to them. Harry thinks – or so Ava guesses – that Ava wants to be forgiven. And she does want to be forgiven – forgiven for all the things she kept secret from Louis, really. But all Harry says is, 'He'll turn up. Be patient.'

Ava tells herself: at worst, he will simply never arrive. He won't send anyone after Harry, not Louis . . . not ever. But as the wait goes on, she begins to wonder.

Then, one afternoon when her mother has driven the Model A up the coast to retrieve more supplies, Ava hears a far-distant automobile winding along the highway. It is too early for her mother to be back already, so the sound catches her attention. She listens, wondering if it is merely a motoring tourist headed down the highway, past the turnout for the path that leads to their little cabin. But for some reason she knows: this one is different. She hears it pull off the highway and into the turnout, its tires spitting rock and dust and crunching to a stop. She hears a door slam shut.

'Harry!' she shouts. 'Harry!'

Harry comes inside from where he was attempting to dig a vegetable garden.

'I heard it, too,' he says.

Harry drops his trowel and wipes the soil from his hands. Together they begin to walk the narrow path back up to the main road, each step bringing them closer to their friend.

ACKNOWLEDGMENTS

This book was inspired in part by a few real-life family connections. I would like to acknowledge the late Barbara Matsui. Barbara was a close friend of my mother's who spent time with me as a child and who happened to be legally blind. When I asked my mother about the trouble with Barbara's sight, she told me a little bit of Barbara's past: Barbara had been born in an internment camp, where her mother had contracted German measles while pregnant. That these camps ever existed in America, much less in my home state of California, shocked me as a child. In recent years, remembering Barbara's story led me to research more about the internment camps and the kinds of health problems former internees suffered (and some continue to suffer). Barbara's personal story left an impression on me. She was simply a delightful and uplifting person to be around (a teacher and a talented musician, no less). I'm grateful to have known her.

My other influences include my great-grandmother Jessie, who owned an orchard and ranch in Penryn, California, and who relayed the story of the Japanese-American foreman and his family who lived on her property up until the time the US government ordered their internment. On the other side of my family, my grandfather Norbert grew up picking fruit in the orchards of Placer County. He recalled the large number of Japanese-American settlements and properties that abruptly disappeared after Executive Order 9066. Like Louis, he became a flight instructor during World War II for the US Army Air Corps. His daughter, my mother, also learned to fly and got her wings.

And my father eventually flew F-111s for the US Air Force during Vietnam. I myself am terrified even to fly commercial (must've missed that gene), so I'm not sure I would have or could have written this particular book without the influence of my many flying family members, or the numerous air shows our family attended when I was a kid.

In the book world, I would like to thank the following people for their guidance and support: Emily Forland and everyone at Brandt and Hochman, Jake Morrissey and his assistant Kevin Murphy, Ivan Held, Sally Kim, Stephanie Hargadon, Alexis Welby, Madeline Schmitz, Ashley McClay, Emily Ollis, Brennin Cummings, and all the amazing people at Putnam. I am also very lucky to have Michelle Weiner of CAA as a champion of my work. I am grateful for the many friends who have kept me company through the writing process over the years: Jayme Yeo, Susan Shin, Julie Fogh, Brendan Jones, Georgia Clark, Lyndsay Faye, Amy Poeppel, Elizabeth Romanski, Brian Shin, Melissa Ryan Clark, Julia Masnik, Ning Zhou, Eva Talmadge, Joe Campana, Susan Wood, Sophie Gouyet, Cécille Pradillon, and Sophie Weeks. I'd also like to thank Kimi de Cristoforo, daughter of translator Violet Kazue Cristoforo, for her help in gaining permission to include the poem 'Rain shower from mountain' by Suiko Matsushita. Again, I'm thankful to my family members: Sharon Rindell, Arthur Rindell, Laurie Rindell, Melissa d'Armagnac, Phillipe d'Armagnac, and Rémy d'Armagnac. And finally, to Atom and the Poppet: I could not have written this book without your love.

Suzanne Rindell recently earned her PhD in English literature. Her first novel, *The Other Typist*, has been translated into fifteen languages and has been optioned for film with Keira Knightley producing and starring. Rindell has enjoyed subsequent success with *Three-Martini Lunch*. Before she turned to writing, she worked at a New York literary agency and lived in a cheap apartment above a funeral home. She now divides her time between California and New York.

suzannerindell.com
@SuzanneRindell